MW01136463

Bronx Justice

A Novel Straight from the NYPD Files

Bronx Justice

A Novel Straight from the NYPD Files

By Bob Martin

Bronx Justice

A Novel Straight from the NYPD Files

ISBN-13: 978-1540793614
ISBN-10: 1540793613
ASIN:B01NBFTZK6

Edited by: Lorna Collins
Cover design by: Melissa Summers

"There are no crime stories quite as good as a New York crime story. With ***Bronx Justice,*** Bob Martin adds another good read to that list."

Bill Bratton, former NYPD Police Commissioner

"If there is an extra dose of realism in this taut suspense tale, it is because the author, a veteran NYPD cop, lived ***Bronx Justice*** and stories like it. The novel is filled with good guys and bad guys and wise guys—a perfect recipe for a really fine page-turner of a novel."

Bob Drury & Tom Clavin, NY Times best-selling authors of ***Lucky 666: The Impossible Mission***

"Martin didn't just write ***Bronx Justice***, he lived it. Hence, the reader is treated to an exciting and fact-filled Cops 'n Robbers novel posing as fiction."

Vince Lardo, NY Times best-selling author of ***The McNally Series***.

"A tale of multiple redemptions, ***Bronx Justice*** takes us deep inside a cabal of crack dealing monsters. It also takes us into the complex mind of a truly dedicated, though greatly flawed, NYPD detective, John McGuire, struggling with his own demons as he works to bring down the evil cabal. Great story, great writing, great read..."

John Mackie, author ***Manhattan South***

Contents

Dedication

~~For my wife Marg Martin,
the "wind beneath my wings"~~

~~To those departed: my parents, Anne and Al Martin,
Bill Lecomte, my TPF partner, great friend,
Jack Miller, and John Timoney—"A Bronx cop"~~

~~And for Bobby Bilodeau, Abe Walton,
Tommy Pegues, Lee Ford, and Frankie Sledge,
five NYPD colleagues, friends, and heroes
who made the ultimate sacrifice~~

Acknowledgements

A first-time author needs all the help he can get. I was blessed to receive guidance and support on this project from my mentor, Vincent Lardo, a *New York Times* best-selling author.

I am grateful for these *New York Times* best-selling authors, who also encouraged and advised me: Tom Clavin, Marijane Meaker (and her Ashawagh Hall Writers Workshop.)

I am also indebted to my Street Crime Unit buddy, author of the *Thornton Savage* series, a great cop-great writer, John Mackie and his wife, Bonnie.

Special thanks go to ex Chicago cop, ex FBI Agent, prolific writer John Wills. He not only pointed me in the right direction, he was kind enough to share his editor with me, the phenomenal Lorna Collins.

One - The Escape

The Bronx, New York-November 1990

Roberto Medina took in a deep breath and exhaled loudly. He was grateful to hear the air moving past his lips. He got as comfortable as he could while lying in the pitch-black trunk of a moving auto. Occasionally, the car hit a bump, and Medina's head bounced off the spare tire and hit the trunk lid. He wished his hands were free so he could cushion these blows, but they were bound tightly behind his back. In spite of this, he felt strangely calm.

The savvy Puerto Rican had risen to the top of the Harlem numbers racket with a mixture of tenacity and good street sense. That sense told him there was nothing he could do but lie back and save his energy. At this point, nothing could be gained by shouting or trying to kick open the trunk. He had no idea where his two captors were taking him, but he was certain this was a one-way ride. When the car reached its destination, the driver and his companion would open the trunk, take him out, and shoot him. Medina knew he had only one chance to escape this fate, and so he nervously waited for the moment to arrive.

* * *

Steven "Pooh Bear" Jennings drove at a leisurely pace. The last thing he wanted was to be pulled over by some overzealous Bronx cops. The guns in the car would be hard to explain. Roberto Medina's presence in the trunk, even harder. Jennings knew cops well enough to know that the timing of this job could not be better. It was just after seven a.m. on a Sunday morning. The cops who had worked the busy overnight shift would not be looking to get involved in anything during the last hour of their tour. Saturday night was always the busiest night in any precinct, and doubly so in the South Bronx. The weary cops, finishing the late shift, would be checking their watches, looking to EOT (end of tour), signing out, going home, and catching some sleep.

Jennings slowed the car even more as he turned onto Park Avenue. This road in the Bronx was a far cry from the Park Avenue in Manhattan. The Manhattan version housed some of the most exclusive apartments and elite restaurants in the world. Many of the Fortune 500's top companies had their corporate headquarters there. The Bronx avenue, however, was an ugly stepchild. Lined on one side with run-down factories and boarded-up garages, the opposite side was bounded by a time-beaten chain-link fence, beyond which was the ugly open depression or "cut," which contained the tracks for the Metro-North Railroad. The tracks ran thirty feet below Park Avenue. Rising from the tracks to the street was a steeply sloped hillside made up of spindly trees and twisted shrubs all fighting for survival against unbridled weeds, and a twenty-year accumulation of Bronx garbage and eyesore trash. Old sinks and refrigerators, rusted stoves, and busted-up couches cluttered the hill. It also appeared any tire, taken off any vehicle, anywhere in the world eventually found its way to the Park Avenue cut.

At 169th and Park, Jennings came to a stop as he saw what he had been seeking. A large section of fence was missing. He leaned over and whispered to his friend Rontal Cheery, "You wanna do him?"

Cheery hesitated.

Jennings then murmured, "One of us has to do it."

Cheery blinked rapidly and let out a long sigh. "Wh—why us? Da—Dee killed all the others. Ha—how come we got to do this?"

Jennings put his finger to his lips and motioned toward the trunk. "Quiet, bro."

He leaned closer to Cheery. "Dee says it's time for us to step up. He wants us to have some blood on our hands." He noticed the perplexed look on his friend's face. "Think about it, Rontal. Once we do this, ain't no way we can ever make a deal with the cops and testify against him if we get caught. Dee's no fool."

"No. He, he's a psy—psycho."

"Straight up. Killing don't bother him at all. But, he ain't stupid." Jennings put a hand on Rontal's shoulder. "So?"

Cheery slowly nodded his head, his large Afro bobbing up and down.

"I made a lot of cash s—since you got me into Dee's crew. I—I owe you. I'll d—do it."

Pooh Jennings exhaled and nodded gratefully. "Thanks, brother. You the man. Now, here's how it goes down. When I open the trunk, I'll take him out and tell him everything is cool. Tell him we got the ransom money and we're letting him go. We walk him right up to the edge of the cut and tell him we're going to take the handcuffs off. You cap him, one shot to the head, his body will roll down the hill into the trash. They won't find him till it gets warm and he starts stinking."

He looked into his friend's eyes. "You ready?"

Cheery nodded.

"Let's do it."

They stepped out of the car and walked to the trunk. Jennings put the key into the lock.

* * *

Roberto Medina felt his skin tingle as every inch of his body quivered in anticipation. He curled himself into a ball with both feet inches from the center of the trunk lid. He knew he'd get only one try. If he failed, he would surely die.

His kick had to be timed for the exact instant it was unlatched. The element of surprise was the only thing working in his favor. Too soon or too late, he was dead. He heard the click of the key in the trunk lock. He was ready.

At the sound of the lock releasing, Medina kicked upward with all his might. The trunk panel shot up, catching one man solidly under the chin, driving him backward. In reflex, the second man took his eyes off the car and reached for his falling friend. This gave Medina the millisecond he needed to throw his legs out of the trunk. He landed shakily on the street, saw the second man lean over the fallen one, and whipped a vicious kick to the guy's ribs.

He heard a sharp "Oof" as air burst from the man's lungs. Had his hands been free, Medina would have attacked the black sons of bitches, but with them handcuffed behind him, he had only one option: to run.

He took off, his legs pumping furiously. A glance back over his shoulder showed the man he'd kicked getting to his feet, holding a gun. The other man still lay sprawled on his back.

Medina instinctively bent forward from the waist to make himself a smaller target, but unable to pump his arms for balance, this maneuver almost caused him to crash forward onto his face. He knew if he fell, he'd be dead.

He straightened up and ran.

The sound of the first shot made him run still faster. The second shot tore through his right arm and glanced off of his rib cage. The third ripped into his buttocks. It felt as if someone had rammed a white-hot poker into his ass.

He stumbled and almost went down but was able to keep his feet under him. He had no idea where he was, but about twenty yards ahead he saw what looked like a major street.

He saw cars traveling on this road and prayed he could reach the corner. He hoped the gunman wouldn't pursue him there and shoot him in front of witnesses.

Like a wounded animal, he ran on. Three more shots rang out, but all missed their mark.

Medina neared the corner and saw the street sign: "Washington Avenue." He knew by the white letters on a blue background he was in the Bronx. He cut sharply to his right and looked wildly from left to right, hoping to spot an open store or gas station in which to seek safety. Washington Avenue curved slightly. As he rounded the curve, the road ahead forked. On a triangular patch of ground in the middle of the fork stood an ancient red brick building. His heart leapt. It looked like a school or courthouse or perhaps a government building. As he got closer, he sighed. "*Gracias a Dios*." The building had green lights hanging on either side of its front doors. Roberto Medina knew he had stumbled upon a police station, and safety.

* * *

Long Beach, Long Island, New York

The clock radio went off with a loud buzz and the louder voice of Vanilla Ice singing "Ice, Ice, Baby."

NYPD Detective John McGuire rolled over and looked at the time through bloodshot eyes.

"God, I hate this song and the stupid prick singing it." McGuire reached out, smacked off the alarm, and sat up to find that he was sharing his bed with the cute redhead he had been drinking with at The Saloon, his local bar, some hours before. He ran a hand through his thick brown hair. *Jean? Jan? Jen? What the hell is her name?* He surveyed the tiny room and saw his and her clothes mixed in with empty Guinness Stout cans and a half-filled bottle of Peppermint Schnapps. *Wondered why my mouth tastes like Scope.* He noticed the wings on her blue uniform jacket. It started to come back to him. *Oh, yeah. Jean, TWA, flight attendant. "Don't call me a stewardess".*

Long Beach, located in Nassau County, a short drive from Kennedy Airport, was home to many airline employees. McGuire had moved there three months earlier when his wife left him. While he disliked the small basement apartment, he enjoyed being one block from the beach, the many bars, and the active night life.

He looked at the clock. Seven-ten a.m. He glanced again at Jean, sleeping peacefully, the sheet not completely covering her.

He shook his head. *Don't even think it. You absolutely must get to work on time today.*

He found a blanket, covered Jean, and took three steps to the bathroom. He'd let the hot shower soothe him for a minute, soap up, rinse, and then switch to cold to wake him up. He'd just started to lather when the shower curtain was drawn back. Jean, naked, held up a washcloth. "Want me to get your back, Detective?" Her face wore a sly smile.

McGuire looked at her, and felt his resolve start to go. He stepped back against the wall. "Babe, I'd love to, but I got to get to work on time today. I was late twice last week. My sergeant and my partner are really on my case."

Jean moved closer. She took the soap from McGuire and began to scrub his chest.

"Come on, John. Just a little while. I know you'd rather stay with me."

He grabbed her hand, holding it away from his body. "Part of me wants to stay, but the other part says I have to get to work."

She freed her hand and began moving the soap slowly down his stomach, stopping between his legs. She looked down. “Wow. I think I know how this part is voting.”

He groaned and pulled her to him. “Half an hour. My partner will cover for me.”

He brought his mouth down on hers.

Two - The Four-two

Sergeant Brian Flaherty was settling in. As the desk officer on the 42nd Precinct's day tour, he had gotten off to a good start. He'd "turned out the troops," giving the ten cops their assignments at roll call. Flaherty would have preferred going out on patrol, but today, he would handle the desk, taking care of all the mundane administrative tasks to be done in every precinct.

He'd assigned his steady driver, Leroy Dixon, to Special Post 1, also known as "the Palace Guard." Leroy would assist Brian in the station house, checking the cells, doing the property inventory, and ensuring Brian would have a quiet tour.

Leroy had made a run to the bakery and newsstand and returned with today's *Daily News*, *Post* and a dozen bagels.

"Coffee's ready, Boss," he called to Brian, who was busy making entries in the Log, the precinct's official record of the day's events.

Flaherty walked to the coffee pot, poured a cup, and grabbed a whole-wheat bagel.

Detective Joe "Go-Go" Gomez came down the stairs next to the desk, saw Brian, and snapped a military salute. "Permission to come behind the desk, Sarge. Want to check the 61s in your basket?"

Gomez was a slim, five-foot seven inches, originally from the Dominican Republic. He wore his black hair short. His, small mustache, glasses, and sharp three-piece suit made him look more like a banker than a detective. His nonstop energy and doggedness when on a case had produced his nickname, "Go-Go Gomez," from a character in the old *Dick Tracy* cartoons.

Brian returned the salute. "Sure thing, Joe, and thanks for asking. Some of these new kids don't have half your manners. They have the balls to come behind the desk without even asking, like they belong here. I worked with a lieutenant when I first made sergeant. Christ, I was afraid to come behind the desk when I relieved him for his meal. He owned the desk, and God help anyone who walked behind it without his permission."

"I had good people break me in when I came on the job, Sarge. I was taught whenever you came into the house to salute the flag and never go behind the desk without the DO's permission. It's just a habit now."

"Can't hurt, Joe. Doing the day tour? Didn't see you come in."

"Did the turnaround tour. Slept over up in the dorm."

Gomez referred to the detective schedule. They performed two night tours—four p.m. to one a.m., followed by two day tours—eight a.m. to four p.m. The third "turnaround" tour required the detective to be back in the squad seven hours after going off duty. Those who lived upstate or on Long Island got off at one, drove home, hit the rack, got maybe five hours of sleep, and then have to get up and be in by eight a.m., hence the term "turnaround" tour.

Many detectives found it easier to bunk in the precinct on the turnarounds, saving gas and mileage on their cars, and not having to worry about fighting traffic on the way in. While the accommodations were not the Ritz Carlton—two bunk beds in a small windowless closet made up the Four-two's dorm—for many, they beat the alternative.

Gomez stayed over but had been unable to talk his partner, John McGuire, into doing likewise. McGuire insisted on driving home to Long Beach. He'd assured Gomez he would get to work the next morning on time, but Gomez had serious doubts. Since McGuire's separation, his drinking had gotten out of hand. On a hopping Long Beach Saturday night, Joe knew John had either gotten lucky and was waking up next to a flight attendant—whose name he would not remember—or had drunk himself into a stupor. In either case, odds were long against McGuire showing up on time.

"Your partner upstairs, too?" Flaherty asked.

"No, John went home, but he should be here in a few minutes."

The sergeant raised an eyebrow and looked Joe directly in the eye. "He should be, but will he, Joe? I like McGuire, but I'm glad I don't have to supervise him. He's a great detective, but it's obvious that he's been hitting the bottle lately. It's starting to show."

"He's going through some tough marriage problems, Boss, but he'll be fine."

"I hope so. I've seen too many good guys go down the tubes on this job because of the booze."

Gomez finished looking at the crime reports. "You're right, Boss." He tried to change the subject. "Nothing major in your basket. I'll be upstairs if you need me."

"Grab a bagel, and take one for McGuire. Hopefully it won't be stale when he gets here."

"Thanks, Sarge." Gomez grabbed two bagels and ran upstairs to the squad room.

It was ten minutes to eight, ten minutes to the start of their tour. He picked up a phone and dialed McGuire's number. "Please be on your way. And please, John, be sober." The phone rang and rang.

* * *

Downstairs, Sergeant Flaherty had buttered a bagel and sipped his coffee. "Leroy, Jets-Dolphins, one p.m. kickoff. Want to take a 1300 meal and watch the first half? Relieve me for my meal at 1400, and we'll see the Jets kick ass on the Fish."

"No problem. Should be a nice, quiet Sunday."

A loud crash caused both men to spill their coffee. The massive wooden front doors burst open. A wild-eyed man, with his hands cuffed behind his back, had crashed through. In slomo, he stumbled to the front desk, where he collapsed, unconscious, in a rapidly expanding pool of blood.

Sergeant Brian Flaherty looked over the desk and down at the crumpled body, the blood, and the handcuffs. "Leroy, call an ambulance and go up and get the detectives. I think our nice quiet Sunday has just ended."

Three - "You Got Some Detecting to Do"

Joe Gomez ran downstairs. He saw a trail of blood starting at the front door, bits of glass from the door's broken window, and a body.

Sergeant Flaherty had a towel wrapped around the victim's arm, slowing the bleeding from a wound. "Joey, toss this mutt."

Gomez knelt and ran his hands over the man's body, into his pockets, over his crotch and legs, searching for a weapon. He found nothing, no weapon, no drugs, no wallet, no identification. "He's clean."

"Get the cuffs off him so I can look at this chest wound."

Gomez took out his cuff key and attempted to open the set on the victim. The small key fit into the hole, but turned without releasing.

"They're not ours." Gomez looked up. "Not Smith & Wesson's. They're some kind of cheap, knock-off set. I can't open them."

"I didn't think this guy escaped from one of our cops. We'd have heard a pursuit over the radio." Flaherty frowned.

Gomez took a ballpoint pen out of his shirt pocket, twisted it open, and removed the ink cartridge. He turned this upside down, inserted the open end into the cuff lock, pressed down hard, and turned. The cuff flew open. He did this with the second shackle and examined the victim's arms and hands. "He's no junkie, no tracks, looks clean."

He continued to check the man's hands. "Gets his nails done."

The examination stopped at the arrival of the ambulance. When two EMTs rushed into the station house, Gomez and Flaherty stepped back to give them room to work.

"Looks like he took one through the right arm. It glanced off his chest." Flaherty pointed.

"What about the blood all over his pants?" The EMT rolled the man onto his back and was checking for an open airway and heartbeat.

"The blood on his pants dripped down from the arm wound, Doctor Watson." Flaherty laughed.

The EMT unbuckled the victim's belt, opened his pants, and rolled him back onto his stomach. He pulled the pants down, revealing the wound to his right buttock.

"Hey, Sarge," the EMT shouted. "Call the *Guinness Book of Records*. I think we just found the first man ever born with two assholes. And, the assholes must have had a helluva fight, because one of them is bleeding like a stuck pig."

"Fuckin' know it all," Flaherty muttered. "Joey, where's your partner? Looks like you got some detectin' to do."

"He's on his way, should be here in five minutes," Gomez lied. "I want to get the Polaroid and get some pictures of this guy and the cuffs."

He ran upstairs to the squad, grabbed a phone, and punched in McGuire's number again. He looked at his watch. One minute after eight. Their tour had officially started, and all sorts of brass would be likely to show up soon. A handcuffed shooting victim stumbling into a police station was unusual, even for the Bronx. Gomez knew there was no way McGuire was en route to work. The phone began to ring. “Pick up John, please pick it up.”

Four - "I'm On the Way"

McGuire hadn't gone straight home as promised the night before. He certainly should have. Hell, he'd been tired, and it was almost two a.m. when he reached Long Beach. He'd have to leave his house by seven to get back to the squad by his tour's eight a.m. start. It made sense for him to get home and catch four and a half hours' sleep. More sense, it would seem, than he'd apparently had.

His route home took him right by his favorite Long Beach watering hole, The Saloon. He'd slowed and looked into its front window. The place was hopping. He'd hesitated, pulled to the side of the road, and checked his watch.

I'll have just one, he'd said to himself. He could hear the bar's jukebox before he reached the front door. "Catch a Wave." The box was filled with Beach Boys records favored by the aging surfers who frequented the place, most of whom had last actually caught a wave when Nixon was president.

He'd opened the door and was hit with a wave of noise and smoke. Fifty conversations strained to be heard over the mega-decibel music. All took place within a thick cloud of cigarette smoke. The bar was packed, a nice clientele, male, female, young, and old. The airport crowd mixed with cops, firemen, stock brokers, nurses, secretaries, and construction workers.

Squeaks O'Toole, the bartender, immediately drew a pint of Guinness Stout, McGuire's beverage of choice.

McGuire worked his way through the crowd, exchanging handshakes and hellos as he went.

Squeaks caught his eye. “Johnny Mac, got a spot for you at the end of the bar.” He held the Guinness high and pointed to a corner where five older men, Saloon regulars in their 50s and 60s, sat. Squeaks placed the stout on the bar and addressed the group. “Guaranteed, John will know the answer.”

An elfish-looking man in his 60s, wearing a kelly green, Fighting Irish-Notre Dame, sweatshirt, took a pipe from his mouth and blew a stream of smoke toward the ceiling. “And how the fook would John know what the five of us haven’t been able to figure out in the last twenty minutes?”

“Ah, you know John’s real good with the sports trivia, Barney,” another answered.

Squeaks nodded. “Not just sports, but movies, TV shows, history, current events. The man’s a walking *Encyclopedia Britannica.* I guarantee my man knows the answer you guys are stumped on. Anyone care to make a bet?”

“I got twenty says you’re wrong.” Barney threw a bill on the bar. His four friends did likewise.

“What’s the subject?” McGuire took a swig of his Guinness.

“Baseball trivia.” Squeaks reached into his pocket and peeled five twenties off a roll and slapped them down on top of the old-timers’ bets. “You ready, Johnny Boy?”

McGuire took a long pull of his Guinness and nodded.

“Okay, here it is,” Squeaks said. “Six members of the 1961 Yankees hit over twenty home runs. Can you name them?”

McGuire shook his head slowly as he looked at the bettors.

"This is what has the five of you stumped? And Barney, you're a lifelong, die-hard Yankee fan. You should be ashamed of yourself."

"Stop flapping ya gums and give us your answer, Mr. Wise Guy." Barney scowled.

"All right. First base, Moose Skowron-twenty-eight. The outfield, of course Roger Maris broke the Babe's home run record with sixty-one. The Mick, Mantle had fifty-four."

"We got them and one more," Barney said. "The fifth and sixth ones are tough."

"I'll tell you why it's hard, my Lucky Charms-looking friend. Like most people, you probably went position by position. I bet the fourth one you got was Yogi, the catcher with twenty-two."

"Right, Bucko, Yogi Berra. Now who are the last two?"

"Well, Barney, forty some years of drinking and smoking your pipe has rotted your brain. You've forgotten that while Yogi's in the Hall of Fame as a catcher, he spent most of the '61 season playing left field. Elston Howard did the catching. He had twenty-one round-trippers."

"Shit. I forgot Yogi played the outfield and Howard caught. So, who's the sixth player? You covered eight of the nine positions, and we all know a pitcher didn't hit twenty homers?"

"No, but the backup catcher, Johnny Blanchard, blasted twenty-one dingers in only 243 at-bats. Skowron, Maris, Mantle, Berra, Howard, and Blanchard. Six Yankees who hit over twenty homers in 1961." McGuire took a small bow.

"Game, set, and match, boys." Squeaks whooped while he scooped up the pile of twenties.

"I told you Johnny Mac has all the answers." He put two of the twenties in front of McGuire.

McGuire stared into his Guinness. "Squeaks, my friend, if I had all the answers, I'd still be married."

The old-timers grumbled into their drinks.

McGuire drained his glass and flipped the forty dollars back toward Squeaks. "Buy the senior citizens a drink on me."

The grumbling stopped.

The bartender took McGuire's empty glass back to the taps, filled it halfway, and as it settled, worked the far end of the bar. A few minutes later, he was back, and put the fresh pint in front of McGuire. "The lovely lass at the other end of the bar wants to buy you this drink."

McGuire looked, but through the haze of smoke and peoples' heads, he had trouble seeing the bar's far end. He was able to make out three women, all wearing identical blue jackets. "Which lovely lass would that be, Squeaks?"

"See the three TWA Stews in the corner in blue? The cute redhead on the right."

"Wow. Guess I should go down there and thank her." McGuire picked up his pint.

"Always the gentleman." Squeaks winked at his friend. "Her name is Jean."

* * *

McGuire heard the phone ring. He sat up and held his pounding head with both hands. *Shouldn't a had that second pint, or the tenth one either.* He thought he'd heard something a few minutes earlier but couldn't be sure. Maybe it was his neighbor's phone. The houses in Long Beach were close. It didn't stop.

He walked into the tiny living room and picked up the phone.

"John, it's Joey. Where the hell are you?"

"What kind of detective are you, Partner? I believe you called me, so odds are I am now standing in my palatial waterfront estate in beautiful, bucolic Long Beach."

"You know what I mean. I asked you to stay over last night. You had to go home but swore you'd be in on time. Well, on time is now, and you haven't even left your house yet."

"Relax, it's Sunday. Sergeant Ramos is off, and whoever is covering us won't be around for hours, if he even bothers checking up on us. If the covering boss calls, tell him I'm in. If he wants to talk to me, tell him I went out for bagels. I'll take a quick shower and be there in forty-five minutes."

Sergeant Vic Ramos, the CO of the Four-two Detective Squad, was off on Sundays and Mondays. The detectives would be covered this tour by a "covering boss," a sergeant from one of the other Bronx squads. "John, we have a handcuffed shooting victim lying in front of the desk. I'll have to call the covering boss soon. He'll call the detective duty captain, who'll call the Chief of D's office, who will then let the PC's office know. I need you here now. You're putting my neck on the line."

"Ah shit, different scenario. No shower, give me half an hour to get in."

"Make it quick, but for God's sake don't get in an accident. I'll cover things until you get here, but John, this shit has to stop."

"You're right, Joey. I fucked up, but I'm on my way. See you in half an hour."

McGuire hung up the phone and walked into the bathroom. He leaned over the sink, turned on the cold water and checked his face in the mirror. His blue eyes looked good, nothing a couple of bottles of Visine wouldn't fix. There was little he could do about the dark circles under his eyes and the new puffiness of his jaw line. His face was showing the effects of too many late nights and far too many pints.

He splashed cold water onto his face, dried it, stood to his full six-foot-two inches and examined his upper torso. His two-hundred-pound body was toned and muscled. He pinched the small roll of flab, which hung over his waist, and addressed his mirrored reflection. "Tomorrow, ten mile run, a hundred sit-ups and no drinking until Friday. Have you back in fighting shape in two weeks."

He grabbed the wash cloth from the shower, wiped himself down, dried, and put on a few extra sprays of Right Guard. He then combed his medium-length brown hair and did a quick once-over on his face with an electric razor, which set his five o' clock shadow back to three. He went into the bedroom, donned clean Jockeys, a crisp white shirt, khaki chinos, brown belt, black socks, and brown penny loafers.

McGuire snapped his holstered .38 Colt Cobra onto his belt. His shield went into his left front pocket, his money clip into his right. From the top of his dresser, he took a small can of fish food and sprinkled a few flakes into the glass fish bowl.

"Breakfast, Clubber," he said to his goldfish, named after the notoriously brutal NYPD Inspector Alexander "Clubber" Williams, who'd ruled the West Side of Manhattan with an iron fist in the 1870s.

"There is more law at the end of a policeman's nightstick than in any Supreme Court decision," was a Clubber quote McGuire loved.

Jean was sound asleep. He thought about trying to wake her, but decided rousing her would take time he didn't have. He didn't like the idea of leaving someone he barely knew alone in his house but rationalized to himself. *I got my gun, shield, money. What can she take? Clubber ?*

He scribbled a quick note: "Jean. Fun night. You're a special lady. I have to bring law and order to the wild, untamed South Bronx. Help yourself to anything you want in the fridge. See you soon, John."

The note failed to point out McGuire's refrigerator contained only eight pint-sized cans of Guinness, a bottle each of mustard and ketchup, and two containers of Chinese food, long past their use date. The freezer held a copious supply of ice cubes and a half bottle of Stoli.

McGuire retrieved sheets and blankets from the floor, covered Jean, and left the note on the pillow. He grabbed a red tie and blue blazer from the closet, dropped his keys into his pocket, and headed toward the door.

"Be kind to our guest, Clubber. She's a redhead, just like you."

He quietly left the house, jumped into his beat-up blue '85 Chevy Caprice, let out a sigh of relief when it started, and headed to the Bronx.

Five - Dee

Pooh Bear Jennings drove slowly down the Grand Concourse. Beside him, Rontal Cheery moaned softly. He held his right hand to the left side of his rib cage and leaned forward at an awkward angle.

“P—P—Pooh, you got to g—get me to a hospital. I th—think my ribs are broken.”

“No can do, Rontal. We don’t want your name on any records. I’m going to the crack house on Tiebout. We’ll get you some coke. You’ll be fine.”

“Sh—Shit, don’t go th—there. I can get some bl—blow anywhere. We go to T—Tiebout, we might run into Dee. I don’t wa—wanna see him. He’s going to be p—pissed. Let’s not tell him w—what happened.”

“Rontal, you know Dee is gonna find out Roberto got away. We got to man up and tell him. Better he hear it from us. He’ll get mad, but don’t you say nothing. Let me do all the talking, and we’ll be all right. He’s going to meet us in twenty minutes. Remember, if Dee asks you anything, hush up. Let me handle it.”

They turned off the Concourse and headed toward Tiebout Avenue. Jennings cruised past an abandoned house, made a U-turn, and came back. Satisfied the location was not being surveilled by the police, he parked around the corner. He and Cheery climbed the rickety steps, knocked twice, waited, and then knocked three times. Behind the sheet metal-covered front door came the sounds of bolts opening, metal bars being moved. The door opened an inch.

"It's us, Marvin," Jennings said.

The door swung open to reveal the three-hundred-plus pound Marvin Williams, who ran the Tiebout crack house. Jennings and Cheery stepped into darkness. All of the windows were boarded up. What little light there was came from candles spaced around the room.

Bare and filthy mattresses, trash, and hundreds of brightly colored plastic crack vials covered the floor. The only thing worse than the sight of the house was its smell. With no running water or electricity, the toilet had long since become full. The crackheads now relieved themselves in buckets. They crowded the small bathroom, and the smell of feces and urine was overpowering.

Pooh Bear Jennings did not use drugs and was sickened whenever he had to come here. As his eyes adjusted to the darkness, he looked around and swore softly. The place was empty, the usual throng of spaced-out junkies nowhere to be seen.

"Where is everyone, Marvin?"

Williams did not answer but looked toward the back of the room. From its darkness, like a ghost floating toward them, came the big man, Dee.

Six-foot five, two hundred-forty pounds on a muscular frame, shoulders twice as wide as hips. Though having never lifted a weight, his seventeen-inch biceps strained the sleeves of his knee-length black leather trench coat. A turtleneck, jeans, and motorcycle boots, all black, completed the look. Dee's skin was just a shade lighter than his coat.

His shaved head and diamond stud in his right ear reflected the sparse light.

"I wanted to speak to y'all in private," he began. "Just what the fuck happened?" Dee's angry voice hovered about five floors below *basso profundo*. He spoke slowly and enunciated each word, which emphasized the low rumble of his speech. His voice, wardrobe, and physical presence exuded menace. If asked to describe him in one word, "Evil" would probably do.

Pooh Bear Jennings explained how he had been knocked down by the trunk lid. Dee lifted his hand to Jennings' jaw. "You got a welt there, looks swollen. Better put some ice on it."

Dee turned his gaze toward Cheery. "And what did you do as our man escaped?"

"He tried to—" Jennings attempted to answer before Dee cut him off.

"I'm asking Rontal." Dee's unblinking brown eyes never left Cheery's face.

"I'm s—s—sorry Dee. But sh—sh—shit happens."

Dee stood with both hands gripping his lapels. As he slowly turned his head to the left to look at Jennings, his right hand slid under his left into his coat. He snapped his head back and with it came his right hand, holding a Charter Arms stainless steel .44 caliber "Bulldog" revolver. The gun swung smoothly until it almost touched the center of Rontal Cheery's chest.

Dee pulled the trigger once. The "Bulldog" barked, the sound deafening in the small room.

Cheery staggered back, and looked once at the smoking hole in his chest. His eyes rolled back. He was dead before he hit the floor.

Dee held the weapon to his nose and snorted the smoky gunpowder wafting from the barrel. He slid the gun back into the shoulder holster beneath his left armpit.

"Oh God, Dee, why, why?" Jennings moaned

"Sh—Sh—Shit happens."

Dee snapped his fingers. Marvin Williams knelt down, removed Cheery's wallet from his front pants pocket and handed it to Dee. Williams then slipped two bright-red crack vials into the same pocket.

"Soon as it gets dark, get this stuttering motherfucker outta here. Got to get the crackheads back, and make some damn money," Dee said.

"Where should we dump him?" Marvin Williams asked.

"I don't give a fuck. Drop his ass on second base in Yankee Stadium for all I care. Ain't no thang. Honky cops will be happy. One less nigger junkie to worry about. You think Reverend Al will be marching for justice for Rontal, or Mayor Dinkins will break a sweat? No way, baby, this is the Bronx. Nobody, I mean nobody, gonna give a shit about one more dead brother."

Six - Watch Your Back

Gomez spotted McGuire's car pull up. He ran downstairs, saw McGuire, and pointed to the alley next to the precinct. "John, this is it. I can't keep covering for you."

"I'm sorry. I swear to God. I try but—"

"Save the excuses. No time. Listen."

McGuire hung his head.

"Stark, the new sergeant from the Four-seven, is covering us. He just got into the bureau, and word is he's shaky. He got here ten minutes ago. I told him you were at Jacobi getting info on our victim. Just spoke with a nurse I know there. The vic's in the OR now. Took a round in the ass and one in the arm, which grazed his ribs but didn't penetrate."

"We got a name?"

"Still John Doe, but won't be for long. Not a junkie. Somebody must be looking for him. Lost a lot of blood but going to be okay. We should be able to talk to him in an hour."

"How we gonna play it with Stark?"

"Wait five minutes, then come up, and fill him in on all you found out at the hospital."

"Joe, did you ask your nurse friend to hold onto his clothes and any rounds they recover? Not throw them in the trash?"

"Done."

"You get smarter every day."

"Yeah, I get smarter and I get to work on time." Gomez walked up the steps.

"That's why you're my partner," McGuire called before Gomez disappeared inside.

In the police world, partners were like brothers. They bonded while BSing on quiet tours and faced danger together on busy ones. When two cops were paired on a steady basis, they read each other's minds, anticipated what the other was about to do, communicated without words. They shared a sacred bond.

McGuire moved toward the front of the precinct, still out of view of the detective squad's second-floor windows. He found a spot of sunshine and leaned against the wall of old building. It was a crisp fall day. He hadn't bothered with a top coat. He rested his back against the warm wall and it felt good. The stone retained some of the sun's heat. He had closed his eyes when a loud voice startled him.

"Hey, Detective, you holding the building up?" A big smile covered the pretty black face of PAA Wanda Stith.

"No ma'am, this place don't need my help. They built them to last back then."

"Back when?"

"1904."

"Were they afraid of Indians? Place looks like a fort from an old movie."

McGuire smiled. "Not Indians. People who designed police stations and armories at the turn of the century learned from Civil War Draft Riots forty years earlier, when mobs overran and burned precincts where the cops were trying to protect your people."

"From your people."

McGuire grimaced. "You got me there. Not the Irish's finest hour, although most of the cops doing the protecting were also Irish."

Wanda pointed at the precinct. "So?"

"Three stories, the first limestone, next two brick. Heavy metal screens over the windows. Built to be imposing and tough for a mob to overrun or set fire to."

"Still say it looks like a fort."

"Lot of cops agree with you."

"What?"

"You know what the cops call the Four-one—"

"Fort Apache."

"The Four-0?"

"*Little House on the Prairie.*"

"Yeah, and Brooklyn has three precincts: the Alamo, Fort Surrender, and Fort Zinderneuf."

"Fort Zinderwhat?"

"Zinderneuf. Old Gary Cooper flick, *Beau Geste.*"

"Never heard of it."

"You're too young. Go to Blockbuster and rent it. A classic. Not many films have four Oscar winners in them."

"Four?"

"Gary Cooper, Ray Milland, Broderick Crawford, and Susan Hayward."

"I know Gary Cooper. 'Today, I consider myself the luckiest man in the world.'"

"Close enough. Yeah, he did *The Lou Gehrig Story.*"

"McGuire, I heard you know all about sports. How you know all this other stuff? Your brain must be full of—"

"Useless information. It's what my wife used to say."

"Heard about that, too. I'm sorry."

He looked at his watch. "You going in?"

They walked up the steps. McGuire held the door for Wanda, who stopped at the 124 Room where she would spend her day typing. She reached a hand up and touched his cheek. "Take care of yourself, John. That's an order from the precinct's best Police Administrative Aide."

"Thanks, Wanda, I'll try."

He turned to the front desk and fired a salute to the flag.

Sergeant Flaherty saw him. "Detective, hold on, I want to talk with you."

"Sure thing, Sarge." McGuire wondered if he was in trouble with the uniform boss.

"Come up, John." McGuire stepped to the side of the desk, opened the brass gate and stepped up. Flaherty pointed to a small room behind the desk and led McGuire into it.

"Are you okay, Mac? You don't look so good."

"I'm fine."

"Wanna give you a heads up. Do you know your covering boss, Sergeant Stark?"

"Haven't met him yet. I was over at Jacobi getting—"

"Yeah, you were at Jacobi. Stick with it, but I wanna warn you, Stark just came down and asked if I saw you today. Told him I got ten cops and a rookie sergeant to look out for. I don't keep tabs on detectives not under my control. This guy's a real prick. He was in IAB as a detective, wanted to go right back out of sergeant school. He didn't get it. Sent him to the Seven-one. He's there about two weeks, got everybody pissed off. Stripes went to his head. The cops hated his guts, went on a slowdown when he was working."

"How's he go from uniform in the Seven-one to the Four-seven Detective Squad?"

"They had to get him out of Brooklyn. Not just the cops, the other bosses, everybody thought he was a dipshit. The troops gave him two nicknames: Stark R.M. and The CO."

"Stark R.M.?"

"Stark Raving Mad, John. Stark Raving Mad. He's been looking for you. Be on your toes when you go upstairs."

"What about The CO?" McGuire raised an eyebrow. "The Commanding Officer?"

"No, but you're a sharp detective. I bet you'll figure it out when you meet him. Now get your ass upstairs, and stay on your toes."

"Thanks, Boss, I really appreciate it." McGuire headed slowly up to the squad. His usual bounce and confidence stayed behind at the desk.

Seven - Cat and Mouse

McGuire put some pep in his stride, a smile on his face, and began to whistle a tune as he neared the squad room. He pushed open the old door covered with so many coats of green paint it no longer closed all the way, and entered the office. Nothing had changed since he'd left the night before. Green paint peeled off the walls, steam pipes hissed, dirty windows, five green metal desks were covered with papers, reports, and case folders, and trash cans were still filled to the brim.

"Yo, Partner, I'm back from Jacobi. You solve this case yet?" he loudly exclaimed.

"Still working on it, but arrests are imminent." Joe rolled his eyes toward the supervisor's office. "Sergeant Stark from the Four-seven is covering us. He's in Vic's office."

McGuire heard a chair scrape and walked to the sergeant's office. He knocked twice on the frame then turned into the room. Sergeant Roy Stark came around from behind the desk. McGuire had to suppress a laugh. The sarge was, maybe on a good day, five-foot-seven. He weighed well over 200 pounds. His belly protruded over his belt, and his shirttail hung outside his pants. The pièce de résistance, though, was Stark's hair style. He had very little, and he wore what was left very long and badly dyed jet black. It was combed from just above his left ear, slicked down over the crown, and came to rest near his right ear.

McGuire now knew why the boys in Brooklyn had christened him "The CO." It had to be "The Comb Over."

McGuire stuck out his hand "Hi, Boss. John McGuire."

Stark took his hand in a viselike grip and pulled him in very close. He went up onto his toes so his nose was just a few inches from McGuire's face.

"You been drinking, McGuire?"

"No. Oh wait, I did have a dram of sherry last night while I was reading *War and Peace* at home in my library."

"I heard you're a wise guy, McGuire. You want to get wise with me?"

"Not at all, Sergeant. I did have a beer, off-duty last night, nothing more."

"You sure it was only one beer? I hear you been pounding them down since your wife left you. I saw plenty of that shit when I was a detective. 'Boo hoo, my wife left, give me another beer.' Guys in squads with a six pack in the fridge and an open one in their desk drawer. Drunks. Disgrace to the job."

McGuire, stunned because Stark knew of his personal problems, had no reply.

"And where you been? Your partner tells me you were at Jacobi interviewing the shooting victim, but you're not signed out in the Movement Log, as required."

"Sergeant, we got a shooting victim who runs into the house and collapses in front of the desk. I figure he must have been shot somewhere close by. I took a walk down Washington Avenue and some of the side streets, asked some people if they saw or heard anything. There could be another victim lying out there needing medical help. When I got back, the bus had just left. I told Joe to hold down the scene here, and I went to the hospital hoping to get a statement from the victim."

Stark had gone behind the desk and sat down. He leaned back with both hands behind his head, put one black shoe, which badly needed a shine, up on the corner of the desk. "And how did you get to the hospital?"

"How did I get there? Jacobi is a bit too far to walk to, so I drove, of course."

Still leaning back, Stark's gaze bore into McGuire. "You drove? In your private car or a department auto?"

McGuire's mind raced. *Where is Stark going with these questions?* He couldn't take his eyes off of Stark's dirty shoe resting on the corner of his fastidious boss, Vic Ramos's desk.

"In a department auto, of course, Sergeant."

"What one?"

"Do you mean which one of the squad's autos did I use?"

Stark's face was turning red. "You know exactly what I mean. What car did you take?"

"I took 4196."

"Let's see, 4196 is one of three cars assigned to this squad, correct? And you took it to Jacobi?"

"Yeah, Sarge, it's the car I took."

Stark swung his foot off the desk and stepped past McGuire to the corner of the office. A small, brown wooden box with a door was mounted on the wall, about five feet off the floor.

Stark opened the door and stared at McGuire. "Then explain to me, Detective, if you took auto 4196 to Jacobi, how is it the keys to 4196 and the other two vehicles assigned to this squad are hanging in this box? Tell me how you can drive a car to Jacobi when the keys are right here. Please explain, Mr. Hot Shot detective."

McGuire drew in a deep breath and exhaled slowly. He was trying to keep his cool. He expected to be grilled about where he had been, but Stark's comments and his obvious disdain for working detectives pushed him to his limits. The reference to his marriage crossed the line. His rage had to come out somewhere.

"I would be happy to explain, Sergeant. First off, you never worked in a precinct detective squad, correct? I know you got the gold shield in IAB. What kind of cases did you work? The female cop in Manhattan who got two scoops of ice cream at Baskin-Robbins and was only charged for one? You know what real detectives, precinct detectives, work on? You been readin' the papers? We work on homicides, people getting killed. We had over 600 here in the Bronx last year."

"How dare you talk to me like that? I'm a sergeant and..."

"Now, in response to your question, how could I drive a car when the keys are up there in the key box, let me explain. Quite often a detective, finishing an eighteen- or twenty-hour tour after catching a fresh homicide might forget to turn in the keys to a car. He goes home with them in his pocket. So, you know what a sharp detective does?" McGuire reached into his pants pocket, took out his key ring, and jingled the numerous keys on it.

"A sharp detective has keys made for all the cars in his squad and puts them on his own key ring so he never has to worry about finding a missing set. It's how this hot shot detective got to Jacobi without taking a key from the locker, Sergeant."

Stark's mouth hung open as he obviously struggled to come up with a reply. Unable to think of one, he turned and stalked out of the room.

McGuire followed closely behind.

Stark stopped at Joe's desk. "Gomez, I'll be at the Boro, call me if anything breaks on the shooting."

Joe was about to answer when McGuire stepped in front of him. "You'll be the first to know."

Stark turned and headed for the door.

McGuire called to him, "Sarge."

Stark stopped just outside the squad in the empty hallway. McGuire came out, put a hand on the man's shoulder, and leaned in close. "Want a little advice from a hot shot detective? You're in the Detective Bureau now. You're a boss. You need to look sharp."

Stark's face turned bright red and the blue vein pulsing in his forehead looked ready to blow. "Fuck you, McGuire. You better watch your ass."

"No sense both of us watching it."

Stark started down the stairs.

McGuire leaned over the banister. "One last fashion tip: you might want to get yourself a nice snap brim fedora like the old-time detectives wore. Maybe buy two. You could give one to your CO."

Stark flew down the rest of the stairs.

McGuire turned, bounced on his toes and threw a three-punch combination into the air, left hook head, left hook body, right hand jaw. He was starting to feel better.

Eight - You May Have Won the Battle, But...

McGuire was still bouncing as he walked back into the squad.

Gomez jumped up. "*Ay, dios mio,* John, what did you do?"

"What did I do, Partner? You saw what I did. I couldn't help it. The fat prick had to be taken down a notch or two."

"God, I thought he had us. I signed you in, but never thought to sign you out in the Movement Log. I never called the Boro. Stark didn't call. He dropped in unannounced. I was sure we were dead meat when I heard him ask you about the keys. I didn't know you had copies made for your key ring."

"I don't have any squad car keys on my ring."

"John, you told Stark you did. I heard you jiggling your keys."

"Joe, you have to listen more carefully when I speak. I did not say I had keys made. What I said was it's something a sharp detective might do."

"Then why did you rattle your keys in his face?"

"Stark seems very childlike. It amuses the shit out of my two-year-old nephew when I do it, so I figured he might enjoy it."

"What were you going to do if he asked to see the key for 4196 on your ring?"

"He wouldn't do it, Joey. Sergeant Stark is a coward and a bully, and I—"

"Don't like bullies. I certainly know how you feel, but Stark is a supervisor, not some cop you can just punch the crap out of. You embarrassed him. He can make our lives miserable."

"I embarrassed him? Joe, did you see the man? He's a walking embarrassment. Shit, he's a supervisor in the Detective Bureau of the largest police department in the world, and he walks in here looking like an unmade bed. Shirt tail out, belly popping the buttons of his twelve-dollar Alexander's special shirt I wouldn't wear to change my oil. Must have spent about fifty bucks for that shitty, ill-fitting suit on Orchard Street. He probably climbed into the St. Vincent de Paul drop box behind St. Raymond's to get the shoes, depriving some homeless man of some nice kicks. And putting his foot up on Vic's desk—what balls. Vic eats at his desk, and this shitbird comes in, brand new in Bronx Detectives, and puts his filthy shoe on a squad commander's desk. If Vic had walked in and seen it, the shoe would have gone out the window with the fat bag of shit's foot still in it."

"John, you're right. But still, this is the NYPD. Stark is a boss. We are the peons. He can hurt us, ruin our careers."

"Relax. First off, when Vic comes in Tuesday and finds out what happened, I bet he goes right up to the Four-seven and has a little talk with Stark. Straightens him out about the courtesies expected when covering another sergeant's squad. Second, the only time he can mess with us is on Sundays and Mondays when Vic is RDO. There are six other sergeants beside Stark who have Fridays and Saturdays as regular days off, who get the coverage. The most we should see him is maybe once a month. Don't sweat it, Joey. We'll be fine."

"I hope you're right, John."

"Of course I'm right. I happen to be a hot shot detective. Now whadda ya say you and I get over to Jacobi and speak with our victim and find out why somebody handcuffed and tried to kill him."

"Yeah, let's go. We should be able to talk with him now. What car you wanna take?"

"Same car I used before, of course, 4196. Engine should still be warm, Partner."

Gomez walked to the key locker and took down the set for 4196. As he signed them out in the Movement Log, he turned to look at McGuire. "I got your parting shot about buying a hat, but why would you tell him to buy one for his CO? Chief Philbin has a full head of hair."

"Let's go. I'll tell you in the car. We got a case to solve."

Nine - Just the Facts

Joe Gomez pulled into the service road of Pelham Parkway and made a right into the entrance for Jacobi Hospital, parking between two ambulances. He and McGuire entered the emergency room and headed to the nurses' station. The desk was staffed by three nurses, who were true representatives of their borough: one black, one Latina, supervised by an older, stout Irish woman. Gomez caught the eye of the pretty Hispanic nurse. "*Hola Maria, cómo estás?*"

"Detective Gomez, we can converse in English here. This is the ER not the DR."

"*Lo siento, Maria.* I'm sorry, but when I see you, I think of Santiago and home."

When most Americans thought of the Dominican Republic, they pictured themselves lying on a beautiful beach in Puerto Plata or Punta Cana. Santiago, where Maria and Joe both hailed from, was not one of the tourist destinations. It was a tough, gritty city, far from the coast and the *touristas.*

"Sorry, Joe, no time for a stroll down memory lane. We're busy as hell. You looking for your shooting victim?

He's in seven." She looked down at a clipboard. "His name's Roberto Medina. Doc Singh just sewed him up. You should be able to speak with him."

McGuire and Gomez walked to Treatment Room seven. Their victim was on a gurney, lying on his left side, a large dressing covered his right buttocks. His right arm, also bandaged, was in a sling.

Gomez bent down and looked the man in the eyes. "*Yo soy Detective Gomez y mi socio, Detective McGuire.*"

"I speak English, Detective," the man said.

"Your Spanish is sure going over big here today, Partner." McGuire grinned.

"Okay, how about telling us who you are and how you ended up shot, in handcuffs, in the Four-two Precinct?" Gomez asked.

"Sure thing. Name's Roberto Medina, I'm a numbers guy, run the action on the East side, Eighty-sixth street to 125th. Spanish Harlem is mine."

"You push drugs also, right?"

"Detective, I just told you, I'm a numbers guy. I make a very nice living. Once or twice a year, your friends in Vice bust me, and I pay my lawyer a few grand to keep me out of jail. The longest I've ever been in is one week in twenty years. Why would I want to sell drugs and risk going away for life? I would never push poison to my people."

"Bullshit." Gomez raised his voice. "You're such an upstanding member of the community. You would take the last dollar from some poor old widow if she lost her bet with you. You low-life scumbag."

McGuire was surprised at the reaction from his normally quiet, calm partner. "Hey Joe, why don't you go out and speak with Maria for a minute while I have a chat with Roberto."

Gomez started to protest, but McGuire stopped him. "I got this, Partner. It's okay."

Gomez stalked out without a reply.

"Hey, Roberto, sorry. Don't know what got into my partner."

"*No es nada.* He's Dominican. I'm Puerto Rican. There's a little rivalry here. No big thing, like the cops and firemen. Family friction is all."

"How'd you know he's Dominican?"

"We can tell. Dominicans talk very fast."

McGuire pulled over a chair and sat near Medina's head. "Roberto, my job is to find out who shot you. I could give a flying fuck about the numbers racket. *No es mi problema.* Why don't you just start at the beginning and tell me what happened."

He let the man speak for five minutes, never interrupting, not taking notes, nodding his head occasionally. One of McGuire's great strengths as a detective was he was a good listener. He found most people liked to talk, and one of their favorite subjects was themselves. Whether he was speaking to a victim, like Roberto Medina, a witness, or a perp, he started by asking one simple question. "What happened?" He let the person talk until they were finished. He then asked questions to clear up any murky points. If he was grilling a perp, he'd point out the inconsistencies he'd discovered, but even then, he was calm and detached. It was like peeling an onion to McGuire. Take a story one layer at a time and either believe it or shoot it down.

When Medina finished, McGuire said, "Wow, it's some story. You're lucky to be alive. Okay Roberto, tell me what happened again." This was the point where McGuire, who had a great memory, looked for any discrepancies, anything which didn't jibe with the man's first version.

Medina again described what had happened. On Friday evening, he'd been in his office, the back room of a bodega in Spanish Harlem, when he heard a commotion out front. He walked out and was confronted by what he thought were two cops, very large white men, in plainclothes with police badges on chains around their necks. One man carried a police walkie-talkie. He had been arrested numerous times before. It happened in his profession. The vice cops who had busted him had always been, if not polite, at least businesslike. They had a job to do just like he did. This time, something about these cops bothered him. They seemed nervous, unsure of themselves, like this was new to them.

The leader, a big man with a ponytail, who looked like the actor, Steven Seagal, said they had a warrant for his arrest. *A warrant? For numbers?* It had never happened before.

"May I see the warrant?" Roberto had asked.

"No. Shut the fuck up. Vinny, cuff him."

Vinny was really huge, six-foot-four, maybe 260 pounds, a weight lifter. Roberto recalled this cop sweated profusely.

"It's November, chilly out, and this guy is sweating making a two-bit numbers collar. Something ain't right. I yell to Benny, my guy in the bodega, 'Call my wife and lawyer, tell them—.' That's all I get out. Vinny and Seagal each grab an arm, cuff my hands behind my back, lift me off the ground, and hustle me out into the back seat of a car at the curb."

"What kind of car?" McGuire asked.

"Dirty, dark blue, piece of shit Crown Vic, like you guys drive. Oh, sorry."

"No apology needed. Then what happened?"

Medina then described how Seagal had driven, with Vinny sitting in the back with him. When they drove off the block, Vinny pushed Roberto down onto the floor and placed a canvas bag over his head.

"I know we're going north on First Avenue. We go onto the Triborough Bridge."

"How'd you know if you got a bag over your head?"

"Detective, I could still hear. We went up a hill and stopped. Exact change lane. I hear the bell, and we take off. I think we are going to the Bronx. Then five minutes later, I'm sure."

"How could you be sure?"

"It's quiet in the car, no talking. Suddenly Vinny says, 'The house that Ruth built.' Seagal yells, 'Shut the fuck up, you moron.' I know we just passed Yankee Stadium. We stay on the Deegan another five or ten minutes and get off. Maybe north Bronx, maybe Yonkers. Hard to tell."

The car came to a stop, and Medina heard a garage door open. They drove in. Medina was pulled roughly from the back seat.

"I hear Seagal talking to a new guy. Sounds like a black dude. Seagal says, 'He's all yours.' The black voice gives a nasty laugh and says, 'We'll take good care of him.' This guy's voice is real deep. Sounds like Barry White. I hear the car leave."

Medina now heard three people, all sounding like black men, talking. He is pushed down into a chair.

"I still have the bag on my head, but I can look down and see the floor. I see a pair of black boots, big. The deep voice, Barry White says, 'How you feeling, *amigo*?' Something hard is pushed against my ear. I hear a clicking noise and a loud snap. This prick is dry firing a pistol into my ear. I'm scared, but I know if they wanted to kill me, they could have just blasted me in the bodega. I ask him what they want."

"We want a hundred grand. We know your organization and wife can raise it. If we don't get it by tomorrow night, I put the bullets in. We get the money, or you get dead."

Medina then told McGuire how his captors had handcuffed him to a chair in a small, windowless room. He was allowed to remove the bag from his head, but he had to put it back on when one of them entered the room to bring him water or food. He had no idea how long he was in the room.

"Finally, this morning, I hear Barry White again. Sounds like he's pissed off. I hear him say, 'I ain't asking you. I'm fucking telling you. Do it. That's all.' Door opens and a tall black guy comes in, all smiles. Lots of gold chains. Black Converse sneakers.

"He says, 'Great news, Roberto. We got the ransom money. We're going to take you back to Manhattan and let you go.' This ain't Barry. Much softer voice. I put on a big smile and say, 'I knew my boys would come through,' but I know he's full of shit. They're going to kill me."

"How'd you know, Roberto?"

"Because, Detective, when he came in, he didn't ask me to put the bag on. For how many hours they did not want me to see their faces? Now they're going to let me go, and they don't care? I know he's lying. They're going to kill me. I thought about attacking them, but they—"

"Gotcha."

"Well, anyway, Converse and a skinny guy with buck teeth come in. Bucky and Cons get me out of the chair; cuff both hands behind my back. Cons is in charge. I notice Bucky stutters. They push me out the door, and I see we are in some kind of garage. Car is right there with the trunk open. They throw me in."

"What kind of car?"

"Don't know. Happened real quick. I decided when I heard the trunk open, I was going to kick the lid with all my might and see what happened. Thank God, it worked. I kicked, saw Cons on the ground, kicked Bucky, and ran for my life. Bucky was the one shooting. Guess he was groggy. Think I heard six shots. Only hit me with two. I never ran so fucking fast in my life. Those green lights outside your precinct were the sweetest sight I ever seen."

"Give me a description of Cons." McGuire leaned forward.

"Light-skinned black man. Maybe six foot, skinny, wearing one of those 8-Ball jackets with leather sleeves, black cons."

"Anything stand out?"

"Oh yeah, the gold chains. Lots of them. Had the Mister T starter set. One of them was strange. He had a chain with a cute little figure on it. A fat little bear. Like that cartoon bear that always wants honey."

"You mean Winnie the Pooh?"

"Yeah, right. I thought it was weird. Dude wearing a little cute bear is going to kill me."

"What about the other guy?"

"Buck teeth, big afro, stuttered, is all I remember." Medina's eyes drooped.

"Okay, amigo. You did great. You're tired. Get some rest. I'll call your wife. Let her know you're okay. I'm gonna try and get a uniform cop to baby sit you for a while. Until I do, I'll get hospital security to keep an eye on you. When we come back, I'll make sure my partner is in a better mood."

"Detective, I am a numbers man. I break the law. But I have never hurt anybody. I do not use or sell drugs. I want the guys who did this to me caught. They should not be allowed to do this to anybody else. I will come to court and testify. On this you have my word."

"Roberto, no guarantees, but I promise you my Dominican partner and I will do our very best."

Roberto Medina reached out with his left hand and took McGuire's hand in his. "Detective McGuire, I do not know you, but I have a feeling when you try your very best, there is little that you cannot do. *Que dios le bendiga*—May God bless you."

McGuire was touched. He reached out and gave Medina two light taps on the cheek. "Get some rest, amigo. We're on the case. Be back in a little while."

Ten - The Players

The dirty, blue Crown Victoria exited the Cross Bronx Expressway at Third Avenue and headed west. The police radio sitting on the dashboard put out a constant squawk. "Report of shots fired, Melrose Ave and 1-8-0 Street, Signal 10-30. Robbery in Progress, Grand Concourse and 171 Streets." The driver of the car looked at the passenger. "Busy fuckin' place."

Tony Falcone drove slowly. He rolled down the window and let the chill November air into the car. He also wanted to let the smell out. Tony was sweating. Not the usual sweat he produced when lifting weights, this sweat had a distinct tang. It was the smell of fear.

Since exiting the Cross Bronx, Tony had not seen one white face, other than his companion, Vinny Bongiorno. Tony knew Vinny wasn't scared. This was not because Vinny was so much braver than Tony, but more likely because Vinny was too fucking stupid to be afraid.

Vinny was the dumbest man Tony knew, but he was also the most loyal friend one could ever hope to have. They'd been tight since the first grade. Tony had helped Vinny pass his tests by letting him copy his answers, and

Vinny had protected Tony from the older grade bullies. Even in grammar school, Vinny had been big. He had continued growing, and a recent regimen of heavy lifting and massive doses of steroids and human growth hormone had filled his six-foot-five-inch frame to a muscle-loaded 270 pounds. The steroids had also produced some side effects. Zits covered Vinny's back. He was losing his hair, and would occasionally lose his temper, big time, for little or no reason. Tony has seen Vinny break a beer bottle over a friend's head in their favorite topless bar because the friend had the unmitigated balls to claim Willie Mays was a better center-fielder than Mickey Mantle. The 'roid rage would hit Vinny suddenly, and then just as quickly disappear.

Tony did not worry about this. Never in a million years would Vinny even think of hurting Tony. It was fortunate because, although Tony was a well-put-together six-foot, 195-pounder who occasionally juiced, the truth was his fighting skills were the equal of Vinny's intellect. He could not punch his way out of a wet paper bag, but the only person close to him who knew this was Vinny. Tony was good at playing the tough guy. After growing his pony tail, he'd adopted the Steven Seagal swagger. He sometimes issued threats in the raspy whisper favored by the martial arts star, and he claimed to have a black belt in aikido.

In truth, his martial arts training had consisted of one complementary lesson at a neighborhood dojo when he was twelve. His vision of becoming a bully with a black belt ended when the *sensei* had Tony grapple with an orange belt girl half his size. He had grabbed her *gi*'s lapels and was pulling her across the dojo floor when she suddenly executed a perfect leg sweep. He later remembered floating through the air, looking at the ceiling before she brought him crashing to the hard wooden floor, driving her elbow into his stomach as they landed, forcing all the air out of his lungs. He decided then it would take a lot of hard work for him ever to reach the black-belt level. It was easier to stay best friends with Vinny, who asked so little in return. They were a good pair. Tony had the brains, Vinny the brawn.

Tony's flop sweat came from a simple truth. Although they were in the Crown Vic, had the police radio, six-shot Smith and Wesson .38s on their belts, and detective shields in their pockets, they were not cops. They were gangsters, which was not an advantage on the mean streets of the South Bronx.

A real cop in trouble could pick up the radio and call a signal 10-13, Officer Needs Assistance. This call was the NYPD's highest priority. Every cop, detective, and supervisor within a two-mile radius would drop whatever they were doing and head, lights and sirens, to their colleagues' assistance. Coffee and sandwiches would be thrown out radio car windows. Cops in the station house would run out, jump in their cars and take off to assist their own. This camaraderie, the "one for all, all for one" mentality was what made the job so different from any other. It was the thing all cops said they missed the most when they retired: the feeling of being part of the tribe, of knowing your buddies had your back and you theirs. This glue held the job together.

Tony and Vinny were not part of this tribe. As such, they were on their own as they drove through the Bronx. They looked enough like cops as they stopped at traffic lights, the young black faces on the corners started to whistle. "Yo yo yo-five-0," they called out, both as a warning to friends up to no good, and to let the plainclothes cops know that they knew who they were. Of course, it wasn't real difficult to make two white guys in a beat-up, dirty Crown Vic as cops. Had the street corner loungers been truly observant, they would have seen a small difference in the way Tony and Vinny reacted to them, as opposed to genuine cops.

Real cops would give a hard stare to the men on the corner, hoping to spook them into doing something stupid. A mutt carrying a gun, under the intense stare of a cop, might adjust his shirt or place his hand over his pocket to cover the weapon's bulge. Someone wanted on a warrant might decide to take a quick walk. Either one might find an observant cop out of the car and headed his way.

Tony and Vinny did not possess the street smarts, did not have the savvy of the real cops. When they stopped, they didn't stare. They avoided eye contact, a telling signal if one was truly observant. In truth, Tony was intimidated by the hostile black faces he encountered.

"I bet there ain't ten white guys within a mile of us." He swallowed hard.

Vinny gave his usual reply to any comment he did not fully understand, which encompassed almost anything said to him. "Whatever."

"Ever see this many black guys before, Vinny?" Tony put the car in motion.

"Yeah."

"Where?"

"Last fuckin' Tarzan movie I seen." Vinny giggled like a child.

"Remember to tell that joke when we meet Pooh Bear and his crew. I'm sure they'll think you're real amusing. Right before they shoot you."

"Ah, I'm just kidding, Tony. I know you really like Pooh and his home boys. Just don't know why."

"Vinny, I told you ten times why. When I did my three months in Rikers, he was my cellmate. He had loads of juice on the Island, kept the animals off my ass, got me booze and grass. Nobody fucked with him: inmates, guards, nobody."

"Is he tough?"

"He's tough, but he's also smart. Not book smart, didn't graduate high school, but he's one cool operator. In Rikers, he knew the system, how to play it, and always came out on top."

"Like how?" Vinny seemed unusually interested.

"Like this one time, a couple of weeks into my stretch, we get a head-case in the cell next to us. Crazy, totally nuts. All night long, he howls like a wolf. Me and Pooh get no sleep. Next day I ask him if he can do anything. I know he gets along with the guards. If he asked, they would probably move Nutsy to a different tier. He says, 'I could ask, but then I'd owe the guards one, better they owe me a favor.'

"'What are you going to do?' I asked him.

"'I'll take care of it,' is all he says.

"I find out later, he gets one of his boys to get him a shiv, which he plants in Nutsy's cell. Pooh tells the captain of the guards he got word Nutsy is gonna try to kill a guard. COs do a shakedown of our whole tier, find the shiv, Nutsy gets sent to the hole, we can sleep again, and all the guards tell Pooh they owe him one. Simple, but only a guy with real smarts thinks, 'What can I get out of this?' When I got put into his cell, he didn't think, 'Who needs this white boy?' The way his mind works he thought, 'How can I use this white boy?' After we got to know each other, we were sitting in the cell smoking a joint, and he says, 'You know, you look like an undercover cop. You got any white friends, look like you?'

"I tell him most of my friends look something like me. I guess they could pass for cops. I don't tell him almost all my friends are white. He's my only black friend. He tells me he's working on an idea and give him some time. Few days later, he lays it out for me. He's a low-level drug dealer, but he knows all the major players in the Bronx and upper

Manhattan drug scene. He wants to move up and make big bucks, eliminate the competition.

"Surest way is steal all their money, take all their product, or kill them. He came up with the plan. He gives us the targets, we go in like cops, arrest them, turn them over to his crew. They negotiate the ransom. We get a third of it."

"Why we only get a third? Should get half." Vinny frowned.

"Hey, asshole, stop bitching. They do the hard work. What do we do? Go in, flash the badges, grab the mark, and drive away. Nobody fights us. They think we're cops. Nobody gonna report it to the cops. What they gonna say? 'Some bad people took me and stole my drug money.'

"We made thirty-three large on that PR we took near the Whitestone Bridge, not bad for about twenty minutes' work."

"We make thirty-three grand, and I got six gs. How's that fair?"

"For the last fucking time, let me lay it out. The PR's people paid a hundred grand to Pooh. We got thirty-three thou. Our crew—you, Davey Boy, and Ski—got six each. I got ten. Without me, you wouldn't have had shit. The last five grand went to my Uncle Carmine. We ever want to get made, we have to show respect and kick back something from our scores to the organization. We don't do that and they find out, we're fucked."

Uncle Carmine was Carmine Laturza, a distant relative of Tony's and a captain in the Westchester branch of the Genovese organized crime family. Carmine owned Chances, the topless bar in Pelham Tony and his crew hung out in. Carmine used Tony's guys for odd jobs, like collecting overdue debts, chasing drug dealers off his turf, the occasional beating.

Tony dreamed of one day becoming a made man and knew his and Vinny's chances of doing so rested with how much they made for Uncle Carmine. He also knew the others in his crew: Dave "Davey Boy" Fallon of Irish descent, and Gene "Ski" Sikorski, a Pole, could never become made men. They could, however, be "associates" and stay in Tony's crew.

On Tony's last day in Rikers, Pooh slipped him a note. "You got a month till I get out, plenty of time to get these."

Pooh gave Tony a list of things he'd need for the kidnap plan to work. Some .38 caliber Smith & Wesson revolvers, Motorola walkie-talkie radios, programmable to the NYPD frequencies, NYPD detective shields, two 1987 Ford Crown Victorias, dark blue or black.

Tony had gotten everything.

Pooh Bear called Tony shortly after getting out. "You get all the stuff, Tony?"

"Yo, bro, got everything you wanted. Got two nice cars in great shape. Look almost new."

"Like new, fuck it, homey. I don't know what the cops up in Whiteyland where you live drive, but down here in the ghetto, ain't no new-looking cop cars. Maybe the fucking commissioner got a new car, but the average pig-mobile looks like it's on its way to the junkyard. You bring a new-looking car down here, the po-leece will know you ain't real. Take those cars you got and beat the shit out of 'em. No hubcaps, lots of dents and scratches, put some holes in the dashboard."

Tony had done it, and his partnership with Pooh had proved profitable.

Their first score, last June, the kidnapping of the Puerto Rican drug dealer near the Whitestone Bridge, had gone perfectly. They were averaging two jobs a month. Roberto Medina had been their twelfth operation. Six of the capers had been successful with the victims' crews paying the ransom, always at least thirty-thou. In five cases, the ransom demands were not met. Five bodies had been dumped on the streets of the Bronx by Pooh's crew.

"It's the perfect crime, Vinny. Pooh and his boys do the hard work. If it goes well, we score big bucks. If it goes bad, Pooh's guys do the dirty work. We got nothing to do with the hits. We're clean." Tony was a little fuzzy on how the law looked at accessories to a crime. Anyone aiding and abetting the commission of a felony, which murder, even in the Bronx, still was, was as guilty as the one actually committing the crime. But Tony and Vinny were happy in their ignorance. "We got nothing to worry about. Nobody gives a shit when a *moulie* or spic drug dealer gets popped." Tony used the Italian slang word for *moulignon*: eggplant, a derogatory name for blacks.

"What about the cops? Don't they care?" Vinny asked

"Nah, the cops couldn't care less. One less drug dealer makes them happy. Forget about it."

"So what's the deal with Roberto? Do we get anything? Not our fault he got away."

"That's why we're meeting with Pooh today. I'm sure we can work something out. We don't want to kill the goose that laid the golden egg."

"Or the *moulie* who did either." Vinny laughed.

Eleven - "*El Orgullo*" - The Pride

McGuire and Gomez pulled out of Jacobi Hospital onto Pelham Parkway. Gomez drove. Neither spoke, Tension hung in the air.

Finally, when they stopped for a light, McGuire asked, "Want to tell me about it?"

"About what?"

"About why you blew up at our victim back there."

"I didn't blow up at him."

"You didn't? You gotta be kidding me. I've seen you treat homicide perps better than you treated Roberto. What's up with you?"

"Want to know what's up? I'll tell you."

The honking horns let Gomez know the light had turned green. He pulled the car up onto the parkway's island, put it in park, and turned to face McGuire.

"First off, the difference between a homicide perp and our victim is the perp knows he's a perp. He doesn't act like he's a respectable businessperson like your friend Roberto. Like being a numbers man is the same as being a banker or a stockbroker. Like we should show him respect because he's such a hard-working guy and not involved with drugs.

Well, hooray for Roberto, such an upstanding citizen. What bullshit. He's a no good skell."

"Joey, he's a numbers guy. In the big book of what's fucking up this city, I would put numbers back on the last page. Guns, drugs, and thousands of kids with no fathers in the house would take up pages one and two. Schools, which graduate kids who can barely read and write, would be on page three. Numbers ain't the worst thing in this world."

"John, it's gambling and illegal. End of case."

"Yeah, you're right, Joey. Gambling is illegal and should be abolished. Do me a favor. On the way back to the house, stop at the OTB on Tremont Avenue. I want to bet a few ponies today. Then I'll go to the candy store next door and play the lottery and buy some scratch-off tickets. And that will prove what a moron I am, because if I win at OTB or the lottery, I'll collect about half of what a bookie or numbers guy would have paid me."

"But it's—"

"See, the state has to withhold taxes so it can build new schools with all the money they make on bets. See any new schools around here? OTB is the only bookie in the world that loses money. The whole system is a cesspool of malfeasance, corruption, and nepotism. The pits. Compared to them, Roberto don't look too bad." McGuire gazed out the window. "Is there something else about Roberto bothering you?"

"What do you mean?"

"Well, Roberto thought it might be a Dominican-Puerto Rican thing."

"You told him I was Dominican?"

"No, he told me. Said he can tell. You talk too fast. Is it what this is all about?"

Gomez took in a deep breath and exhaled slowly. "You wouldn't understand." He sighed.

"Try me, Partner."

"It's not a PR-DR thing. It's a Latino thing."

"What do you mean, Latino thing?"

"John, the average Anglo can't tell a Dominican from a Puerto Rican from a Mexican. We all look the same. We're all wetbacks, greasers, beaners, spics. We're lazy, drug dealers, welfare mommas, and numbers guys. I busted my ass, stayed out of trouble to come on the job. You know how hard I've worked since we teamed up. I always know what I do, who I am, reflects not just on me and my family, but on all Dominicans and Latinos."

"Joey, you don't have to—"

"We're a proud, hardworking people, but we're judged by what the average person sees on the six o'clock news. They see the drug markets in Washington Heights and say, 'Latinos.' They see the drug homicides and say, 'Who cares? The spics are killing each other.' No other race has to overcome this bias. What pisses me off about a guy like Roberto is he makes us all look bad."

"Joey, I hear what you're saying, but I can't agree with everything. Yeah, the Dominicans are in the spotlight now. You know why? 'Cause, you're the new kids on the block. Look at the history of this country. Each new group of immigrants who came over got the shit end of the stick until they got accepted, and a new group took their place. Except for the Indians, who were here first and still got shit on. Each group had its shitheads who made things bad for the hard-working, honest folks. And don't give me the shit about no other group has to fight bias. Think my people had it easy when they got here in 1847?"

"But at least people didn't think all Irish were criminals."

"Oh no? Joe, when you make a collar and have to take the prisoner to court, what do you call?"

"The wagon."

"The what wagon?"

"The Paddy wagon."

"That's right, Joe, the Paddy wagon. Not the spic, spade, guinea, or hebe wagon. The Paddy wagon, cause when people saw it go by they assumed it was full of drunk Paddies. Isn't it a great heritage for my people to live down? What I'm saying is we all got bad dudes in the family. We just got to make sure the good guys come out on top."

Gomez drummed his fingers on the steering wheel, exhaled, and looked at McGuire. "Okay, John. You're right. You know I'm with you." He put the car in gear and pulled out.

"Don't forget I want to hit the OTB on Tremont." McGuire grinned.

"You should know a lot about horses."

"How's that?"

"Because, Partner, you are the original north end of a horse walking south."

"Okayyyy, Wilbur." McGuire did his best *Mr. Ed* imitation.

"I have no idea what you mean. How about we get back to the house and get working on finding out who tried to kill Roberto?"

"*Comprendo, mi amigo. Andele, Arriba.* We're on the case." McGuire playfully punched his partner's shoulder.

Twelve - Putting It Together

McGuire and Gomez got back to the squad room just past noon. They had made a quick stop at Gambino's Deli on Arthur Avenue, in the Italian Belmont section, for hero sandwiches. McGuire went in while Gomez stayed in the car monitoring the police radio. They also hit a Carvel for a chocolate thick shake, McGuire's favorite hangover remedy. They took their lunch into the squad's tiny meal room and began to eat.

"What do I owe you for the hero, John?"

"Nothing. It's on me. Sorry for all the trouble today."

"No apology necessary. I know it's been tough on you. What's the latest on the divorce? Cathy still going through with it?"

"Yeah, supposed to get the papers this week." McGuire sucked on his shake.

"You going to have to pay alimony?"

"No way. Cathy makes five times what I do. She's a Wall Street big shot now. She should pay me alimony. I'd take half of her Christmas bonus and be happy."

A phone rang in the squad. Gomez went to answer it. McGuire stared into his drink and thought of the last time he had seen his wife.

He couldn't believe Cathy had left him. The girl he'd met in grammar school. Close friends, who started dating the day she went to his last high school football game. They'd been together ever since, engaged the day he graduated from the academy, married a year later. Now, after twelve years of marriage, she was gone. He blamed her rapid rise up the corporate ladder of her Wall Street firm for their problems. She resented the time he spent with his cop buddies when off duty, his crazy love of the job.

Who cares who's at fault. I thought we could work it out.

McGuire's reflections were interrupted by Gomez. "Guess who was on the phone?"

"Not Lynda Carter looking for me again?"

"No, but close. It was your favorite sergeant, Stark. He wanted to know when we got back. I told him we just got in and were grabbing a quick bite. He said to make sure we sign in to the meal log."

"What a moron."

"It gets worse, Partner. He gave me a list of things he wants us to do, his investigative checklist."

"Three days in the Detective Bureau, and Stark's telling us how to work a case. He's got to be kidding."

"You ready? Number 1. Check area for security cameras."

"Great idea. What area would that be, since we don't know yet where Roberto got shot? Did you tell the follicle-challenged nitwit that security cameras are not real big in the Bronx since they get stolen? Remember when the check cashing place on Prospect Avenue put a camera outside the door? Last image the owner got on tape was a toothless black guy grinning into the camera as he ripped it off its mountings."

"Number 2. Canvas the crime scene area for possible witnesses."

"Yeah, we usually do when we know where the crime took place."

"So where do you think the shooting happened, John? Has to be fairly close. Did Roberto give you any ideas?"

"He's not sure, not familiar with the Bronx. He remembers seeing a chain-link fence when he got out of the trunk, running down a street, turning right on Washington Avenue."

"Wrap up your hero, John. Let's take a ride. The chain-link fence info gives me a hunch."

"Let me eat. There's probably over a thousand of those fences in the precinct. Every driveway, parking lot, schoolyard, and factory. We gonna check them all?"

"No, but we are going to check the only fence that runs straight for one mile through the Four-two. The Metro-North cut."

"Shit. I shoulda thought of it. Good thinking, Partner. Let's go, but remember, Sergeant Shit-for-brains is covering us. We have to sign out of the meal log, sign out in the Movement Log, and sign out the car in the vehicle log. Am I forgetting any logs?"

"Think that covers it." Gomez put his and McGuire's heroes in the refrigerator. They drove slowly up Park Avenue scanning the street for anything out of the ordinary. At 169th Street, sunlight glinted off something near the curb on the track side of the street.

"Hold up, Joey. We got something over there."

They walked over and found six shell casings, their brass shining.

Gomez inserted the tip of his pen into the open end and picked one up.

"Nine millimeter." He held it to his nose and passed it to McGuire who did the same.

"What do you think, John?"

"God, I love the smell of gunpowder in the morning."

Gomez rolled his eyes. "What?"

"Robert Duval? *Apocalypse Now*? Forget it." McGuire sniffed again. "These are fresh, recently fired. This must be the spot."

"Want to start a canvas, Joe? I'll take this side of the track. You take the other."

McGuire's side had four collision shops, all closed. Gomez gazed across the tracks to the Butler Houses. New York City Housing Authority. The projects, as they were called, consisted of six twenty-one story buildings, almost 1500 apartments and 5000 residents.

"Just kidding, Partner. Let's bag these casings up and go over to Butler and see if any of our friends from Housing PD want to give us a hand."

The Housing Police Department was not part of the NYPD, did not have to assist them in any way if they chose not to. Many NYPD cops looked down their noses at their Housing brothers, considered them a second-rate department. Treated them with little respect when their paths crossed. McGuire and Gomez always went out of their way to aid any Housing cop who needed help, treated them as equals. It paid off. They were greeted like old friends when they entered Butler's police office, a converted apartment.

McGuire explained what they needed. Perhaps a tenant looking out their window this morning had seen the shooting.

The desk sergeant, who McGuire had helped on many occasions, nodded. "No problem, Mac. I have five guys working. I'll have them start at the top floor and knock on doors of any apartments facing the tracks and work their way down. We'll cover what we can, and then I'll get the four-to-twelve crew to continue it. I'm in tomorrow-days. We'll hit it again. Tenants' association meets tomorrow night. Good group, people who give a shit about this place. We'll let them know, ask them to keep their ears open. They love to play detective. Let you know if anybody saw anything."

"Thanks, Sarge. We owe you one."

McGuire and his partner drove back to the squad. Gomez stopped at the desk. He would voucher the shell casings, have them officially logged into the Precinct's Property Inventory, and sent to the police lab for testing. The round metal cases rarely revealed a usable fingerprint, but it was worth a try. Vouchering them would also ensure an unbroken chain of custody, which could be crucial if something developed and the case went to trial. If Gomez needed the shell casings for a court appearance, he would have to submit paperwork to the Property Clerk, show his badge/ID card, be photographed and fingerprinted before they would be released. These strict rules went into effect after the NYPD was embarrassed in 1972. Four-hundred pounds of heroin and cocaine, seized in the famous French Connection case ten years earlier, had disappeared from the Property Clerk, replaced with milk sugar.

McGuire was wolfing down what was left of his hero when Joe came in.

"Voucher's done. Ready to get back to Jacobi?"

"I assumed we'd eat first, Joey."

"Wrong. Let's go now. We'll eat when we get back. Want to get the Polaroid, go back to the scene, and take some shots. Show them to Roberto. Might jog his memory for some more information."

"Okay, Joe. Give me a minute. I wanna get my big gun."

Like most NYPD cops, McGuire and Gomez carried two guns when they worked. Both .38 caliber revolvers. The big on-duty gun had a four-inch barrel, the smaller two-inch, usually worn when off duty, was now carried as a backup. The NYPD had been using these same weapons for the last eighty years. While dependable, they were no match for the firepower they now confronted on the street. A .9mm Glock, a perp favorite, held sixteen bullets, dwarfing the cops' six-shot capacity. Until the NYPD updated its weapons to cope with this threat, most street cops had begun to carry two guns.

McGuire turned the combination and opened his locker. His gun was on the top shelf. As he pulled it out, his uniform hat fell to the floor. He picked it up and was placing it back when a flash of color from inside the cap stopped him. He brought it to eye level. Inside the plastic liner, looking out at him was a picture of Cathy. It had been taken two summers before when they had vacationed at Gurneys Inn, Montauk, on the eastern tip of Long Island. Cathy stood with her back to the ocean. The royal blue water, the breaking waves, and white foam formed the background. With a huge smile on her pretty freckled face, Cathy's red hair and green eyes danced in contrast to the water. They had never been happier. For a full week, McGuire did not think about police work, and Cathy left all her worries on Wall Street. They swam, jogged on the beach, climbed to the top of the lighthouse, ate lobster, drank champagne, and made slow, passionate love every night. *God, I wish I could go back to that day*. He stared at the photo until he felt a hot tear form in his right eye. His body shook as he suppressed a sob. He swore softly, threw the hat into the locker, slammed the door, and snapped the lock shut. He rubbed his eye, took a deep breath, and walked into the squad.

“You okay, John?”

“Yeah, I’m fine.”

Gomez stood and touched his partner’s arm. “John?”

“Man, it hurts.”

“John, Cathy and you have been together since high school, right? Of course, it hurts. It’s going to take time, brother, going to take time.”

“Time. I’ve got plenty, Partner. Let’s go.”

Thirteen - A Not So Merry Christmas

The magic McGuire and Cathy had experienced in Montauk quickly eroded as fall turned to winter. The tension had built. Her Wall Street lifestyle contrasted sharply with McGuire's love of the cop culture. She got VIP tickets to sporting events and popular Broadway plays and ate dinners at the city's best restaurants. McGuire would rather spend time with his cop buddies. Playing on the department's football team, drinking with his teammates after games and practice. Stopping after work with "the boys" for beers in the local cop dive bar.

Cathy had become a major player in her firm. The benefits came and the attention she got from some of the men in the firm's upper echelons was intoxicating to this young girl from Brooklyn. She tried to include McGuire in her after-work adventures, but gave up after he found excuse after excuse not to go. In truth, he was much more comfortable staying with his tribe, the cops he worked or played football with.

This came to a head when McGuire reluctantly agreed to meet her at her firm's Christmas party. The setting was the City Lights restaurant, a beautiful spot on Pier 17 at the

South Street Seaport. Its third-floor location afforded patrons a gorgeous view of the East River and the Brooklyn Bridge. McGuire got there after finishing a day tour. The party was just kicking into high gear when he arrived. Cathy quickly introduced him to the company's upper management, older men, who were genuinely pleased to meet a working detective. They commiserated with him on the state of the city and the lack of respect shown to those in law enforcement.

Then she made introductions to the younger set, the up-and-coming, aggressive brokers, fresh out of college, hungry to make their first million. McGuire quickly picked up on their vibe. They did not have respect for the difficult job the police did every day. They didn't realize if the cops ever stopped doing their jobs, they, the Masters of the Universe, would not be able to do theirs. The rules society had in place had to be enforced for people to go about their daily routines, to live and work in peace. As Cathy introduced him, he heard a handful of similar responses.

"Oh. The cop. You're not going to arrest me, are you?"

"Guess you can't wait to do your twenty years and get out."

"I got a speeding ticket last week. Can you do anything about it?"

"It's a shame what they pay you guys. Can't blame you cops for doing as little as possible."

McGuire bit his tongue, not wanting to embarrass his wife at her party. As she worked the room, he found a spot in the corner of the crowded bar. Cristal champagne, Patron tequila, and Glenfiddich single malt Scotch flowed like water. The bartender working McGuire's end of the bar, his face a map of Ireland, came over.

"What can I get you, Sir?"

"Pint of Guinness, please."

The barman took a closer look at McGuire.

"You're not one of them, I see." He nodded his head to the Wall Street folks.

"What gave me away? I'm not wearing an Armani suit?"

"Yes, and your nose looks like it's been busted a time or two. Also, you said, 'Please,' when you ordered. First time I heard the word tonight. And, none of these people would want a Guinness." He stuck out his hand. "Liam O'Brien."

"John McGuire." He shook the offered hand.

"What precinct you in, John?"

"Who said I was a cop?"

"Sure, I would have guessed it myself, but a few of the Armani lads mentioned it. Seemed very concerned. I was wondering why."

"Wanna know why, Liam? Check the conga line going in and out of the men's room. These guys either have extremely weak bladders or they're into the Peruvian marching powder in a big way."

Liam was called away, and as McGuire sipped his stout, he noticed something at the other end of the bar. Two men, both mid-forties, upper management types, one looking like a weight lifter, the other, a fat guy in an expensive suit, who could be "Muscles's" boss, were in the corner with a very young-looking girl. They were all doing tequila shots, the salt, the lime, the whole bit. McGuire pegged the girl to be about nineteen, probably a secretary, not old enough to drink legally, and these two morons were pouring Patron down her throat. She was having trouble standing, and Fatso had his arm around her to keep her from hitting the floor. After a few minutes and another round of tequila, the two men put their heads together then headed for the men's room, with the young girl between them. The fat guy went in with her, leaving Muscles at the door. McGuire put down his drink and walked to the men's room. He did not want to create a scene at Cathy's party, but he had to take some action.

He approached Muscles, who said, "Out of order, pal. Have to use the ladies."

McGuire leaned in like he wanted Muscles to hear him over the music. He then grabbed a handful of the creep's balls, squeezed hard, twisted, and lifted. The air whooshed out of the guy's mouth, and McGuire moved him out of the way. The door was locked. McGuire put his shoulder into it, and it popped open. When he entered, he saw the kid sitting on a toilet with the fat prick standing in front of her.

McGuire delivered a side kick behind Fatso's knee which brought him to the ground. He reached into the stall, got his arm around the girl, and walked out with her.

The party was going full blast, the music cranking, nobody seemed to have noticed anything amiss. Cathy saw McGuire with the girl, and he motioned for her to meet him outside in the mall. He placed the kid in a chair as Cathy approached. He quickly described what had happened, complete with a description of the two jerks.

"Mr. Mathis and his side kick, 'Steroid' Sam Schwartz," she said. "Two losers. They think they're God's gift to women. Always saying inappropriate things. They give us the creeps."

McGuire pointed to the young girl. "She work with them?"

"Yes. Nancy Ryan. From the Bronx. Started last month as an intern. Mathis quickly had her assigned to his office."

"We gotta take her home, Cath."

"I can't leave the party, John. It would look bad."

"Shit, I don't want you looking bad in front of all these nice people. What would the child molester Mathis think?"

"John, there are going to be presentations and awards given out later. I'm giving a speech. I can't leave. Why don't you take Nancy downstairs and put her in a cab?"

"Put her in a cab? Are you nuts? The kid can barely walk. I'm not putting her in a cab and hoping she makes it home."

"Well, John, I don't know what to do, but I can't leave."

McGuire though for a moment. "Okay. How about this? I'll take the kid over to my pal's place, Mike's Irish Pub, on the other side of the pier. You go back inside and find a girl who's looking to leave the party and would like not taking the subway home. From the Bronx would be good, but not necessary. Have her meet me and Nancy at Mike's. Call the limo company your firm uses. Have them send a town car over to take the two ladies home. I'll handle it from there."

Cathy gave him a quick kiss. "That'll work. Thanks for not getting too crazy playing cop and ruining the party."

"Yeah, I was the one who could've ruined your party."

McGuire walked Nancy across the pier to Mike's. Thank God the place was quiet, three customers, Mike behind the bar perusing the *Racing Form*. Seeing McGuire enter with the cute young girl on his hip, he called out, "McGuire, are you daft man? With your wife's company partying not fifty yards from here. What are you thinking?"

McGuire settled Nancy into an overstuffed lounge chair so she couldn't fall and approached the bar. "Mike, it's not what it looks like. I—"

Mike laughed and put a Guinness in front of McGuire. "Relax, John. I know all about it. Liam called me a minute ago. I was expecting you."

"Oh. Guess I forgot about the faster-than-the-speed-of-light Irish bartender telegraph system. I take it you know Liam then?"

"Sure. Mullingar's a small town. Word gets around when someone's coming over. I got Liam the job behind the stick at City Lights."

McGuire took a long sip of his stout. "Got your own little Celtic employment agency going, do you?"

"Can't blame us. Wasn't that long ago our folks who were looking for work saw the No Irish Need Apply signs."

Their conversation was interrupted when a striking young blond, wearing a red turtleneck sweater with a Frosty the Snowman pin on it, entered and approached McGuire.

"Hi, Mr. McGuire. I'm Heather." She shook his hand. "I can ride home with Nancy."

"Where do you live, Heather?" McGuire took his hand back from Heather's strong grip.

"I'm in the Bronx, too. Riverdale. Nancy's from Norwood, not too far from me."

"Good." Pleased, McGuire nodded and took a sip of stout.

"Aren't you going to buy a girl a drink?" Heather looked at McGuire.

"I'd love to, but I really want to get Nancy on her way. Hopefully, the car service will be here soon."

Heather let out a long disappointed sigh. "Cathy said the car's downstairs waiting for us."

McGuire told Mike he'd be back, gathered up Nancy, and led Heather through the kitchen to the service elevator. He did not want to run into Mathis, Schwartz, or any of their buddies as he left. A line of town cars waited on South Street, one with a sign, "McGuire" in the window. The driver jumped out. They got Nancy into the back seat. Heather lingered.

"Did I mention I love cops, John?"

"You did not, but we certainly appreciate support from citizens like you." He eased her into the back next to Nancy.

He shut the door and turned to the driver. “Can I see your driver’s license, pal?”

“Sure thing, Sir, no worries.”

McGuire caught the brogue for the first time. “Patrick Kelly, 2047 Nostrand Avenue, Brooklyn.” McGuire read the license aloud. “Here’s what I need from you, Paddy. I need you to drive both these ladies home, not stopping anywhere, not going for a drink, even if the cute blonde begs you to.”

“Not a problem, Sir.”

McGuire handed the driver a slip of paper. “You will drop Nancy off at this address in Norwood. Please walk her to her door and make sure she gets in and the door gets locked. Okay?”

“Not a problem, Sir. I have three daughters of my own, about these girls’ ages. Not to worry.”

“Good. After dropping off Nancy, please take Heather to Riverdale and make sure she gets into her apartment safely.”

“Lovely. Again, no worries.”

“Great. Then when both ladies are home, Patrick Kelly of 2047 Nostrand Avenue, I would appreciate it if you could call me upstairs at Mike’s Pub to let me know. The number is—”

“Oh. I know the number, Sir. You see—”

“Don’t tell me. You’re from Mullingar too?”

“Actually, Dublin. Mike got me the driving job. He’s my cousin.”

McGuire laughed, slapped Kelly on his shoulder and put a twenty-dollar bill in his hand.

* * *

McGuire and Cathy made it through the holidays, but the tension built. The Wall Street versus cops arguments grew louder and longer. One night, after McGuire had downed a pint, they went at it again. Cathy came home from work in a foul mood.

When McGuire suggested they go out for dinner, she snapped at him.

"Why are you in such a bad mood, babe? Did I do something?" McGuire asked.

Cathy took a long sip from a glass of Chardonnay. "Why am I in a bad mood? I don't know. Maybe because I was up for a promotion with a nice raise, a bigger office, and guess what? I was passed over. Didn't get it."

McGuire popped the top on another can of Guinness. "Passed over? Why? Nobody works harder than you."

Cathy banged her wine glass down. "I was passed over because Mr. Mathis spoke to two of the people on the selection committee. He has it in for me over what you did to him at the Christmas party. You couldn't not be a cop, not be 'on the job,' for five minutes."

It was McGuire's turn to bang down his drink. "What I did. What I did? You know what I did, Cathy? I stopped that young kid from being sexually abused, maybe raped. You know very well. And you have the balls to suggest I shouldn't have done anything. I was playing cop at your party?"

He took a long drink from the overflowing stout can. "And, if I really had my cop hat on that night, I would have marched that fuckin' degenerate Mathis out in handcuffs. Put his fat ass in jail, where it belongs."

"He says he didn't do anything. Nancy said she was going to throw up. So, he took her into the nearest bathroom. He actually considered pressing charges against you. Said you kicked him for no reason."

McGuire felt his face grow bright red. "No reason?" he shouted. "You know he's full a shit. That whole fuckin' story of his makes no sense. He couldn't get one of the other girls to take her into the ladies' room? He puts his dickhead steroid freak buddy out front as a lookout. Why'd he lock the door? You knew as soon as I told you what the guy looked like, who he was, and said he was up to no good. Thank God I was there for Nancy and on the job."

He drained the can and threw it angrily into the trash. "I'm sorry you didn't get the promotion, but I wouldn't change one fuckin' thing I did."

Cathy sighed. "That's the problem, John. You won't change. You can't change. But I have. You love hanging with your cop friends, your buddies on the job. On the job. You guys never say you're NYPD, or cops, or work in law enforcement. No. You're on the job. *The Job*. Like any other job is bullshit because you guys are on the only job that matters." She finished her wine and poured some more. "Well, if it's such a great job, why do the guys who pick up our garbage make more money than you do? Why does the average person at my firm make five times what you do, and we don't work nights, weekends, or holidays? And, the biggest worry the wives of the guys I work with have is: will their guy come home drunk after meeting a client or not come home after getting a hot young secretary? They don't have to sit home alone and get the shit scared out of them every time they hear of a cop getting shot on the news."

She put her glass down. "And, if I go to one more of your cop buddies' barbecues, out on the Island in Wantagh, or Merrick, or East Cupcake, with the tiny backyard with the four foot above-ground pool, where the guys play volleyball and pound down beers, and the wives inhale wine and talk about what's on sale at Pathmark, my head will explode."

"I'll take my cop buddies over your Wall Street phonies any day." He opened the refrigerator and grabbed another can of Guinness.

"My friends are out on the streets every night, making things better in this city." He popped the top and drank deeply. “What do your pals do? Play with other people’s money. You think I should change to fit in with them? Fuck them. Ain’t gonna happen.”

“You hit the nail right on the head, John. You won’t change.”

They made it through the rest of the year by staying out of each other’s way. Cathy spent more and more time with her Wall Street friends. McGuire devoted all his energies to the job, his work, and the NYPD football team. The following summer, they did not go to Montauk, revive their love at Gurney’s. No lobster, champagne or long nights of making love.

This year was different. On Labor Day, Cathy announced she was leaving and would file for divorce. Two weeks later, he moved into his apartment in Long Beach. Cathy moved into Manhattan. To a Park Avenue apartment. With one of her firm’s partners.

Fourteen - No Commission

January 1991

The drug dealer kidnappings had continued. Two successful snatches in December, netting a hundred grand, had made for a very nice Christmas for Dee, Pooh, Tony, and their crews. In the seven months since they had gone into business, the gang had kidnapped fourteen victims. They'd received ransoms from eight, killed five when the demands were not met, and had one escapee: the numbers man, Roberto Medina. They had made 300 thou, but the New Year brought a challenge, which had Dee mad enough to kill again.

He had noticed a drop off in business at the Tiebout Avenue crack house. January was usually a good month. The crackheads had to get out of the cold, and admission to the Tiebout house came only with the purchase of drugs. But, there was a definite fall off in visits.

Dee began asking questions and found out a new crack house had opened on Valentine Avenue, just a few blocks away. He was enraged. What pissed him off even more was the newcomers were Hispanic.

"Mother fucking wetbacks come up from Mexico and think they can move in on my turf. This is the bullshit we got to put up with? President Bush better start enforcing our immigration laws. The shooting is going to start."

"They're Dominican, Dee," Pooh Bear Jennings said.

"Don't make no difference. I like shooting cans."

Dee saw the puzzled look on Jennings's face. "Mexi-cans, Puerto Ri-cans or Domini-cans, all the same to me. Fuck 'em, think they can move in on us. They going to find they got themselves a little problem."

"Want me to try and set up a meet?" Jennings asked. "We can tell them they have to shut down, move farther away from our spot."

"Oh, no. They knew we were here when they moved in. They knew exactly what they were doing. They're challenging us. Think because they got some cartel with a lot of firepower behind them we'll take their shit. What these spic fucks don't know is we got us a secret weapon. Something they ain't never seen before. Gonna surprise the shit outta them."

"What's that?" Pooh asked

"The fuckin' white boys."

* * *

Pooh called Tony Falcone, and a meeting was set.

Tony and Vinny drove to the Patterson Houses, another Housing Authority complex on Third Avenue and 143rd Street. Dee had an apartment there as he did in three other projects. They got in the graffiti-covered elevator.

"What a stench. Smells like piss," Vinny moaned.

"They all smell like this, Vinny."

"Who pisses in an elevator in their own building?"

"Fuck if I know, maybe the Urine Fairy comes every night. Hold your breath."

They got off on the tenth floor and went to the last door on the left. Pooh Bear Jennings answered their knock and let them in. Two of Pooh's crew sat at the kitchen table playing cards and drinking wine. Dee stood in a corner by himself. Introductions were made, but Dee did not speak and never left his spot. Tony had heard of Dee's ruthless reputation and was nervous. He also knew Vinny couldn't care less.

Jennings showed them pictures they had taken of the Valentine Avenue crack house, explained the security set-up, and outlined the plan. Tony and his cops would hit the spot on a Saturday night when Felix and Jorge, the two Dominican honchos who ran the spot, would be there. They and any other workers would be taken.

"Might be two others," Jennings said.

"We're taking four guys? Why? Are we going to get four ransom payoffs?" Tony asked.

Dee moved from his corner. "Ain't gonna be no ransom."

"Then why are we doing it?"

"Because we're asking you to do it."

"And what do we get?"

"Nothing."

Vinny started to stand. "Nothing? Why should we stick our necks out for nothing?"

Tony pushed Vinny back into his chair. He'd noticed Dee's right hand inside his jacket.

Dee's hand was visible again. "How much have you guys made working with us?"

"Something like a hundred thou? I think you owe us one, no? We need a little favor is all. If there's any cash or crack handy when you go in, feel free to grab it. It's a little bonus for you."

"But, you'll want to get in and out as fast as you can," Jennings added. "Taking four guys ain't going to be easy. Get it done quick before somebody calls the real cops. You guys pull up in your Crown Vic. We'll wait outside in a van. Cuff them, bring them out, and throw them in the van. That's all you have to do. Okay, Tony?"

"We can do it. You're right. We owe you guys. We'll be ready Saturday night."

"Cool. Here's how we going to get you guys in. The Dominicans' security is pretty good, but we can get you by the front door. The Domos won't fight if they think it's a routine bust. Crackhead zombies won't bother you except for their smell. This is how it will go down." Pooh then laid out the plan.

Tony thought it made sense.

* * *

On Saturday night, Tony and Vinny were in the black Crown Vic. Ski and Davey Boy followed in the blue car. They both parked alongside Echo Park, a short drive from the crack house. Ski and Davey jumped into the back of Tony's car. At ten minutes to midnight, a black van pulled in behind them. Jennings got out with a young, skinny, sick-looking Hispanic man and approached Tony's car.

"Guys, this is Ramon. He's a regular at the house. They all know him. He's going to walk up the steps right at midnight. When they buzz him in, he's going to make like he's sick and pass out in the doorway. You guys go in right behind, just like we planned. Pull up your cars past the front door. Leave room for the van right in front. Do your cop thing, cuff the spics, hustle them out, and throw them in the back of the van. Let's try and get in and out in less than two minutes, right?"

Tony was so nervous he could barely utter, "No problem, Pooh."

"Let's do it." Pooh gave Tony a fist bump. "Start walking, Ramon. These nice po-lice officers will be right behind you."

Davey Boy and Ski got back in their car as Ramon walked away. The two cars followed a block behind him. They hung back as Ramon climbed the steps of the crack house. When they saw the door open, both drivers gunned their cars, roared up, and screeched to a stop just past the house. With badges dangling from chains around their necks and guns in their hands, they bounded up the steps. Ramon was on the floor, his leg wedged into the door. The door guard, a very large, fat, Hispanic man, seeing the four white men running toward him, slammed the door on Ramon's leg but could not get it closed in time.

Vinny was the first to reach the doorway. He hit the door with all his weight, knocking the guard on his ass. He brought his gun down hard on the man's head, drawing a scream and a spray of blood. Vinny was barely able to click the handcuffs over the guard's huge wrists.

Tony and Ski had gone right to a small room where the managers were counting money. Tony ordered both against the wall. Ski did a thorough pat down which produced two .9mm Glocks. He cuffed both men. Davey was choking another guard.

"Davey, we need him conscious. He has to walk out of here. Stop choking. Cuff him," Tony yelled.

Tony and Ski grabbed bundles of twenty dollar bills and some crack vials, putting them in a small nylon gym bag Tony had brought. When they'd taken all the money in sight, Tony looked at his watch. "Two minutes. Let's go."

Each took a prisoner and headed out the door. Ramon still lay on the floor, moaning in pain. Tony tossed some twenties and a few crack vials at him as they left.

Jennings stood at the back of the van. Both rear doors were open. The four Dominicans were unceremoniously shoved into the van, landing hard on the metal floor.

"What kind of police van is this with no seats?" one asked.

"Relax, it's just a short ride to the precinct." Jennings slammed the doors.

The Crown Vics had already left.

Jennings jumped into the driver's seat and pulled away.

"Officer, I want to call my lawyer, and my friend needs a doctor." The Dominican spoke perfect English.

A low rumbling laugh came from the passenger seat. The large black man turned to face his captives. "Y'all won't be needing a lawyer, and lucky you, I happen to be a doctor." Dee pointed his .44 Ruger Bulldog at the man's face. "They call me Doctor Death."

The van pulled into the Butler Houses parking lot, away from the buildings, close to the Metro-North Railroad cut.

* * *

On the sixth floor, Mrs. Olivia Robinson, seventy-five years old, looked out her window. She'd had two cars stolen from the lot in the past year and kept close watch over her latest. She was getting too old to walk to church services. She had the phone in her hand when the van slowed down near her Honda Accord. She relaxed somewhat as it passed and parked near the fence.

As she looked, she saw four distinct flashes of light spring from the van's windows. A large black man got out, opened the rear doors and hefted a bundle unto his shoulder. He walked to the fence and dropped it. He was on the third bundle when Olivia picked up the phone. "Father, you may forgive them for they know not what they do. But, I know what they are doing, and I don't forgive the lazy no account bums. Dumping trash in my parking lot. Yes, hello, police."

Fifteen - Working the Scene

McGuire and Gomez had gotten the calls from their boss, Sergeant Vic Ramos, shortly after two a.m.

"We have four dead in the Butler Houses' parking lot. Get in as quick as you can."

Ramos had been called at home by the Night Watch. This squad, one sergeant, six detectives, worked strictly midnight till eight a.m. They responded to major crimes anywhere in the Bronx after the precinct detectives went off duty at one a.m. They would do the preliminary investigative steps, secure the crime scene, interview witnesses, get the complainant's story. They would turn the case over to the precinct detectives when they came in at eight a.m., or earlier if the crime was deemed serious enough to call them at home and bring them in on overtime. This was such a case.

McGuire and Gomez had met at the squad at three a.m. and drove to the Butler Houses. McGuire was happy to see that the uniformed Housing PD had done a nice job in protecting the crime scene. He and Gomez had to park on Webster Avenue since no cars were allowed into the lot. As they walked down the alley, they were stopped by yellow crime scene tape manned by a very young-looking, uniformed, black, Housing officer with a clipboard.

Both McGuire and Gomez had their detective badges visible on their coat pockets.

“Sorry gentlemen, but I have to bother you for your names, shield numbers, and command for the crime scene log.” The young cop held his position.

McGuire was pleased to see the rookie taking this task to heart and not letting anybody sporting a badge enter the crime scene. He looked at the officer’s name plate. “It’s no bother at all, Officer Jefferson. How long you on the job?”

“Got out of the academy right after New Year, Sir. This is my first crime scene.”

“Well, you’re doing a hell of a job. It’s very important we know everybody who gets back there. Crime scenes are like first impressions—you only get one shot at them. And you can save the sirs for sergeants and above. I’m John. This is Joe.”

“Pleasure to meet you, Sirs.”

McGuire laughed and gave the rookie the required information. He had seen many crime scenes get screwed up by people who had no business being there: nosy neighbors, the press, off-duty cops who lived in the area, or working cops from neighboring precincts who had to “stop by for a look.” The fewer people tromping around the scene the better. Anyone walking through the scene could be taking important evidence out with them or leaving something that hadn’t been there. Hair, fibers, blood droplets could make or break a case.

“I saw the Crime Scene van out front.” McGuire addressed the young officer. “Did they check in with you?”

Jefferson looked down at his clipboard. “Detectives Sherman and Ott are in the back, Sir.”

"Hal's got this job? Well, at least I know we'll have a few laughs."

"Laughs? Sir, perhaps you don't know, but there are four dead people back there."

"I do know, officer, but I also know Hal Sherman, the best CSU detective on the job, is also certifiably insane. One very funny guy."

"He was dressed a little odd."

McGuire reared back. "Not the red boots?"

The rookie nodded yes.

"He's too much. Nice talking to you, officer, keep doing a good job out here."

"Where do you know Hal from?" Gomez asked as they neared the lot.

"We play on the PBA Volleyball team. Go to the Police Olympics up in Albany every June."

"Hal plays volleyball?"

"Hard to believe, right? Short, chubby, Jewish guy—but he can play. Very soft hands, a great setter. Can put the ball right where all of us spikers want it. He's good! Plus, a great guy to have as a teammate. Keeps you laughing all through practice and games."

At the lot, they encountered more crime scene tape.

"Housing guys are sharp, Joey. Set an inner and outer perimeter."

The outer perimeter and Officer Jefferson were meant to exclude all unauthorized persons from the crime scene. The inner perimeter was the territory of the Crime Scene Unit until they turned it over to the detectives and the Medical Examiner.

"There's Hal." McGuire pointed to a figure clad in the white one-piece coveralls, complete with boots and hood worn by CSU detectives working a scene. They did not want to be the ones to ruin a pristine location.

Sherman acknowledged McGuire and Gomez and came over to the tape.

"Hi, Joe. Still stuck working with the Irish boozehound I see." Looking at his watch, he turned to McGuire. "Twenty after three. The bar closed and you came right over, John? And, where did you get the tie? A gift from Stevie Wonder?"

"Oh, that's rich," McGuire shot back. "Fashion tips from a guy wearing red cowboy boots under his little white booties. By the way, Hal, you know with the white jumpsuit and hood, you bear a striking resemblance to Poppin' Fresh, The Pillsbury Dough Boy."

"*Touché*, bunky. Want to call it a draw and get down to business? You and Joe catching this?"

"Yeah, probably work it with some of the Housing guys."

Hal lifted the tape. "C'mon in. I'll show you what we got. Walk right behind me. We still have some work to do."

McGuire and Gomez walked single file directly behind Sherman. Ten feet from the bodies, they stopped. The four victims were almost touching each other. A large pool of dark red blood ran down the curb onto the asphalt lot.

"So whatta we got, Hal?" McGuire took in the details.

"Four male Hispanics, each shot once in the head."

"I can see that from here. Can you tell us anything else?" McGuire pressed.

"Sure. My best guess is the shooter is left-handed, walks with a limp, high school graduate, maybe some college, hates his mother. She made him eat broccoli as a kid."

"Where'd that come from?" Gomez asked.

"Oh, I just made it up, but it's how they do it on TV, right? Come on, let's take a closer look."

They followed Hal to the bodies. He turned on a large four-cell flashlight.

"Let's start at the left. Be careful not to step in anything. Here's something I noticed. From the left, the first three guys, all medium height and weight, all shot once in the back of the head. All face down."

They stepped slowly from left to right, taking in the carnage.

Hal stopped at the last body. "Now our rather chubby friend here is tall, six-foot-two or so, and must weigh well over 300 pounds. He took one right in the forehead. He's face up." Hal squatted and picked up the victim's right hand. "Notice the nice hole in the hand. My guess is he got his hands in front of his face before the shooter pulled the trigger."

McGuire squatted and studied the hand. "Looks like we have some stippling here." He had noticed a pattern of dark spots around the hand wound, most likely caused by gunpowder.

"You are most observant, number one son. Probably got his hand up very close to the weapon. See how the stippling runs directly around the entrance wound on the palm? He must have been almost touching the gun's muzzle."

"What about the other three? Stippling on them?"

"Hard to tell now with the massive head wounds. The ME will get them cleaned up and let you know."

"Thanks, Hal. Joey, we better find Sergeant Ramos."

"He was with the Housing Major Case Lieutenant," Hal said. "Think they went to find the witness."

As Sherman and Gomez walked away, McGuire lingered. Bowing his head ever so slightly, he made a very small sign of the cross, touching his forehead, chest, and each shoulder. He paused in front of each body.

"May God have mercy on your soul," he murmured softly four times. Once more, a small sign of the cross. He turned and caught up to Gomez and Sherman.

"Volleyball practice starts in March, Hal." McGuire shifted gears in his head.

"I'll be there. You guys don't stand a chance without me setting."

"Show Joey how high you can jump, buddy."

"Ready, Joey? Watch this. One–two–three." Hal threw his hands up. His feet never left the ground.

"Wow. I'm impressed, Hal. You sure can elevate. For a white man." Gomez and McGuire walked away.

"*Adios, amigos.*" Hal called out. "McGuire, get a new tie. The Salvation Army Thrift Shop on Fordham Road opens at nine."

"Later, Poppin' Fresh. Thanks for the tour."

McGuire and Gomez found Sergeant Ramos in the Housing PD office speaking with HPD Lieutenant Lance Montgerry. Both men stood six feet tall. Ramos was built like a bull. His face showed signs of his short career as a professional boxer.

Montgerry was a tall, thin, light-skinned black man. His men sometime called him L-T Billy Dee, for he bore a striking resemblance to the actor Billy Dee Williams.

Both were dressed impeccably, and would not be out of place on the cover of *GQ*—although *The Ring* might seem a more apt publication for the sergeant's mug.

Ramos waved them into the room. "Men, you know Lieutenant Montgerry, right?"

"Sure thing, Boss. How you doing, Lou?" McGuire shook his hand, followed by Gomez.

"Hell, Vic." Montgerry grinned "Everyone in Bronx Housing knows these guys. Two of the best. Happy to have them on board with this."

"Who do you have catching this, Lou?" McGuire asked

"Angelo Cutrone. He's up talking to our witness, Mrs. Robinson."

"Great. Joey and I have worked four or five cases with him. Top-shelf guy. Very thorough."

"John, Joe, just so you guys know right off the bat, Housing is up on this one," Ramos referred to the informal agreement between the two departments. When working a case jointly, they took turns as to which one's detective would get credit for the arrest. Cutrone, the Housing detective, would be the arresting officer if and when one was made.

McGuire frowned at this information but said nothing.

Gomez broke the tension. "Okay, but can I go out and do the press conference?"

There was no press at the scene. Montgerry, a lieutenant, was the highest-ranking police official. "Yeah, Joe." Montgerry nodded. "You can do it. If you find any press out there, they probably want directions to Manhattan. Nobody gives a crap about a homicide, even a quad homicide in the Bronx. We should count our blessings. If this was just over the river in the Big Apple, we'd have the press and brass up our ass. Thank God, we work in the Bronx." He grabbed a clipboard off a desk. "I'm going to get Angelo and find out if Mrs. Robinson had any more information for us. Meet you guys back here in fifteen minutes to compare notes?"

"Sounds good." Ramos nodded, as Montgerry left.

McGuire turned to Ramos. "Boss, this is bullshit. We should be up. Housing caught the New Year's Eve homicide."

"I know, John, but another Bronx sergeant did an end run around them last week. Had a double homicide case with them, identified and located a perp. Housing was up. They all agreed to do a five a.m. takedown of the mutt. This sergeant and one of his detectives got a tip the perp was going to rabbit. They went out at four without Housing and made the collar. They fucked HPD. I want to make it up to them."

"Sure, Boss, no problem, right thing to do. What sergeant would do a fucked-up thing like that?"

"Why your good buddy Stark of the Four-seven squad, of course," Ramos punched McGuire's shoulder.

Sixteen - Payback's a Bitch

Dee and Pooh Bear Jennings sat in the Tiebout crack house counting money. Four days had passed since Sunday morning's killings. Dee was in a great mood. As he had predicted, the finding of the four bodies in the Butler lot had drawn little notice—one or two quick stories on local news programs and nothing on the national scene. The major channels were too busy getting their reporters into camo and over to Kuwait to cover the Gulf War to worry about a few killings in the Bronx. Dee had not noticed any additional police presence or pressure. Business had picked up in the previous two days. Life was good. He'd sent one of his lackeys to the liquor store with a hundred-dollar bill. He returned with a bottle of Courvoiser XO Imperial, a cognac Dee loved.

"I'm feeling good, my man." Dee counted and drank with Pooh. "We in the clear now. No worries, it's a beautiful night." They clinked snifters.

The mood was broken by the sound of glass shattering in the front.

"What the fuck? We ain't got no windows." Dee and Pooh ran toward the sound.

Marvin Williams, the crack house manager—with no view outside the house—had his hand on the front door. "I'll take a look, Dee."

"No," Jennings yelled as Williams opened the door and was immediately cut in half by a burst of automatic weapon fire.

Jennings ran to the door, which was now on fire, slammed, and locked it. Gunfire came pouring through the plywood-covered windows. Both men hit the floor.

"Front of the building is on fire," Pooh yelled above the noise. "They must have thrown Molotov cocktails at the door."

"Grab the fucking money. We can get out through the basement," Dee yelled back.

They crawled back to the money room, loaded the cash into two bags, and headed for the cellar. The four crackheads in the house began to laugh. People crawling on the floor. The bullets flying over their heads and the large dead man at the door went unnoticed.

The shooting had stopped, but Dee and Pooh took no chances. Staying on their bellies, they made it to the stairs and slid head-first to the cellar below.

Dee's car, a dark blue Eldorado, was parked one block over on Folin Street. He never parked on Tiebout. Cops were known to take plate numbers there. Parking on Folin let him slip down the alley behind the crack house without being seen by anybody watching the Tiebout side.

They cautiously opened the cellar door and let their guns lead them out. Breaking into a sprint, they ran to Dee's car. Pooh was quicker, and pulled open the passenger door. Both froze when the interior light came on. Somebody was sitting there. Pooh jammed his gun into the person's chest and was pulling the trigger when both recognized the face.

It was Ramon, the crackhead who'd helped them get into the Dominican crack house.

"What the fuck are you doing here?" Pooh yelled as Dee trained his gun on Ramon from the driver's side. Getting no response, Pooh grabbed Ramon's coat and pulled.

Ramon's body tumbled out onto the street.

His head stayed in the car.

Seventeen - Someone Cares

Four-eight Precinct Station House
Detective Borough Bronx Headquarters

McGuire, Gomez, Sergeant Ramos, Lieutenant Montgerry, and Detective Angelo Cutrone sat in the conference room drinking coffee. Montgerry had brought a box of Dunkin Donuts which were quickly disappearing. They had been summoned to the Four-eight by Chief Mike Philbin, the CO of Bronx Detectives. As the chief entered, Ramos called, “Ten-Hut.” Everyone jumped from their seats and stood erect.

“Relax, men. Not necessary.” Philbin motioned for them to sit.

Philbin had been assigned to Bronx Detectives shortly after Labor Day and had made an immediate hit with the troops. Low key and polite, he had a smile and a greeting for everyone, from the captains on down to the janitors.

Ramos introduced Montgerry and Cutrone to the chief.

“I appreciate your coming on such short notice, Lieutenant. I want to get a handle on this ASAP.”

“Our pleasure, Chief.”

"So, gentlemen, who's going to tell me about all these January homicides?"

Montgerry nodded to Ramos, who spoke. "Chief, as you know on Sunday January thirteenth, four male Hispanics were found shot to death at 0100 hours in the Butler Houses parking lot in the Four-two. With help from Narcotics, we have identified the four as Dominicans, who ran a crack house on Valentine Avenue. They had been in business for less than two weeks when they were killed. Four days later, Thursday the seventeenth, over fifty rounds were fired into a crack house on Tiebout Avenue, in the confines of the Four-six Precinct. It appears a Molatov cocktail exploded against the reinforced front door. Inside was the body of Marvin Williams, a male, black, twenty-seven. He was shot numerous times. Narco ID'd him as the manager. He had five previous arrests, all narcotics related. Uniform then did a search of the area, and discovered the body of Ramon Vega, male, Hispanic, twenty-eight, a junkie with a long rap sheet, on Folin Street, the block behind the crack house. He'd been tortured. Three of his fingers were cut off, and he was beheaded."

"What was the cause of death, Vic?" Philbin asked.

"The ME feels after his fingers were cut off, he was strangled. The head came off post mortem. The tongue is missing."

"So it looks like we have a crack war going on, with bodies dropping in two precincts, one of them on Housing Authority property?"

"Correct, Chief."

"Gentlemen, I've been the Bronx Detectives CO for almost five months. I know all about the theory nobody cares what happens up here. In some ways, I have to agree. I haven't gotten one call from the PC's office or City Hall about these killings. The media doesn't care. They want murder at a good address. But, let me tell you this. I care. I am not going to be the chief in command when we set a record for homicides in a year. We have fifty, and we're not out of January, which is usually one of the quieter months. We had 620 murders in the Bronx last year. If we keep going at this pace, we could break 700 this year. Not on my watch."

Everyone nodded in agreement.

Philbin continued, "I'm starting a Task Force. Vic, you, Gomez, and McGuire are coming off the chart. You'll work these two cases. Reassign any open cases McGuire and Gomez have to someone else. I'll get a sergeant to cover your squad. This is priority number one. Lieutenant, I would love to have you on board, but your chief tells me he can't spare you full time. He did give us Cutrone, though. Glad to have you, Angelo. I expect Housing will play a big role in this."

"Thanks, Chief."

"Vic, you can work out of the Four-two. I'm going to get you one detective from Homicide and one from the Four-six. If you need anything, let me know. I want a progress report every day. Any questions?"

"No, Sir."

"Good. Thanks for coming. Now get to work."

* * *

Ramos, Gomez, and McGuire returned to the squad. Cutrone went back to Housing to clean up his open cases. He would join them tomorrow.

"Guys, take a look at your cases," Ramos said. "If you can close any out, do it. Give me your active ones. I'll spread them around to the rest of the squad."

"What about the Roberto Medina kidnapping, Sarge?" McGuire asked.

"John, you heard the chief. Homicides. Nobody's losing any sleep over the Medina case."

"Let us keep it, please. Joe and I have been working our asses off on it. I made a promise to Roberto. Nobody else is gonna give a shit about it."

"John, we have a full-time job—six homicides to solve."

"How about if we work it on our own time?"

Ramos looked to Gomez. "You okay with it, Joe?"

"Yes, Sir."

"All right, keep it. But, if I think it's interfering with our case, it goes. Got it?"

"Yes, Sir. Thanks."

"Get working on those cases. I have to make a few calls."

Twenty minutes later, Ramos called McGuire and Gomez into his office.

"My pal, Lieutenant Rudden in Homicide, says we can pick whoever we want for the task force from his squad. Any suggestions?"

"How about the kid they just picked up from Narcotics? Tyrone Crawford," McGuire offered.

"He just came over. Has no real investigative experience. I have no idea how he went from Narco to Homicide. Must have a huge hook. Why him?" Ramos shrugged.

Gomez laughed and pointed at his partner. "You're looking at Tyrone's hook, Boss. Detective John Alfred McGuire. Tell him the story, John."

"You tell him. I wanna grab a cup of coffee." McGuire left the office.

Ramos looked at Gomez. "Why can't he tell the story?"

"You know him. He's not big on taking credit for the good things he does."

"So, tell me what he has to be humble about."

"When we got out of the Academy we were assigned to Brooklyn, the Six-nine Precinct. Mostly Canarsie, but our sector was up in Brownsville. We covered the Brownsville Boy's Club on Linden Boulevard."

"Cool place. I boxed in a tournament there once as a kid." Ramos nodded.

"Yeah, nice spot. Has a pool, basketball, weights. Keeps the kids off the street."

Ramos sipped from his coffee cup. "Good idea. Brownsville's a rough neighborhood."

"So, during the summer the club had a field day. Had the street out front blocked off. They had the shower spray caps on the fire hydrant, barbecue, games, music. John and I covered it, in uniform. At the end of the day, they had a series of foot races for the kids."

Ramos put his coffee cup down. "I think I know where this is going."

Gomez laughed. "You know John. One of the counselors asked us if we wanted to race. John was twenty-three, starting safety on the Finest Football team, was, and still is, very fast."

"So, he took the counselor up on..."

"Before I could blink, he handed me his gun-belt, shirt, shield, and he was on the starting line. Forty-yard dash. Six black kids, four Hispanic, fourteen, fifteen years old, wearing shorts and sneakers, and Officer McGuire in uniform shoes and pants."

"I'm glad he didn't strip down to his jockeys."

"Me, too. Anyway, they got ready, whistle blew and they were off. It was a two-man race, a black kid and John. Kid won by four yards. John came back and said, 'That's the fastest kid I've ever seen.'"

"He asked the counselor. Found out the boy was Tyrone Crawford, local kid, single mom who worked two jobs. Kid had never been in serious trouble but looked like he was headed that way. Played one year of football at Samuel

Tilden High School but quit and was talking about dropping out of school. He'd started to run with a local gang, the Brownsville Bangers."

"Typical story. The gang becomes the family these kids want." Ramos took another sip.

"John's thoughts exactly. Two days later, he took Tyrone to Nazareth, a Catholic high school in the precinct. Dom Laurendi, a cop John played with on the Finest team ran the football program there. They went out on the field. Dom had a stopwatch. He had Tyrone run two forty-yard sprints."

McGuire walked back into the office with his coffee.

"Finish the story, Partner." Gomez grinned.

McGuire smiled. "So, Dom looked at the stopwatch and got a huge smile on his Italian mug. 'Four-point-six seconds. Ty, are you Catholic?'" Dom asked.

"'No, Sir. Mom's Baptist.'

"'How 'bout your dad?'

"'Don't know. Never met him.'

"'Great, so he's a Catholic. Just what I wanted to hear.'"

"How did it work out?" Ramos asked.

"Fine. The kid just needed a little discipline. Dom and Nazareth gave it to him. I stayed in touch, went to most of his games. He made All-City as a running back his senior year. Not big enough for any major college programs but played at Nassau Community College and got his B.A. Came on the job six years ago. Plays with me on the department football team. Got into Narco three years back, and just got picked up by Bronx Homicide."

"Narco to Homicide. No stops at a precinct detective squad? I wonder how that happened."

"Funny you should ask, Sarge. Well, I ran into Lieutenant Rudden at Glacken's one night. We were having a beer and he told me about this new Homicide Apprehension Team he'd just started. They weren't doing investigations. They go out, do surveillance, and grab perps who are wanted for homicides. I told him, 'Hope you have some guys who can run on your team.' He offered me a spot. I told him I was too old, but I knew a kid who could catch anybody he sicced him on."

Ramos shook his head. "John, obviously you think the world of this kid, but he has zero investigative experience."

"Sarge, Ty is strong as an ox, runs a 4.6 forty, and speaks pretty good Spanish. Three skills we might need on this case. Joey and I can teach him how to be a homicide detective."

"Okay, John. Ty Crawford it is." Ramos looked down at a notebook on his desk. "The Four-six is giving us a guy named Hanlon."

"Fuck no, Boss. Call them back. Not Fat Pat Hanlon. The guy is a piece of shit."

"His boss told me he's a first grader," Ramos said.

"First fuckin' grade detective, my ass." McGuire scowled. "He couldn't find a Chink in Chinatown. His uncle was President of the Emerald Society. Put him into Intel six months out of the Academy. Got him his gold shield a year later. Second grade two years afterward. He drove O'Dwyer, the President of the City Council for the last ten years. A fuckin' chauffeur. Got the bump to first grade when O'Dwyer retired. Lives up in Goshen. Intel dumped him. Ended up in the Bronx for a shorter commute. Never was in a precinct squad. Never caught a case. Loudmouth, empty suit, hairbag. You don't want this prick, Sarge."

"Too late, John. His transfer just came down on a telephone message from the Boro. It's official. We got him. Give it a chance. You might end up liking him."

"Yeah, Boss. And I might like a raging case of hemorrhoids."

Eighteen - The Boys Are Back in Town

Dee and Pooh had fled the Bronx after the Tiebout Avenue shooting. Dee to a girlfriend in Brooklyn, Pooh to a cousin's house in Newark. One week later, as planned, they met at the Butler safe house.

"My man tells me that things are quiet again. We need to get back in business quick. The crackheads will be walking over the bridge to Harlem if we don't get a house up and running soon. Find us a new spot by tomorrow, Pooh. I got enough product here to get us going. We may have to call the white boys and do another snatch job to get money to resupply. Start thinking about someone we can grab for some quick cash. Don't have to be a big score, twenty or thirty grand will do us fine."

"Got it, Dee. Can do. We got to get back up before the Dominicans do."

Dee let out a soft, deep chuckle. "Domos ain't getting back up. Domos be going down. Down for the count. Think they can fuck with us, shoot up our house, kill my friend Marvin, and get away with it. No fuckin' way, bro. This shit gonna end real soon."

Pooh did not wish to remind Dee the Tiebout house shooting and the killing of its manager, Marvin Williams, was a direct result of Dee's shooting the four Dominicans taken from their Valentine Avenue crack house. He had also seen enough true crime shows on television to know Dee did not have any friends. Marvin was a useful tool to Dee. He had kept order in the crack house and didn't rip off any of the profits. He would be replaced.

Pooh also knew Dee judged people by what he could get from them. He could play the part of the caring friend, as he did with Pooh. But Jennings knew if the day came when he didn't have anything to offer, Dee would drop him like a bad habit. Or worse, terminate their friendship like he had done to Rontal Cheery, who Dee blamed for Roberto Medina's escape. A bullet in the chest at point blank range was Rontal's reward for years of service to Dee.

Pooh had seen a documentary about the '70s serial killer, Ted Bundy, who was suspected of raping and killing over forty young women in Colorado, Washington, and Utah. He was convicted of the murder and rape of two Florida State coeds and a twelve-year-old girl. Pooh was surprised at how many characteristics Bundy and Dee shared. He was so impressed he had written down those traits. Bundy was said to be manipulative, glib, charming, had total lack of remorse or shame, a grandiose sense of self, incapacity to love, and the need for constant stimulation, usually satisfied by sex, gambling, or ultimately, the biggest thrill of all, murder. Pooh went down the list and checked those which also applied to Dee. When he had checked them all he circled the word the psychologist on the show had used to describe Ted Bundy: sociopath. Pooh did not have to look up the meaning of the word. He knew Dee was one. A sociopath, as much or more so than Ted Bundy, the man that the state of Florida had smoked in the electric chair two years earlier.

Jennings hoped to put Dee and the Bronx far behind him soon. He had been saving his share of the kidnap money. He didn't use drugs and drank moderately, so he didn't squander money like Dee and the others in the topless bars of Manhattan and the Bronx.

One or two more decent scores. and I'm out of here. Back home to Georgia and buy the farm that my mom used to work on. Live the life of the country gentleman—me, mom, and my brother. Life will be sweet.

"Yo, Earth to Pooh, you hear what I'm saying? My man got me the location the Dominican honchos are at. It's a bodega on Tremont Avenue right off Webster. They meet every night in a room in the back. Tomorrow night, we hit it. Eliminate these fuckers once and for all."

"Who is this 'my man' you keep talking about?"

"My man is my man. You got your make-believe cops. I got a real one. Don't come cheap, but the info he gives me is worth it. Like where to find the Domos who killed Marvin. Tomorrow we gonna send them boys home to the DR in boxes."

"What's the plan, Dee?"

"My girl, Yolanda, will go into the bogey, scope it out. We'll be outside in a van. If she comes out and walks to the left, they ain't in there, and we wait another night. If she turns right, it's a go. We go in fast and hot. Wait till you see what I got for us. We go in spraying lead. Get to that back room and punch the Domos' tickets and get out. Get one of your GLA guys to boost a van and be the driver. Make sure he's got some balls. Don't want to come out of the bodega and find the fuckin' van gone."

"I'll get Shorty Brown. Best car thief in the Bronx. He could drive NASCAR races if he went straight. We give him two-hundred bucks. He'll wait till hell freezes over for us."

"Good. Now check out our new friends." Dee opened the refrigerator and took out two small packages wrapped in what looked like wax paper. He gently placed them on the table and pulled the paper back. The black metal glowed like a pair of new shoes.

Jennings's eyes bulged. "Holy shit, Dee, are they—?"

"Uzis, my man. Uzis." Dee picked one up. "Seven point two pounds. Eighteen inches long, fires 600 rounds a minute on full automatic, which these two have been converted to." He pulled down on the front stock and held up the ammunition clip. "These will take fifty .9mm rounds. Let me show you a trick my Special Forces uncle showed me." Dee took another clip from the package, turned it upside down and held the two clips side by side with about three inches of clip protruding at each end.

"Hold these tight." He gave the clips to Pooh. He took a roll of black electrical tape out of his pocket and tightly wound it around the center of the two clips Pooh held. He took these from Pooh and rammed one into the stock. "See this little switch up here? Push it forward for full auto. If you hold the trigger you going to use the fifty rounds in twelve seconds. So, squeeze and release. Three-second, twelve-round bursts. If we fire a lot before we get to the back room, hit the button on the right, the ejector. Pull the clip out, flip it over, back into the stock, and you got fifty more rounds." Dee demonstrated the maneuver, then handed the Uzi to Pooh.

Pooh did it three times. "Got it."

Dee smiled, opened another bag, and took out two small dog leashes.

"Don't tell me we're going to walk dogs into the bogey." Pooh raised an eyebrow.

"No, my friend. Not dogs. We're going to walk death into the bogey. Death at the end of these leashes." Dee took a leash, put the clip end through the handle forming a loop, which he put his right arm through. He pulled the loop onto his shoulder, took the Uzi, and clipped its rear stock to the end of the leash. The gun hung just below his waist as he stood and pulled on his long black leather coat. "See anything that looks like a gun?"

"I see a big black man in a big black coat. Nothing else."

"Good. Wear your black leather trench tomorrow night. We meet here at eleven. Make sure Shorty has the van and waits downstairs." He whipped back his coat and brought the Uzi out in one swift, smooth motion. "Two black men in two black coats gonna be the last thing some Dominicans ever see."

Pooh was apprehensive. Even with the Uzis, the Dominicans might prove formidable. *I hope I don't buy the farm before I have a chance to buy the farm.*

Nineteen - The Postman Cometh

McGuire pulled up to his house in Long Beach. He felt great. The assignment to the task force could be the break he was hoping for. He had gotten his gold detective shield seven years before and was aching for an overdue promotion to second grade. Sergeant Ramos had put him in for it three times over the previous two years. There was no way of knowing if his name made it to One Police Plaza and the Chief of Detectives' office where the final determinations were made. But, working on a case the Bronx boss, Chief Philbin, was tracking had to help his chances.

He got out of the car whistling Amy Grant's "Baby, Baby," opened the front gate, and headed to his basement apartment when his landlady, Mrs. Murphy, called to him from her front door.

McGuire walked up the steps wondering what she wanted. He always paid his rent early. She wore a green terrycloth robe, belted at the waist, and fuzzy pink bunny slippers. The former Playboy Bunny was pushing sixty. Though still pretty, like a lot of the local women, her face showed the effects of too much sun and too much vodka. Her body was a different story. She hit the gym every day, and her large breasts did a good job of fighting the years and gravity.

Gomez, who had met her when he helped McGuire move in, had been impressed. "She must have been a knockout back in her day."

McGuire, remembered a line from *Caddy Shack*. "Yeah. She was hot before electricity."

From the clear liquid swirling in his landlady's glass, McGuire guessed Happy Hour had begun.

"C'mon in, John, I have something for you. Would you like a drink?" She pointed to a frosty bottle of Stoli, which sat on a table in her small living room.

McGuire was tempted but had promised Gomez he would be bright-eyed, bushy-tailed, and standing tall when they met at the Four-two at six a.m. tomorrow. They would have two hours to work the Medina kidnap case—on their own time—until Sergeant Ramos and the newly formed task force reported for their first day duty at eight.

"No thanks, Mrs. Murphy. Got to get up early."

"Oh, too bad. I hate drinking alone. And please, call me Claire." She moved to the table, picked up an envelope, and handed it to McGuire. "The mailman asked if I would sign for you. It's registered mail."

McGuire looked at the envelope. It came from a law firm in Manhattan. He opened it, and, as he suspected, it was the official notice Cathy had filed for divorce. McGuire saw both their names and the words "Irreconcilable Differences."

Like our honeymoon night. She came to bed in an exquisite short satin night dress from Victoria's Secret. I had on my NYPD Football gym shorts.

He put the letter in his pocket. "The drink offer still stand, Claire?"

"Of course, Handsome." She picked up the bottle and gave McGuire a view of her ample cleavage.

Twenty - Time Flies

"The first one's always the hardest," Claire said.

McGuire had shared with her the contents of the letter. How he and Cathy had been together since high school. As the vodka went down, the hurt came out.

She told McGuire about her three failed marriages and latest disappearing act by her boyfriend of two years. As they talked, they emptied the bottle.

McGuire stood to leave and thanked Claire for the drinks.

"Do you have to go, John? It's so nice to have someone to talk with."

"Yeah, Claire. I want to go down, take a shower, grab something to eat, and hit the sack. Promised my partner I'd be in at six."

Claire stepped into the kitchen and reappeared with another bottle of Stoli. "We could call for a pizza and crack this open while we wait."

"Thanks, Claire, but really I have to—"

"Please, John, one more drink and a few slices of pizza won't hurt you." She gazed at McGuire with pleading eyes and looked much older than when he'd come in.

McGuire felt sorry for her. If she was hurting half as much as he was, he understood her need for someone to talk to.

"Okay, Claire. Call for the pie and give me one more drink. One more, a couple of slices, and I'm out of here."

She smiled and looked twenty years younger. "One drink and a pizza coming up. A pleasure to serve one of New York's Finest. And handsomest."

It wasn't lost on him. Claire eyed him like a junkyard dog gazing at a meaty sirloin. He caught her running her eyes up and down his six-foot-two, 200-pound frame.

"Where did you get those shoulders, John? And those biceps? You must work out." She walked over to McGuire, linked her right arm through his left, and led him back to the couch, making sure that his arm and elbow were firmly planted in her right breast.

Claire spun him onto the couch, leaned forward, and placed both hands on his cheeks. "Thanks for staying, Gorgeous."

He looked up into her face. *Fuck. She's older than my mother.*

He moved back farther onto the couch. "How 'bout calling for the pizza, Claire. I'm really hungry."

She sighed, walked into the kitchen, and placed the order. On the way back, she filled McGuire's glass. "Delivery in twenty minutes. Want to look at some old pictures?"

"Sure thing, Claire."

She went to a bookcase and came back with two albums. "First, my modeling days."

McGuire opened the book's old red leather cover. A young and beautiful Claire had appeared in a number of print ads. One was for Chevrolet. McGuire looked at the car. "1955?"

"Fifty-six."

McGuire read the ad copy out loud. Claire leaned back, a faraway, contented look in her eyes, a smile on her lips. McGuire went slowly, page by page, with Claire filling in the backstory of each ad.

He noticed Claire's rack was nowhere near as impressive in the ads as it was now.

As he closed the book, Claire handed him a second. "I don't let just anybody see this one." McGuire placed the large black leather-covered portfolio on his lap and opened it.

"These are the proofs from my Playboy shoot."

"I knew you were a bunny. But, you were in Playboy?"

"Miss November 1961."

McGuire scanned the first three pages. Photos of Claire, fully clothed in a chair as her makeup and hair were done. Somewhere between 1956 and 1961, her breast size had doubled.

Claire snuggled up next to McGuire. "Turn the page, here come the money shots."

The doorbell rang.

"Perfect fucking timing." Claire sighed. She untangled herself from McGuire and went to the door.

McGuire looked and saw the frayed robe, pink bunny slippers, and 1961 immediately gave way to 1991. He closed the book.

Claire came back with the pizza. She put out some napkins and paper plates. As she took the book from his lap, her hand rested for a moment on his thigh.

"I'm starving. Let's eat," he said.

She filled both their glasses with Stoli and poured two large snifters of Irish Mist. "I like to have my after-dinner drinks with dinner."

McGuire started to inhale a slice of pizza.

Claire downed half of her vodka and chased it with the entire glass of Irish Mist.

My God. She puts it away like an Irish cop at an open-bar retirement party.

McGuire quickly finished his second slice. He started to stand, had some trouble, and fell back onto the couch.

"You can't leave without seeing the best part." She placed the album flat on McGuire's lap. She leaned in close with her lips almost touching his ear. She opened the book.

McGuire stared at a full-page black-and-white shot of Claire in a barn, sitting on a hay bale, wearing a straw hat and coveralls. The top of the coveralls hung down to her waist. The straps hung over her shoulders but didn't even begin to cover her huge breasts.

A very subdued picture compared to the *Penthouse* and *Playboy* magazines McGuire had grown up with. No pubic hair, no degree in gynecology needed to enjoy it. Just a gorgeous, full-breasted American girl, looking like the farmer's daughter, topless, sitting on a bale of hay.

McGuire instantly grew hard.

Claire chuckled. "Officer McGuire, is that a nightstick in your pants, or are you just happy to see me?" She kissed him hard on the mouth. She pulled back, her robe now almost completely open. He stared with glassy eyes.

McGuire was torn. He had never cheated on Cathy in all their years together. Now she wanted a divorce. Why should this feel wrong?

Claire stroked his ear, saying something he couldn't understand. He gulped some more vodka.

Got to go for it. How many chances does a guy get to nail a Playboy Playmate of the Month? I don't give a shit that I was six that month.

The urge McGuire was feeling was quickly overridden when he was hit with an even more overwhelming urge. To piss. Right now. Downing almost a quart of vodka can do that.

He got shakily to his feet. "Where's the bathroom, Bootiful?"

Claire pointed. "Second door on the right. Hurry back, Officer Nightstick." She downed her vodka glass, refilled her Irish Mist snifter, and finished half before McGuire stumbled to the bathroom.

He closed the door and pulled down his zipper. He pulled his jockey shorts to the side and his dick sprung out of his pants.

Looking down at his penis, McGuire smiled. "Curse of the Irish, my ass. Dick's so hard a cat couldn't scratch it."

He finished, wobbled to the sink, and ran the cold water. He washed his hands, helped himself to a bit of Claire's toothpaste, put it on his finger and brushed his teeth.

Spitting it out, he grabbed cold water in his hands and doused his face. Satisfied, he patted the bulge in his pants. "Ready, Tiger? Get your game face on. I think we're in for one hell of a night."

He returned to find Claire passed out, snoring, her mouth wide open, Irish Mist running down her chin onto her neck. McGuire's Rocky the Tiger became Limpy the Noodle.

"Son of a bitch."

He slapped Claire's face gently, but she was out cold. The Irish Mist bottle lay on its side. McGuire picked it up, found a towel, and mopped up the booze on the coffee table. There were three fingers left in the bottle.

Getting ready to go, he reached into his pocket for his keys and came out with the letter from the law firm. His knees buckled, and he fell back onto the couch. He read the letter once more. The words spun in front of his eyes. He sucked in a mouthful of air. His hand reached for the Irish Mist. He sat back on the couch and brought the bottle to his lips.

* * *

He awoke not knowing where he was. Sunlight streamed through the window. McGuire vaguely remembered eating some pizza. He scanned the room and saw the two dead Stolis and a bottle of Irish Mist on life support. No wonder his head felt like midgets were doing calisthenics in it. He looked at his watch.

Six fuckin' thirty.

He shot off the couch, remembering his promise to Gomez.

He was almost out the door when he turned and saw Claire, still asleep on the couch.

He grabbed an afghan from a chair and tucked it in around her.

He raced down to his apartment, grabbed the phone and dialed the squad.

"Four-two squad, Gomez."

"Joe, John. I'll be there in—"

Click. The line went dead.

Twenty-One - Better Late Than

McGuire made it to work in one hour. There were, perhaps, two traffic laws he did not break en route. He ran up the stairs to the squad, sweating heavily, despite the January chill.

Gomez was at his desk typing.

"Joe, I'm sorry but—"

Gomez did not look up. "Sergeant wants to see you."

McGuire froze. He had promised Sergeant Ramos he and Gomez would work the Medina case on their own time. He had fucked it up on the first day. He walked into Ramos's office expecting an ass chewing, to be told that the Medina case would be reassigned. "Sarge, I—"

"John, glad you're in early. Appearance control called. ADA Torelli wants you in her office ASAP. You got a Huntley hearing this morning on the gun collar you made last September."

McGuire held in a sigh of relief. He looked at the clock behind Ramos. Seven-forty a.m.

The sarge, complimenting him for getting to work on time, meant he did not know McGuire had reneged on his promise to Gomez to be in at six. Ramos had probably gotten in his usual half hour early, seen Gomez, who was always early, and thought nothing of it. Gomez had said nothing.

The Huntley hearing, a proceeding to see if statements given by a defendant would be admissible in court, would be easy. Patching things up with his partner would be difficult.

McGuire walked out of the sergeant's office and noticed Gomez wasn't at his desk.

He found him in the meal room, alone. "Joe, I'm really sorry but—"

Gomez's face grew dark. His knuckles, wrapped around his coffee cup, were white.

"I know, John, you're sorry. You're always sorry. You've been a sorry excuse for a partner for the last five months. I'm sorry. I'm sorry Cathy left you. I'm sorry you have to hide your sorrow in the bottle. You're the one who begged the sergeant to let us keep the Medina case, and you can't get your ass in on time the first day we're going to work it? I'm tired of your bullshit excuses, tired of your lies. And right now, I'm tired of having you as a partner."

McGuire took a deep breath. "If you don't want to be partners anymore, ask Ramos to hook you up with someone else."

Gomez stood and brushed past McGuire. "I might just do it." He slammed the door behind him.

* * *

McGuire drove to court trying to remember all of the details of the September gun collar. He had trouble doing this. His mind kept replaying the scene with his partner and best friend.

He and Gomez had been returning to their command from court when they spotted an older black man getting out of his car. He stood up, adjusted something behind his right hip, and pulled his shirt down over it. Both partners had seen this move many times before.

"Bingo," McGuire said.

"He's packing," Gomez replied.

The duo knew people who were not accustomed to carrying a pistol were always checking it, patting it, making sure it didn't show. To NYPD cops, required to be armed both on and off duty, the gun became part of their bodies. They knew it was on their hip, ankle, or under their armpit. There was no reason to constantly touch it.

The elderly man's adjustments had tipped the detectives to the fact he was carrying, and was most likely not a retired cop or corrections officer. They had been partners for so long, they each knew exactly how this situation would be handled, what tactics would be used. The suspect had not seen them and was walking down the sidewalk.

Gomez exited the passenger seat, slowly and quietly closed the door, but did not let it latch. He fell in behind the man, keeping a gap between them. McGuire drove well past, pulled to the curb, got out, and appeared to be looking for an address. If this spooked the man and he turned, it would be Gomez's stop. He kept walking however, and when he was about ten feet from him, McGuire stepped into his path, his gun visible in his hand but not pointing at the suspect. "Police. Don't move." McGuire called in a loud, clear voice. He did not bother to remove his badge from his pocket. It would tie up his non-shooting hand, which he would need if this turned into a struggle. Besides, a four-year-old kid in the South Bronx knew when he saw a white man on the street he was probably a cop. Washington Avenue attracted few tourists or ladies who lunch. The man stopped.

"Nice and easy, put your hands on your head."

The man complied without a word.

"Keep your hands up. Do not drop them, okay, pal?" McGuire moved in closer.

Gomez had come up behind the man when he stopped. He stood just to his right to give McGuire a clear field of fire, if necessary. Had the suspect reached for whatever was under his shirt, Gomez would have been on him before he knew what hit him.

"My partner is going to take a quick peek under your shirt. Do not turn around."

"I have a gun, officer."

Gomez reached in and held up a silver revolver. "Bingo, John."

Gomez holstered his own weapon, and with the silver gun pointed safely toward the sky, continued to search the subject. More than one cop had been killed letting his guard down after taking a gun from a perp who carried two.

The search completed, McGuire asked, "Don't suppose you have a permit."

"No, Sir."

McGuire holstered his gun and pulled out his handcuffs. He gently brought the old timer's hands behind his back to be cuffed. "What's your name, pal?"

"Amos Jenkins, Sir."

"Amos, you know it's illegal to carry an unlicensed firearm in New York City, right?"

"Yes, Sir. I know."

"Then why you packing, Amos?"

"Officer, I would rather you catch me with it than the young thugs catch me without it. I been robbed three times in the last year. Beat me up pretty bad the last time. I had enough. Bought it down home in South Carolina. Just want to be able to protect myself."

McGuire looked at his partner and gave a deep sigh. "How old are you, Amos?"

"Seventy-two, Sir."

The handcuffs still dangled from McGuire's hand. He motioned to his partner to come closer. "Joey, I don't wanna collar this poor old guy. Let's put him in the car, drop him off a few blocks over, throw the gun down a sewer. Everybody's happy."

"John, you see all the people watching us. We can't do it."

A crowd had formed and was moving closer to them. As if on cue, a large black man, thirtyish, with jailhouse tattoos on his neck and arms, stepped forward and got into McGuire's face. "Why you hassling the brother? He ain't doing nothing."

McGuire took in the bad tats, the jailhouse muscles. A recent graduate of Greenhaven or Attica was his guess. "Give us a minute, Bro. We're working this out. Just back off a bit."

Amos, who'd heard the partners' conversation, addressed the big guy. "Back off, Fool. Let these men do their job."

"Shut up, old man. These are our streets not these pigs'." He put a large hand on McGuire's chest and pushed. "Time for the pigs to leave." He left the hand on McGuire's chest.

McGuire gave an almost imperceptible nod to Gomez, who did not need any signal. He knew what was coming. McGuire could put up with a ton of verbal harassment, but anyone placing hands on him did so at great personal risk. His right hand, holding one cuff, shot behind Tattoo's hand, his left grabbed the other cuff. He pulled in tightly, locking the creep's hand onto his chest and bent forward violently from the waist.

This all happened much too quickly for his adversary to react. His hand, with nowhere to go to relieve the pressure McGuire's weight was exerting, bent backwards beyond its normal range of motion. His wrist snapped with a loud crack.

McGuire, still locked onto Tattoo's hand, spun from the waist, locking the man's arm out. He slid his forearm behind Tatoo's elbow and applied pressure, dumping him face-down on the sidewalk. He dropped his 200 pounds on one knee directly onto his opponent's spine, pulled both of Tattoo's hands up behind his back, and slapped the cuffs on them.

Amos looked at Gomez. "You must be Robin." He saw the puzzled look on Gomez's face. "You got to be Robin, 'cause your partner definitely be Batman."

Gomez chuckled. "Nah, not Batman, but he knows how to handle himself." Gomez was one of the very few who knew McGuire, in addition to his boxing background, had also attained a Black Belt in *Kempo* karate and had studied the Chinese martial art *Chin Na*, which emphasized seizing, locking, and controlling an opponent's limbs and joints.

"The karate and boxing are great, but we don't usually square off with a mutt on the street we're looking to collar," McGuire had told Gomez when he had asked about the *Chin Na.*

"Our fights are usually more like a hockey fight, right? You grab on, get in tight and try to bring the skell down to the ground where you can get the cuffs on him. You're hoping to get their hands behind their backs and cuffed before they can do any damage to you. *Chin Na* is great. It's not about strength. It's all leverage and joint manipulation. And, in case somebody is taping it, you're not punching or kicking the shit out of some poor peace-loving civilian and won't be the lead story on the eleven o'clock news."

McGuire lifted Tattoo off the ground and dumped him into their car's rear seat.

"Police brutality, police brutality!" Tattoo screamed.

"Thanks to your big fuckin' mouth, the old guy's getting collared, Jerk Off."

A bottle sailed off a roof and broke next to McGuire's head. Two more followed.

"Amos, Joe, let's go. Get in the car." Amos ran over to McGuire and turned with both hands behind his back, waiting to be cuffed. "Just get in, Amos, no time for formalities."

Gomez shoved Tattoo over, put Amos in the middle, and got in the rear seat behind McGuire. "Go," he yelled before his door closed as another salvo of bottles and bricks exploded around their car.

Safely back at the squad, it was discovered Tatoo, whose real name was Mustafa Jaleel—AKA Richard Porter—had gotten out of upstate's Greenhaven Prison three days earlier. He had been paroled after doing ten years for manslaughter. He owed eight years and would now be going back to finish his sentence. After complaining of wrist pain, Jaleel had been taken to Jacobi Hospital by two, young, Four-two uniformed cops. He now sat in the squad's holding cell, a cast on his left hand and wrist.

Amos sat next to McGuire's desk, not cuffed, sipping a Coke and smoking a cigarette, both of which McGuire had bought for him in the precinct's vending machines. Someone walking into the squad might take Amos for a retired detective stopping by for a visit with his old partner.

Gomez had run Amos's and Jaleel's names through NCIC and discovered Amos had never been arrested. Mustafa Jaleel had a rap sheet longer than his arm. He had taken collars for burglary, drug sales, assault, rape, robbery, and finally completed his Criminal Justice degree with the manslaughter arrest.

Gomez had gotten this information with a simple query on the squad's new computer. The NYPD was getting a very late jump into the information superhighway computers provided. Many smaller police departments had used them for years. But, the NYPD, the world's largest police force, did not change rapidly. The department was often compared to a huge, lumbering aircraft carrier. Its size made for comfortable travel, plowing straight ahead on a stormy sea, but it could not change direction quickly.

When the computer had arrived, Gomez immediately asked Sergeant Ramos if he could attend a one-week training course at the academy. He followed up months later, going back for more advanced studies. He could make the machine sing.

McGuire did not know how to turn the machine on. "Joey, it ain't that I don't see their usefulness. No doubt they will be a big deal in the future. You're great with it. It's why we're a good team. We each got our own talents."

Gomez had printed out Mustafa Jaleel's sheet and brought it over to McGuire's desk.

"What the hell is wrong with this guy, he wants to go back to jail?" Gomez asked.

"He Mus-ta-fa few screws loose." McGuire chuckled.

Gomez rolled his eyes. Amos burst out laughing.

"Mus-ta-fa screw loose. Now that's some funny shit, Detective." The old man finally stopped laughing.

McGuire picked up the sheet and studied it. "He's an Institutional man. He's thirty-six. Last twenty, he's been outside all of four years. He likes prison. It's his home. He gets to hang with his homeboys, a warm bed, cable TV, weightlifting, and three square meals a day."

"Don't forget the butt fucking," Amos added.

McGuire and Gomez rolled with laughter.

"Yeah, Amos. Can't forget about that." Still smiling, he turned to Gomez. "Joe, I'll run Amos down to Central Booking, okay? Get those two young uniform kids to drive you and Mustafa down, but give me an hour. Be careful with that prick. You're not going to be able to cuff him with the cast."

"I don't think he'll be a problem. Like you said, he's probably hoping to get back to Greenhaven ASAP."

"Might be his book club meets tomorrow night, Joe."

McGuire walked into Bronx Central Booking with Amos at eight p.m. Cops who had made collars the night before waited for their cases to be called in Night Court. McGuire used all of his charm and considerable prestige to jump to the front of the line. None of the cops who were on overtime objected, especially when told the details of the arrest.

McGuire spoke to the judge before Amos was arraigned. A low bail was set. A bail bondsman McGuire knew came forward. Amos walked out before midnight.

Now, four months later, McGuire had to come up with a way to prevent Amos from going to trial. His age and clean record notwithstanding, he was looking at a minimum one-year sentence. The carnage on the streets of New York, and in the minority neighborhoods in particular, had to be stopped. The number one cause of death for African-American youths in the city was not accidents, as it was for whites, but homicide by gunfire. The city's five District Attorneys had taken a hard line on weapons possession.

ADA Gina Torelli's office was in the Bronx Supreme Court building on the Grand Concourse and 161st Street. She was a rising star in the DA's office, having won a number of very high-profile cases. This status had gotten her an office on the eighth floor with a great view into Yankee Stadium. McGuire and Gomez had done a number of cases with her. She was sharp and took no shit from anyone. She was welcome at all the Bronx cops' promotion and retirement parties and was very popular with the collar guys, the active cops who appreciated having an ADA, and a female one to boot, who they felt had their backs.

She was thirty-two, five-foot-two, and cute, with long, straight black hair from her Italian father and bright green eyes from her Irish mother's side. Unfortunately, the long days in the office, downing fast food, pizza, coffee, and bagels had added some unwanted pounds to her small frame.

No matter, McGuire could not have been happier she had been assigned this case.

He stopped at Gina's secretary's desk and put down a bag holding a dozen bagels.

"Thanks, John." Mary Glavey, a redheaded looker, married to a cop John knew, pushed a button on her phone. "Detective McGuire's here, Gina."

He heard her reply. "Send him in, please."

"Good morning. How is the best ADA in the City of New York doing today?" He breezed through the door.

McGuire wondered if Gina, like other females in the Bronx DA's office, thought he was good looking. He'd overheard a couple refer to him as "a hunk." The rumor his once happy marriage was on the rocks was common knowledge. He noticed her frown when she spotted his wedding ring.

"I'm great, John. This case. The gun collar you made on Washington Avenue last September. Talk to me about your original stop of Amos Jenkins. The statement he made on the street. 'I'd rather you catch me with it than the young thugs catch me without it,' is great. A spontaneous admission, no need for Miranda. We just have to articulate the reasons you suspected he might have a gun."

"Gina, have you seen his record?"

"Yes, John, his first arrest. Nevertheless, he's carrying a gun on the street."

"I asked him if he'd ever carried a gun before. You know what his answer was? 'Only other time I carried a weapon was in Italy in 1944.' He was mugged three times last year. No arrests made. Shit, Gina, if the system can't protect him, do you blame him for wanting to protect himself?"

"John, I don't have to tell you, we had over 600 homicides in the Bronx last year, most caused by guns. He's going to have to do some time. Maybe because of his age, we can plea him down to attempted possession. Get a year, do three months in jail, nine months' probation. Okay?"

"No jail, he's gotta walk."

Gina pointed to her window. "You know, just like the Yankees over there, I have to keep my average up. I can't strike out on a gun case. It would look bad on my record."

"How about if you decided it was a bad collar. I had no lawful reason to stop him."

"What was your reason for the stop?"

"I stopped him because he was black."

"And, he was the only black guy on Washington Avenue, right? John, you have to do better."

McGuire looked straight into Gina's green eyes. "Counselor, sometimes we just have to do the right thing. This is not a guy who belongs in jail. You tell me what you need me to say for you to 343 this case, and I'll say it."

She stared back at McGuire. They held each other's eyes for what seemed a minute. She sighed, turned and opened a file drawer. "Detective McGuire, I am filling out form 343. The Bronx District Attorney's Office is declining to prosecute this case. The arresting officer cannot articulate a lawful reason for his stop of the defendant. I will notify Mr. Jenkins's lawyer all charges have been dropped at this time."

McGuire stood and took Gina's hand in both of his. "I said you're the best ADA in the city, and I meant it. Thank you, counselor. I owe you one. How about lunch some day?"

"Detective, I'm thinking more along the lines of dinner and a movie."

Twenty-Two - Enough

McGuire was in no hurry to get back to the office. He wanted to put off finding out if Gomez had asked for a new partner. He needed time to grasp everything. While he knew they were coming, the divorce papers had rocked him. Losing Gomez would be more than he could handle. He would be hurt and embarrassed. Word would spread quickly throughout the Bronx police world. He could live with everyone knowing about his divorce. It was a common byproduct of police life. But partners who had worked together for as long as he and Joe rarely split.

In his mind, Cathy bore as much responsibility for the divorce as he did. But Gomez? Only one person was to blame for their mess, and it wasn't Joe.

McGuire killed some time with another ADA, Hank Dwyer, with whom he had an upcoming homicide trial. He and Hank spoke of how they would counter the defense strategy and some of the finer points McGuire had gotten when he had taken the killer's confession.

"I'm expecting him to cop when we pick the jury, John. Open and shut case. Let's grab lunch. Alex and Henry's. I'm buying." Alex and Henry's was a first-rate steakhouse. It survived in the rundown South Bronx by being the closest watering hole to the courts. Every borough had one: a restaurant/bar near the courthouse where judges, cops, defendants, ADAs and defense lawyers put aside their differences in search of a decent meal, and perhaps a drink or three. McGuire was tempted. He wasn't hungry, still very much hung over from last night's binge. But a strong Bloody Mary, lots of ice, pepper, Tabasco, a stalk of celery, double shot of vodka—he could taste it. A couple of those would do the trick. As much as he wanted it, he needed something more. To be alone, to think, to figure a way out of his problems.

"Thanks, Hank, I'll take a rain check. Got a few things to do." He picked up his coat and headed for the door.

"Okay, John. Take care. Give my best to Joe."

McGuire took a deep breath. "Sure thing, Hank," he mumbled without turning around.

* * *

McGuire checked his watch: two-thirty. He had two hours to kill to ensure Gomez and the rest of the task force would be gone when he got back to the squad. He drove from court to his favorite place in the Bronx, The Botanical Garden. No one manned the gate on this cold January day. He walked straight in. Except for a few workers, McGuire had the place to himself. He had discovered the place early on in his Bronx career. He had been at the scene of a gruesome murder of two young children in an apartment on the Grand Concourse. Despite his best effort, he had been losing it. Feeling like he might puke. An old-time uniform sergeant took him by the arm, put him in his patrol car, and drove to the garden.

"Take a walk. I'll pick you up here in an hour."

The Botanical Garden became his sanctuary, his place to go when the job overwhelmed him.

He stopped by a waterfall in the Rock Garden. *How'd my life get so messed up? Cathy and I had a lot of problems. What's causing my troubles with Joe?* McGuire looked into the falling water. The answer to the question was obvious. *My drinking. Every time I screwed up with Joe, it was the drinking. God help me. Please don't let me lose him, too.*

McGuire thought back to when they'd first met, fourteen years earlier when they were accepted to the same Academy class. McGuire, of Irish-American descent, brought up in Brooklyn, a natural athlete, was outgoing and confident.

Gomez, born in Santiago, the Dominican Republic, had come to New York with his parents when he was fifteen. Speaking only Spanish, his first year of high school had been hell. He learned English quickly but was still shy and quiet. Their friendship had blossomed during boxing lessons in the third week of academy training.

McGuire was good with his fists, a skill learned on the streets of Brooklyn and later polished in the PAL gym near his home. He had fought as a light heavyweight in the Golden Gloves and made it to the finals, where he lost to an opponent who would later turn pro. Still, he was happy with his four wins/one loss record and treasured the miniature pair of silver gloves he was given as the sub-novice light heavy runner up.

The recruits stood in two lines facing each other. McGuire was paired with a short kid named Abe Selig. Sensing Selig was uncomfortable facing a much larger opponent, McGuire smiled and touched gloves with him.

"You boxed much, Abe?"

"Not at all."

"Want a little lesson?"

"Yeah, it would be great."

Abe was getting the hang of things when a flurry of motion to his right caught McGuire's attention. Two bouts over, he saw a heavily muscled white guy whaling away at a skinny Latino recruit. At first he thought the two knew each other and wanted to have a real go. He quickly realized this was not the case. The thin guy, while fighting back gamely, was completely outclassed. His foe knew how to throw a punch and put his body into each one. Again and again, his heavy right hands jolted his opponent.

McGuire looked to the instructors, hoping they would stop the fight, but they were busy watching two recruits who were going at it toe to toe. As he watched, the skinny kid took two hard rights and went down on one knee. Mercifully the whistle blew, ending the round. But, just as the rookie started to get to his feet, Muscles threw one more right to his body. It doubled the kid over. McGuire stepped over to the pair.

"You, okay?" he asked.

"Yeah."

McGuire waved Abe over.

"This round, why don't you and Abe hook up?" He turned to the bruiser. "What the fuck was the beating about?"

"I was giving the spic a boxing lesson, pal. What's it to you?"

"How about givin' a mick a lesson this round?"

"My pleasure, Dickhead."

The whistle blew and Muscles charged in like a wounded bull. McGuire sidestepped the charge, and was throwing a left when he felt an explosion of pain in his left leg. The cretin had tried to knee him in the groin. McGuire saw red. A knee injury could end his police career before it started. This fight had to end quickly.

As he waited for the caveman to get back in range, McGuire's mind locked onto a three-punch combination he thought would work against this jerk. He threw a lazy left hook at Muscles' head, and with satisfaction, saw his foe raise his right arm to block it. The combination would work. McGuire threw a sharp left hook to the head and doubled up with a quick left hook to the body. Bluto blocked the first punch. The second landed on his rib cage, and he reflexively leaned forward, right into a crushing right hand, which caught him square on the jaw. His head snapped back, and he fell to the floor. McGuire knew he wouldn't get up soon. He had put his entire body into the punch, had felt the power start in his toes, travel up his body as he turned from the waist, and got all of his 200 pounds into it. He knew while big biceps might impress the girls, a punch's power came from the legs and the turning of the hips.

This one had it all, and the results proved it. Muscles was trying to get up, but his arms and legs were not working well. The punch had short-circuited the messages from his brain to his limbs.

McGuire looked at the instructors. They hadn't seen him demolish his adversary, but Abe and the skinny kid had. They both stared at him with their mouths open. He looked back at them and shrugged.

When the whistle blew, he stepped behind his dazed foe and lifted him into a seated position.

"You, okay?" McGuire asked.

"That was a lucky punch, you prick."

"Yeah, lucky it didn't take your head off." He pointed toward Abe and the Latino recruit. "Fuck with them, you got a major problem."

Later, after McGuire had showered, he was in the locker room getting back into his gray probie uniform when the skinny rookie approached.

"Why'd you do that?" The kid held an ice cube to his swollen lip.

"No big deal. I just got a thing about guys who think they're tough and try to prove it by bullying someone. It bothers me. Besides, we're all cops and should be looking to help, not hurt each other."

"I'm Joe Gomez. I appreciate what you did. If I can ever—"

"Thanks, Joe. John McGuire. I just might take you up on the offer someday." The two shook hands.

"I'm going to Ptomaine Teddy's for lunch. Wanna come with me?"

"Sure thing," Gomez replied.

They began a friendship which had endured through fourteen years. McGuire's recent behavior was threatening to end it.

* * *

At half past four, he circled the precinct and, not seeing Gomez or Sergeant Ramos's cars, went up to the squad room. The night crew was working. Pleasantries were exchanged. He did not pick up on anything out of the ordinary. If Joe had made the move, everyone would know.

Feeling relieved, he picked up the Medina kidnapping case file from Gomez's basket and took it into the meal room. He'd spent about ten minutes reviewing it and making notes, when the door closed. He looked up to see Gomez. "Joe, I can't tell you how sorry I am."

"John, please don't say anything, just listen. This is it. Your last shot. Come in late, come in drunk, I'm gone. Ask me to cover, to lie for you, adios. It's all up to you. Understand?"

"I swear—"

"John, do you understand?"

McGuire stood. "Yes. I just want to say—"

"I got it. *Hasta aqui se acabo.* It's over. Forget it, okay? Now, what are you doing?"

"I was just making some notes on Medina."

Gomez walked to a closet and came back with an easel. He pulled back the cover sheet.

It bore a mug shot of Roberto Medina, his B number, a list of his arrests. Gomez pulled the next sheet down.

"Addresses where he was collared and where he was living. These are the phone numbers he called after each arrest. Visitors he had at his short stays in Rikers, their numbers. Calls he made out from there. Associates he was collared with. Their phone numbers, numbers they called."

He turned another page. "Numbers the ransom demands came from. No matches with any of the others. Two public phones, both in the Bronx. One stolen cell phone, legit owner, no connections. Call was placed in upper Manhattan."

He turned yet another page. "Ballistics. The one slug they pulled out of his ass. A .9mm, no matches with any others at this time."

McGuire shook his head. An inside job was always the first thing a detective looked at in a kidnapping. Who knew who had money, where he would be? Who would they call with the ransom demand? He had anticipated spending dozens of hours working the angle. Gomez had just knocked it out.

"Looks like you've been busy, Joe."

"Real busy. I'm doing the work of two men."

"Not anymore. What do you need me to do?"

"Aren't you going home?"

"Nah, I want to put in a couple of hours on this and then catch some sleep in the dorm. Don't feel like driving home."

Gomez sat down. “I’m good till ten o’clock.” He picked up a folder and handed it to McGuire. It contained arrest photos of twenty white males, looking at the camera and in profile.

“Over a hundred reported police impersonations in the city last year.” Gomez pointed. “None for kidnapping, most for shaking down store owners or motorists. Thirty arrests made. I ran them all. Ten are still in. These mopes are out, either beat the case or out on bail.” He took the folder and stood. “Want to take a ride into Manhattan? I called Medina this afternoon. He and Benny, his guy who was there with him, will meet us at the Gracie Diner on Eighty-sixth and York whenever we say.”

“He didn’t want to meet in his bodega?”

“Nah, it was my idea. Wanted to get them off their home turf. You never know IAB or the feds might be watching his place.” Joe picked up a phone. “Seven o’clock good?”

“Make it eight. I might feel like eating by then.”

Twenty-Three - Coming in Hot

Pooh and Dee sat in the back of the stolen van, Shorty Brown at the wheel. All eyes were on the door of the Tremont Avenue bodega. They had gone through this last night. Dee's girl, Yolanda, had entered and, seeing no activity in the back room, had exited and turned left. Mission aborted.

* * *

Domingo Flores, the bodega manager, eyed the woman warily as she approached the counter. She had come in last night and left without buying anything. Now she was back again. His hand gripped the sawed-off shotgun he kept under the counter. "Can I help you, *Señora*?"

The woman approached and seemed strangely interested in the three men sitting at a table in the room behind Domingo's counter.

"Do you have any dog food?" she asked.

"No, *Señora*. There is a pet store around the corner on Webster."

"Thanks. I'll try there. Good night."

Domingo watched her leave. She turned right. He looked up at the three security camera monitors. The outside camera showed two men in black getting out of a van, heading quickly toward the store.

"*Cuidado. Ahi vienen los prietos,*" he warned those in the back room.

* * *

Dee and Pooh entered, the Uzis rising from beneath their coats. The man behind the counter fired one round from a shotgun as he slid into the back room, pulling the heavy door closed. Pooh ducked behind a stack of cans, Dee let loose with the Uzi on full auto. Fifty .9mm rounds left the weapon in twelve seconds. The first five hit the door, the rest went into the wall and ceiling as the muzzle of the gun climbed higher with each shot.

Pooh wisely stayed behind the cover of cans and hit the door more effectively. He fired short bursts, three or four rounds with each trigger squeeze, and kept them all on target.

Dee emptied his clip, ejected, reversed it, and rained lead on the door. They both waited to hear screams from the Dominicans inside. They'd have a long wait.

They might as well have been shooting spit balls at a battleship since the Dominicans had planned for just such an assault. Behind the sheetrock and plywood, the wall and door to the back room consisted of half-inch steel plates covered with bullet-resistant Kevlar. Not one round penetrated this fortress. They also had placed two small ports on the wall from which two of the men were firing back at the intruders. The store was filled with smoke, killing visibility.

Pooh was to the right and rear of Dee. During a brief break in the barrage, he yelled, "Dee, let's book." Neither could hear well. The blasts of gunfire had left their ears ringing. Dee turned to look at Pooh.

Javier Boren, a fourteen-year-old neighborhood boy who worked in the bodega, had been in the bathroom when the shooting started. He had stayed there, and now, with the quiet, saw his chance to escape.

Suddenly, Pooh Bear Jennings saw a kid running down the aisle behind him. Apparently, Dee had also seen him and swung his Uzi in the kid's direction, uselessly pulling the trigger on his now-empty weapon as the kid dove to the floor. Pooh turned and saw a young boy with a look of terror on his face. Dee quickly pulled his .44 Bulldog from his shoulder holster as the kid was getting to his feet.

"No," Pooh screamed.

Dee fired three rounds. Pooh dove to his right. The kid ran two steps and crashed into a display of El Pico coffee cans. Pooh saw blood pour from him. He and Dee ran from the store, jumped into the waiting van. Tires screeching, it took off.

* * *

McGuire and Gomez were headed back to the office. Medina and Benny hadn't recognized any of the faces in the photo spread. It had not, however, been a wasted trip. Medina had assured the detectives the passage of time hadn't taken away his desire to see his kidnappers caught and punished. Gomez, true to his word, had forgiven McGuire. They were a team once again. That and the chocolate thick shake he finished in the diner had him feeling human again.

McGuire drove over the Triborough Bridge into the Bronx. The conversation was about the upcoming Super Bowl. They turned from the Major Deegan onto the Cross Bronx Expressway. They'd pass the Jerome and then the Webster Avenue exits before getting off at Third Avenue. They'd just passed Jerome when the police radio crackled.

"All units—report of a robbery with shots fired—Santiago Suprette—1475 Tremont Avenue—confines of the Four-eight precinct."

McGuire pulled into the right-hand lane and slowed down. "It should be near Webster. We're close. Could be real. What do you think?" They weighed their options. The report could be false. Quite a few were. Store employees frequently called 911 to report a robbery when the crime was shoplifting—someone walking out with a can of beer without paying.

If this call was in fact a bodega robbery with shots fired, McGuire and his partner were perfectly placed if the robbers were in a car and fled onto the Cross Bronx.

The dispatcher came on again, this time preceding her announcement with the repeated electronic bleep that signaled a priority message. "All units, we now have numerous reports of shots fired—1475 Tremont, cross street: Webster Avenue—Santiago Suprette—numerous reports—shots fired. What units responding?"

"Four-eight Adam."

"Four-eight David, two minutes out."

"Four-eight Sergeant responding. Any description, central?"

"Units stand-by, central on landline with a caller, stand-by one."

McGuire hit the gas and rocketed down the Webster Avenue exit. "Fuck it, let's go. It's two blocks away." Detectives did not have to respond to radio calls, but McGuire and Gomez frequently did.

Gomez picked up the radio. "Central, be advised Four-two squad is responding in plainclothes. Let uniform know—two detectives responding—male white, male Hispanic."

Gomez pinned his badge to his coat lapel. He did not want to join the list of plainclothes cops who had been shot in "friendly fire" tragedies by their uniformed comrades.

They were the first unit to arrive. They hadn't used their emergency light or siren, choosing to make a silent approach. McGuire double parked thirty feet from the store. He and Gomez, six-shot Smith & Wesson .38s in hand, slowly made their way on opposite sides of the street toward the bodega, McGuire on the store side. The perps could still be in the store. They could have back-up on the street or sitting in any of the cars the duo passed. McGuire reached the edge of the storefront and stopped. On the other side of the doorway, broken glass sparkled on the sidewalk. He nodded to Gomez, who crossed over and took up a position behind a car, his gun on the hood, covering McGuire.

McGuire crouched low and quickly looked into the store. One body on the floor, a man kneeling over it yelling in Spanish. He looked at Gomez and held up two fingers. Gomez nodded, pointed to his eyes and gave the rounded thumb and forefinger zero sign. He saw the same two McGuire saw, and from his better vantage point, no one else. McGuire, kept low and sprinted to the door, entered, crouched behind a stack of soda cases and pointed his gun at the kneeling man.

"Police. Don't move!" he yelled.

The man turned and started to rise. Had McGuire not had the cover of the cases, he might have fired. Being behind something gave him a half second's luxury. He saw a quizzical look on the man's face.

"*Manos arriba.*" The man immediately raised both hands.

Gomez, now stood behind McGuire. "I got it. Cover." He spoke in Spanish, and the man knelt with both hands behind his head. He and Gomez exchanged a few words.

"He's the manager. No one else here now according to him. Perps are two male blacks, fled in a white van."

"You believe him?"

Gomez asked a few more questions. "Yeah, he's the manager. From Santiago, my hometown." Two marked cars pulled up.

The sergeant recognized McGuire. "Whatta we got, Mac?"

McGuire quickly gave him the description of the perps and getaway car. "Place needs to be searched top to bottom, Sarge, just to be sure." The sergeant put the description out over his radio and began giving orders to his men. McGuire ran to the body. A young boy, having trouble breathing, blood pumping from his shoulder.

"Kid who works here," Gomez said.

McGuire, who was EMT qualified, knelt and examined the wound. He placed two fingers in the hole, slowing the bleeding.

"Ambulance two minutes out," the sergeant called.

McGuire, keeping his fingers in the wound, scooped up the boy. "Can't wait. He's got a severed artery. He'll bleed out." He ran to the door with the boy in his arms. The sergeant followed. As they hit the sidewalk, another Four-eight car pulled up. The sergeant opened the rear door and helped McGuire put the victim in. McGuire straddled him, keeping pressure on the wound.

"Closest hospital, Sarge?"

"St. Barnabas. Hit it, guys. I'll let em know you're coming." He slammed the door as the car took off.

* * *

McGuire sat in St. Barnabas's nurse's lounge sipping coffee, grateful for the fondness cops and nurses seemed to share for each other. A nurse and an orderly had been waiting outside the emergency room with a gurney when they'd pulled up. The kid, now known to be Javier Boren, had been rushed into surgery. McGuire, exhausted, had dropped into a waiting room chair. The adrenaline rush over, he closed his eyes.

"You want to get out of those clothes?" he heard a female voice ask. Thinking he might have dozed off and been dreaming, he opened his eyes. A tall, tough-looking black nurse stood over him.

"Excuse me? I don't understand."

"Your clothes." She pointed at him.

He looked down and noticed for the first time he was covered, from chest to knees, in the victim's blood.

The nurse held out her hand. "I'm Sara Williams, the night supervisor. Come with me, Detective. We'll get you cleaned up."

McGuire introduced himself and followed Sara. "Is the boy gonna make it?"

"Yes. Thanks to you. He lost two pints of blood. Any more and his chances would have been slim." She opened a door with a key. "Nurse's lounge. A shower back there. Got a set of scrubs for you to change into. Take your time. I'll make sure none of my nurses disturb you."

"Thanks, but it's not necessary. You must be busy."

Sara smiled. "Coffee's over there. You can wait in here. I'll check back in a while."

Ten minutes later, cleaned and in the fresh scrubs, McGuire began to relax. The door opened.

Sara entered. "You have company." She escorted Gomez in. "Doctor Williams will be in to talk to you in a minute."

McGuire raised an eyebrow.

"Yes, my husband."

"What's the scene look like, Joe?"

"Had to be over a hundred shell casings. Unreal. *Gunfight at the O.K. Corral.* Two black guys with Uzis, full auto. Trying to kill some Dominicans in the back room."

"Did they?"

"Nah. Room's like a vault. A safe room. Over a hundred rounds. None penetrated."

"Drugs?"

"Room was clean, but you know it has to be. Never saw a bodega with a room like this. The kid's legit. Stockboy. Goes to Cardinal Hayes. No record. Helps pay his tuition by cleaning up."

A very tall black doctor entered. "Hey, Detectives. Steve Williams. The boy's going to be okay, thanks to you guys."

"Can we speak with him, Doc?"

"No. He's sedated. Tomorrow morning at the earliest."

"Doc, did you recover—?" McGuire stopped.

Doctor Williams held up a plastic bag with a bullet in it. "Went in the shoulder, took it out near his neck. Knew you'd want it."

"Oh, we want it. Thanks, Doc." McGuire held up the bag and looked closely at the bullet.

"Joe, the hundred shell casings. What caliber?"

"Nine mm. This looks bigger."

"Looks like a .45. Very interesting."

"Ready to go, Doc?" Gomez asked.

"Go where?" Doctor Williams replied.

"Sorry, Doc. I was asking Doctor McGuire."

Twenty-Four - Ballistics Bonus

McGuire slept in the squad's dorm. Like most detectives, he kept a change of clothes in his locker. Working a homicide could entail going forty-eight or more straight hours without a chance to go home. Fresh clothes were a nice luxury to have. He woke at six, showered, shaved, dressed, and was at his desk by six-thirty.

Gomez arrived from home a few minutes later.

Sergeant Ramos entered the squad at seven and was briefed on the bodega shooting.

"It's a Four-eight precinct case, but it has to be part of our drug war," McGuire said.

"I'll call Chief Philbin later. I'm sure he'll give us the case. The Four-eight will be happy to get rid of it." Ramos nodded. "They're still digging out from last year. Led the city in homicides with a hundred-thirty-seven."

"Yeah, they had one-thirty-seven, but cleared eighty-seven of them with one collar. Bet they have a better than eighty percent clearance rate." McGuire referred to the horrendous Happy Land Social Club fire in the Four-eight the previous March. A deranged man, after fighting with his girlfriend who worked there, bought a gallon of gasoline and doused the staircase to the only entrance to the illegal club. The patrons, most of them from Honduras, were trapped. One arrest, eighty-seven homicides solved.

Ramos studied a folder on his desk. “Close, John. The Four-eight had a seventy-five percent homicide clearance rate last year. We were lucky to clear sixty-six percent. It was the citywide average. If we were much lower, I’d probably be back in uniform now.”

“I’m glad you’re still here, Boss, but ain’t it pretty fucked up? It’s acceptable if we solve two thirds of our homicides. This is some city.”

“At least we know we’ll never get laid off for lack of crime.” Ramos scowled.

McGuire and Gomez went back to their desks. “I’m going to give Ballistics a call, Joe. Want to see what caliber slugs they pulled out of the four Domo druggies from Butler Houses.”

He looked up the number and dialed.

A male voice answered. “Ballistics, Technician Pierce.”.

“Good morning, Technician Pierce, Detective McGuire Four-two squad calling. Need a favor. Can you tell me if we got any usable slugs from a quad homicide in the Four-two on January thirteen? Case number 42-065.”

“Let me check.” McGuire heard papers being shuffled.

“Okay, found it. The ME took a decent slug out of one victim. Let me see, ‘Bullet appears to have entered the victim just above left eye after passing through his right hand.’”

“Great. What caliber is it?”

“Doesn’t say. Hasn’t been tested yet.”

“Hasn’t been tested? The shooting was over two weeks ago.”

“Well, we only got the bullet a week ago from the Medical Examiner.”

"And in seven freaking days, nobody in Ballistics thought it might be a good idea to examine a round from the gun, which may have killed four people?"

"It's above my pay grade. I just work here. We're a little busy. You may have heard, there were over two-thousand homicides in Fun City last year. Two guesses as to weapon of choice in the majority. I will accept handgun or firearm as a correct answer. So, Detective, it's not like we're down here sitting on our asses playing pocket pool all day."

McGuire knew better than to fuck with someone whose help he needed. He looked at Gomez and made the "I'm being jerked off" hand motion. "Pal, I know you guys work hard. I was just hoping this case would get a special look. Maybe pushed to the front of the line."

"That's what every detective who calls or stops here wants. We do the work in the order received."

"I understand. No problem. Is it possible for me to speak to a sergeant?"

"Sergeant Boyle will be in at eight."

"Okay, Pierce. I appreciate your help. Sorry if I came on a little strong."

"No problem, Detective. One develops a very thick skin working here. Have a nice day."

McGuire went back into Sergeant Ramos's office and explained the problems at Ballistics.

"I got the slug they pulled out of last night's victim. It's not one of the nines from the Uzis. Might be a .45. Thought I'd take a ride down to Ballistics and see if I can find someone to compare it to the Butler House bullet. The four Domos were whacked with something large, like a .45. Got a better chance of getting results in person than on the phone."

"Good idea, John. Go ahead, but leave Joe here. I have a ton of stuff I need him to run through the computer. When the other guys come in at eight, I have plenty for them to do, too."

"Ten-four, Sarge." McGuire turned to leave.

"John, hold on a second. Almost forgot. President Bush is coming to town on Saturday. You interested in doing an overtime tour in uniform? Come in on your day off? Have to get at least eight hours OT."

McGuire quickly envisioned standing outside the Waldorf Astoria, in uniform, freezing his ass off, maybe having to listen to a thousand protestors screaming about whatever their latest beef with the prez was. "No thanks. I'll pass."

"No problem. Gomez will have to get by without you."

McGuire signed out in the movement log and got the keys to one of the squad's autos. He went back into the meal room which had become their office and found Gomez. "Joe, I'm running down to Ballistics to see if I can get one of the lab nerds to do some work for us. Sarge wants you to hang and do some of your computer magic for him."

"I'll do my magic. You do yours at Ballistics, and get us some results."

"Will do." McGuire turned and then stopped. "You took the OT tour on Saturday? I'm surprised. I know how much you Dominicans love the cold. It'll be blood money. And, when you do finally get paid, a third of what you made will disappear in taxes. I passed on it."

"Yeah, it'll be a bitch, but money's tight. I'll wear my long johns and hope for the best. Call me when you're heading back to the squad. Remember, if I'm out, call me on my cell."

McGuire laughed. Technology-savvy Gomez was the very proud owner of a new cell phone. He was one of the few detectives in the Bronx who had one. "I've called you ten times since you got it. Think I got through once. I got a better chance of reaching you with a carrier pigeon. I'll beep you when I'm leaving Manhattan."

***

It took McGuire over an hour in rush-hour traffic to drive the seven miles from the Four-two to the Ballistics Lab located in the Police Academy on East Twentieth Street in Manhattan. It took another half hour to find a semi-legal parking spot. He popped the Department Auto ID plate on the dashboard and hoped for the best. A cop would not write him a ticket, but a meter maid might.

He entered the Academy, passing two companies of recruits in their gray uniforms on the muster deck. He walked faster, not wanting to compete with them for the building's two ancient elevators when he remembered he could slow down. Probies were not allowed on the elevators. They had to take the stairs. Small miracle, an empty car waited and took him to the fourth floor. He approached the Ballistics Unit reception desk where a bored-looking cop in uniform sat reading the *New York Post*. Without looking up, the cop asked, "Picking up or dropping off?"

"Actually, neither. I was hoping to speak with Sergeant Boyle."

Still reading his paper, the cop hit a button. "Sarge, someone to see you."

Two hours ago, I hear how busy they are, can't check ballistics from a quad homicide. Looking at Officer Eveready, I can see why they're so backed up. Fuckin' dead wood growing here. He looked at the cop's belt. *No gun. Ah, that explains it. A limited duty man. Had his guns taken away. They can't put him on the street. Probably a headcase. Rubber gun squad.*

"Can I help you?" McGuire turned to see a tall, beefy, man in a suit, looking as Irish as can be. "Sergeant Boyle?"

"Yeah, what can I do for you?"

"Sarge, Detective McGuire, Four-two squad. I have a round from a shooting last night, and you guys have one from a quad homicide from two weeks ago. It hasn't been examined yet. I was hoping we might get them looked at today. I know you're busy, but maybe a little favor from one Emerald Society man to another?"

The sergeant laughed. "I see. The name Boyle and my mug makes me an Emerald man, right?"

"I figured–"

"You figured wrong, buddy. My dad is Sean Boyle. My mom is the former Louisa Ehrenzweig from the lower east side. I was raised Jewish. Member of the Shomrim Society. Nice try, though. Leave the round. We'll get to it."

Boyle had his hand on the door, stopped, walked closer and pointed to a pin on McGuire's lapel. A miniature police badge rested on a football. "What's that?"

"I play on the department's football team."

"What position?"

"I'm a d-b. Defensive back."

"I thought you looked familiar. I was at the Fire game at Shea Stadium in '89. Didn't you take an interception back fifty yards for the game-winning touchdown?"

"Yeah, I got lucky."

"We both got lucky. I was with my hose-head, big mouth, fireman brother-in-law. We had a hundred-dollar bet on the game. He almost cried when you scored. You woulda thought he lost a grand. Fucker's tighter than a clam's ass. What a great night. Come inside."

Five minutes later, McGuire and Boyle watched as Technician Pierce placed the round from the Dominican homicides under a microscope. He removed it, then weighed and measured it.

"Definitely .44 Caliber. Probably semi-wad cutter. The flattened tip expands when it hits something. One purpose: to kill whatever it strikes."

McGuire reached into his jacket and out came the bag containing the round taken out of Javier Boren last night. He handed it to the technician, who weighed and measured it with small calipers.

"Another .44," Pierce declared. "Let's compare them." He placed both rounds into a side-by-side microscope and began to play with the adjustment screws on one, then the other. He stepped back and smiled. "Want to take a look?"

McGuire put his eyes to the scope. It took a moment, but he could make out both bullets. The lands and grooves placed inside a gun barrel to make a bullet spiral when it exits and not tumble end over end, had left their marks on both rounds. To McGuire's untrained eye they looked similar. "They kind of look the same to me."

"Not kind of, identical. Every gun barrel leaves its own individual markings." Pierce smiled. "Like fingerprints. I could testify in court both bullets were fired from the same gun."

"What about the other rounds from the Dominican shootings?"

Pierce opened an envelope, placed three lead balls on the table and examined them.

"Too deformed. No way to match them to a gun, but they're .44s. So, Detective, looks like you have five people shot, four killed with the same weapon."

"What kind of gun?"

"My guess would be a short-barreled .44 revolver. Maybe a Ruger Bulldog. Berkowitz is still in, right?" He referred to David Berkowitz, who had terrorized New Yorkers in the late seventies, killing six. The Son of Sam's weapon: a Ruger Bulldog .44.

"Yeah, Dave's still in, and he's the wrong color anyway. We're looking for a big male, black. Thanks, Pierce. Sarge, thanks a lot. This really helps me out. I owe you one."

"No, I owe you, John. Keep beating those rubber men so I don't have to take any shit off my asshole brother-in-law. Call me if you need anything else."

"Will do. I'll get you two tickets to this year's game, on me."

"Get one, John. Shit for brains can pay for his own ticket."

Twenty-Five - Brainstorming

McGuire rushed back to the squad. He wanted to share the good ballistics news with the rest of the task force. He was surprised to find only Gomez, hard at work on the computer. He wondered where the other task force members, Angelo Cutrone, Ty Crawford, and Pat Hanlon, were. The regular day-tour team of three detectives was also absent.

"Hey, Joey, where is everybody?" McGuire called out.

Gomez put a finger to his lips and waved McGuire back out into the hallway.

"Vic is really pissed off. I thought he was going to knock Hanlon out."

"Not the great first grader. What did Fat Pat do to rile Vic?"

"I forgot. You were in court yesterday. Task force's first day? Tour starts at eight? Hanlon walks in at twenty after. Sarge gets us all together, talks about how important this case is. Stresses we're a team and everybody has to pull their weight. Looks right at Hanlon and says, 'This includes everyone getting in on time.'"

"Don't tell me he's late again today."

"Strolled in at half past. Signed in at eight. Had a bag with coffee and a roll. He went into the meal room, sat his fat ass down, started feeding his face and reading the *Post.*"

"What fuckin' balls."

"It gets worse. Sarge was looking for him since eight. He saw him in the meal room and went in, closed the door, all hell broke loose."

"Boss musta tore him a new asshole."

"He started out fairly calm, warned him again he has to be on time. We could all hear it. Then I heard Hanlon say, 'I hit some traffic. What's the big deal?' That did it. Vic screamed, 'Two days in a row. You hit traffic, you're late, but you still stopped for coffee and you signed in at eight. Next time you're late, you go back to the Four-six, Mister First Grader.'"

"I told the boss Hanlon was a piece a shit. So, where is everyone?"

"He sent Hanlon and Ty to do surveillance on the bodega. Get plate numbers of any cars stopping by. Angelo's in court. The day tour team very quickly went out on an old case."

"Smart move on their part. Has he calmed down?"

Gomez shrugged, and they went back into the squad.

Sergeant Vic Ramos appeared in the doorway of his office, coffee cup in hand. "Johnny Mac, tell me you got something positive from ballistics. I need some good news."

The three huddled in Ramos' office where McGuire explained what he had learned.

Ramos nodded. "So, we have the same gun used at the Butler House and bodega shootings. Four dead, one kid wounded. The shooter's Uzi must have jammed. He had the .44 as a backup. After the Butler killings, we have the retaliation at the crack house on Tiebout Avenue. Two dead there. Has to be the Dominicans giving payback for Butler.

Last night, tit-for-tat, the blacks looking to off the Domos in the bodega. Joey, what kind of description did we get on the perps last night?"

"Nothing much. Two male blacks in black-leather trench coats. The manager said one guy was very tall. Place had three security cameras recording to tape. I pulled the tapes, and guess what?"

"They're no good."

"Worse. They forgot to reload two of the tapes from the inside cameras, or that's what they told me. The outside camera had a tape which has been used for the last two months, recording over and over. Got a grainy image of the white van. Two black guys got out. One looked pretty big."

"Mrs. Robinson, our witness at the Butler Houses, also said the guy who got out of the van and 'dumped the trash' was a big guy." McGuire added. "Right now I think the Butler shootings are the key to this case."

"Why, John?" Ramos asked.

"Couple of reasons. Butler was the first incident. First we know of, anyway. The Tiebout crack house and last night's bodega attacks are, as you said, payback and payback. And both of them are simple, all-out assaults. Heavy automatic weapons, lots of rounds fired. All the action happening at the place of occurrence."

"Good point," Gomez said. "Based on Mrs. Robinson's story, we know the four Dominicans were killed in the van in Butler's parking lot and dumped by a tall male black. We now know they were shot with the same gun, a .44."

"You think it was a drug rip off? The black guy killed the Domos and stole their drugs?" Ramos scratched his head.

"I don't think so." McGuire shook his head. "You'd have to believe one, maybe two black guys are going to rip four Domos who, if they were doing a sale, would be armed."

He locked his hands behind his head and leaned back in his chair staring at the ceiling.

Ramos and Gomez remained quiet, lost in thought.

Suddenly McGuire leaped to his feet. "Got it, goddammit."

"Got what, John?" Ramos asked.

"The four Domos. Three face down, shot in the back of their heads. The one good slug we got, the big guy, face up, bullet went through his right hand into his forehead. How do one, maybe two, black guys get the drop on four tough-as-nails Domo drug dealers?"

Gomez and Ramos start to nod their heads.

"Their hands were tied or cuffed behind them," McGuire said.

"Then how did the big guy get his hand in front of the gun?"

"Sarge, the dude was six-two, three hundred pounds. I lifted his hand to examine the stippling around the wound. It was as big as a catcher's mitt. They couldn't get his hands behind his back. They cuffed or tied him in front."

"Does the Medical Examiner's report mention any signs of ligatures on the wrists?"

"No, but they weren't looking for them. Cause of death was pretty obvious. Nobody got too worked up over another drug homicide."

"John, this could be important down the road. Call the ME, and ask him to reexamine the four bodies with emphasis on the wrists and hands."

McGuire walked out of the room. Two minutes later, he was back with his coat on and the keys to the car in his hand. "Boss, the three normal-sized guy's bodies were claimed by the families and shipped back to the DR. Nobody claimed the big boy."

"Okay, so where you going? The ME keeps unclaimed bodies for thirty days." Ramos looked at McGuire. "You and Joe can go down to the morgue tomorrow and watch the ME examine the big man's hands."

McGuire nodded. "Unclaimed bodies are kept for thirty days. It's the law—under normal circumstances. Unfortunately, because we have so many bodies dropping, the morgues are over capacity. The mayor signed an emergency order last week. Unclaimed bodies are now held only for two weeks. Big boy left the morgue this morning for his last boat ride. He was on the ten a.m. Corrections Department ferry from City Island to Hart Island. Last stop, Potter's Field."

Ramos grabbed a phone. "You guys get over to City Island. I'll get Corrections to have the ferry waiting."

"I called the Morgue Unit. They're sending one of the Missing Persons guys from Jacobi morgue to meet us at the ferry."

"Bon voyage." Ramos punched in a number as the other two ran out the door.

Twenty-Six - Change of Plans

Steven "Pooh Bear" Jennings got off the Greyhound bus in Atlanta, Georgia. His boyhood friend, George Jackson, waited in the terminal to drive him the eighty miles south to their Macon hometown. Pooh spotted him, and the two friends exchanged hugs.

"Pooh, my man. I was surprised to get your call. After seeing you last year, I thought you'd come back home driving a Rolls, not riding the dog down from the Apple."

"I could have rented a car but didn't want no paper trail. When you want to go somewhere and don't want no one to know, you pay cash, jump the dog. Travel in-cog-nito."

"There a need?"

"I'll tell you in the car." They walked out of the terminal to Jackson's new blue Impala. Pooh threw his duffle bag into the trunk and got in.

"New wheels. Doing pretty good for yourself, brother."

"Not bad. You know I was share cropping a piece of land on the old Stanford Farm."

"Hell yeah, place my mom used to work."

"Well, old Mr. Stanford died last November. Mrs. Stanford asked me to run the place. Gives me a thousand a month to be her handyman, keep an eye out, make sure none of the other croppers don't put up any shacks or start growing anything the po-lice might be interested in. I get the thou plus the money I make selling my crops. Doing okay." Jackson put the Chevy in drive and began working his way out of downtown Atlanta.

He pointed to a Styrofoam cooler on the rear seat. "Thought you might be hungry. Some Cokes and a barbecue pork po-boy in the sack."

"Thanks, man, I'm starving."

Pooh reached into the back and took out two cans of Coke, popped them and handed one to Jackson. "And a barbecue pork hero is in this bag." He put a napkin under his chin and took a huge bite. "Mmm. Outfuckinstanding. Can't get barbecue like this in New York. Now, I'm home. Thanks, bro." He took another bite and washed it down with a gulp of Coke. He wiped his lips with the napkin and turned to look at Jackson. "My mom always said the Stanford's were good folks, treated people fair. What's the lady plan to do with the farm now?"

"She wants out. Both her kids are down in Florida, somewhere near Tampa. They want her to move down. She's pushing eighty."

"So she has the farm up for sale?"

"Not yet. Still some legal stuff with her husband's will. But, she plans to soon as all that shit's cleared up."

"Any idea what she's going to ask?"

"I heard she could get close to a million if she subdivides. Probably sell it to some developers who want to put up a bunch of houses. Hundred acres, nice piece of property, but she don't want to do it."

"Why not?"

"She's sentimental. Says it's been a family farm for almost two-hundred years, should stay a farm. Lot of her kin are buried there."

"You think she might take less if the buyer says he'll keep it a farm?"

"She might. She loves the old place. And, I heard the state has some kind of deal where they give something to farmers so they don't turn every farm into a Monopoly-board subdivision."

They grew quiet as Jackson steered onto Interstate 75, heading south. Traffic was light. Jackson glanced at Pooh. "You ready to tell me why you had to take the bus down?"

Pooh filled in his friend on the ongoing Bronx drug war. "Remember the dude, Dee, I told you about?"

"Yeah. Real bad ass. You said he was a stone-cold killer."

"That's him, but now I find he don't give a shit who he kills. Shot my friend, Rontal Cheery, point blank in the chest 'cause he didn't like the way poor Rontal spoke to him. We got us a war going with some Dominicans moving in on our territory. The other night, we go to their bodega, going to punch their tickets. Dee sees this young kid behind me trying to run away. He pulls the trigger on the Uzi. If he hadn't already put all of the rounds from the clip into the ceiling, he would have cut me in half."

"The kid got away?"

"Nah, Dee got him with his pistol. Young boy, not one of the dudes we were looking for. Kid was in the wrong place, wrong time. I heard he lived, but the cops are pissed. They don't get too worked up over niggers shooting Domo drug dealers and vice versa, but fucking Dee capping the kid has turned up the heat. It's why I had to get out of town. I'll chill down home here for a week or so and then get back up to the Bronx."

"The heat will be off so quick?"

"Shit, bet there'll be three kids shot up there before the week is done. Cops will forget our bodega kid soon as the next one gets popped. Nature of the beast."

"Pooh, you ever think maybe you pushing your luck? From what you just told me, it seems like going back to the Bronx gives you three possible outcomes."

"What?"

"One: You get caught by the cops. Spend the rest of your life in jail. Two: You get killed by the Dominicans. Three: You get smoked by your good friend, Dee. Not a good choice in the bunch. Why don't you stay down here? You said you got some money socked away."

"I do. Over a hundred thou."

Jackson let out a whistle. "Pooh, you gotta be kidding. You have it and still want to go back North and risk getting your ass shot up? A hundred thou could buy you anything you want down here."

"I want the Stanford Farm. I always dreamed of coming back, taking care of Mom and my brother. If I go back and hook up with the white boys for one more score, a really big one, I might be able to swing enough to offer Mrs. Stanford four-hundred large."

"You can make so much from one job?"

"I could, but I have to give a third to my white boys and split the rest with Dee."

"I just did some quick math in my head." Jackson frowned. "Hell, Pooh, you'd need like nine-hundred thou, for you to walk away with three-hundred K with the split."

"Or, we could do one big job, I collect the ransom, and the only splitting I do is me splitting the Bronx and coming home. You up for running the Jennings Farm?"

"You gonna mess with crazy killer, Dee? Are you looking to die?"

Pooh took another bite of his sandwich, chewed slowly, and swallowed. He looked at his friend and smiled. "Damn, this is some good po-boy."

Twenty-Seven - Heart to Hart

McGuire and Gomez drove through Pelham Bay Park, passed the NYPD Firing Range at Rodman's Neck, and crossed the small bridge onto City Island.

Gomez stared out the window. "I've never been here without being at the range first."

"Yeah, I don't know how many times I left here after I stopped for 'just one' after qualifying at the range." McGuire turned onto City Island Avenue.

"Hard to believe we're in the Bronx. Looks more like New England." Gomez shook his head.

"Cool place, very nautical. Was 'the place' back in the day when sailing was a big sport. A lot of the America's Cup winners were built in the shipyards here." He turned on Fordham Street, passing a number of large buildings. "These are all condos now, Joe. Used to be lofts where the sails were made."

At the street's end was a gated chain-link fence topped with razor wire. A large sign read: NO TRESPASSING - BY ORDER OF THE NYC DEPARTMENT OF CORRECTION. A young man, dressed in boots, jeans, and a black ski jacket, stood just inside the gate. He held a clipboard and leaned against an unmarked car. McGuire rolled down his window.

"Where do we—?" McGuire addressed the figure.

The young man raised his head. "Hey, John. Park over on the side. We have to go over in my car."

"No problem, Phil." McGuire backed into a space.

"Who is this guy?" Gomez asked.

"Phil Higgins. I know him from the Emerald Society. Good guy. He's one of the ghouls from Missing Persons, assigned to the Morgue Unit."

"That has to be a depressing job."

"They like it. They're all morticians, have second jobs with the funeral homes. Phil's family has owned Higgins' Funeral Parlor on Coney Island Avenue in Brooklyn for like a hundred years."

Higgins slid the gate open, and McGuire and his partner walked through. Introductions were made. McGuire noticed for the first time that they were not standing on a pier. Higgins's car was on the ferry. A quarter of a mile across the Long Island Sound lay their destination, Hart Island.

Higgins waved to a man sitting in the forward wheelhouse. The ferry's engine roared to life.

McGuire immediately opened the door to Higgins's car and slid into the passenger seat.

"John," Higgins said. "It's not too cold out today. Ride outside with us. I'm going to give you guys my ten-dollar tour."

McGuire cracked his window two inches. "Give it to Joe. I've heard it before."

"Your choice."

***

Higgins and Gomez walked to the bow of the boat. "Is Johnny boy hung over?" Higgins asked.

"Nah, not at all. He's tired. We had a busy night." Gomez quickly described the bodega shooting and McGuire's rushing the wounded boy to the hospital.

"John's aces. One of the best detectives I ever met. I just wish he'd cut back on the beer a bit. And this is coming from a fellow Emerald man."

"He's trying." Gomez shrugged. "So tell me about the island. I've never been here before."

"Very few people have, even guys on the job. Ready? Stop me if I get boring." Higgins waited, but Gomez remained quiet. "Hart Island is one hundred-thirty-one acres. There are over 800,000 bodies buried here, making it the largest publicly-funded cemetery in the world."

"Eight hundred thousand? How long have we been burying people here?"

"First recorded burials were of Confederate POWs held here during the Civil War. The city bought it in 1869. It's been a lunatic asylum, TB hospital, and a prison. Was also used for German POWs during WWII, and it had Nike missiles on it during the Cold War."

"Interesting." Gomez grabbed a handrail as the ferry hit some waves mid-channel.

"How did you get to know so much about it? Thought you worked at the morgue in Jacobi."

"I'm assigned there but spend a lot of time over here. When we get a John or Jane Doe body, we try to ID it and notify the next of kin before they get buried. If we can't, they get laid to rest here. Even if we ID them, sometimes there is no next of kin or anybody who cares, so they end up here. Sometimes we'll get an inquiry from a family member years later, which gives us enough info to figure out who our Doe was. Then it's my job to find out where we put them."

"Is it hard?"

"Used to be a mess. There are no name markers. We have a pretty good system now."

The boat bumped into some pilings and eased into the Hart Island berth. They walked back to the car. Higgins slid behind the wheel. Gomez got in the back.

"Feeling okay, tiger? You look a little green around the gills." Higgins looked at McGuire and chuckled.

"I feel good enough to kick your donkey ass. Thanks for asking."

A ramp in the front of the boat was lowered, a gate pulled back, and Higgins drove slowly off onto the island.

"Who actually does the burials?" Gomez asked.

"Total Department of Corrections show. They had the prison here until Rikers Island opened in the '60s. They moved all the inmates over there but kept control of the burials here. They bring over about twenty inmates every day. They do the work."

"You have to work with inmates?" Gomez questioned.

"Not any hard-core guys. Misdemeanors, petty shit. Have to be serving less than a six-month sentence. Volunteers, they love it. They're paid fifty cents an hour and get off The Rock for a day. Look around. Is this beautiful or what?"

Both detectives nodded. A flock of Canada geese came in for a landing on a small pond just off the road. The water—sparkling blue—stretched east over the Long Island Sound to Queens and Nassau County."

"It is beautiful. I can see why the inmates would rather be here than in Rikers," McGuire said.

"And why I prefer the island to the basement morgue in Jacobi. Here we are."

They had pulled off the road next to a large open trench. Three pine coffins were perched at the other end. Four inmates, two black, two white, stood nearby.

"We do about fifteen hundred burials a year, close to half are babies. The backhoe digs the trench. Morgue truck pulls up. For the adults, they put a ramp from the truck down into the trench. The coffins are plain pine. The guys slide the coffins down the ramp into the trench. Adults are stacked three high and two across. Babies take less room, so they go five high, twenty across. Sit here a minute while I talk to the guys."

Higgins got out of the car and walked over to the workers. "Good morning, captain," the oldest-looking black inmate called out cheerfully.

"Captain? Don't they know he's a detective?" Gomez asked.

"They call anybody in a position of authority 'captain.' It's a New York thing. In prisons down south, the prisoners say 'boss,'" McGuire answered.

"How do you know what prisoners in the south say? You ever been to a southern prison?"

"No, but I saw *Cool Hand Luke* when I was a kid. My man, Paul Newman. 'Taking it off, Boss.' Should have won an Oscar. Rod Steiger got it in '68 for *In the Heat of the Night*. Shoulda been Paul's."

"You know, I have no idea what you're talking about, John."

"'What we have here, is failure to communicate.'"

"Again, I'm lost. As happens frequently when you go into your trivia routine."

As they watched, Higgins seemed to have a good rapport with the prisoners. They were laughing and pointing at one of the coffins. Higgins took something from his pocket and handed it to their leader. He walked back to the car, opened the door, and leaned in.

"What are your guys so happy about?" McGuire asked.

"Well, as I told you, adults go in three deep. Of course, your Dominican gentleman, Mr. Bravo, weighing over three hundred went in first. Two on top of him. When you called me at the morgue, I rushed over here right before they were going to cover up the grave. Asked the guys to bring Bravo out. Of course, they had to take out the two on top of him first to get to your man. Then it was simple physics. Lot easier to slide a body down a ramp than push it up. They were joking you had to pick the heaviest guy on Hart Island to bring up. Ready? Let's take a look."

The prisoners had taken the lid off the coffin and stood back respectfully. McGuire looked in. "Looks like the ME did a nice job. He looks pretty good for a body nobody wants."

"Yeah, they do what they can. A week from now, a family member might come forward and claim the body. It has to be somewhat presentable, even if it's likely this will be his final resting place." Higgins put on a pair of heavy rubber gloves. "You wanted to see the hands, John?"

"And wrists, please, Phil."

Higgins squatted next to the box and slowly worked one of Bravo's arm up a bit. McGuire and Gomez both squatted beside him. Higgins pointed to an indentation around the wrist. "This what you're looking for guys?"

"Yep. How 'bout the other one?" McGuire asked.

Higgins shifted and grabbed the other hand. "Same thing, maybe a little worse on this one."

"Like we thought, he was cuffed. In front. You have a camera in your car, Phil?"

"Of course."

"Can we get a few shots? Tight on the wrists. I'll call Crime Scene to come over and take the official photos. Can we keep him up for a while?"

"No problem. The crew is happy."

"I thought they were bitching," McGuire said.

"They were until I gave them each a five spot. You owe me twenty bucks."

Twenty-Eight - The Ties That Bind

McGuire and Gomez returned to the squad. Sergeant Ramos waited for them on the station house steps. "I'm starving, guys. Let's talk over lunch."

They walked down the street to Pedro's Diner and took a booth in the back. Ramos, as the boss, got the seat all cops wanted, back to the wall, facing the entrance. McGuire and Gomez slid into the booth opposite him.

"How'd we make out?" Ramos leaned forward.

"Great," McGuire answered. "Our Domo victim had abrasions on both wrists. No doubt the four of them were handcuffed before they got popped in the van."

"Let's see if I got this." Ramos sat back. "The four Dominicans whacked in a van in the Butler House parking lot were handcuffed and all shot with the same gun, a .44?"

"Check." McGuire nodded. "Same gun shot the kid in the bodega last night."

Pedro's daughter, Mercedes, the waitress, glided up. The cops all smiled and greeted her warmly. They had watched her grow up. She and Pedro were part of the Four-two family. She put down place settings, silverware, and three cups. She filled the cups with coffee. “Hi, guys. Your usuals, or do you need to see a menu?”

All three answered, “The usual.”

“Two *chile relenos*, one bacon cheeseburger well done coming up. You gonna stick with coffee or you want something else to drink?”

McGuire’s eyes shifted to the Corona beer sign behind the counter. Just one cold one, with a wedge of lime, would fix his pounding head, but he couldn’t, not with Ramos sitting there.

“Coffee’s fine,” he said as Gomez and Ramos agreed.

“Mercedes,” McGuire asked, “make the bacon extra crispy, please.”

“John, I’ve waited on you for four years. I think I remember how you like your burger.”

McGuire smiled at the pretty eighteen-year-old. “Just making sure. You see, my Dominican partner tells me Puerto Ricans often suffer from frequent memory lapses.”

Mercedes looked at Ramos. “You hear, *Jefe?* Us Puerto Ricans have memory problems.”

“There might be some truth there, Mercedes,” Ramos blew on his coffee. “I think I might have forgotten to put these guys’ names in for promotion.”

They all laughed, and Mercedes headed off to the kitchen.

McGuire drained his cup and, with trembling hand, reached for the coffee pot Mercedes had left on the table.

Gomez quickly grabbed the pot and filled McGuire’s cup.

“Thanks.” McGuire was starting to drag. The last twenty-four hours had felt like a week.

“So what else do the two cases have in common?” Ramos asked.

McGuire took a large sip and set his cup down. "Two descriptions of a very large black man. From Mrs. Robinson at Butler Houses, and the bogey owner last night."

"And the surveillance video from last night, bad as it is, shows a very large black male," Gomez added. "Boss, back to the cuffs. Who's going to get four tough Domo drug dealers handcuffed?"

"Well, you have evidence of a big black guy, and probably a black driver."

"As the shooter and driver." Gomez nodded. "John and I think they did the hit, but somebody else had to get the cuffs on our vics. Someone they wouldn't fight—like, maybe cops."

Ramos almost choked on a mouthful of coffee. "The black guys could have had shields, done a police impersonation." His voice sounded like a high-pitched gurgle. He cleared his throat.

McGuire handed Ramos a napkin. "It's not what we're thinking." He gestured to his partner. "Joe?"

"Sarge, you know Dominicans are very color-conscious. Our four victims were light skinned. I don't see them letting two black guys cuff them."

"What if the blacks had badges?"

"I still don't see them going down easy. These were four very savvy, street-smart tough guys. They had to be made to feel comfortable enough to let their guard down."

Ramos nodded slowly and shook his head.

Mercedes arrived with their orders. She placed three plates on the table. The aroma of steaming *chile relenos* filled the booth. She also brought a fresh pot of coffee.

"Do you need anything else, gentlemen?"

Ramos sighed and rubbed his temples with both hands. "*Mi hija,* I feel a headache coming on. Could you find me a couple of aspirins, please?"

"A sus ordenes, Jefe." Mercedes walked away.

Gomez and McGuire dug right into their food. McGuire watched as Ramos tucked his napkin under his chin, protecting his Hermes tie and custom-tailored shirt. Ramos started to cut his chile, stopped, and looked across at his detectives.

"Please don't tell me you think it was real cops."

"Can't rule it out." McGuire lay his burger down on the plate. "But, Joe and I think something else. Remember the kidnap/shooting we caught last November? Roberto Medina? The one you wanted us to drop when the task force started, but we talked you into letting us work it?"

"On our own time." Gomez patted his lips with his napkin.

"Yeah, I remember, but what's the connection? The guy was a numbers man not a drug dealer, right? And, he was snatched in Manhattan, not the Bronx."

"But, he was shot in the Bronx after being held for ransom." McGuire took a sip and picked up his burger. "They were going to kill him, but he escaped. Two black guys were going to whack him, but it was two big white guys who initially grabbed Medina. They came into his bodega, badges, radios, said they had a warrant. He thought they were cops at first, but when he got suspicious and started asking questions, they picked him up and threw him in a car."

Gomez nodded. "And he says while he was being held, a black guy with a deep voice and huge feet threatened him. Said he would kill Roberto if they didn't get the ransom."

"Deep voice, big feet. What the hell kind of description is that?"

"They had a blindfold on him. But, he could look down. Says the guy had to be wearing size fourteen boots and had a deep, deep voice. Roberto said he'll never forget the voice."

The conversation had McGuire's adrenalin pumping, and the coffee had given him a second wind. "The big guy wasn't one of the two who were going to do him. Roberto could hear those two talking while he was in the trunk, definitely not bigfoot. But, dollars to donuts, bigfoot was the shooter of the four Domos in the van at Butler Houses and the kid in the bogey last night."

Mercedes stopped at the table and handed a bottle of Excedrin to Ramos. He opened it, popped two into his mouth, washed them down with coffee.

"So? Any leads on the white guys?"

"Negative, Boss," McGuire answered. "We showed photo spreads of white police impersonators to Roberto. No hits."

"And, bigfoot? All we have is male black, deep voice, big feet?"

Gomez looked down at the table. "Yes, Sir."

Ramos began massaging his temples again. "The two black guys who were going to kill Roberto Medina? Please tell me we have something more than average-sized feet, normal voices."

Gomez perked up. "Yeah, he got a good look at one of the guys who put him in the trunk."

"Let me guess. High-pitched voice, tiny feet?"

Gomez furrowed his brow, clearly unsure of what Ramos had meant. McGuire extended his hand, palm up across the table for a high five from Ramos. "Good one, Boss."

Gomez finally got the joke, smiled, and continued. "No, regular feet, wearing high-top black Converse, 8-Ball jacket, and here's the kicker, lots of gold jewelry, including a chain with a Winnie-the-Pooh figure on it."

"Did you come up with anything on that?"

"Ran it every which way through the nickname file. Nada. Plenty of Bears—Grizzly, Cubby, Polar, Yogi, Smokey, Huggy—but nothing with Winnie. We even reached out to Corrections. The COs at Rikers and the Tombs keep their own nickname files, but again came up zilch."

Ramos said he felt better. "Listen, you guys are two of the best detectives I ever met. My two all-stars. Once you sink your teeth into a case, you're relentless. Like a loose thread on a sweater, you keep on pulling until something pops. Then you guys will pull that thread until the entire case unravels."

Ramos dug into his meal with gusto, finishing everything on his plate, while McGuire and Gomez still worked on theirs. When done, he removed his napkin, stood, and put his coat on. "I have to get back. Take your time. I have faith in both of you. You guys will figure this all out. And if you don't, *no problema*. I still look pretty good in uniform."

"We'll crack it." McGuire put down his napkin. "We need to keep the department's best-dressed sergeant in the Detective Bureau where he belongs."

"Thanks, guys. I'll take care of the bill. You leave the tip. See you back at the house."

McGuire slid into the seat Ramos had just vacated. His eyes once more fell upon the Corona sign. He took three Excedrins out of the bottle and washed them down with a swig of coffee. He finished his burger, reached into his pocket, opened his money clip, and threw a ten-dollar bill on the table. "For Mercedes. Give me five, Partner."

Gomez cleared his throat. "John, I'm a little short. Can you lay it out for me until payday?"

McGuire looked his friend in the eye. With a wife and three small kids, Gomez lived paycheck-to-paycheck. But, he rarely ate out, did not hit the bars after work, and usually had a couple of bucks in his pocket. McGuire sensed something was wrong.

"Want to tell me what's going on?"

"Nothing, I'm just tapped out right now."

"You don't have five bucks to spare three days before payday? You took an overtime tour where you're going to freeze your nuts off in uniform Saturday night? Talk to me, Joey."

Gomez toyed with the salt shaker. "Raysa's mom. The Alzheimer's. She's bad. We took her in. Raysa had to quit her job. Has to stay home and watch her. Money's really tight."

McGuire opened his money clip and took out a twenty.

"No John. I won't take it."

"It's a loan, Partner. Pay me back Thursday. It's twenty I won't have to worry about leaving on some bar."

Gomez took the twenty. They walked back to the squad in silence.

***

When they entered the squad, Ty handed McGuire a yellow sticky note. "John, you got a call from a sergeant in Ballistics."

McGuire walked into the meal room, grabbed a phone, and dialed. Sergeant Boyle answered.

"Sarge, John McGuire."

"My favorite defensive back. I got something for you. I had Pierce run your .44 slug through our computer database. He's a whiz. Turns out, he got another hit. The ME pulled a .44 slug out of a guy, shot once in the chest, body found in Ferry Point Park in the Four-five last November. It matches yours. He was a John Doe, no ID, couple of crack vials on him. Morgue guys printed him. Comes back as Rontal Cheery, male, black, twenty-seven. Bronx guy, last address on Longfellow Avenue. Took a couple of collars for drugs. Swanson in the Four-five has the case."

McGuire's adrenalin was really pumping now. The thread on the sweater had popped. He thanked Boyle and filled in his partner on the latest news. Gomez immediately logged onto the computer and began to search.

McGuire called the Four-five squad.

His luck held. Swanson answered. He quickly filled in McGuire on the Rontal Cheery homicide. "Late November. Ferry Point Park. You familiar with it, John?"

"I see it when I drive over the Whitestone Bridge. Pretty desolate."

"Over 400 acres, lots of salt marshes. Goes right down to the water, Long Island Sound. They keep talking about building a golf course there, but now it's strictly a nature center. Couple of dirt roads, but mostly small paths you have to hoof."

"It get many visitors?"

"Not many, but it's big with the bird watchers. Old couple, the Dolans from Throggs Neck, hot on the trail of a Scarlet Tanager—pretty bird, red with black wings. They push through some reeds. Do they find their *piranga olivacea*?"

"Thought they were looking for a Scarlet something?"

"Tanager. They were, my friend. *Piranga olivacea* is the bird's scientific name. All animals have them, so scientists who speak different languages will know when they're talking about the same species."

"Swanson, I'm almost afraid to ask. But, how the fuck do you know all this shit?"

"I stopped drinking four years ago. My wife gave me a choice. Had to choose between her and the kids or my good friend Jack, as in Jack Daniels. She won. Been sober since Christmas of '86."

"And?"

"And, I now have lots of free time. It's amazing how much time you gain when you ain't spending all night drinking and all day nursing a hangover. I got into golf and bird watching."

"That explains it." McGuire looked at the notes he was taking. "So, your bird watching couple, the Dolans, didn't find their *piranga olivacea*?"

"No, but they found *drugdealius nomorus*. The body later identified as Rontal Cheery. Six collars, mostly drug sales, low-level shit. Had two crack vials on him. Took one in the chest at close range. Powder burns on his jacket. Bullet comes back a .44. ME said he'd been dead about a week. The rats and racoons had a picnic with his face."

"The Dolans must have been shaken up."

"You could say. I got a nice buy on a great pair of binoculars. The Dolans have taken up bridge."

McGuire laughed. "You think Cheery was popped in the park?"

"Nah, definite dump job. We get about five a year there. Perfect spot. If the former birdwatchers hadn't stumbled across him, he'd still be there."

"No Missing Person report?"

"No. Had a hard time finding any relatives. One sister down in South Carolina. I'm trying to help her now. The body was unclaimed, buried in Potter's Field. She wants to bring him home. Bury him with his parents in Beaufort."

"Anything else?"

"Nah. My boss wasn't authorizing any overtime on this. Just another druggie killed, probably not even in the Four-five. But, you know, wherever the body is found. I did what I could, but dump jobs are hard. I have forty open cases right now. Had to move on."

"I understand, pal."

"What's your interest in this, John?"

McGuire explained. “So, we now have five homicides and one kid wounded with the same gun. A .44.”

“Shit, Brother, sounds like you have your hands full. Let me know if you need anything from our end. Happy to help.”

“Thanks, Swanson. I’ll let you know when we solve this. Get you a clearance on your homicide. You can buy me a drink when we do.”

“Can’t do it, John. I don’t go nowhere near Mr. Daniels anymore. How about I take you out for a day of birdwatching instead?”

“You got a deal, buddy. Can’t wait to see my first *piranga olivacea.*”

Twenty-Nine - The Thread Comes Loose

McGuire hung up and walked into the squad. Gomez was at the computer, a phone in one hand and yanking papers from the printer with the other. He looked at McGuire with a huge smile on his face.

"Thanks, Officer Miller, you've been a huge help. I'm going to get my boss to do a forty-nine to your CO, letting him know what a great job you did." Gomez hung up, picked through a pile of papers, and with a flourish, handed one to his partner.

McGuire scanned it and shrugged. "Okay, it's an arrest report for Rontal Cheery. Collared in the Four-five. June of '89 for Criminal Possession Controlled Substance—cocaine. I told you he had six previous." He made tight eye contact with his partner. "Why the shit-eating grin?"

"Keep reading."

McGuire examined the report. Captions the arresting officer, J.P. Miller of the Four-five Precinct, had filled in by hand with a pen. Time, date, place of occurrence. The penal law charge. In the details box, the officer wrote he observed Cheery blow a stop sign, and when asked to present his license and registration, Cheery attempted to kick something under the driver's seat. Miller observed, in plain view next to the driver's foot, six glassine envelopes containing a white powder, believed to be cocaine.

McGuire looked up. "Looks like a routine collar. What am I missing?"

Gomez took the report, placed it on his desk, clicked his pen, and circled one section near the bottom. The box read: Phone Calls Made. A defendant had a right to make three phone calls after being arrested. The arresting officer was supposed to dial and note the number, time, and name of the person called in this box. Few cops bothered. Miller had.

McGuire squinted. The printer was always low on ink. He made out a phone number and looked closely at the name which accompanied it. He looked again. "Holy fuckin' shit."

Rontal Cheery had called one Steven "Pooh Bear" Jennings on the night almost two years earlier.

McGuire thrust one fist in the air. "Outfuckingstanding. But, why didn't this pop when you checked the nickname file?"

"That file is when a cop gets a nickname from someone he arrests. This was just a phone call from a person arrested. J.P. Miller is one sharp cop."

"Fuckin' A right he is. What else you got?"

"I spoke with security at the telephone company, retired cop named Mike Caburis. The number came back to 248 Fordham Road, Apartment 3A. Account in the name of Steven Jennings. Active from April to October, 1989, when it was terminated for non-payment."

"How was it paid when it was? Check, credit card?"

"No luck such. Cash, every month, at the telephone company office on the Concourse."

McGuire smiled. His partner spoke excellent English but still had a problem handling the slang, the idioms, the nuances of the language. "That don't help."

"No, but this does." Gomez took another sheet from the stack and handed it to McGuire. "I ran 248 Fordham. Last five years. Anyone collared there. Anyone arrested who gave the address. Twelve hits, but I think you'll like this one."

McGuire perused the arrest sheet. Steven Jennings of 248 Fordham Road had been arrested in Manhattan in May of 1989 for "Theft of Services." He had hopped over the turnstile at the Times Square subway station and been grabbed by the Transit Police.

McGuire punched Gomez's shoulder. "*Excellente mi hermano*. My computer genius." They now had a name, DOB, description, and NYSIS number for Steven "Pooh Bear" Jennings.

"He has three more collars, John, small-time drug stuff. Two different Bronx addresses." Gomez handed his partner the reports. McGuire's head was pounding. He squinted at the papers, barely able to make out the words. The lack of sleep and lack of drink was overtaking the rush the good news had produced. His mouth felt like it was full of sawdust. He thought of the Corona sign in Pedro's. *Fuck it. Just one. Hair of the dog.* One and he would feel a whole lot better. He stood, grabbed his coat, and headed toward the door.

Gomez watched but said nothing.

McGuire stopped in the hallway. He wanted the drink, wanted it badly. He looked back into the squad. Gomez was back at work on the computer. His partner, who less than twenty-four hours earlier, he'd promised he would not let drink affect his work or their relationship.

He started down the stairs. *Just one, it's not really drinking. I'm just thirsty.* He stopped halfway down. *If you're really thirsty, drink a glass of water, jerk-off.*

He pictured the devil in red with a pitchfork sitting on one shoulder and a beautiful angel in white on the other. He exhaled loudly. *I know who's winning this fight.* He turned and walked back up the stairs. *Twelve years of Catholic schools. Fuck you, Devil. I have enough guilt, thank you.*

He entered the squad, shook off his coat, and headed to the meal room. Gomez followed him in.

In the harsh light of the bare bulb hanging from the ceiling, McGuire thought he must look twenty years older than he was.

"You okay, John?" Gomez studied his partner's face.

McGuire grabbed his coffee mug off a shelf and picked up the pot.

"John, the slime's been sitting there since this morning. I'll make us a fresh pot."

"This is fine." He filled his cup, opened the sugar bowl, and scooped three heaping teaspoons in.

"You like coffee with your sug—?" Gomez trailed off when he saw McGuire's haggard face turn toward him.

"I'm trying, Joe. I'm really trying."

He drained his cup and made a second, identical to the first, rubbed his eyes, stretched, and yawned. He walked back into the squad, picked up Jennings's arrest sheet, and sat down. His head spun. The sugar rush fought the alcohol withdrawal. The adrenalin battled the lack of sleep. He looked out the window toward Pedro's, shook his head, and read the arrest report. Nothing jumped out at him. He reached into his shirt pocket and took out a business card. Assistant District Attorney Gina Torelli. She had written her home phone number on the back of the card. He thought of her and felt himself grow hard. *I have the hangover hornies.*

He was always amazed when he drank too much and felt like shit, the first part of his body to come back to life was generally his dick.

He picked up the phone, hesitated, put it back, and stared out the window. He suddenly snapped forward and grabbed the last arrest report from the bottom of the pile. His hands shook so badly he had to put the sheet down on the desk. He went over it caption by caption. Jennings and two others had been arrested in September when Bronx Narcotics took down a crack house on Morris Avenue. The two others arrested: Rontal Cheery and one Dwayne Dillon. He looked closely at Dillon's physical description.

Male, black, thirty-two, six-five, 240 pounds.

He jumped from his chair, held the sheet over his head, and looked at his partner. "Got him."

Gomez looked to where McGuire pointed. He ran back to the computer, pounded the keys, and brought up the Roberto Medina kidnapping. Scrolling through it, he stopped when he found what he had been seeking. "Thought so. Remember Medina spoke about the guy with the deep voice, big feet? This Dwayne Dillon, AKA Dee, has to be our big man. He not only fits for Roberto Medina's kidnapping, but also the hits on the four Dominicans, Rontal Cheery, and shooting the kid in the bodega."

The other detectives in the team began to shout questions.

Sergeant Ramos, apparently hearing the commotion, stepped out from his office. He was quickly filled in.

Gomez went back to the computer. "Last address we have for Dillon is 2119 Tiebout Avenue, right down the block from the shot-up crack house."

"Think he's still there?" Ramos asked.

McGuire grabbed his coat. "Only one way to find out. Let's hit it, Boss."

"Wait a minute, John. We have to do this right. Call Emergency Service Unit. Draw up a tactical plan."

"Sarge, we could lose hours. ESU won't hit a place without a warrant. This prick has already killed five people and wounded the kid. We have six guys here. The place is five minutes away. Let's do it." McGuire bounced from foot to foot, hangover forgotten. Pure adrenalin now surged through his veins.

Ramos took a deep breath. "The book calls for ESU with their automatic weapons, Tasers, flash/bang grenades, and apprehension expertise. But, Mac, you're right. They'll want to see a warrant before they take down a door. And it could take hours." Ramos was a good street boss and trusted his men—most of them anyway. "Fuck the book." He clapped his hands. "Okay, we go. I want two guns and vests on everyone."

Fat Pat Hanlon raised his hand. McGuire knew the know-it-all was about to tell Ramos what he was doing was wrong.

Sharp as ever though, Ramos must have known what was coming. "I need one volunteer to stay here and cover the phones." Hanlon's hand was still up. "Thanks, Pat, you got it. Everyone else, let's saddle up."

The men went to their lockers to get vests and second guns.

Gomez continued to work on the computer. When the team reassembled, he read from the screen. "Five-story walk up. Dillon's apartment is on the top floor, on the right of the stairs, Five-F. Shotgun apartment. Front door, hallway, kitchen, bathroom, bedroom. Fire escape off the bedroom." He handed Ramos a crude drawing he'd made of the layout.

The boss studied it. "McGuire, Gomez, and me at the door. Crawford on the roof. Cutrone, backyard. I do the entry."

"Sarge, it's my case," McGuire said.

Ramos shook his head. "Okay, entry will be McGuire and Gomez, but let me warn you. If either of you guys is killed, I will never speak to you again." The team gave the nervous laughs of brave men trying to hide their fear. "Guns, vests?"

Each team member opened his coat to show Ramos they were properly equipped. He poked each one in the chest, with the exception of Hanlon and Gomez, who was still on the computer. "Let's do it."

***

Starting down the stairs, Gomez stopped and turned to McGuire. "Have to get my vest. Meet you at the car."

Gomez walked back into the squad and saw Hanlon on a phone. The man stared out the window, watching as the team walked to their cars. Apparently, Hanlon hadn't noticed his return. Gomez got his vest and was walking out when he overheard Hanlon. "Sergeant Super Spic is gonna get someone killed."

Gomez bit his tongue and hurried down the stairs to his waiting partner.

***

Two unmarked cars pulled up silently several doors down from 2119 Tiebout. Quickly and quietly, the men entered the building. Angelo Cutrone went to the basement to find the door which led to the yard. The other four, guns now in hand, crept up the stairs, keeping plenty of room between each other with Sergeant Ramos in the lead. He slowly climbed to just below the fifth-floor landing, high enough so he could see the door to Apartment 5F. He pointed to Ty Crawford, who continued onto the roof, while Ramos trained his gun on the apartment door.

Thirty seconds later, Ramos signaled he'd heard two clicks in his radio's earpiece. Ty was in place. Three clicks followed. Cutrone was ready. Ramos nodded, and McGuire and Gomez moved up the stairs.

They each took a position on either side of the apartment door, backs to the wall, crouching low. They squatted and listened for sounds coming from inside. McGuire could hear his heart beating as he strained to hear any movement. Salsa music played down the hall, and a dog barked somewhere below, but nothing from inside. McGuire looked at Ramos, pointed to his ear, and shook his head.

Ramos thumbed his radio and whispered, "Ty, go down the fire escape and take a peek."

Long seconds passed.

"Place looks empty." Crawford finally whispered through his radio.

"Nothing in the bedroom, and I can see straight through to the front door. The only room I can't see is the bathroom. It's on your right as you come in."

Ramos moved next to McGuire. "Ty says it looks empty."

"I heard."

"Want to knock?"

McGuire rapped on the door and shouted, "Gas Company." He stopped, waited, listened. Nothing. Crawford reported no movement. Ramos looked to Gomez.

"Joe, see if you can find the super."

Two minutes later, Gomez returned with a nervous-looking Hispanic super. After listening to Ramos explain they thought they smelled gas coming from 5F, the man produced a key to the apartment. Ramos thanked him and told him to wait downstairs. The super, happy to get away from whatever was about to take place, quickly departed.

McGuire inserted the key and slowly swung the door open. "Police! Come out with your hands up." He slid into the room, his weapon at high port.

Although no one had been seen or heard inside, they played it safe. Someone could be hiding in a closet, under a bed, or in the bathroom. The bathroom worried McGuire. He didn't want to get caught in the apartment's hallway, with no place to seek cover, if someone was to pop out shooting.

Cops were taught at the range their best friend in a gunfight was cover, something solid to get behind. The hallway leading to the bathroom, two walls, was a no-man's land McGuire dreaded. He slowly inched his way into the apartment, crouched low, gun now trained on the bathroom doorway. Sweat dripped into his eyes. He raised his left hand to wipe it away when something flashed out of the bathroom doorway.

"Freeze." McGuire's finger tightened on his trigger. The blur stopped and looked up at him. McGuire dropped his arm and stifled a laugh. It was a pretty goddamned calico cat.

Gomez and Ramos slid passed McGuire and searched the rest of the apartment. No one was hiding anywhere. Ramos called McGuire into the kitchen and pointed at the stove. The burner was on. A pot of tomato soup had boiled over onto the floor. A cigar sat in an ashtray on the table. McGuire picked it up. "Macanudo. Expensive. Still lit. Someone bugged out of here in quite a hurry."

Ramos turned off the stove and picked up his radio. "Ang, Ty, nobody home. You guys stay here and keep your eyes open in case Dee comes back. I'll get someone to relieve you in a little while."

They exited the apartment and locked the door behind them. Ramos handed the key to Gomez. "Joe, go tell the super we're done. We turned off the gas. Tell him we'll keep the key for a while, and make sure he knows not to talk to anyone else about our visit."

Back at the squad, Ramos made a call. The Bronx Homicide Apprehension Team would watch the Tiebout Avenue address in case Dillon returned.

Twenty minutes later, Crawford and Cutrone walked into the squad. While disappointed they'd come up empty at the apartment, the entire team felt energized. They now had a target. The case was starting to come together. McGuire and Gomez had found the loose thread.

Ramos looked at his watch and clapped his hands. "Everybody, get out of here. It's almost ten. Go home and get some sleep. Tomorrow is gonna be a busy day. See you all at seven."

"You look beat, John. You're not going to drive all the way home, are you?" Gomez looked concerned. "Want to stay over at my place?"

"No thanks, Joe. Take off. I gotta make a few phone calls."

Gomez said goodnight and left.

McGuire took out Gina Torelli's card. He picked up the phone. This time he did not put it back down.

Thirty - The Fat Lady Sings

McGuire felt torn. He wanted to see Gina but almost wished she hadn't answered her phone. Was this a date? He was nervous. He was a novice in this world. He had not dated since he and Cathy had become an item in high school. Seventeen years later, his usual self-confidence had deserted him. He felt like a rookie cop on his first night out on patrol.

Gina had not seemed surprised by his call and, despite the hour, readily agreed to meet him for a drink. She lived on Manhattan's Upper East Side and suggested meeting at Elaine's, the famous Second Avenue watering hole. The place was known as much for its larger than life—in so many ways—owner, Elaine Kaufman, as for the non-stop parade of celebrities who showed up there every night. While the food was edible, Elaine was the magnet who attracted the glitterati.

McGuire pushed open the door and saw Gina sitting at the crowded bar. *Man, she cleans up nice.* Gina, in full makeup, with her black hair blown out, emerald earrings complementing big green eyes, and a killer red silk blouse, looked very different from the austere Assistant District Attorney he had spoken with yesterday morning.

Was it yesterday? It seemed like weeks ago, so much had transpired since then. He checked his watch: *ten-thirty p.m. Last night this time, I was up to my elbows in Javier Boren's blood on the floor of a dirty Bronx bodega. Tonight, I'm meeting a pretty woman for a drink in the hippest bar in Manhattan. One great thing about being a cop—it's never boring.* He made his way through the crowd and squeezed in beside Gina. She flashed a smile. Unsure of how to greet her, he held out his hand, which she took in both of hers.

"Sorry I'm late. There was an accident on the Triborough."

"No worry. I just got here a few minutes ago myself."

As the bartender approached, McGuire caught his eye, shook his head and winked.

Gina made the introduction. "Ted, this is John McGuire." The men shook hands.

"What can I get you, John?"

"Would you have a Guinness?"

"We would." Ted then pointed to Gina's almost full glass of Chardonnay.

"No, I'm good, Ted." She covered the glass with her palm.

Seeing how nice Gina looked, McGuire suddenly wished he had taken time to shower and shave before leaving the Bronx. "Counselor, I have to tell you, you look fantastic."

The lady smiled.

"I hope you'll excuse my appearance, but we've been running all day."

"You look fine, John. Fine, but tired. We didn't have to do this tonight you know?"

"Nah, I'm okay. Nothing some Guinness won't cure."

Ted reappeared and put McGuire's drink in front of him.

He picked it up and held it toward Gina, who raised her glass. "*Sláinte*, Gina. And thanks again for your help with the case yesterday." He clinked his glass on hers.

Gina clinked their glasses again. "Well, as you said, 'Sometimes we just got to do the right thing.' And, you were correct. Old Mr. Jenkins did not belong in jail. I'm glad you pushed me to do what was right."

"Wasn't much of a push. More like a nudge. Glad you feel good about it now."

McGuire drained his glass and called for another.

Gina had barely touched her wine. "John, do you want to get something to eat? I don't know Elaine, and we're two commoners, but we might get lucky and get a table."

"Sure, we can try. I'm starving." Ted brought his second Guinness. "Ted, do you think Elaine could find us a table?"

"She's in the back. Let me ask." The barkeep turned and walked away.

Two minutes later, the rotund grand dame herself approached. She stopped at McGuire and cocked her head. "You have your passport, buster?"

Gina looked on, clearly baffled.

"No, Ma'am."

"Then get your ass back to the Bronx where you belong, Johnny Boy." She grinned before wrapping her large arms around McGuire and planting a wet kiss on his cheek. McGuire returned the hug and introduced Gina to Elaine.

"This is a great guy you got here, Gina. The finest of the Finest. Wish he would honor us with his presence more often." She turned. "Ted, for God's sake, give us a drink."

"So, how did you meet John?" Gina asked.

Before Elaine could reply, McGuire said, "I did a favor for a friend of hers."

"That's right. Stay here, I'll be right back." She moved toward the rear of the restaurant, returning quickly with a framed photograph which she handed to Gina.

Gina gazed at the picture of Elaine, McGuire, Joe Gomez, and another man at a table. Then she looked closely at the thin man in the center dressed all in white. "Is that—?"

"Tom Wolfe." Elaine nodded. "When he was researching *Bonfire of the Vanities*, he asked me if I knew any detectives up in the Bronx. I didn't but called my friend, the Chief of Detectives, and asked if he could hook my pal up with two of his good ones. Tom spent two weeks with them, going out on cases, seeing them deal with victims in the hospital, homicides, locking up bad guys, going to court. He said he never would have been able to capture the flavor of the Bronx without their help. Adores John and Joe." She took the glass Ted handed her and took a sip. "Have you read the book, Gina?"

"Oh, God, yes. It's practically required reading at the office. I always wondered how he captured the underbelly of the Bronx so well. The poverty, the crime, the cops, the courts." She gazed at McGuire. "Now I know. He had a pretty good teacher."

"He had the best." Elaine hugged McGuire once more and grabbed Gina's hand. "You guys are hungry. Let's eat."

***

Gina took McGuire's arm. They followed closely behind Elaine as the big woman weaved her way out of the crowded and smoke-filled bar. She led them to a large table already occupied by four men and two women in the front dining room. Two waiters appeared with three chairs and Elaine made the introductions.

Gina recognized an aging actor with a much younger blonde trophy wife, whose low-cut white cashmere top showed off her abundant cleavage. The rest of the group consisted of a Wall Street big shot with his wife, and a writer and his foppish boyfriend.

Elaine passed the picture around, and they all toasted John for his contribution to the book. Empty bottles and glasses littered the table. The volume of their voices—and flush of their faces—led Gina to believe they had been partying for quite some time.

Elaine waved a hand, and a waiter appeared with four bottles of wine, two red, two white. He pulled the cork on the first bottle and handed it to Elaine. She bounced it off the waiter's head.

"For Christ sake, Charlie, just pour. What? Am I going to send it back?"

Gina held back, waiting to see who was drinking what. After a few moments, she realized everyone was drinking everything. It didn't seem to matter. Red, white, mixed drinks, whatever was closest at hand was consumed. The talk grew steadily louder, competing with the racket that filled the room. Every table was full. It felt almost like a family gathering with people getting up from one table and plunking themselves down at another, all under the watchful eye of Elaine, who seemed to be the ringmaster of this happy circus.

Elaine constantly got up to greet people. She then led them to a table and sat them with people she thought they would find interesting. Everyone mixed and seemed to get along. Those Gina could see in the front room anyway. She had read somewhere that the rear dining room was referred to as "Siberia," a place where newcomers and regulars who had pissed off Elaine for some reason would find themselves. As she scanned the nearby tables, Gina, a big sports fan, was greatly impressed. Right next to them was a table of New York Ranger hockey players.

All-Star Mets first baseman, Keith Hernandez, was deep in conversation with an older, gray-haired man at another table. She was stunned when the man approached their table, and she recognized him as the owner of the Yankees, George Steinbrenner. She was even more shocked when, after kissing Elaine, Steinbrenner shook McGuire's hand. "John, good to see you. How've you been?"

McGuire replied he was fine, and introduced her as ADA Torelli.

The Yankee owner took her hand. "A Bronx detective, and a Bronx District Attorney. I better watch my step around here." He waved and walked away.

Charlie, the waiter, arrived with a huge tray filled with plates of pasta, fish, shrimp, and clams. These were passed around. Everyone took what they wanted and handed it off to the person next to them. Gina had grown up in a large family in Queens and felt quite at home with the eating arrangement, but this was definitely not Queens. This was magic, a magic hard to find outside of Manhattan.

Gina had finished her one glass of wine. She felt tipsy, but decided it wasn't the alcohol but the excitement of this special night. It was also not lost on her McGuire had drunk red wine, white wine, and a third pint of Guinness Ted had brought back. She also noticed Carla Cleavage, the actor's wife, had taken Elaine's empty seat and now sat on McGuire's left, hanging on his every word—literally hanging, as she had a hand on his shoulder with one breast resting on his arm.

"Ssso tell me Mr. Policeman, have you ever ssshot anybody?" Ms. Cleavage was sloppy drunk and slurring.

McGuire glanced across at Gina and offered a sheepish smile. “Not today. Not yet anyway.” He elicited a big laugh from the others.

Gina hoped the actor might notice his wife flirting with John, but he was deeply engaged in conversation with the writer, whose boyfriend silently pouted. She tuned in to Wally Wall Street on her right, droning on about a deal which had netted him a million dollars. All the while, she kept John in view out the corner of her eye.

The blonde was stumbling, trying to make a point while touching John’s thigh repeatedly. Gina was about to say something when John suddenly excused himself and headed for the men’s room. He stopped for a moment to whisper something to Elaine, who returned and stood by the table.

When he came back, Elaine sweetly told the blonde, “Move back over honey. I have to speak with John.”

Reluctantly, the woman moved, but not before giving McGuire’s leg a parting squeeze.

With McGuire now once again safely ensconced between Elaine and herself, Gina relaxed. She leaned over and placed a hand on his shoulder. “Are you ssshure you didn’t ssshoot sssomebody today, Mr. Policeman?”

McGuire and Elaine had a good laugh at the dead-on impression.

“Where’s the ladies’ room, Elaine?”

McGuire put a hand on her shoulder. “Elaine, tell her what you told the tourist who asked where the men’s room was.”

“Head to the back and make a right at Michael Caine.”

The table exploded in laughter.

Elaine pointed Gina in the right direction as more wine was poured.

When she returned to her seat, she saw a fresh Guinness in front of McGuire. *It has to be his fourth pint, plus I don't know how many glasses of wine.*

She remained standing and looked at her watch. "It's getting late, John. I have a trial in the morning."

He held up his glass up. "One for the road. Five minutes, okay?"

She sat again. "So, how do you know George Steinbrenner?"

"We both work in the Bronx."

"Come on, John, you have to do better."

"Okay. He's a good man. Loves the cops. Hosts the Silver Shield game every year. Money goes to the Police and Fire Widows and Orphans. I did him a few favors."

"You seem to do favors for a lot of people. Steinbrenner, Tom Wolfe, old Mr. Jenkins."

McGuire took a long pull on his Guinness. "What can I tell you, Gina? I like to help people. One of the reasons I became a cop."

She kissed him lightly on the cheek and took his hand. "C'mom, Sir Galahad, let's go. I really have to get up early."

"Just let me finish this." McGuire raised his glass. He had almost finished when Keith Hernandez approached the table.

"Hey, John. Keith Hernandez. George Steinbrenner told me you were a top cop. Just wanted to say hello and tell you how much I admire the work you guys do."

"Thanks, Keith. I'm a big fan of the '86 Mets. You guys were the greatest." He introduced Gina.

"Can I buy you guys a drink?" Hernandez asked.

"Thanks, but we were just leaving," Gina said.

"Gina, come on. One drink with Keith. You don't get a chance to talk to an All-Star, World Series winner every night. C'mon babe."

"John, I have to leave." She stood. "But, you stay. We'll catch up some other time."

She said goodnight to Elaine, the folks at the table, and Hernandez. McGuire walked her to the door and held her coat while she put it on. She noticed he seemed unsteady on his feet.

"You sure you're all right with this Gina? Want me to walk you home?"

"No, I'll catch a cab. You stay, but you might want to pass on any more drinks. I think you've had enough."

He walked her out and flagged down a cab. He started to kiss her, but she pulled back. "How 'bout I get in the cab and you take me home with you?"

"That ship sailed five minutes ago." She got in the cab. "You don't get a chance to talk to an All-Star, World Series winner every night. Lucky you. Tonight's that night." She pulled the cab's door shut.

Thirty-One - Two Weeks' Notice

One week after arriving in Georgia, Pooh Bear Jennings was back in the Bronx. As he had predicted, five days after the shooting of the kid in the bodega, a bigger case had popped. A young Assistant District Attorney had gone into a deli opposite the Bronx courthouse to get a sandwich. As he waited at the counter, a drug dealer whose case was on the docket walked by. The dealer had beaten some people out of a large amount of money. A car screeched up, three men jumped out and began firing. The dealer escaped unhurt, but a stray bullet entered the store. Young ADA Seamus O'Grady, hit once in the head, died on the dirty floor.

Jennings read the news. "Bad for him. Good for me." He couldn't wait to get back to plan the big job, his last one. Win, lose, or draw, he had made the decision: one more and out. He was tired of the thug life, tired of lying to his mother about where his money came from, and, he was very tired of working with the fucking psychopath, Dee.

He knew Dee could just as easily have killed him the day he shot Rontal. But, Pooh knew he was useful to Dee because he was the connection to the white boys, the fake cops who made the kidnappings work. It was the reason he was still alive. *One more job. I take the money and kiss Dee, the Bronx, and all this gangsta bullshit goodbye. Take Mom and Gerard and we go home to Macon. No more killings, no pushing dope, no more time in jail. One more is all I need.*

He called his mother as soon as he got home. The following day, Sunday, he paid her his usual visit. She had a nice apartment in the Edenwald projects, not a bad place as projects went. He stopped and bought some flowers for her and some comic books for Gerard. As he rode the elevator up, he felt a sense of relief. For the first time in years, he had a plan.

He knocked on the door.

Gerard answered. “Big Brother.” Gerard picked him up in a bear hug, almost crushing his ribs.

“Gerard, young man, you put your brother down this minute.” Mother had come into the hallway. She would not want Gerard to get too excited. Three years younger than Pooh, at twenty-eight, he was mentally handicapped, operating at the intellectual level of a ten-year old. He could not be left alone. Momma dropped him off at his school each morning on her way to work and picked him up on her way home. Days off were spent together. He wouldn’t have lasted one day on the mean streets of the Bronx by himself.

Pooh handed the flowers to his mother and gave her a long hug. Gerard looked on excitedly knowing his brother, Steven, never came empty-handed.

Pooh stepped back and opened the bag he carried. He took out the comic books. “Let’s see, Gerard, we have Batman, Spiderman, and The Incredible Hulk. Your three favorite superheroes.”

Gerard eagerly took the comics and went inside.

Pooh turned to his mother who was smiling. “Truth be told, son, Gerard’s biggest hero is you. You’re all he talks about, his big brother.”

Pooh took his mother in his arms once more, softly kissed the top of her head. Any doubts he’d had were now gone. He was no hero. Just a guy who wanted to get his brother to a place where he could take a walk without fear of getting beaten up. Take his mom back home where, for the first time in years, she could stop working and feel some peace.

He could do it. He just needed one more job. And a plan already started to take shape.

Thirty-Two - Unraveled

The elevator opened, Pooh Jennings strode out. *Fuckin' hall stinks as bad as the damn elevator.* He walked down a dark hallway, barely able to make out the numbers on the apartment doors. He knocked on the last one.

A deep voice asked, "Who?"

"Pooh."

A lock clicked and the door opened. Dee stood with the .44 Bulldog in hand.

"Get in quick," the big man said. "You check the block for cops?"

"Yeah. I got your message. Street's clear. Why the paranoia?"

"Pigs hit my crib on Tiebout last night. Looking for me for the Domo hit."

"How you know what they looking for you for?"

Dee put the gun into the holster under his left armpit and locked the door. "My cop came through. Called and said they ID'd me."

"How?"

"We didn't have much time to talk. Said the cops were on their way. Shit, I saw them pull up." Dee's eyes widened. "It was fuckin' close, man."

Jennings scoped the place as they walked to the living room. The centerpiece was a large screen television atop a plastic milk crate. A badly stained mattress occupied the floor in one corner, and a lopsided and tattered orange beanbag chair another. An emaciated black girl slouched in the chair watching cartoons. An unlit crack pipe dangled from her lips. She gave Pooh a toothless smile.

"Yo, Shavell, get your ass into the bedroom," Dee barked.

Jennings watched as the girl stood and moved slowly into the next room. *Girl's probably twenty. Looks about sixty. Crack's some bad shit.*

"She gives good head." Dee watched her leave. "All gums, no teeth. Wanna blow job?"

"No thanks." *I'd rather stick my dick in a blender.*

"I gotta get out of this town for good, quick." Dee took a long pull from a bottle of Courvoisier. "Need one last score. You got anybody lined up?"

Thanks for opening the door. "Maybe we could snatch Flaco over in Spanish Harlem."

"Thought the skinny spic was up in Greenhaven."

"He got out last month. Right back in business."

"Didn't one of his guys take over the operation?"

"Yeah, some guy called El Gato was running it the last two years, while Flaco was upstate."

Dee took another swig and offered the bottle to Pooh, who shook his head no.

"How much we asking if we do Flaco?"

"I hear he's doing good. We could ask for three hundred thou, see what his crew comes up with."

Dee was at the window, checking the street below. "Three's cool. One fifty each."

"It would be one hundred each, Dee. The white boys get a third."

"Our last job. Fuck the white boys. They did fine with us. Never going to see them again anyway. Fuck em."

Never see the white boys or you after this job, you psycho. Fuck you, too.

"Sounds good to me, Dee."

"Where and when?"

"One-sixteenth and Second Avenue. I'll check it out tomorrow. Get hold of the white boys. Go for it Thursday night."

"Should work."

"I'll call you after I scout the location."

"No. No calls. They leave a trail. Cop said it's how they got onto me. Some old phone calls from an arrest report."

"What should–"

"Meet me at midnight tomorrow." Dee turned from the window and looked at Pooh. "Our old crack house down on Tiebout."

"You think it's a good–"

"Just another abandoned house now. Cops won't be looking at it. I got some cash hidden in the basement there I need to get."

"Why don't we meet at–"

"You got shit in your ears? I say where we meet."

"Okay. Tomorrow, midnight, the old house." Pooh headed toward the door.

"Hold up." Dee held the gun in his hand. He unlocked the door, opened it an inch, and peered out. "Okay. Clear." He holstered the weapon. "Hey. This El Gato dude? He just stepped down when Flaco got out of the can?"

"More like fell down. Dead. Got shot."

Dee's chuckle sounded like a bass drum's beat. "Funny. I thought cats were supposed to have nine lives."

"Flaco musta believed the same thing."

"Why?"

"He shot El Gato ten times."

Thirty-Three - A Terrible Web

Assistant District Attorney Gina Torelli always arrived early for work. Today she was five minutes late. She had consumed more than her normal one glass of wine limit last night and had a slight headache. Her best friend, fellow ADA Yolanda Simons, was waiting as she entered her office.

"Girl, were you out late last night?" Yolanda appraised her appearance. "And us with a trial starting today."

Yolanda Simons was in her fourth year at the Bronx DA's office and a rising star. Gina, a Fordham Law grad, had met her years earlier when she'd been asked to speak to the incoming freshman class at the Bronx school. She'd encouraged Yolanda to take her LSATs, graduate Fordham Law, and pass the bar exam. It was a foregone conclusion she'd join Gina in the DA's Office.

Yolanda was bright, articulate, hard-working, eager to learn, attractive, and had something else, which made her very popular in the Bronx Criminal Justice system. She was Hispanic. And black. Her mom the former and her dad the latter.

This combination was a definite plus in the Bronx, which had the lowest percentage of white residents of the city's five boroughs. The jury pools were different from those in Manhattan, Queens, Brooklyn, and very different from those on Staten Island. The Bronx was known as a place where a minority jury, after being presented a slam-dunk case, with a perp caught in the act on surveillance cameras, who gave a full confession to the police, could come back with a Not Guilty verdict because they didn't believe the arresting officer and prosecutor, especially if both happened to be white.

Gina had lost a number of such cases and done some homework on the Bronx's demographics. She found the U.S. Census Bureau considered the Bronx the most diverse area in the country. If two people, of the over one million, three-hundred thousand plus residents, were chosen at random, there was a ninety percent chance the two would be of different race or ethnicity. The latest census had shown the borough to be over fifty percent Hispanic, the only borough with a Hispanic majority, thirty-two percent black and ten percent white.

When Gina had presented these facts to her boss, the District Attorney of Bronx County, Van Jensen, a black man, he was not surprised.

"I've been trying to recruit the best and brightest minority candidates to this office for the last five years. It's the only way we are going to break through with juries, who come in with their own opinions about cops and lawyers."

Gina sighed. "I know, but it's tough. How do we compete against the big firms, the banks, the Goldman Sachs, the Lehman Brothers?"

"Hard to get a kid who grew up in the Bronx, makes it into Fordham Law, graduates with huge student loans to pay off. Are they going to work for us at forty grand a year, or go to Wall Street where they would get triple that as a Christmas bonus? Unless we get them early and develop a relationship like you did with Yolanda, we don't stand a chance."

Gina was proud her efforts had worked out so well. She had mentored her protégé through the tough first years in the office and was now watching her bloom into a top-notch prosecutor.

The trial beginning today would be Yolanda's first as the lead prosecutor, the first chair. Gina would be there to support her friend as co-counsel, second chair, but was confident Yolanda was ready for her debut as lead in an attempted homicide trial. Yolanda had repaid Gina's kindness by being a true friend, had become like one of her family. Gina had grown up with four brothers. Yolanda was the little sister she had always longed for.

Little sister looked at her as she popped two aspirin and downed them with coffee.

"So? You going to tell me where you went last night?"

"I met a guy for a drink at Elaine's."

"Ooh, Elaine's. Very nice. And who was the guy?"

Gina took a bagel out of a bag. "Let's go over your opening statement."

"Sure. Right after you tell me who the guy was."

Gina chewed the bagel. "One of the cops."

Yolanda put her coffee down. "One of the cops? One of the cops? One of the cops you told me to stay away from? Not to date." Her smile grew. "This must be a very special cop. Name?"

"McGuire."

"Come on, Gina, more info. Half the cops in the Bronx are named McGuire or O'Hara. What precinct please?"

Gina swallowed. "The Four-two." She paused. "Detective Squad."

Yolanda stood. “The Four-two squad. *Dios mio.* Do not tell me you went out for drinks with Detective John McGuire of the Four-two squad.”

“Well, I did. Why? Do you know him?”

“No, but I wish I knew him. Gina, he’s a doll. He’s very popular with the ladies in this building. I know two of the girls in the typing pool who would do him right on the court house steps after work and not even put in for overtime. But, isn't there a little problem? Like he’s married?”

“Not anymore. Going through a divorce.”

“I hear they all say that.”

“This time, it’s true. One of the court officers confirmed it for me.”

“What a shame. So, tell me about last night.”

Gina filled in Yolanda about dinner at Elaine’s, all the celebrities who were there, how everyone from Elaine on down seemed to know and like McGuire.

“It was a great night, *si*?” Yolanda leaned on Gina’s desk, smiling sweetly. “So how did it end?”

Gina sat back in her chair. “Started out great. Ended on a downer. It’s a shame. Until then, it was a fantastic time, but the man drinks way too much.”

“Yeah, I heard. Will you see him again?”

“I don’t know.” Gina turned, looked out her window and stared down into Yankee Stadium. After a few seconds, she snapped back around. “Enough about last night. We have the People of the State of New York versus Anton Jones, charged with Attempted Murder in the Second Degree. Are the people ready?”

“Yes, your honor. The people are ready.”

“Counselor, the court will hear your opening statement.”

Yolanda went over her opening twice. Gina suggested two subtle changes to make it more effective. They were getting ready to move down to the courtroom when Gina's phone rang. She picked it up and, after a short conversation, hung up, sighing in frustration.

"That was the Leprechaun. Our defendant refused to get on the bus at Rikers Island this morning. We'll have to reschedule the trial."

"What a shame, Gina. I was ready."

"I know you were."

Yolanda walked to the door, stopped, looked back at Gina. "So? You going to see McGuire again?"

"Don't you have some work to do?"

As Yolanda left, Gina's secretary entered. "A detective waiting to see you."

"Fine."

A man entered. Gina didn't recognize him. She stood. "Good morning, Detective."

He shook her hand. "Actually, I'm a sergeant."

"What squad are you from?"

"No squad. Internal Affairs. I'd like to speak with you about a particular Bronx detective."

"Which one?" Gina began to feel uncomfortable.

"John McGuire of the Four-two squad."

Gina felt her stomach drop. She looked at the sergeant and noticed for the first time his cheap suit and ridiculous attempt to cover his bald skull with a classic comb-over. She would have laughed if McGuire's name hadn't been mentioned. "What did you say your name was?"

"Stark. Sergeant Ray Stark. Counselor, how well do you know McGuire?"

"I know he's a fine detective. I've had a number of cases with him."

"Do you see him socially?"

"I don't know what you're—"

"It's a legitimate question."

"How is it any of your business who I see after office hours?"

"We have a case on McGuire."

"What kind of case?"

"Information has been leaked to known drug dealers. McGuire is a suspect."

"Have you looked at his record? He leads the Bronx in cases closed, arrests, and convictions. He has more commendations than you can count. You're barking up the wrong tree."

Stark pulled his chair closer and leaned over the desk, invading Gina's space.

The aroma of cheap cologne caused her to sit back.

"Am I? I know McGuire. He's a wise guy. Has no respect for authority. Going through a divorce. Has a gambling problem. A major drinking problem. But, I guess you know about it, right?"

"How would I—?"

"Last night? Elaine's?"

Gina blinked. "How—"

"One of my detectives recognized you."

"Are you tailing—?"

"So, did you see McGuire talking with any unsavory characters last night?"

Gina stood, folded her arms over her chest. She could feel her Sicilian blood pounding in her ears. She stared at Stark and said nothing.

"How much did he drink?"

She did not reply.

"Did he pay for the meal?"

She took a deep breath. "Get out. Out of my office." Each word was spoken softly, slowly.

Stark began blinking rapidly. "Let me remind you, Madame District Attorney, as an officer of the court, you are required to assist in this investigation."

"No. Let me tell you something. I am required to assist in a criminal investigation. I am not, however, required to assist a fat slob who shows up at my office unannounced, asking me to help him nail a fine detective. Unsavory characters in Elaine's? Yeah, Elaine and George Steinbrenner. Go talk to them. Did he drink too much, pay for his meal? I believe if either of these charges were true, it would constitute at most a minor violation of Police Department guidelines. Not a criminal offense."

She leaned down into Stark's face. "Now get out of my office. I don't want to see or hear from you again unless you have a subpoena."

Stark started to rise. "I will count on you to keep our conversation private. Don't tell your boyfriend what we spoke of. Don't let him know I'm on to him. If you do, you could be charged with impeding an investigation." The man turned to leave.

Gina felt her face redden. She followed Stark to the door. "Sergeant."

He stopped in his tracks.

"Do you have five dollars on you?"

"Yeah. Why?"

"There's a shoe shine stand in the lobby. Stop and get one. You look like a bum."

Thirty-Four - The Plot Quickens

Gina was having lunch at her desk. A tap at the door caused her to look up. Court Officer Dan Foley cleared his throat. Thirty-two years before he'd found he was two inches short of the NYPD's then, five-foot eight-inch height requirement. The Court Officers accepted him, and he was now the Bronx court's senior man. Wiry, with shining blue eyes, white hair, still carrying a trace of a Dublin accent, he was known as "The Leprechaun."

"Didn't know you were eating, counselor. I'll come back."

"No. Come in, Dan. Help me finish this." She pointed to a huge pastrami hero on her desk.

Foley sat opposite Gina. "Thanks, but I ate already. Just wanted to let you know. Anton Jones?"

Gina nodded while wiping her lips with a napkin. She pushed half of the sandwich toward Foley. "Yes. What's the story there?"

"I spoke to Corrections. Reason he refused to get on the bus?" He picked up the hero, took a big bite.

Gina waited while he chewed. She reached back to a mini refrigerator, took out a can of Coke, popped it, and slid it across the desk.

The Leprechaun drank, sat back and sighed deeply.

Gina handed him a napkin.

"Well, it seems the reason he didn't get on the bus was he was waiting for an ambulance instead." He took another bite, another sip.

Gina waited patiently. She was used to listening to law enforcement people talk about the most horrendous incident as if discussing the weather. "And, he needed the ambulance because?"

Foley patted his lips with the napkin. "Somebody slit his throat."

It was Gina's turn to sigh deeply. "Do we know what happened?"

"Corrections ain't saying much. Usual jailhouse sticking. Jones was at breakfast. Fistfight started on the other side of the mess hall. Distraction. COs broke it up. Came back and found ya man doing the horizontal lambada in a bowl of bright red Cheerios."

Gina's headache suddenly returned. She rubbed her temples. Foley had the sandwich at his mouth.

"Dan, Jones?"

"Alive. Elmhurst Hospital. Attacker did a poor job. Missed the jugular. Once they get him stabilized, they'll ship him over to the prison ward at Bellevue. Looks like Yolanda will have to wait a bit for her big debut."

"Did you let her know?"

"She's out to lunch. Figured you'd want to know straight away."

"Thanks."

Foley stood to leave.

"Dan, one more thing."

"Yes, Gina."

"John McGuire, Four-two squad. You said he's getting divorced. You sure?"

"Told me so himself."

"You know him well?"

"I do. I coach the Court Officer's Hurling team. It's an Irish game where—"

"People beat the hell out of one another while hitting a ball with flat wooden bats. I've seen it on Wide World of Sports." She rolled her eyes.

"Lovely, yes. Well, John is quite the athlete. Plays football for the PD. I recruited him to give the hurling a try a few years back."

"Does he play for your team?"

"No. He did the one year, was learning the game. Would have been good, a natural, but it conflicted with the football, so he stopped after the one season. May I inquire as to why the interest, Counselor?"

"Oh, I've done a few cases with him. Interesting man."

"He is indeed."

"There are rumors he drinks too much."

"There was an explosion in a boarding house, love. Roomers flew all over. I only mentioned the divorce because himself told me about it. It's a fact out there. I will not sully a good man's reputation with idle chatter about the drink. It may or may not be true."

"I appreciate it, Dan. Thanks. And, thanks for the news on Anton Jones."

"You're welcome." The Leprechaun turned to leave.

"Dan, take the rest of the hero."

"Only if you're done, Counselor." He grabbed up the remaining piece. "Meself, I've already eaten."

***

"Who would want Jones dead?"

Yolanda stared out the window, looking down at the green grass of Yankee Stadium. She turned to Gina. "I'm sorry, Boss. I thought it could be July, not winter and thirty degrees. Who'd want Jones dead?"

Gina nodded.

Yolanda answered her own question. "Well, besides me and Jermain Dickens—the guy he shot—I would say anybody he ever met and may ever meet. His mother may have liked him, but I doubt it."

"He's so bad?"

"Pure evil. I wanted to take a long shower and scrub with a Brillo pad after meeting him."

Gina popped a stick of Doublemint gum in her mouth. "Run the case by me again."

"January six, two a.m. Four-Six cops on patrol heard shots fired, Fordham Road and the Concourse. Turned the corner, saw Jones running down the street, gun in hand. They hit him with the car, bounced him off a wall. Got him and the gun. Jones, of course, isn't injured."

"Naturally."

"Cops found Dickens on the ground, shot in the leg. They tried to roll him over to check for any other wounds, and he refused. They tossed him and came up with a gun, a nine."

"Which he carried because—"

"Protection. Said he was mugged."

"Lot of that going around lately."

"His story, he was walking home, heard yelling. Saw a black guy and a Spanish guy in a dispute. Kept walking, heard shots, took a round in the left leg. Claimed to be an innocent bystander."

"You ever met a guilty bystander?"

Yolanda laughed. "You've got a point there, Gina, but I believe him."

Gina mused aloud. “Something about Jones getting stabbed today, when the trial was going to start, bugs me.”

“Boss, you know better than I do. It’s pretty common in jail. Guy ties up the phone, switches channels on the television, pisses someone off, they pay.”

It was once again Gina’s turn to look out at the stadium. “I know, but the way The Leprechaun described it, this was a planned attack, not some spur-of-the-moment beef. Maybe someone thinks he’s cooperating with us?”

“No chance. When Dickens told me the story about Jones and the Spanish guy, I thought it was worth checking to see if it had anything to do with black/Spanish drug war going on. I spoke to Jones’ attorney. He agreed to bring him in for a Proffer hearing last week. Gave him ‘Queen for a Day,’ offer of immunity if he cooperated, but no dice.”

Gina whirled from the window to face Yolanda. “Yoli, tell me Jones had some other case in court when you brought him in for the Proffer.”

“No, he—”

Struck suddenly with a likely scenario, Gina held up a hand and buzzed her secretary. “Mary, Elmhurst Hospital, patient Anton Jones, inmate from Rikers admitted this morning with a throat wound. I need to speak to whoever is guarding him, now.”

She looked at Yolanda. “You never, ever, bring an inmate over and try to turn him without having some other reason for his being in the building. He goes back with a rat jacket, cooperator or not. Dig up an old case, a warrant, an old traffic summons, something.”

“I’m sorry. I didn’t—”

“Who’s his lawyer?”

“Legal Aid. A new guy, Benson.”

“Figures. Only a novice would—”

The intercom squawked "Officer Negron from Elmhurst on line one."

Yolanda paced back and forth as Gina spoke to Negron. After three minutes, which probably seemed like thirty to Yolanda, Gina hung up.

"Gina, I am so sorry. I—"

"Stop wearing out my carpet. Have a seat. It's okay. The cop guarding Jones will keep a close eye on him. He thinks they'll ship him over to the Correction Ward at Bellevue tomorrow. We'll get him isolated there." Gina leaned back, yawned and stretched her arms toward the ceiling. "This could work out for us."

"How so?"

"Jones may be in a mood to talk with us now. They tried to pop him once. We can offer protection, maybe a reduced sentence if he cooperates. Worth a try."

"You want me to—"

"Call his lawyer. Let him know what happened. Pitch the protection, reduced sentence. If he agrees, which he probably will, we can hold a Proffer with Jones in Bellevue."

"You think—"

"Hey, your idea about digging for something on the drug shootings was a good one. Let's see where it leads."

"I'm on it." She stood.

"When you did the Proffer last week, did Jones have anything to say?"

"Matter of fact, he did. He invited me to have sex."

"Sex. With that creep?"

"Not exactly. He was not participating. Told me to go, uh—have intercourse with myself."

"Lot of that going around, too."

***

It was late morning the following day when Gina and Yolanda arrived at the reception window of Bellevue

Hospital's prison ward. The correction officer slowly perused their IDs and paperwork they slipped under the bulletproof glass partition.

"Anton Jones is in Room 112." He passed their documents back. "Have him solo as you requested. His lawyer's in with him. Left side after you clear the ward." He then keyed a microphone. "Two on the gate."

The steel-barred gate to their right slid open with a metallic hum. They entered a hallway which led into a larger room. The ward had ten beds. Each held a prisoner. Most were asleep. The occupant of the last bed, a young Hispanic, studied Gina and Yolanda intently. He had one wrist cuffed to the bed rail.

"*Hola, Bonita.* Lady, don't you remember me?" The kid looked wild-eyed as they approached.

"Keep moving." Gina was aware of the inmate's uncuffed hand moving rapidly under the sheets as he pleasured himself.

A huge black guard appeared. "Sanchez, I told you if you don't stop playing with yourself you're going to go blind."

"And, I told you I'll stop when I need glasses."

"Sorry 'bout that, ladies. Please follow me." The guard turned.

They found Anton Jones sitting up in bed speaking with his lawyer. Except for the gauze bandage around his throat, he looked fine. After introductions were made, Gina took the lead. She would not normally have come to the hospital, but was worried there might be repercussions from Yolanda's error. She wanted to ensure her friend's mistake didn't come back to haunt her. She was pleased when neither Jones nor his attorney seemed to blame Yolanda for the attack.

"Mr. Jones, your attorney, Mr. Benson, has explained to you how this proceeding works. Correct?"

"Yeah, said if I give you something, I might cut a deal with y'all but I ain't no snitch. Fuck no."

Gina stood. "Well then, we have nothing further to discuss. Good luck back in Rikers."

"Counselor, could I have a minute alone with my client?" The Legal Aid lawyer stood and took a step toward her.

Gina and Yolanda went out into the hall.

Three minutes later, Benson popped his head out. "My client will speak with you now."

"What are you offering me?" Jones asked.

"Depends on what you give us," Gina replied. "Right now, as a predicate felon, you're looking at minimum of ten years for the shooting–if you take a plea."

"Maybe I go to trial. Take my chances."

"Mr. Jones. If you go to trial, we have the victim, Mr. Dickens, who will identify you. We also have the two cops who caught you running from the scene with a gun in your hand. Ballistics has identified the gun as the same one which put the bullet into Mr. Dickens's leg."

"Fuckin' cops hit me with their car." Jones scowled, showing misaligned, jagged, and rotting teeth. "That shit ain't right."

"You should have crossed at the green, not in between. In any case, there is no doubt in my mind if you go to trial, you'll be convicted."

"What kind of time I be looking at?"

"Let's see. With your extensive criminal record, a conviction on these serious charges would bring–" Gina looked out the window and did the math in her head. "To put it bluntly Mr. Jones, on the day you're convicted, there's a very good chance the person who will one day become your parole officer will not yet have been born."

"Huh? Say what?" Jones looked questioningly at his attorney.

"She means you will be an old man before you get out, Anton."

"On the other hand, if you cooperate and supply information of value, we might consider a reduced sentence."

"I got to go back to Rikers?"

"Depends on what you give us. We're interested in finding out what you know about the shootings between the black and Dominican drug dealers."

Jones again looked to his lawyer who nodded yes.

"I don't wanna go back to Rikers. Dominicans be at war with some bad dudes. People you don't fuck with."

"Give me a name, Anton." Gina was surprised to see tears well up in the man's eyes.

"I give you this. I go back to Rikers, I die."

"Give me a name and maybe you don't go back."

Jones took a deep breath, placed both hands onto his throat. Tears now ran down his face. "Dude be called Dee."

"What's Dee's name?"

"Just know him as Dee. Should be easy enough to find. He's like seven feet tall and built like the fuckin' Kingsbridge Armory."

"How do you know this Dee?"

"I did some work for him. He don't like spics pushing dope on his turf."

"Was this what led to the altercation between you and the Spanish man which resulted in—"

Benson interrupted. "My client will not answer the question at this time."

"Fine, Counselor. We can discuss it at a later date. Does your client have anything else he wants to tell us?"

Benson leaned down and whispered into Jones's ear. Jones nodded. The lawyer stood and looked at Gina. "My client has information on a very sensitive subject. If we reveal it, I want your guarantee he will not go back to Rikers, and will be put into witness protection."

"It's possible. Depends on what he gives us. If it's good, you have my word."

Benson cleared his throat. "Police corruption." He looked to Jones. "Tell them."

"Dee's got a cop on his payroll."

"Name?"

"Gomez."

Gina thought back to the picture she'd seen in Elaine's. Tom Wolfe, McGuire and his partner, Joe Gomez. Had to be a coincidence. Gomez was a very common Hispanic name. "You know this cop Gomez's first name?"

"No, but I know he works out of Washington Avenue. With an Irish guy, McGuire."

Thirty-Five - Fox in The Henhouse

McGuire had slept in the squad's dorm and wakened with a slight hangover. Last night had been fantastic. Gina was bright, funny, easy to talk with, and cute. McGuire had enjoyed his time with her at Elaine's. He felt terrible about the way the evening had ended. He knew he should have left when she wanted, and sorely wished he could take back letting her go so he could drink with one of his all-time favorite baseball players. He definitely wanted to see her again, to make it up to her, but now it was time for work. He showered and dressed.

The Medina kidnapping, the execution of the four Dominican drug dealers, the Rontal Cheery homicide, and the shooting of the kid in the bodega had all come together. Today the team would hunt down the triggerman, Dwayne "Dee" Dillon. If he could wrap these four cases up, his promotion to Second Grade Detective would be put on the fast track. It would also prove to his doubters that he still had it. He'd gone through a rough period after Cathy left, but he was still one of the best detectives on the job.

At five-thirty, he went to Pedro's for breakfast. Greasy bacon and eggs washed down with a chocolate thick shake and *voilà*, he felt better. He brought a dozen rolls back to the squad.

By six-thirty, the place was already hopping. Cutrone and Crawford were at their desks. He was sure Gomez, who was always early, must be around somewhere. Hanlon was not in yet, which was no surprise and, no fuckin' loss.

McGuire stopped outside Sergeant Ramos's office. "I got rolls, Boss."

Ramos gestured for John to enter. "Close the door."

This got McGuire's attention. The door was never closed. He pulled up a chair close to Ramos.

"We have a problem, a big problem."

McGuire's mind raced. Had he fucked up again? "I'm not late. You said we were starting at seven today, right?"

Ramos nodded. He leaned closer and spoke, his voice a troubled whisper. "Remember last night, when we hit Dee's apartment on Tiebout? The soup boiling over, the cigar still smoking. Somebody left in a big rush."

"Like he got word that we were coming."

"My thoughts exactly. You have to be in a real hurry to run out and leave the range on. Could have burned down the whole building, right?"

"What are you getting at?"

"I sat here last night after you guys left and kept playing out different scenarios in my mind. Kept coming back to one. There were six of us who knew what we were doing. Could one of us have warned Dee we were headed his way?"

"No way. I trust these guys with–" McGuire stopped mid-sentence. Fat Pat Hanlon's face had popped into his head.

"After about an hour, I couldn't come up with anything else which made sense. The tip had to come from one of us. No one else besides us knew you and Joe had identified

Dillon as the shooter. I was sick. Much as I hated to I—I called Internal Affairs."

"Whoa. And what did those idiots come up with?"

"They did a dump on the phone in that apartment. Got the records early this morning. We hit the place last night at nine-twenty. They found a call going in there at nine-fifteen."

McGuire thought back and remembered Fat Pat hadn't gone on the raid. He'd stayed in the office. "Let me guess what IAD found. The warning phone call came from here, right? Had to be Hanlon. It's why he volunteered to stay. I warned you about the guy. Knew he was a useless piece of shit."

Ramos massaged his throbbing temples. "No, the call didn't come from one of the office phones." He pulled open his desk drawer and removed a yellow legal pad. Very slowly he slid the pad across the desk. McGuire picked it up. A ten-digit phone number was written on it in large numbers.

"You recognize the number?"

"No. Don't know where the 917 exchange is. Ain't the Bronx."

Ramos started to speak and his voice wavered. He stopped and cleared his throat. "It's a cell phone, John. Listed to Joseph Gomez of Riverdale. Your partner made the call."

"No fuckin' way. You gotta be shittin' me. My partner? No fuckin' way." McGuire was on his feet, his voice raised, his face crimson, his arms flailing.

"John, calm down. Take a deep breath. Sit, please."

McGuire sat. "I'm telling you, it's gotta be some kind of goddamned mistake. Maybe he lost his phone and some skell found it. Where is he? Let's ask him."

"IAD grabbed him when he came in this morning, six o'clock. He had the phone on him."

"Where is he? I gotta talk with him."

"I know you guys are close. You do know about his mother-in-law?"

"Yeah, she's got Alzheimer's and moved in with them. Big deal."

"Did you know Joe's wife had to quit her job to care for her mom? He's been strapped for cash for the last few months. It's why he's been taking every overtime tour he can get his hands on, like the presidential visit."

"Okay, I know he's been hurting for money. But, there's a huge difference between hawking OT and selling your badge out to a drug-dealing murdering scumbag. And, how did he make the call? We all went out together. Only Hanlon stayed behind."

"It's what I thought, too. But, then I remembered while we were getting suited up, Joe was still working on the computer. He went back up for his vest as we were going down the stairs. He could have phoned from the locker room. The call only lasted ten seconds."

"Where is he? I wanna speak with him."

"IAD took him to one of their discreet locations. I don't know where."

"Discreet location. You mean they fuckin' kidnapped him."

"John, I did what I had to do."

"I know, Boss. I don't blame you. But I know Joey better than I know my two brothers, and I'm telling you there is no way he made the call. No way. Now I gotta do what I have to do. Can I have the tour off?"

"Why?"

"I'm calling Jack Healy, vice-president of the Detectives Union, and getting him and one of their lawyers on this. When we find out where he is, we'll go get him. Fuck IAD, Joe's got rights. We'll find out what the real story is. Then, we'll come back and wrap up this case for you. Me and my partner. I promise."

"Go ahead. You've got the tour. For God's sake, please be careful. I hope you're right about this."

"Guaranfuckinteed, Sarge. Guaranfuckinteed."

* * *

McGuire went into the office and made two calls. Jack Healy, the union VP, a friend of McGuire's, exploded when he heard the news.

"We don't know where they're holding him," Healy said. "Have they arrested him?"

"I don't know, Jack. They scooped him up here when he came in."

"And he hasn't called anyone? You, the sarge, his wife?"

"He'd call me. I know he wouldn't call his wife and get her upset. I just called his cell phone. No answer."

"They're holding him incommunicado, the bastards. Think our guys have no rights. Hell, a homicide perp is allowed to make three phone calls. This ain't some little shit. Let me make some calls, starting with the Chief of Detectives. Soon as we find out where he is, I'll get back to you."

McGuire looked in his memo book then dialed another number.

"TARU, Detective Kelty."

"Mike, John McGuire. I was praying you were working today. I need to pick your brain about how cell phones work. Can you spare a half hour for me?"

"Got a busy day today, pal. I'm sitting on a Pen Register here, and may have to go out later to work on a tap for narcotics in Brooklyn. How about tomorrow?"

McGuire quickly told Kelty about the Gomez situation.

"Hell, yeah. I'll do whatever you need. Give me ten minutes. My partner will be in. I'll get him to sit on the Pen and give you a call."

"Better yet, I'm coming over. Be there in ten minutes."

McGuire hung up and turned to Crawford. "Ty, I'm running over to the TARU at the fort. If Jack Healy calls, tell him to call me over there. Here's the number."

McGuire got into his car, started to get on the Cross Bronx Expressway heading east and stopped at the onramp. As it was for twenty-three hours most days, the traffic in both directions was at a crawl. Luckily, having worked in the Bronx for years he knew how to get to his destination on the city streets. Fifteen minutes later, he was cruising over the Throgs Neck Bridge heading for Queens. His destination was Fort Totten, an Army base built after the War of 1812 to protect New York Harbor from attack from the Long Island Sound side. It had been decommissioned some time ago. Although it was still home to a number of Army reserve units, it also housed commands from the NYPD and FDNY.

McGuire stopped at the gate, showed his shield, and was waved in. The NYPD's Technical Assistance Response Unit, TARU, had somehow gotten themselves stationed in an old mansion right on the water's edge, looking out over the bridge to the Bronx. Mike Kelty was waiting outside as McGuire parked.

"Welcome to paradise, John."

McGuire shook hands with his friend. He usually took a minute to admire the gorgeous view, but not today.

"Mike, you know how much I know about computers and these new cell phones. I need you to give me some clue on what you think might have happened with Joe."

For a detective to be assigned to TARU, he had to have expertise in one of the fields the unit specialized in. TARU was to the NYPD what Q Branch is to James Bond. While no detective ever left Fort Totten driving an Aston Martin with an ejector passenger seat, the unit came up with pole cameras to look around corners, robots armed with cameras and shotguns, that could climb stairs and search for dangerous felons in cramped apartments, and bullet-proof blankets to be dropped over a window where a shooter was firing.

TARU was filled with cops who, before joining the department, had worked as electricians, plumbers, TV, and radio repairmen or, as in Mike Kelty's case, employed by the phone company. Kelty was the go-to guy for wire taps and any kind of phone surveillance or documentation.

Kelty pointed to a picnic table close to the water. "Not too cold today. Let's sit out here." He pulled a cell phone from his belt.

"Let's start nice and simple, John. What is this?"

"It's a cell phone. I've seen one before. Obviously, Joe has one."

"Correct, it's a cell. But it's also something else. Something you use every day."

McGuire looked puzzled, shook his head.

"Think of the portable radio, the walkie-talkie you have in your car. Cells work similarly. The radio lets you send and receive transmissions over the air, right?"

McGuire nodded as a seagull swooped down to raid a nearby trash can.

"Cells do the same. Messages through the air, no wires needed. Now let me tell you what I bet happened to Joe. For a call to get to a cell phone owner, the service provider has to know where their client is. They need to bounce the call to the cell tower nearest the subscriber."

"How would they know where one guy with a cell is? Lots of people walk around with those things now."

Kelty held up his phone. "Right now NYNEX knows where I am. Not the exact spot, but if a call comes for me, they know to bounce it off the cell tower on top of the bridge." He pointed.

"How do they know?"

"Remember I said a cell was like your portable radio? A cell phone, when it's turned on, transmits a message every seven seconds to the nearest cell tower. It says, 'If any calls come in for me, route them to this tower.' If I get in the car and drive, every seven seconds my phone pings information out, looking for the next tower. It puts out my info: the phone number and another number the phone company can identify the subscriber by."

"I think I follow, but what's this have to do with Joe?"

"It took the bad guys about two weeks to figure out how to steal the information cells are transmitting. Radio Shack sells something like a radar detector, known as a reader. Plucks the number right out of the air."

"What good does it do the bad guys?"

"They get a new phone and program the stolen number into it. Sell it to somebody. It's known as 'Cloning a phone.' Guy gets to make free calls for a month until the subscriber gets his bill. It's a huge business now."

"I never heard of it."

"You will. The drug guys and kidnappers are all over it."

"So we won't be able to do a trap and trace?"

"Exactly. We did a job with Secret Service last week. Russian mob set up a reader in an apartment in Brooklyn, near JFK, overlooking the Belt Parkway. All the limo drivers are getting cells now. They plucked hundreds of numbers each day. Had the reader hooked up to a computer, which could download twenty different numbers into one cell phone. They were selling them for five grand. Called them 'forever phones.' Imagine when we get a kidnapping and the perps make ransom calls from one of them."

"So you think someone cloned Joe's cell?"

Kelty waved to a passing NYPD Harbor launch. He received a blast from its fog horn in return. "Has to be."

"But why would IAD grab him? Don't they know about cloning?"

Kelty shook his head.

"How can I know about cloning now and the geniuses in IAD don't?"

Kelty stood and put his phone back on his belt. He gazed out over the water. "Because you asked, John."

Thirty-Six - Where There's Smoke

McGuire and Kelty walked back into the TARU mansion.

"Thanks for the lesson, Mike. Gotta make a call."

Kelty smiled. "Nobody's here now. Sergeant's coming in later. Use his office." He led McGuire through what had been the mansion's living room, now filled with benches holding radios, cameras, televisions, and row after row of hammers, spools of wire, wire cutters, headphones, alligator clips. The tools of the trade for those assigned to TARU.

He stopped at an oak doorway surrounded by stained glass panels, opened the door, and gestured.

McGuire took two steps in. "Jeez."

Kelty laughed. "This was the library." Walnut shelves stacked with books, a bow window looking out at the water. He pointed to the far wall. "Working fireplace." He opened another door. "Bathroom with tub and shower."

McGuire looked in. "This bathroom is bigger than my sergeant's office."

"Really?"

"Yeah. Ramos says his office is so small he has to go out into the hall to change his mind. If you run into him, don't mention this. He might ask for a transfer to TARU."

"Captain's office upstairs is even bigger." Kelty pointed to a desk. "Phone."

McGuire called the office. Crawford answered. "No word from Gomez, but Jack Healy says to call him."

He made the call. "Jack, McGuire here. Have you found Joe?"

"Not yet. The IAD pricks are playing hardball, but we should hear something soon. Our lawyer just spoke to a chief there and threatened to get a writ of habeas corpus if Joe is not produced within the hour. Has the wife heard anything?"

"Haven't spoken to her. I know Joe would call me before letting Raysa know and upsetting her."

"Pal, you have to think like these IAD guys. Getting his wife upset could be part of their game plan. Puts more pressure on him to cooperate and tell them what they want to hear."

"Tell them what? He hasn't done a fuckin' thing wrong. Joe's an altar boy, for God's sake."

"My guy there says they got him calling a known drug dealer."

"He didn't make that call. His cell phone's been cloned."

"Cloned? What the hell is cloned?"

"It's too complicated to explain, Jack. Keep the pressure on with the lawyers. I'll give the wife a call and see if she's heard anything."

"John, I'd assume IAD has his home phone tapped. You might want to play it safe. Do you know where she is? At home, or does she work?"

"Home. Had to quit her job. Taking care of her mom. She's got Alzheimer's."

"They still live in the Bronx?"

"Yeah, Riverdale."

"I'd drive up and speak to her in person."

"Will do, thanks. Call the squad if you hear anything. They can get me on the air."

McGuire said goodbye, thanked Kelty, got in his car, and headed back over the Throgs Neck to the Bronx. Hitting the inevitable traffic jam on the Cross Bronx, he bailed, taking the Bruckner to the Deegan. Exiting at W. 231 Street brought him to very familiar territory, the Kingsbridge neighborhood.

Stopped for a light on Broadway, he surveyed the intersection, shook his head. There was a bar on each corner. The Piper's Tune and The Borstal Boy on the East side. *They'll be rocking on Paddy's Day*. Across the street, The Liffey and Ehring's.

McGuire's swallowed. His mouth was dry. *Hit the Tune for a quick pint of Guinness*? But, Ehring's, the old-fashioned German restaurant had a lot to offer. McGuire loved their sauerbraten with red cabbage and dumplings. Even better, they kept their beer steins on ice. He could picture Willie, his favorite Ehring's bartender, pulling one from its bed of crushed ice and filling it with the dark, malty Weltenberger Bock. His daydream was interrupted by a blaring horn.

"The light don't get any greener, asshole." The truck driver behind him gently prodded him to move.

He drove across Broadway, up a steep hill, and turned north.

Entering Riverdale, it was as if he was leaving the Bronx, or the Bronx most people thought of when picturing the borough.

As he drove through the most northern part of New York City, the landscape changed dramatically. No projects, no graffiti, no packs of dogs roaming wild, no boarded-up apartment and storefront windows. No bodegas, no OTBs, no cars double parked, and no radios blaring. The other Bronx receded in his rearview mirror. Before him was a town from a different planet. Wide, clean streets, large private homes with immaculate lawns still showing green mid-winter. *I think this is where Leave it to Beaver grew up.*

He roared past Horace Mann and then the Riverdale Country School. Graduate from either, and you were probably on your way to Harvard or Yale. McGuire came to a mansion on Independence Avenue and made the sign of the cross.

He always said a quick prayer when passing the boyhood home of John F. Kennedy.

Just before hitting the Yonkers border, he came to a commercial area on Riverdale Avenue. Two upscale restaurants, a beauty parlor, a dry cleaner, and a funeral home. The Gomez family lived in a walk-up apartment over the cleaner.

McGuire parked and was about to get out when the door leading up to the apartment opened. Joe's wife, Raysa, came out. McGuire sat back in his car. Something was wrong with this picture. *Where's the sick mother she left her job to care for? Why is she dressed like she and Joe are going out to a Broadway play, hair and makeup done, stylish brown leather coat over a conservative black dress?* She was talking into a cell phone and smiling brightly. Obviously, she was not speaking with Joe.

McGuire hunched down in his seat. He'd seen Joe's beat-up Chevy Nova parked at the station house. It was their only car.

Has Raysa called a car service? Or maybe she's going to get picked up by someone. If she's fooling around on Joe, it will kill him.

McGuire suddenly felt nauseated. What he saw next made him feel worse.

Raysa took a key out of her purse and walked toward a parked car. She got in and quickly pulled out. A Budweiser truck delivering to the restaurants had blocked McGuire in. He couldn't catch the plate number. He didn't need to write down the make, model, and color of the car. One didn't see many brand new, bright red, Lexus SC 400 Coupes in the Bronx. Not even in Riverdale.

Thirty-Seven - Decisions

In the car ride back to the Bronx after leaving Bellevue, Gina was quiet. Yolanda drove, talking excitedly about how Anton Jones' information could break the drug homicide cases wide open. "Won't take us long to find out who this Dee character is, Gina. And Gomez. You going to call Internal Affairs, or let Van do it?"

"Don't know."

"This is big. Maybe the call should be made by the District Attorney himself. You know how much Van likes to get involved with cases which lead to major press coverage. He's up for reelection next year, gonna love this."

"I don't know if we're telling Van or IAD anything right now. Relax, Yoli. We have to think on this a little."

"Gina, you're the boss, but I don't see what there is to think about. We've been given information about police corruption."

"By a career criminal drug dealer looking to beat a shooting rap."

"Who we went to see, and asked him what he knew. Now, you don't like what he told us? I don't get it. I don't—oh wait a minute."

She pulled the car into the curb, turned and looked at Gina. "Is all this because Gomez is McGuire's partner? Are you going to put your career on the line because a guy you went out with once might be working with a dirty cop? Gina, Jones didn't say McGuire was on Dee's payroll, only Gomez. McGuire probably has no idea his partner's dirty."

Gina thought back to her visit from the obnoxious Internal Affairs Sergeant Ray Stark and his suspicions about McGuire consorting with drug dealers. He had not mentioned Gomez, only McGuire. She hadn't thought much about it at the time. Criminals frequently claimed a cop was dirty, trying to get back at officers who'd arrested them. But, this was different. The information Anton Jones supplied, coupled with Stark's, had her feeling sick. She took a deep breath, knowing what she had to do.

"Let's get back to the office, Yoli. We have to brief Van right away."

***

Seated at her desk, Gina couldn't keep her gaze from wandering out to the stadium. She and Yoli met with District Attorney Van Jensen and told him about their Proffer with Anton Jones, his information about the killings, and the allegation regarding Gomez. Sure enough, and true to form, he reacted exactly as Yolanda had predicted.

"Great work, ladies. This is huge. Not only will we start making arrests on all the homicides, but we'll take down a dirty cop, too. The papers are going to keep this in the headlines for a month. Excellent."

"Van, you want to make the call to IAD or should I?" Gina asked.

"I'll do it. Go right to the top, Chief of Internal Affairs, Nelson. Want to make sure they can't cover this up. Thank you, ladies. Go get some lunch. Gina, I'll call you later, after I speak with Nelson." Jensen swept from Gina's office.

After a moment of dead air, Yolanda finally broke the uncomfortable silence. "Want to take a walk and get something to eat?" Her concern for her friend was apparent in her words.

"No, I'd better stay here and wait for Van's call."

"Come on, we have time. The fresh air will do you good. What say we take a ride over to Arthur Avenue, get you a nice Italian hero?"

"Thanks, but I'm really not hungry. You go. I'll call you after I speak with Van."

Gina stared at her phone, wishing it would ring, then praying that it wouldn't.

What would she say to McGuire if he called?

She hit the intercom. "Mary. I'm waiting on a call from Van. I don't want to speak to anyone else, okay?"

"Got it, Boss."

Gina played back the last few days in her mind. McGuire had asked her to drop the gun charge against senior citizen Amos Jenkins. He had, of course, been right, she now realized. She'd used the favor to get a dinner invitation from the detective, which led to her finding he was something of a celebrity when they went to Elaine's. The wonderful time there was ruined when he got drunk. The visit from IAD Sergeant Stark, and now the allegation against Gomez. Her head spun. She had not noticed Yolanda enter the office.

She took something out of a large paper bag.

"What have you got there?"

"Went to Sal's. Told him I needed something to cheer you up." She unwrapped a fifteen-inch hero. "The Frank Sinatra, he said it's your favorite."

"I told you I'm not hungry."

“We’ll split it. C’mon. Look, Italian ham, fresh mozzarella, provolone, stuffed red peppers, and mortadella on their great home-baked bread.”

“I don’t know.”

“Sal said to remind you his mortadella is imported from Italy. ‘Not like the Boar’s Head crap some d’udder delis ’round here serve.’” She did a fair Brando Don Vito impression.

Gina laughed and looked at the sandwich. “The mortadella has pistachios and pepper in it.”

“Try a little. You’ll feel better.” Yoli placed half the hero on a paper plate and pushed it across to Gina, along with a Coke, and some napkins.

Gina picked it up and was bringing to her mouth when the intercom squawked.

“That’s Van on line one.”

She put down the sandwich. “Yes, Sir?”

“Spoke to IAD, Chief Nelson. He said he’s had a team working on some unsubstantiated information along the same lines as what you got from Jones today. I told him you would touch base with them and compare notes. Got a pen? Call a Sergeant Ray Stark at—” He gave a number which she didn’t hear.

She hung up and pushed the plate back to Yoli.

Thirty-Eight - Color My World

Pooh Bear Jennings spent Saturday night scouting the headquarters of East Harlem drug kingpin, Raul "Flaco" Carrera. Things had changed since his last visit here.

Flaco's crew was now working out of an apartment building on 116th Street and Pleasant Avenue, an area, which until a year before had been a longtime Italian stronghold.

Fuckin' Eye Talians can't be too happy about this. First they lose most of Little Italy to the Chinks, now they got spics on Pleasant Avenue. He looked south toward a small red building on 114th Street. *When Rao's becomes a bodega it's all over.* There was small chance of it happening, however. Rao's was the Italian restaurant one had to call a year in advance and then still be lucky to get a reservation.

He wrapped up his surveillance at five a.m. The kidnapping of Flaco would be easy.

The drug dealer had grown comfortable since his release from prison and the elimination of his former lieutenant, El Gato. Jennings would report his finding to Dee. They would plan the abduction, meet with the white boys, and work out the fine points. Confident all would go smoothly, he drove home for a few hours' sleep.

Waking at ten a.m., Jennings knew his mother and brother Gerard would be home after going to church. He drove to the Edenwald projects and waited patiently for the always slow elevator. When the door opened, his mother's elderly neighbor, Mrs. Brown, got off.

"How is he, Steven?"

Jennings was puzzled. "How's who, Mrs. Brown?"

"Oh, Steven. I thought you knew. Your brother was beaten up by some thugs down the street. The police came and took your mother to Our Lady of Mercy."

He bolted to his car and drove the short distance to the hospital. There, he found his mother and brother in the emergency room, and a doctor swabbing cuts on Gerard's face.

"Momma, what happened?" He wrapped his arms around her. "Is he all right?"

"Steven, it's all my fault. We got home from church, and I was making breakfast when I saw we needed milk. I've been letting Gerard walk to the corner by himself. He likes being independent."

The doctor turned. "He should be fine, some bumps and bruises, a few small cuts, but nothing major. Want to do a few tests, probably have him out of here in an hour."

Jennings took his brother's hand. "Who did this to you, Gerard?"

"They said I was a creep."

Pooh looked to his mother who motioned for him to step out of the room.

"He came out of the bodega with the milk, and these boys started asking him questions. He had on a baseball hat, and they took it. Juan, the bodega owner, knows Gerard, keeps an eye on him. Thank God, called the police. When

Gerard tried to get his hat back, they hit him, knocked him down. Could have been worse, but they heard the cop car's siren and ran off. The police brought Gerard here, and Officer O'Neal came and got me."

"The cops took him and then got you?" He reared back, incredulous. "Cops don't do that."

"I told you I've been going to the Community Council meetings at the precinct. I met Officer O'Neal there. He's in Community Affairs. We were talking after a meeting, and I mentioned Gerard. Turns out, the officer has a son with similar problems."

"The cop told you–"

"Yes. Invited me to bring your brother to a meeting, which I did. O'Neal and the other cops made a big fuss over Gerard, gave him one of the shoulder patches they wear on their uniform. He put it up on his mirror soon as we got home. We've been back twice. He loves going. They all treat him so well."

"So who do your cop friends think–"

"The Bloods. The gang. We've been hearing at the Community meetings they're here now."

"Yeah Ma, spreadin' from California. Heard they took over a social club on White Plains Road. But, why would they hassle Gerard?"

"He had his Mets hat on which is–"

"Blue, the Crips color. They called him a Crip, not a creep."

"That's what Officer O'Neal said." She shook her head in exasperation. "Steven, I just don't understand."

"Mom, the Bloods and Crips hate each other. Bloods wear red, Crips blue. Edenwald is Bloods' territory. Anybody wearing blue on their turf gets a beating."

"For wearing a hat?"

"It's sick. Guy in Tremont, Willie Morales, brother plays for the Pittsburgh Steelers—"

"Baseball."

"No Ma, professional football. So Willie wore a Steeler's jersey, black and gold. Bloods came up and asked him if he was down with the Latin Kings, Spanish gang."

"Why would—-"

"King's colors. King's colors are black and gold. Willie told them he was no King. They told him to prove it, take the jersey off, and stomp on it. He said no, so they shot him. He's okay." Jennings shrugged. "But he'll never wear a Steeler's jersey anywhere but in Pittsburgh now."

"Lord, have mercy."

"It's a mess, Mom."

They walked back into the room. The doctor placed a bandage over Gerard's right eye. "Not too bad. Doesn't need stitches." He looked at Gerard. "You feeling better, big guy?"

"Yes, thank you, Doctor."

"Okay. I want to take a look at the X-rays we took. Be back in a minute."

The doctor left. Pooh hugged his brother.

"Why did they say I was a creep, Steven?"

"They're the creeps, brother. Bullies. And sometimes creeps and bullies get just what they deserve."

"Steven, let this go. I don't want you doing something stupid." His mother shook her finger.

He moved to her, kissed her gently on top of her head. "Something gonna be done, Ma. Nothing stupid. But, something's gonna be done."

* * *

Pooh Bear cruised down White Plains Road. The street was dark. The elevated subway above kept the road in constant shadow, day or night. He checked his watch—just past midnight. He was beginning to feel nervous. Had he missed the Bloods' social club? Then he heard the noise, the thumping speakers, the bass note coming through his car's closed windows from a block away. As he got closer, his windows actually rattled. The music came from what had been a storefront church, now the Bloods' social club headquarters.

There was little doubt as to who controlled the building. It was painted bright red. The windows were boarded up, and as he drove slowly by, he could make out the Bloods' symbols painted on the wood. A large letter B with an arrow pointing up next to a smaller letter C, arrow pointing down: up Bloods–down Crips. The front door bore the logo CK, meaning "Crip Killa." The El support pillar in front of the club had also been painted red with a series of three white triangular dots. He knew this was the same symbol the Bloods had tattooed on their arms. The dots were supposed to resemble a dog's paw print, a tribute to the greeting Bloods exchanged when meeting a fellow gang member: "Yo, Dog, whazzup?"

Jennings circled the block, returned, and found a dark spot to park with an unobstructed view of the club. Five Bloods stood on the sidewalk passing a bottle. A car pulled up. Four gang members wearing red bandanas got out. Three did the tell-tale adjustment to their waistbands. Jennings knew all too well. *Gotta make sure the gun on your hip is nice and secure, right dog?*

The three escorted the fourth man past the sidewalk drinkers, who parted like the Red Sea upon his approach.

Pooh Bear smiled. "This must be my lucky night."

He had no doubt one of the gang's leaders had just entered the club. *Wonder what his title is? Do they call him Mr. Big Blood, True Blood, Bad Blood?* He started to laugh. *Nah, he has to be The Big Dog.* He shook his head.

These people were unbelievable. They sold drugs. He sold drugs. His crew tried to stay under the cops' radar, wore clothes to blend in. These motherfuckers wore uniforms.

His crew looked for out-of-the-way locations to set up their crack houses, hoping to do business as long as possible before being noticed by the cops. The Bloods might as well have had a damn parade and sent out a freaking press release announcing the opening of their new clubhouse.

"Well, Dogs, hate to rain on your parade but—"

He got out of the car and walked to a nearby phone booth. *This is my lucky night.* Unlike many of the phone booths in the Bronx, this one had a receiver and a dial tone. He put no money in. He dialed three numbers. It rang four times and a woman's voice answered. "Nine-one-one. Operator twenty-seven. What is your emergency?"

He yelled into the phone. "Detective Jenkins-47th Precinct. My partner's been shot! My partner's been shot! Five male blacks with guns, red bandanas. Bloods' club. 2545 White Plains Road."

Operator twenty-seven began to ask a question, and Pooh hung up. Using his handkerchief, he wiped down the phone. He had just reached his car when he heard the sirens. He got inside and closed the door as the first patrol car careened around the corner, lights flashing, siren wailing. It screeched to a stop in front of the club. Two big cops, one white, one black, ran to the door. Guns in one hand, nightsticks in the other.

The Blood standing guard held up a hand. "You got a warrant?"

Whack. Not breaking stride, the black cop brought his stick down on the guard's head. He went down like he'd been shot. The two cops barreled into the club.

"Yeah, Officer, beat him like the fucking dog he is."

Four more marked patrol cars roared up. The cops jumped out, leaving doors open, and raced into the club.

From his position across the street, he could hear bottles breaking and men cursing. It sounded as if a full-blown battle was going on inside.

More cops arrived, and from the numbers on the cars, he knew three different precincts had responded. Some were unmarked cars with cops in plainclothes, some with long hair and beards. Badges swung from chains around their necks.

There came an unbelievably loud air-horn blast as a large Emergency Service truck pulled up. So many police vehicles crowded the street it stopped just past his car. Lights on the big truck lit the entire block. He hunched down in his seat and watched and listened as the two older cops walked to the back of the truck, unlocked the door, and slid it up. Inside he saw weapons of every size and shape.

The younger of the two cops asked his partner, “Whadda ya think, Al?”

Al, who had to be pushing sixty, surveyed the front of the club, now bubbling with cops and bloodied Bloods, some in handcuffs, some still fighting. He looked from the chaos to the weapons rack. “Might be more action, Artie. And it’s probably tight inside there.”

Like a caddie recommending a club to a professional golfer, Artie grabbed a weapon. “Wanna go with the room cleaner?” He held up a semiautomatic sawed-off Remington shotgun.

“That’ll work.” Al took the gun. “You take the MP5, in case we need real firepower.”

Jennings saw the second cop take a machine gun from the rack. They both donned bullet-resistant helmets and walked calmly to the club.

Shit, these dudes are old enough to be grandfathers. This is like another day at the office for them.

A few minutes later, cops came out of the club, dragging and pushing handcuffed prisoners. As they were put into patrol cars, Pooh noticed some of the prisoners were bleeding, mostly from head wounds.

"Hey, now you really are the Bloods. Be sometime before you heroes beat up on a kid just going out to get some milk."

Jennings took one long, satisfying look at the scene before backing down the block. What was this world coming to? Young black men, his brothers, had beaten his real brother and terrorized a neighborhood made up mostly of hard-working blacks and Hispanics. And, who had shown compassion to Gerard? The cops—the fucking cops.

Shit, I don't know what this world is coming to, but I know this. Snatching Flaco will be my last job. Win, lose or draw, I am getting Mom and Gerard out of the Bronx. Out of the Bronx-for good.

Thirty-Nine - No Way

McGuire left Riverdale, slipped back on the Deegan Expressway, and headed south. No matter how he spun what he had just seen, he could make no sense of it. Raysa, going out, her mother not with her, dressed to the nines, cell phone, and the fuckin' car. He kept coming back to it.

If I keep thinking, I might be able to come up with a reason for the other stuff, but the car— Lost in thought, he almost rammed into the rear of a stopped pickup truck. *Why is this jerk stopped in the middle of a highway?*

McGuire threw his auto in park and was about to get out when he saw the reason. They were at the tollbooths for the Triborough Bridge. He had missed the exit for the Cross Bronx Expressway, which would have taken him back to the Four-two. Waiting for a break in the oncoming traffic, he made a totally illegal U-turn and headed back north.

He had driven less than a half mile when a strange noise startled him. He was driving on the cobblestoned shoulder of the road. He continued a short distance until the next exit and got off.

He pulled to the curb, stopped, and took a deep breath. *Enough. I won't be able to figure this out until I talk with Joe.*

It had been some time since he'd checked in with the squad to see if there was any word on his partner. He spotted a gas station on the corner with a phone booth in front. McGuire smiled. Gas stations were busy, less likely someone had used the booth as a urinal. He dialed the squad.

"Four-two squad. Hanlon."

McGuire sighed. This was not his day. He really did not want to talk with Fat Pat.

"Sergeant Ramos, please."

"Who's calling?"

"McGuire. Can I speak with Sergeant Ramos, please?"

"Any luck finding your partner?"

"No. That's why I'm calling. Has anybody heard—"

"Ya got ya cuffs on ya, Johnny Boy?"

McGuire suspected what was coming. "May I speak with the sergeant, please?"

"'Cause when you find your partner, slap the cuffs on that little prick. Coulda got somebody killed the other night. On the take, thieving bastard."

McGuire saw red, but he tried to stay in control. "If anybody was going to get hurt it wasn't gonna be you, was it? Your fat ass never left the office."

"Hey. Don't talk to me like that. I'm a first-grade detective."

That's it. McGuire now screamed into the phone, "You're a first-grade asshole. Now give me the sergeant, you useless, fat—"

The line went dead. McGuire redialed.

"Four-two squad. Detective Crawford."

"Ty, its John. Put Hanlon on."

"No can do. He just walked out."

McGuire took a deep breath, tensed all his muscles and exhaled loudly.

"Ty, have we heard from Joe?"

"I haven't, but hold on. The boss wants to speak with you."

Ramos quickly came on the line. "Anything, John?"

McGuire told Ramos about his visit to the TARU unit and what he'd learned about cell phones.

"So you think it's what happened? Somehow somebody got hold of Joe's cell info. But who? Why? A lot of people are getting those things. Out of all those, your partner just happens to be the unlucky one who gets clomed."

"It's cloned, Sarge."

"Cloned, clomed, whatever. I'm just thinking, what are the odds that somebody in this big city gets Joe's cell info and uses it to call Dee and warn him we're coming?"

McGuire suddenly felt eighty years old. "You gotta be kidding me. You actually think he did it?"

"I'm hoping and praying he didn't. But, I have to look at the possibilities. I spoke to a friend at Internal Affairs. He said they wouldn't be holding him this long if they didn't have a case."

McGuire rested his head against the graffiti-covered glass. "No way." But he felt half the certainty he'd previously had.

"What did Joe's wife have to say?"

"What?" McGuire swallowed hard.

"Jack Healy called to see if we'd heard anything new. Said you were going up to Riverdale."

"Yeah, I did. Nobody home. She must have taken the mother to the doctor or something."

"Just as well. Listen, Ty has a snitch who claims he saw Dee on the Concourse last night around three o'clock.

I'm sending everybody home to grab a few hours' sleep. We're coming back in at midnight. Are you in?"

"I don't know. I—"

"John, there's nothing more to do. Whatever happens with Joe will play out. In the meantime, we're looking for a psycho who snuffed five people. I need you tonight with your head screwed on right."

"Boss, I just want—"

"I want you to go home and get some sleep. See you at midnight."

McGuire let the phone drop from his hand. *Man, I could use a drink.*

He left the phone booth and looked around. He had not been aware of exactly where he had gotten off the highway. Now, he saw he was on the Grand Concourse. He spotted a bodega across the wide street and headed for it. *One Guinness to clear my mind.* He had to stop on the island in the middle of the street to wait for traffic to go by. As he looked to his right, his eyes drifted up the road and came to rest on a large white building. The Bronx Courthouse. *Shit, Gina. I never called her.*

The traffic had stopped, but still he waited. Thoughts ping-ponged through his mind. *The sarge is right. Nothing more I can do about Joe. But, I know I won't be able to sleep if go home. Unless I have a couple of drinks.*

He pushed off and took three steps, heading to the bodega. Halfway there, he stopped again, turned, and walked back toward his auto. Tires screeched as a truck heading to the Deegan swerved around him. He heard the blare of a horn and saw the upraised middle finger of the driver's right hand.

He smiled and raised both hands. "Sorry," he mouthed to the truck driver.

McGuire, you are so messed up.

Forty - See You Again

After her conversation with Internal Affairs Sergeant Stark, Gina had spent the rest of that day, well into the night, locked in meetings with District Attorney Jensen.

The following day, she called Yolanda. “I’m tied up all morning, Yoli. My calendar is clear at noon. Why don’t you—”

“Want me to pick up lunch for us, Gina?”

“Yeah, my office at noon. Get something light. See you then.”

Gina’s secretary came in with papers for her to sign. She lifted her chin toward the stadium. “Pitchers and catchers report today.”

Gina was lost in thought. “What’s that, Mary?”

“Just saying, pitchers and catchers today.”

Gina flashed a quizzical look.

“Hello. Yankees, spring training down in Tampa. Today’s the day—”

“Oh. I’m sorry my mind was on something else. Yes, pitchers and catchers report.” She turned to the window. “Won’t be long now.”

“Home opener, April fifteenth, White Sox. Think Van will get us tickets?”

Gina stared out the window without hearing her secretary's question. Suddenly she snapped back and turned. "What?"

"Just said I have two requests for subpoenas you have to review and sign." Mary dropped the requests on the desk and left.

Gina spent the morning shuffling papers, not able to concentrate, getting nothing done.

She was relieved when Yolanda entered the office at noon carrying two paper bags. "What'd you get us?"

"Sal's. Got—"

"Sal's? I said something light."

"Relax, Boss. He took some of the dough out of the bread."

Gina started to unwrap her sandwich. "You didn't get the mortadella, I hope."

"No. Just ham, salami, and provolone. Light, like you asked."

"You're killing me, Yoli."

Yoli set the wrapped sandwiches and sodas on the desk. They began to eat.

"So, what's Van's game plan with our corruption allegations, Gina?"

"Like you'd expect with an election coming up. Full throttle, wants indictments, press, the whole nine yards."

"It's a little early to start talking indictments, no?"

"Exactly. It's why I was here till almost midnight with him. Had to keep reiterating, 'Go slow, go slow. This thing could blow up in your face if we don't get it right.'"

"And, he agreed?"

"Finally, after I hit him with one of his favorite sayings. 'Let the evidence make the case.'"

"Not the case make the evidence." Yoli nodded.

Gina took a bite of her sandwich and brought a Coke to her lips.

"How did your conversation with Sergeant Stark go?" Yoli asked

Gina put the soda down, shook her head. "The man is repulsive. Has no social skills. I started to tell him Jones' allegations about Gomez, and all he wanted to talk about was McGuire. He's obsessed with him. I think the only reason he even listened about Gomez was he hoped it might help him take down McGuire."

"Wonder why."

"So did I. Made some calls. Spoke to Detective Thornton Mackie up in the Four-seven squad where Stark worked for a short time before going to IAB."

"Thorn Mackie? Great cop. Cute, too. What did he say about Stark?"

Gina opened her desk, took out a legal pad. "Was so good I had to write it down."

"Can't wait. Thorn can be pretty blunt. Did you know he's also a writer?"

Gina wiped her lips with a napkin. "Doesn't surprise me. He's quite literary. Ready?"

Yoli sat back in her chair and smiled. "Shoot."

Gina cleared her throat and began reading her notes. "In answer to my question: What kind of guy is Sergeant Stark? Thorn replied, 'Stark is a moron of the highest order. He could be a good detective sergeant except he lacks any investigative, administrative, legal, or supervisory skills. The man cannot count his balls twice and come up with the same answer. His assignment to Bronx Detectives undoubtedly left the village upstate, where he lives, bereft of its idiot.'"

Yoli laughed. "Told you Thorn was something. Can't wait for his book to come out."

"He's good. And, when I got him to be serious, he told me McGuire had a run-in with Stark a few months ago. Embarrassed him. One of the reasons Stark bailed from Bronx Detectives and volunteered for IAB."

"You think this is Stark's way of getting back?"

"If you spoke to him you'd have to assume so."

"Doesn't put McGuire in the clear." Yoli took a sip of her soda.

"Doesn't make him guilty either. Remember, we have no allegation against McGuire other than Stark's. Anton Jones only mentioned Gomez."

"Gina, they're partners."

"Yolanda, didn't Fordham Law School teach you about the dangers of guilt by association?"

"They did. But they also taught me where there's smoke—"

"Hello. Anybody home?" The voice came from the outer office. Gina looked at the clock. Mary had gone out to lunch.

McGuire entered, a small bouquet of flowers of the type one typically found in a Korean deli in hand. "Good afternoon, Ladies."

Upon seeing McGuire, Yoli swallowed her Coke and wrapped the remains of her sandwich. "Hi, Detective. Boss, I'll get right on those search warrants you want." Three seconds later she was gone.

McGuire stood awkwardly in front of Gina's desk, shifting from foot to foot.

Gina rose. Her mind was in overdrive. *What should I do? Legally, knowing he's a subject of an ongoing investigation, I shouldn't speak with him. But, if I tell him we can't talk, it will alert him that something besides our personal problem is going on.*

She decided to keep it short. Let him say what he came to say and leave.

She sat. “What can I do for you, Detective?”

McGuire started to sit in the chair Yoli had vacated, then apparently realized he hadn’t been asked to and stopped. “Gina, I had to come in person. Didn’t want to do this over the phone. I can’t tell you how sorry I am. It’s just I—”

“Drank too much. Are you going to cop the plea?”

“Well, it’s part of it. I—”

“So what are you apologizing for? Do you even remember how the night ended?”

“It’s the reason I’m here. I know I kind of bailed on you.”

Gina was on her feet. “Kind of bailed on me? You made a choice. Keith Hernandez was more important to you than me.”

“Gina. I’m sorry. I blame the booze.”

“You do it a lot?”

“What?”

“Blame the booze. Yeah, it was Ted the bartender’s fault. He poured all those drinks down your throat. John’s not at fault for ruining a wonderful evening. Let’s put the blame where it belongs: the Guinness Company for bringing their delicious stout from Ireland into this country.”

Gina saw McGuire’s eyes begin to fill up. The big man suddenly looked like an ashamed little boy.

“Sit down, John, please.”

He sat, crushing the flowers in his hands.

Gina looked at them. “You hit up the Botanical Garden on your way here?”

“I, um, they’re for you.” He handed the bouquet to Gina. She took them and said something about finding a vase. She turned and looked through a filing cabinet, stalling, giving her time to think. *My God, this is a complicated man. Complicated, but interesting.*

"Gina, I'm sorry. If you give me another chance, I swear to God you'll see I'm a good guy."

Despite what had taken place, she wanted to see McGuire again. His actions on behalf of Amos Jenkins after his weapons possession arrest marked him as kind and caring. His drinking was a problem, but a problem could be worked on. However, with the cloud hanging over him and Gomez, she knew now wasn't the time for a second date. She'd have to wait and see how it all played out.

"Gina, can we try again? Maybe dinner and a movie."

"John, perhaps we can do coffee sometime, but not anytime soon. I'm starting a homicide trial tomorrow, going to last at least three weeks." She hated to lie.

"When can I call you?"

"How about the first week in April? I should have some time by then."

"Whatever you say, Gina. April. Maybe we could catch a Yankee game?" He stood and walked out the door, stopped and turned. "Today is—"

"Pitchers and catchers." She closed the door behind him.

Forty-One - Parade-No Rest

McGuire went home. He flopped down on his worn-out once-red couch and tried to sleep but could not. He couldn't quiet his mind.

Images of his wife, Cathy, and of Gina competed for space in his head. When he was able to clear them, Joe's face took center stage.

He shook his head, got up, and stretched. He began to do breathing exercises he'd learned in his martial arts training. Inhaling through one nostril, exhaling from the other. Tensing then relaxing the muscle groups throughout his body. Picturing his instructor, Sensei Akimoto, in the dojo instructing him on real life self-defense.

"When confronted, do not think. Deep breath. *Mushin*—no mind. Do not anticipate. React. Brain gets in the way. Rely on training, reflex."

With his mind clear, he lay down again. He continued the controlled breathing, filling his lungs, watching his belly rise and fall. He began to relax. His eyelids felt very heavy. He looked down at his hands. They were covered with blood.

He jumped to his feet and looked again. No blood. He realized he must have nodded off. Somehow Javier Boren, the young boy shot in the bodega, whose life McGuire had saved by rushing him to the hospital, had made an appearance.

He tried once more to quiet his mind, to get some rest, but it was too late. Javier Boren had opened the gates of hell. The parade had begun.

Deep breath, Mushin. Shit.

Timmy Herlihy, ten years old. Cut almost in half when his new stepbrother was showing him around the house and found the "unloaded" shotgun in the closet. Twelve years ago, when McGuire and Gomez were still uniformed cops in the Six-nine precinct. They'd gotten the call, child shot, and rushed to the house in Canarsie. En route, the dispatcher told them the nearest ambulance was ten minutes away.

When they hit the right block, they didn't have to look for an address. Five women stood in front, all with one hand pointing, the other covering their mouths.

Before Gomez stopped, McGuire was out, sprinting up the steps. He pushed his way through a crowd and knelt beside the boy.

Gomez had come in, clearing the hall of everyone except the next-door neighbor off-duty cop, anticipating McGuire scooping up the victim and running back to the car with him in his arms. The hall was clear. Gomez waited. McGuire remained kneeling over the boy.

"John?" Gomez called.

McGuire looked over his shoulder. He didn't have to speak. Gomez understood there was a major problem.

"Joe, backboard, stretcher, something to put him on."

Gomez looked around. He pulled a tool from his gun belt, looked at the cop neighbor and pointed. "Door."

In a matter of seconds, which seemed like hours, they were able to pull the pins from the closet door's hinges and slide it next to the boy.

Gomez's eyes grew large as he realized why his partner had not picked up the boy. The close-range shotgun blast had ripped his midsection apart. Intestines, ripped flesh, and what he guessed was food spilled out. Surprisingly, there was very little blood. McGuire had been afraid the child would break in half if he lifted him under the knees and shoulders.

He looked to the neighbor. "What's his name?"

"Timmy."

He looked down into Timmy's face. Blonde hair, blue eyes, freckles. The child showed no pain, incredibly, still breathing. His mouth opened and closed like a fish.

"Timmy, you're doing great. I have to move you a little now, so stay with me, buddy, okay?"

The blue eyes looked up and the lips continued their movement.

They got the child on the door and out of the house. They needed to leave both back doors open to fit the door into their car. As they did this, Gomez jumped behind the wheel.

McGuire somehow got one leg over Timmy in the back seat. "Two minutes is all we need. Keep breathing, buddy."

Gomez raced to the hospital with lights and siren. They pulled up to Brookdale's emergency room. A nurse and orderly waited with a gurney, loaded Timmy onto it, and headed quickly into the Emergency Room.

They washed up in the ER men's room. McGuire took a handful of paper towels, wet them and began to clean the front of his uniform pants and leather jacket. The jacket cleaned easily. The pants were absorbing a white granular material.

Gomez pointed at his partner. "John. What is that?"

McGuire shook his head. "I'm guessing oatmeal."

They walked back and stood outside the operating room. A large man, who looked distraught, came in, spotted McGuire, and rushed over. "Is he going to be okay, Officer?"

McGuire guessed but asked anyway. "Who are you, Sir?"

"Timmy's father. Tim Herlihy." McGuire heard Galway in his speech.

He put his hand on the man's shoulder. "All I can tell you, Sir, is he was breathing on his own. But, he's hurt bad."

Herlihy put his hands to his face and began to pray. McGuire looked at those hands, big as catchers' mitts, rough and calloused. Those hands could knock a man out with a slap. Now they shook uncontrollably.

Galway man. Looks like a bricklayer.

The door opened. A tall, thin, black doctor came out. He looked at McGuire, who nodded to his right. "This is his father."

The doctor took one of the elder Herlihy's hands in both of his. "We did all we could—" The rest of his message was lost to Timothy Herlihy Senior's anguished wail. The sound would stay with McGuire for the rest of his years.

***

McGuire got off the couch. There would be no sleep. He knew the order. Timmy would be followed by Shavon Sherman, a pretty thirteen-year-old black girl, thrown off the roof of the Glenwood Houses when she refused to suck her twenty-year-old junkie cousin's dick.

Next up would be James Tyler, male, black, sixteen. His crime? An honor student, he wouldn't join the Brownsville Bangers, the gang which ran the Pink House projects where he lived. The Bangers could not let punks like James diss them. They would lose their street cred. Five Bangers forced James to the project's roof where they beat him, doused him with gasoline, and lit it as they pushed him into the elevator shaft. McGuire had found him on top of the elevator, his body still smoking.

No, there would be no sleep. McGuire had seen hundreds of dead bodies. Mostly men, mostly black, shot, stabbed, beaten to death. He had developed the hardness one who deals with death needs in order to go to work every day. But, like most cops, it was the kids. The kids stayed with you forever.

Sorry, Sensei. Mushin *not working today. Have to try a run on the beach.*

McGuire changed into sweatpants and a sweatshirt. He laced up his sneakers, pulled on a dark blue NYPD football jacket, a baseball cap, and headed out.

He slowly jogged the one short block to the ocean. The weather was typical of March in New York, cold, raw, and windy. McGuire liked it. Small chance he would run into anyone he knew. When he hit the beach, he picked up his pace. It felt good to push himself, running into the wind, the waves breaking ten feet to his right, feeling his heart pumping, his mind finally clear.

When he saw Chauncey's, a beachfront bar that he frequented, he slowed. He knew he had done two miles at a decent pace. Chauncey's looked warm and inviting. No matter, he turned and began the run home. Aided now by the wind at his back, he pushed himself. Completely out of breath, he opened the door to his basement apartment.

Four miles and I'm sucking wind? I gotta get back into shape.

He walked to the bedroom and stopped at the dresser. His goldfish bowl sat on top. He grabbed the tin of fish food and sprinkled a pinch on the water. His lonely goldfish gulped down the flakes.

"Sorry, Clubber. I gotta start taking better care of you. Soon as I find Joey, lock this psycho Dee's ass up, figure out what the hell I'm doing with Gina. And—"

He opened a drawer under the dresser. He looked down at a photo in a large silver frame. Cathy and his wedding picture. He quickly shut the drawer.

Damn, I'm thirsty.

He walked into the kitchen, opened the refrigerator, reached down and grabbed a plastic bottle of Gatorade. As he brought it up, he knew something was wrong, it felt very light. He shook the bottle. Silence.

What kind of asshole puts an empty bottle back in the fridge?

The answer to the question came quickly to McGuire, who lived alone.

He tossed the bottle into the trash, reopened the door, and squatted down. On the bottom shelf, four one-pint cans of Guinness Stout. He looked at the clock. Five. Seven hours until he had to report. He reached in and picked one up.

Forty-Two - Point of No Return

McGuire woke to the blaring ring of his telephone. He reached over his head and plucked it from the end table.

"Yeah."

"John, Sergeant Ramos. You okay?"

"Yeah. I was asleep."

"Glad to hear it. Listen, I decided to bring in the team a little early. We might catch Dee on his way out for the night. Can you get here by ten?"

McGuire looked at his watch. Eight-ten p.m. "No problem, Boss. I'll jump in the shower and head in."

"Great. When you get here, I have some good news for you."

"What kind of good news?"

"Don't want to talk on the phone. See you when you get here."

McGuire put the receiver down and headed to his bathroom. He almost tripped over something on the floor. He bent down and picked up a can of Guinness Stout, unopened. He remembered sitting on the couch, his fingernail playing with the pop top, reading the label. "Guinness Extra Stout. Traditionally Brewed. 1759 St.

James Gate, Dublin." He didn't know why it remained unopened but was glad it had. One was too many, and a hundred wasn't enough.

He showered and made it to the Four-two at nine-fifty. He had driven faster than normal, wondering about the good news Ramos had mentioned.

McGuire found a parking spot around the corner and was walking toward the precinct when he heard his name called. He froze. His hand went to the gun on his belt as he tried to track where the voice came from.

He sensed movement in a dark doorway across the street. McGuire approached cautiously, using a parked telephone company van as cover. A solitary figure leaned out cautiously.

Joe Gomez.

McGuire rushed over and picked Gomez off the ground in a bear hug. "Joe, I've been looking all over for you. Where? When did you—"

"John." Gomez grabbed his partner and forcibly pulled him into the darkened doorway. "Be quiet for a second. We don't have much time."

"Time for what? Was your cell phone cloned? Mike Kelty at TARU told me—"

"John, real quick." Gomez's eyes darted up and down the street. "Yeah, my cell was cloned. IAD questioned me at one of their locations in Greenpoint. I couldn't get through to them about the whole cloning thing."

"Mike Kelty could have—"

Gomez put his finger to his lips. "He did. Showed up about five hours ago. Somebody pulled some strings with IAD, and they agreed to listen to him."

"Probably Jack Healy."

"Kelty gave them step-by-step, how a cell works, how numbers can be intercepted and reused. Cloned."

"Yeah, I got the same lesson."

"He told me. Thanks for getting him involved. He saved the day. Mike also explained how one can track the general location where a cell is making or receiving a call."

"Something about towers."

"Exactly." Gomez again scanned the street. "So, Mike calls a contact at the phone company. They run the phone and discover a lot of activity near here and a number of calls bouncing off a cell tower in—"

A car came down the block and pulled into a spot near McGuire's. The door of the new Lincoln Town Car opened, and a large man got out. Gomez brought his right hand to his mouth and whispered into a small microphone protruding from his sleeve, "Positive ID. It's him."

McGuire was totally puzzled. "Who you talking to? Cell tower where?"

Gomez placed a hand on McGuire's chest and gently pushed him deeper into the doorway. "Cell tower in Goshen."

"Goshen?" McGuire recognized the man getting out of the car as Fat Pat. "Fucking Hanlon." He pulled away from Gomez's grasp. "I'll break his fuckin' jaw."

Gomez put more pressure on McGuire's chest. "Wait. Quiet."

Hanlon walked toward them. As he passed the telephone company van, its doors flew open and three men jumped out. All wore blue nylon NYPD raid jackets, had badges around their necks and guns in their hands.

"Police. Don't move," one of the men shouted.

Hanlon looked over his shoulder. "IAD?"

"Yeah."

Hanlon raised both hands. He was frisked. His gun and badge were taken, and he was handcuffed.

McGuire and Gomez stepped out of the doorway. Hanlon saw them. "You. You set me up, McGuire? Fuck you and your spic partner."

Gomez took a step.

McGuire grabbed his arm to stop him. "Hey Pat, I'm sure all the boys upstate in Attica are going to be real impressed having a gen-u-ine first grade detective joining them." McGuire was unable to resist the taunt.

"Eat shit and die, McGuire."

"Pat, one little tip. In the shower up there, you might want to get 'Soap on a Rope.' If you drop it, do not bend over to pick it up."

Hanlon's response, a string of curses, stopped when an unmarked van pulled up. Two of the IAD detectives pushed him into it. They also got in, and the van took off. The remaining IAD man approached Gomez with his hand extended.

McGuire recognized his old nemesis, Sergeant Ray Stark. "I'm sorry for all we put you through, Detective Gomez."

Gomez shook his hand. "It all worked out. Thanks for listening to Mike Kelty."

McGuire, grateful his partner had been cleared, extended his hand.

Stark ignored it.

"I might not be done with you yet, McGuire." He turned to leave.

The warm feeling McGuire'd had a second before vanished.

"Hey, before you get back to me, why don't you learn how to do an investigation and not roust any more innocent detectives."

Stark spun around, his comb over now stood straight up.

"Oh, I know how to do an investigation." Stark sneered. "You still banging the cute ADA, wise guy?"

McGuire was stunned. How would this creep know about Gina? Speechless for a few seconds, he recovered quickly. "Only when your mom is too busy servicing the fleet."

Stark's face turned bright red. "One of these days, McGuire. I'll enjoy putting the cuffs on you. Just a matter of time."

***

McGuire and Gomez entered the squad to applause from their team. Sergeant Ramos, Angelo Cutrone, Ty Crawford all witnessed Hanlon's takedown from the squad's second floor windows. Gomez was hugged, high fived, hair mussed, and back slapped until he finally was able to take a seat.

"Thanks guys, and *muchas gracias* to my partner." Gomez looked at McGuire. "I knew he wouldn't give up. You guys know I would never take a dime."

McGuire and Ramos shared a nervous smile.

"All's well that ends well." Ramos nodded. "They must have a lot on Hanlon to take him down the way they did."

"They have plenty." Gomez looked around the room. "I heard everything IAD found, once Mike Kelty convinced them I wasn't their guy. Began with calls on the cloned phone bouncing off the towers in Goshen. It's when they started looking at Hanlon. They did financials. Jerk deposited two thousand in cash the first week every month into his own account."

Ramos shook his head. "Unbelievable. How could a first-grade detective not know it would be checked?"

"You forget," McGuire said. "He's a first grader who never worked a case. Glorified chauffeur."

"But, he's only been here for a few weeks. Working for Dee? How could he have—"

"Don't forget, Sarge, we got him from the Four-six. He was in the squad there for six months after getting bounced from Intel."

Ramos snapped his fingers. "And the Four-six covers—"

"The crack house Dillon ran on Tiebout Avenue—until it got the shit shot out of it by the Domos in retaliation for their four guys Dee whacked in the Butler Houses' parking lot." McGuire snapped his fingers back at the sarge.

"Now it's starting to make sense." Ramos lifted his coffee cup. He took a long swallow. "Let's forget about Hanlon now. Not our problem. We have a psychotic killer to find. Let's go into the lunch—I mean War Room—to talk about tonight."

They filed into the small room, now even more cluttered than usual.

Three easels lined the wall. One held a large blowup of Dillon's latest arrest mug shot. The second was covered with the names, addresses, and pictures of anyone he had ever been arrested with. The third held a large map of the Bronx. It indicated all the places Dee or his associates had lived or been arrested. All were highlighted in yellow. The three locations where Dillon was identified as a shooter, were circled in red: the Butler Houses parking lot where the four Dominicans were killed, the bodega on Tremont Ave where Javier Boren had been wounded, and Ferry Point Park where Rontal Cheery's body had been found. Dillon's crack house on Tiebout Avenue, where Marvin Williams was shot dead and Ramon Vega's beheaded body found, was highlighted in pink.

Joe Gomez stepped back and smiled. The making of charts and maps was something he usually did. "Very nice. Who did all this?"

Ty Crawford cleared his throat. "Uh, that was me, Joe. We didn't know how long you'd be gone, so the boss asked me to do it."

Over the team's laughter, McGuire said, "And a great job you did, Ty." He looked at Ramos. "Sarge, seems like our football player, fresh out of narcotics, is becoming a real detective."

Clearly embarrassed, Crawford looked down. "With a lot of help from you guys."

They heard a knock, and two cops entered the room. One was a very large black man in uniform, the other a smaller white man in plainclothes.

"C'mon in, men." Ramos turned to the others. "The precinct's lending us two of their best tonight. Does everyone know Officers Washington and Kelly?"

McGuire high fived the black man. "Yo, Wash. Hey, Kel." He turned to Angelo Cutrone, the detective on loan from the Housing Police. "Ang, say hello to the team the skells refer to as Mr. Salt and Mr. Pepper. Best cops in the Four-two."

Angelo stood and with a sly smile shook the black officer's hand. "Nice to meet you, Mr. Salt."

The room cracked up.

"Boss, why's Pep in the bag?" McGuire pointed at Washington's uniform.

"'Cause we're looking for Dwayne Dillon, AKA Dee, male, black, six-four, 250. Pep's built along the same lines. I don't want any mistaken identity, friendly fire shit. Besides, it's always good to have a uniform along if things get hairy."

McGuire nodded. "And it's why you da boss. Also good when the guy in uniform looks like a Coke machine with a head."

"All right, grab some coffee and listen up." Ramos gestured toward the chairs.

When all were seated, he began. "We have five hundred mug shots of Dee. Load up on them and feel free to spread them around. Crawford, Cutrone."

"Yes, Sir."

"Ty, stop at Bronx Narco, drop some pictures. I spoke to the captain there. They're putting all their teams out tonight to do 'buy and busts.' All arrests will be brought here. I want you and Angelo ready to respond and debrief anyone who might have info. Angelo, hit the Housing precincts. Drop photos, let them know to get hold of you with any collars."

"Yes, Sir."

"John, you and Joe check all the locations where Dee's been seen in the past. Press your street contacts. Never know who might have seen him. I'm riding with Salt and Pepper. I want two guns and vests on everyone. If you see Dee on the street, do not attempt to take him down until you have backup. If we find him indoors, we get Emergency Service with their heavy weapons. Remember, this guy has already killed five people we know of. Any questions?"

The room was silent. The earlier levity was gone.

Ramos clapped his hands together. "Okay, guys. Time to rock and roll. Let's be safe out there and get this guy collared. *Vaya con dios.*"

***

McGuire and Gomez got into their beat-up Crown Vic. McGuire drove as Gomez arranged copies of the maps showing Dee's previous locations on his lap.

"Where did you want to start, John?"

"How about Hunts Point Markets?"

Gomez looked at the map. "He's never lived or been collared near there."

McGuire eased the car onto the Bruckner Expressway. "We'll go over and talk to the girls working there. They may know something."

"Good thinking. All the hookers there are crackheads. Might have seen Dee in a crack house somewhere."

The Hunts Point Market was the largest wholesale produce market in the world. Covering 113 acres in the South Bronx, it provided seventy-five percent of all the fruit and vegetables sold in the tri-state area. It employed over ten thousand people and was open from Sunday night to Friday afternoon twenty-four hours a day. A city within itself, the constant steam of trucks coming and going made it a very popular spot for ladies of the night to ply the world's oldest profession. A truck would pull in, the driver would be approached, a deal struck, the prostitute would climb into the cab and service the driver. Some were working girls, some were men, and some were caught somewhere in between. The crack scourge had hit the trade hard. Very few could have made a living at their profession anywhere but the market.

As they drove, Gomez filled in his partner on all the events since he'd been picked up by Internal Affairs. How Kelty's arrival and lesson on cell phones had shifted the IAD spotlight from him onto Hanlon.

McGuire listened patiently, waiting for the right moment to ask the questions he had to ask. He was nervous about confronting his partner with what he'd observed in Riverdale. As they approached the market on Edgewater Road, he decided to act.

"Joe, did you and Raysa get a new car?"

Gomez pointed to four women standing on the next corner. "New car? You kidding me? We don't have a pot to shit in."

As they rolled up, the group spotted the unmarked police car and began to walk away. McGuire tapped the siren twice, stuck his hand out the window, and motioned for them to come over.

As the girls slowly walked toward them, Gomez shook his head. "Can you believe guys horny enough to pay one of these poor creatures for sex? Why'd you ask about a new car?"

The women, two black, two Hispanic, stopped ten feet from the car.

"Ladies, come here," McGuire called out. "We're not Public Morals. We just want to ask a few questions."

The six foot, two-hundred-pound black woman, who was definitely the leader of the pack, tugged down her silver hot pants and adjusted her purple tank top. "C'mon girls, let's see what Handsome wants."

"What's your name?" McGuire addressed her.

"Audrey."

"Audrey, it's too cold out for you to be parading around in that little outfit."

"Officer, the truckers gots to see what they're getting." Audrey leaned down into the open window and gave the cops a look at her breasts. "You do know it pays to advertise."

"You're advertising more than they need to see, Audrey." McGuire saw the bewildered look on her face. He pointed to her hot pants. "You might wanna tuck your balls back in."

All the girls roared with laughter as Audrey made the necessary adjustments. "It's my next operation, Officer."

Gomez handed McGuire the wanted photos. McGuire passed them to the women.

Audrey took one look and gasped. "I seen this motherfucker. He comes down here, uses a girl, and when she asks to get paid, he beats the shit out of her. Broke my friend Alice's nose."

"When did it happen?" McGuire asked.

"Maybe two months ago."

McGuire grabbed another stack of pictures and gave them to Audrey along with a number of his and Gomez's business cards. "Give these to the other girls. Tell them if they want this guy to stop hurting them, call us the next time he shows up down here. Okay?"

As they pulled away, McGuire shook his head. "What a life. You have to feel sorry for them."

Gomez agreed, and mumbled, "New car?"

"We should stop at Public Morals, drop some photos and ask them to debrief any of the girls they collar."

"Good idea. New car?"

McGuire pulled to the side of the road, turned, and faced his partner.

"Joe, I drove up to Riverdale looking for you. I saw Raysa, dressed to kill, getting behind the wheel of a shiny new Lexus. I know she had to quit her job to take care of her mom. So I—"

Gomez choked, then started to laugh. "John, you didn't think I was on the take, did you?"

"Never, Joey, I know you better than that. I just couldn't figure out—"

"Remember Raysa's younger sister, Sophia?"

"Of course. Absolute knockout. Works on Wall Street."

"Worked on Wall Street. She snagged one of the partners from the firm. Moved in with him up in his estate in Bedford Hills. The Lexus was her moving in gift."

"I didn't see her."

"She drove down to watch Mom so Raysa could go out on a job interview."

"Job?"

"Yeah, Sophia talked Mr. Moneybags into popping for a nurse to watch Mom. They're setting up a room for her in their house. We're moving her up next week. So Raysa's in the job market again."

"You never said anything."

"It all just fell into place. Mr. Big wants to marry Sophia. Had to make her happy."

"You happy?"

"Yeah, God is good. Sophia solved one problem. You and Kelty took care of the IAD mix up. Now if we could just bag this Dee prick—"

McGuire gunned the car back onto the Bruckner. "Let's do it tonight, Partner."

They spent the balance of the night hitting all of Dee's known hangouts but came up empty. Dee, Pooh Bear, and the white boys were not in the Bronx.

Forty-Three - The Last Job

Raul "Flaco" Carrera sat at a desk in his second-floor office, which overlooked 116th Street. One floor below him, in El Ponce Bodega, the supermarket he owned, business was booming. His second in command, Juan Oliva, entered the office carrying a gray canvas bag. He dropped it on the desk.

Flaco looked up. "*Cuanto*?"

"Fourteen grand, *Jefe*. Ten from our thing, and four from the bodega."

Flaco looked into the bag and smiled. "Four thousand dollars in one day?"

"*Si. El mercado* is very busy. You were right about the hood needing a big, clean store."

"Our people are moving in. The Italians are moving out. It made sense, and it gives us a great cover. Plenty of people coming and going all hours. The cops watch the place. What do they see? Women buying baby food and Pampers, old men cigarettes and *cerveza*."

"We could expand, maybe one day get out of the drug business."

"Never. I worked in my uncle's bodega for two years when I first came here. He worked twenty-hour days, hoped whoever was covering the store while he slept wasn't robbing him blind. Not a life for me."

Flaco looked at the clock. "See, Juan, it's a little after midnight." He stood. "And, I'm going home." He picked up the bag. "The four grand goes downstairs in the safe. El Ponce is legit. We'll declare this money and pay the tax. I don't fuck with the IRS. It's what brought the great Italian gangster Al Capone down."

"Al who, *Jefe*?"

Flaco was about to answer when the sound of heavy footsteps coming quickly up the stairs caught his attention. He glanced at one of his security monitors and saw two white men. The money went into the desk's top drawer just before the very large men, with badges hanging from their necks, barged in.

One of the men pointed his nine millimeter Ruger at Flaco. "Police. Nobody moves."

The other man quickly frisked them. "They're clean."

"They gotta have guns close by."

"Officers, I run a nice business. I do not need a gun." Flaco smiled.

"Yes." Juan joined in. "We are businessmen. This is police harassment. I want both of your badge numbers."

The cop holding the gun smirked at his hulking partner. "Give the man your badge number, Vinny."

"Vinny" held up the badge which dangled from a silver chain around his neck.

"I can't see the numbers," Juan said.

"I'll write them down for you so you don't forget them."

Like a cat, Vinny sprang. He grabbed Juan by the neck with one hand and pinned his head against a wall. Holding his badge in his right hand, he drove it into Juan's forehead, again and again. Vinny put all of his many pounds into it, and the badge ripped into the flesh of Juan's face like a blade.

Flaco could tell Juan was trying to scream, but the cop's big hand crushed his windpipe and made it impossible.

Flaco froze with fear. He looked at the cop with the ponytail holding the gun on him.

Ponytail shrugged. "Guess he couldn't find a pen."

Vinny dropped the badge and hit Juan with a powerful right hook, which knocked him out.

As Juan slumped to the floor, bleeding heavily, Vinny turned to Flaco. "When he wakes up, all he has to do is look in a mirror. My badge number is tattooed on his forehead."

"Officers, I told you. I, I am legit. I have no gun. This is some kind of, of mistake. Perhaps I could offer you something?" Flaco's trembling hand began to open the drawer holding the bag.

Vinny quickly slammed the drawer shut with his knee as he put all his weight on Flaco's head, pinning it to the desk.

Flaco cried out in pain as his fingers were crushed.

Ponytail tapped Vinny's leg as he grabbed Flaco's wrist.

"Ease up, Vinny."

Vinny moved his leg. Flaco brought his injured fingers to his mouth.

Ponytail pulled the drawer open, brought the bag out, looked in, and whistled. "How much?"

"Fourteen thousand. It's yours if you let me go."

Ponytail flipped the bag to Vinny, brought both of Flaco's hands behind his back and cuffed him.

"And it's ours if we don't let you go." He dragged Flaco to the door. "Comin' down, Ski," the man yelled to alert a third man who guarded the ground floor door.

"Vinny, put the bag under your coat. Go right to our car. Ski, grab an arm."

The cops hustled Flaco out of the store before any of the customers or workers knew what was happening. At the curb, a dark blue Ford van sat behind the fake cops' black Ford Crown Victoria.

A black man opened the van's back door as the group approached. The two cops, without breaking stride, tossed Flaco into the van like a sack of garbage and continued to their car, barely getting in before it accelerated up First Avenue.

The black man jumped behind the wheel of the van and turned east on 116th Street, heading for the FDR Drive. In the rear, Flaco got to his knees. "Officers, I beg you. Let me go. I know nothing about guns."

The big black man in the passenger seat let out a low rumble of a laugh as he turned. "You must know something about guns, you skinny spic. Less you expects us to believe your boy, El Gato, shot his self. Not likely. Be a very special man who could shoot his self-ten fuckin' times."

Flaco looked into the big man's eyes and began to cry. "You, you're not cops."

The big man smiled, thumb up, forefinger pointing at Flaco. "Bingo." He made a popping sound as his thumb came down.

***

Jennings headed north on the FDR Drive, entered the Bronx at the Willis Avenue Bridge, then drove north on the Major Deegan Expressway. Exiting at 155th Street, they passed Yankee Stadium, and two blocks later, pulled into the parking lot of the Yankee Inn motel. While a number of hits had taken place there, none involved baseball. Drug deals gone bad, pimps killing their prostitutes, and garden variety homicides were not unusual. Its location, on the service road of the Deegan, coupled with all the rooms being at ground level with parking directly in front of them, made it a popular spot for those engaged in less-than-legal pursuits.

He parked the van at the north end of the building and walked to the office on the far south side. He opened a grimy glass door to a dark, shabby room with the check-in desk. *Place hasn't seen a broom or mop since Mickey Mantle was a rookie.*

He rang the small bell on the desk and waited. When no one appeared, he rang it again. From a partially open door behind the desk came voices. He leaned closer and heard what sounded like a man and woman screwing. He crept behind the desk and peeked into the room. The lovemaking sounds came from a television. A porn film played to an ancient black man, sound asleep in a wheelchair, a bottle of Old Mr. Boston Lemon Flavored Gin on his chest.

"Yo, Pops. Wake up, man."

The old man's eyes opened. He didn't seem alarmed or surprised. "What can I do for you, young feller?"

"Hate to interrupt your show, my man. But, I need a room."

Putting the bottle on his lap, the man wheeled over and turned the TV off.

"Don't know why I watch this shit. Ain't had a hard on since I don't know when."

"Since Mickey Mantle was a rookie?"

The man laughed, unscrewed the cap and brought the bottle to his lips. "No, when the Mick was a rookie, I was getting tons of nookie."

He was bringing the bottle up for a second swig when it hit him. "Hey...rookie, nookie." His laughter turned into a phlegmy coughing spell.

When it stopped, he looked at Jennings. "The Mick came up in the year nineteen and fifty-one. I was in my forties. Getting me more ass than a toilet seat back then. Mantle hung it up in '68. My johnson retired about ten, fifteen years later." He offered up the bottle. "Wanna taste?"

"No thanks, I'm trying to quit. And bro, while I'm really enjoying this stroll down your sexual memory lane, I need me a fucking room."

They went to the desk. "How long you staying?"

"Till morning."

"Check out's at ten a.m. Give you room number one, next door."

Pooh pointed. "How 'bout the end one down there?"

"Number twenty?" He looked at a board with keys hanging from it. "It's available, but I got to charge you extra. Got a hot tub in it."

"How much?"

The old man looked him over, trying to gauge how much money to ask for the room. "You seem like a nice young man. How about a hundred, cash?"

Jennings put a hundred-dollar bill and a twenty on the desk. "And you seem like a wonderful old gentleman. I would appreciate it if you don't put anyone in the room next to us."

"Likes your privacy, huh?"

"My girl's a screamer."

"Oh, I remember. I surely do." He handed over a key and pointed to a large book. "Care to sign in Mr.?"

Jennings took the key and started to walk out. "You can sign it for me, Pops."

"Sure. What's your name?"

Pooh opened the door, looked back. "Berra," he said. "Lawrence Berra."

"Enjoy your stay, Mr. Berra." The door closed, so did the book. The old man put the one hundred-twenty dollars in his pocket.

***

Pooh Bear opened the door to the room, walked the three feet to the rear of the van, knocked once.

"Ready," Dee said.

In four seconds, Flaco was swept into the room. The two men threw him face-down on the bed.

Dee turned on the TV and looked around. "What a shithole."

"You shouldn't be here more than a couple of hours," Jennings said.

"I'm sure our amigo's people are gonna come up with the ransom real quick. Right, Flaco?"

It took some time for Flaco, still handcuffed behind his back, to roll over and look at them. "How much more do you want?"

Pooh and Dee, in unison, asked, "More?"

"Yeah. Your white friend with the ponytail took fourteen grand from my office."

Dee looked at Jennings. "And you were worried about them getting their share?"

"Fuck 'em. We ain't gonna see them anymore anyway. This is still our last job, right?"

"Yeah." Dee looked at Flaco. "You gonna tell us who we need to call, give us three-hundred thou to let you go."

"I don't know if we have—"

Dee drew the .44 Bulldog from his shoulder holster and placed the barrel gently between Flaco's eyes. "You better pray you do." He pulled the gun's hammer back, cocking the weapon. The clicking sound it made could be heard clearly over the television. A wet stain spread across the front of the handcuffed man's pants.

Three minutes later, leaving Flaco cuffed to the bed, Pooh and Dee climbed back into the van.

"What you think, Pooh?"

"He says they got over a hundred-grand cash in the bodega safe."

"Yeah, but do you think this guy, Juan, will give it all up?"

"When I call, I'll tell him we want two-hundred large or his boss dies. Juan will probably offer what's in the safe. I'd be satisfied with a hundred."

"Fifty thou each and fuck those thieving white boys."

"I'll call you here when I get the money?"

"No. No phone calls. It's how the cops got on to me. How long you think this will take?"

Jennings looked at his watch. "It's a little after one. Shouldn't take long. Back to Manhattan, couple of calls to Juan. If the drop goes smooth–"

"Why you always worry about the drop. It's the easy part–"

Easy for you. You're never there at the drop. Never get out of the van at the snatch. Only thing you're good at is killing people. Though Jennings could not recall all of the people Dee had killed, one he would never forget was his friend, Rontal Cheery.

Jennings took a deep breath. "Snatching the mark is easy. Any dumb motherfucker can grab someone. Our having the white boys makes it doubly foolproof. Nobody gonna fuck with them. The drop, picking up the ransom, is where it gets hairy. Bad guys can show up. The cops mighta been called and are waiting to grab the first guy who touches the money. Lotta bad shit can happen."

"All right, I'll take your word for it. Where's the drop?"

"Highbridge Park, up in Washington Heights."

"Why there?"

"It's Manhattan. Ten minutes from 116th Street, El Ponce. I make the last call to Juan. Tell him he has twenty minutes, has to come alone, money in two bags, drop it in a trash can just inside the park wall, near the pool, off Amsterdam Avenue and West 174th."

"You call from—"

"Pay phone outside a bodega on Amsterdam and 174th. Place's open all night. People hangin' out playing dominoes. I mix in, watch, and wait. He comes with muscle, or the cops show up, we call it a night. Try again in the morning."

"No. Too much heat on me. I wanna be out of town tomorrow. They get one chance. Who's driving you?"

"Meeting Shorty Brown at the safe house on Webster Avenue. We'll swap the van for a clean car he boosted."

"Sounds good. No phone calls. Win or lose, have Shorty pick me up here at eight."

"Eight? Dee, I want to do the drop while it's still dark. Three thirty, four the latest."

"It's cool. Have Shorty drop you and the cash back at the safe house. Don't wanna be driving around in a hot car with the money anyway."

"Why we waiting till eight?"

"'Cause the pigs in the task force looking for me got called in early tonight. My cop says they s'posed to work till six in the morning. At best, the sergeant may let them do one overtime hour till seven. They be back in their homes asleep by eight."

"Where do I tell Shorty he's taking you?"

"Don't tell him shit. Just have him get me here at eight. No sense him knowing where we'll meet to split the money. Less he knows the better. I'll tell him when he gets here. Have him drop me a couple of blocks away."

"Where we meeting?"

"Our old crack house on Tiebout. The basement, like eight-fifteen."

"Doesn't give you much time. Where you gonna let Flaco go?"

"Don't worry. I won't need much time."

Dee got out and went back into room twenty.
Pooh put the van in gear and slowly pulled out of the parking lot, heading to Manhattan.

Forty-Four - The View

Gina Torelli looked out from her apartment. The living room window, facing east, offered a view of the East River. A bell chimed. She turned, walked two steps into the kitchen, opened the microwave, and took out a cup of chamomile tea. Pulling her plush green bathrobe tighter, she sat at a tiny table and looked to the north.

Although this window was much smaller, Gina could see the lights twinkling on the Triborough Bridge. She brought the cup to her lips and took a small sip. Sighing, she placed it down, stood, and looked out at the street below.

At half past midnight, traffic was light on First Avenue. Her eyes were drawn to the corner of First and East 88th Street. She tried to follow it to the west, but her view was blocked by the building next door. Gina couldn't see to Second Avenue but had a clear picture of it in her head. On the Northwest corner, the window with the gold lettering "Elaine's." *What a nice night we had. Until he got drunk. Now, this corruption beef.*

She took another sip. Another sigh. *A really nice night.*

The ring of the phone startled her. She looked at the clock.

This better be good.

"Hello."

"Gina, it's Yoli."

Gina grabbed a pen and small notebook from the counter and sat again at the table. This would be good. Her young protégé wouldn't bother her at home at this hour with anything that could wait until morning.

"Hi, Yoli. What do we have?"

"I'm in the office. Got a call from Brad Kelly, one of the new ADAs. He's riding tonight and–"

"Who's he riding with?"

Yoli hesitated. "Um, no one. He's–"

"He's alone? By himself? A kid who's been in our office three days is going to precincts, interviewing perps, cops, complainants? Taking statements? Maybe getting the perp on a videotaped confession?"

"Well, he—"

"Who's supposed to be showing him the ropes?"

"Willy Tabron. He–"

"Let me guess. Called in sick. He tried to get out of the riding assignment yesterday. Worthless."

"He's not a bad guy."

"Yoli, the only reason he's with us is Mr. Morganthau refused to take him in the Manhattan DA's office. Barely made it through law school, three tries before he passed the bar."

"Just like–"

"Don't say it. Do not try to compare Willy Tabron with J.F.K. Junior. Totally different animal."

"Totally, Gina. One grew up in the Soundview Projects, went to City College. The other, Hyannis Port, the Upper East Side, Harvard, and the Manhattan DA's Office."

"Actually Brown, NYU Law, and, yes, Mr. Morganthau did pick him up."

"And how many tries at the bar did Junior get?"

"All right, I see your point. I'll speak with Tabron tomorrow. Now what did young ADA Kelly want?"

"He got a call from IAD. They want him to respond to one of their locations. They have a cop under arrest."

"Yoli, I know it's late, but could you respond and take Kelly with you?"

"Gina, the call from IAD. It came from your favorite guy, Sergeant Stark."

Gina dropped her teacup, which shattered on the floor. Gomez and McGuire had been the targets of Stark's investigation into who was on wanted killer Dee's payroll, supplying confidential information to keep him one step ahead of the task force's attempts to arrest him.

"You okay, Gina?"

"Yeah, dropped something. Do we know who Stark has?" *Please God, not McGuire, not John McGuire.*

"No. I have his number. Want me to call him?"

"Give it to me. I'll call."

Gina hung up, took a dustpan and small broom from a closet, then immediately put them back. Stepping over the broken china and puddle of tea, she picked up the phone and dialed. It was answered before the second ring.

"Stark."

"Sergeant, ADA Gina Torelli."

"ADA Torelli, how nice to speak with you again."

"I understand you've arrested a cop and need the riding DA. Is this related to the Four-two Detective Squad case we've spoken about?"

"Yes, it is."

"Who did you collar?"

Stark let out a short giggle. "Take a guess, Counselor."

Gina inhaled deeply. She focused on the Triborough Bridge's lights as she exhaled.

"I asked you a direct question. Please answer it."

"Relax. It's not your boyfriend. It's some other detective named Patrick Hanlon. He's given a complete confession. Was on Dwayne Dillon, AKA Dee's payroll. Two grand a month, starting back when he was in the Four-six, before he transferred into the Four-two."

"What about Gomez and McGuire?"

"They targeted Gomez because he's got a cell phone. They cloned it. Know what it is?"

"General idea. New phone, you make calls, comes back–"

"To Gomez's number. Dee tells his crew Gomez is the dirty cop. Meantime, Hanlon's protecting Dee, calling, letting him know where and when the task force is looking for him."

"What's Hanlon say about Gomez and McGuire?"

Gina heard Stark shuffle some papers. "Let's see, 'Gomez is a lazy wetback spic who should be deported back to Mexico.'"

"Gomez is Dominican."

"I know. Hanlon's not too good at geography."

"What's he say about McGuire?"

"Sure you want to hear this?"'

"Yes."

Stark cleared his throat. "Okay, Counselor. Hanlon describes McGuire, as 'a drunken, shanty Irish prick who couldn't find a Jew on Orchard Street.' Also Hanlon says, 'McGuire is banging all the stewardesses down in Long Beach and probably has syphilis, gonorrhea, crabs, and fucking AIDS.'"

"Oh, this Hanlon sounds like a real charmer. Did your investigation turn up anything on them?"

"No. Gomez is straight as an arrow. Family, job, finances, credit cards. He's clean as the driven snow."

"And McGuire?"

"Right now, he's clean."

"As the driven snow?"

"More like two-day-old slush. He's clear on this one, but one of these days, he'll get what's coming to him. Freaking wise guy."

Gina recalled Stark's vendetta stemmed from McGuire's outwitting and embarrassing the sergeant a few months earlier. She looked to change the subject. "So, Gomez has been restored to full duty?"

"Yeah. Him, McGuire, and the task force guys are working till six a.m. looking for Dee."

Gina said goodbye, hung up, and looked at the clock. She fought back an urge to call the Four-two, ask them to raise McGuire on the radio and have him call her.

Instead, she got the broom, dustpan, and cleaned the mess. As she dropped the broken shards into the garbage, she gazed out the window. Looked at the bridge, but saw Elaine's.

Forty-Five - The Drop

Pooh Bear Jennings came out of the safe house and looked up Webster Avenue. Across the street, a car's headlights blinked off then on again. He walked over, saw Shorty Brown behind the wheel, and got in.

"Nice, Shorty. What's it, an '86 Honda?"

"A 1987 Honda Accord." He pointed to the windshield. "Registration, inspection stickers are good, so's the muffler and lights. Half a tank a gas."

"Good job. We want to blend in, not stick out."

"Oh, this Jap rice burner be 'bout invisible." Shorty flipped the directional on, checked the mirror, and pulled out. "Where we going?"

"Manhattan, Amsterdam and 174th." Jennings looked the car over. "Honda's easy to boost?"

"Don't get no easier. Didn't even have to break into it. Owner had one of those No Radio signs. They always leave the car open so the crackheads don't bust a window out to see if they telling the truth."

Jennings laughed. "Talk about giving up. 'I have no radio to steal. I'm not locked so you can check. Please don't take a shit in me if you decide to sleep inside.' This city is getting tough to live in."

"Making it easier to be a car thief." Shorty slowed to a red light.

"How?"

"Couple of murders every night, crack houses all over, keeping the cops busy. Stolen cars be way down on their list." He pulled away slowly when the light turned green. "We all set?"

"Yeah, I made the first call to Flaco's man, Juan. Told him we want two-hundred grand or his boss takes a long dirt nap. He says he may be able to raise a hundred. Flaco said he had over a hundred grand in the bodega safe."

"So, Juan be skimming a few grand for his self?"

"Fuck, yeah. It's not like we're going to give him a receipt or some shit when he drops the two bags. He'll tell Flaco we took it all."

"Why two bags?"

"Hundred thou, crack money. Ain't gonna be no big bills. Fives, tens, twenties. Could weigh a lot."

Shorty signaled and made a right turn onto a highway, staying just under the speed limit. "What we do now?"

"We scope out the drop site. Call Juan back. Had a hard time understanding the prick."

"He no *habla* English?"

"No. One of our white boys tuned him up pretty good when they snatched Flaco."

Shorty laughed. "Sounds like a case of po-lice brutality to me."

They exited the Cross Bronx Expressway at Amsterdam Avenue and headed south. On their right, row after row of six-story apartment houses with bodegas, storefront churches, check cashing, and auto parts stores at street level. On the left, Highbridge Park. Through the twelve-foot-high chain-link fence they saw basketball and tennis courts. Farther on, two softball fields and then, at 174th Street, the Highbridge Pool. A large red brick pool house, shut tight, stood just yards off Amsterdam Avenue. Behind it, an Olympic-size swimming pool, now drained. An entrance to the park led through a gate to a paved path which separated the softball fields from the pool.

Jennings pointed to a parking spot. "Pull in there."

On the other side of 174th, the Santo Domingo Bodega was open for business. Jennings walked to the phone mounted on the outside wall and picked up the receiver. Getting a dial tone, he smiled at Shorty and hung up. An old man in dirty clothes sat beside the bodega's door, a bottle of Presidente beer in a paper bag beside him. He begged for change.

Pooh entered the store, bought two cans of Coke and a bottle of Presidente, which the clerk opened and placed in a brown paper bag. Outside, Pooh gave a Coke to Shorty and squatted down beside the old man. After two minutes of conversation, he stood, patted the man on the shoulder, and left the beer with him.

Crossing Amsterdam Avenue toward the pool, Shorty asked, "What's with the old timer?"

"Nice dude. Jorge. Not drunk. Dominican. Likes Presidente, the DR's national beer."

"This a good time to make new friends?"

"He'll be worth his weight in *cerveza.*"

On each side of the park's entrance gate were two large black-metal trash barrels. Jennings casually scanned them and kept walking. "Both full." Ten yards down the path was a third barrel. Jennings looked around. They were alone.

He glanced into the barrel. "Yes. Looks empty. This'll do." He picked it up, turned it upside down.

"What the fuck? Thought it's empty." Shorty frowned.

"Said it looks empty. People bring their dogs to this park. Don't want the money bags stinking of dog shit." Putting the barrel back, they walked farther into the park. The path curved to the right, ending in a dark alley between the pool house and pool.

Jennings walked closer. "Perfect. Let's go."

They walked back to the Honda. Jennings turned to Shorty. "Here's how it goes down. I call Juan. Give him twenty minutes to get here with the money. By himself. Two bags, drops them both in the can." He pointed.

"What are we doing?"

"Sitting in the car. Easy part. Either Juan shows up and drops the money, or he don't. Us getting the bags from the can and getting out of here is where we got to be careful. Can't be certain Juan didn't call the cops, or have some of his crew jump us when we take the money."

"What if he says he needs more time?"

"Then we know he's setting us up. He's got the money. Just has to drive up and drop it. If he asks for more time, it means either the cops or his crew need it to set up on the site. That ain't happening. He pulls any shit, we leave, and Dee takes care of Flaco."

"How we getting the bags?"

They got back into the Honda. "After Juan makes the drop, we sit here. Wait and watch. Look for a van pulling up with blacked-out windows or a telephone company truck. Cops. When Juan pulls up, we see if he's got another car tailing him. His boys. They'd have to be close. If it looks clear, we get the bags."

Shorty nervously snapped his fingers. "But how, Pooh?"

Jennings gestured to the old man in front of the bodega. "Jorge's gonna help us out."

Shorty began drumming on the steering wheel. "How?"

"Just 'cause we don't spot the cops, don't mean they ain't involved. They're good at this shit, but they never drop real money. They always use tore-up newspaper."

"How you know this?"

"Dee's got a cop on the payroll. So, before we split, we gotta make sure there's cash in the bags, not the *Daily News*."

Shorty now drummed and tapped his feet on the floor. "How?"

"If the cops are watching, they'll let someone take the bag, snatch him up as he walks away. But, they won't let him get in a car."

"Why?"

"They don't want car chases. Guy could get away. People could get hurt. Cops just grab 'em, beat the shit out of them until they give up where the victim is."

"I don't want no beatin'."

"Relax. After the drop, I'm gonna go into the park down at 173rd Street, come up behind to the alley near the pool. You drive up to 173rd and turn around, face north."

"What am I looking for?"

"Our man Jorge's gonna come in the park and take one of the bags. I'm gonna have him walk out and put the bag on the trunk of whatever car is parked closest to the gate. If nobody grabs him, I take a look in the second bag. If you see me walking out the gate with the bag, pull up. We got the dough."

"What if it's the fucking *News*?"

"If the old man comes out and no one grabs him, and I don't come out a minute later, drive around the back of the park to the Harlem River Drive. I'm gonna pull a Jesse Owens, split out the back. You pick me up on the Drive. Got it?"

Shorty nodded yes.

Jennings walked to the phone and dialed.

Juan answered.

"You got the money?"

"Yes. One hundred thousand."

"Listen very carefully now, Juan. You drive up alone. Amsterdam Avenue and 174th Street. You'll see an entrance to the park. Walk in about ten yards. Look for a black garbage can on the right side. Drop both bags in it. Walk back, get in your car, and leave. Repeat what I just said."

Juan repeated the instructions.

"One more thing, *Amigo*. I see anybody who looks like a cop, or one o' your crew, I fade into the fucking night, and Flaco is dead."

Pooh looked at his watch. "It's two-thirty. You got twenty minutes. Not a minute more." He hung up and got back into the car. "Keep your eyes moving, Shorty. Look for any changes in the next twenty minutes."

Eighteen minutes later, a car pulled up, hesitated, then pulled to the curb in front of the park's gate. A Hispanic man got out.

"Is it him, Pooh?" Shorty asked.

"Yep, it's him."

"You seen him before?"

"No, but check out the white gauze on his head. It's Juan."

They watched as the man opened the car's rear door and came out with two black garbage bags which he hefted over his shoulders. He then walked slowly into the park. Less than a minute later, he walked out, got in his car, and left.

Shorty was hyperventilating. "Those bags were heavy. C'mon, Pooh, let's get 'em."

Jennings placed a hand on Shorty's shoulder. "Calm down, bro. This is crunch time. We wait and watch."

Five minutes passed. Nothing on the street or in the park changed.

"Looks good. After I leave, wait one minute then go up the street and turn around. Watch for the old man. If you see me coming out after him with a bag, pull up nice and slow. Make sure the back door's not locked. If he comes out and I don't, follow after a minute."

"I get you down on the Drive. I got it, Pooh. Don't worry, I won't let you down."

Jennings opened the car door, looked back at his friend. "I know, brother. I know."

He walked to the bodega and squatted down next to Jorge. After a minute, he placed a bill in the old man's cup. He then walked up to 173rd Street and entered the park. When he reached the alley behind the pool house, he ducked into the shadows and waited.

A figure entered the park and walked toward him. Jorge. Very slowly, the old man made his way to the garbage can. He reached in and, with some effort, came out with a black bag, turned, and headed out.

Jennings's skin was tingling. His eyes and ears were at a heightened state, waiting, watching, listening.

The old man was out of the park. He placed the bag on the trunk of a dark Chevy and patted his pockets, as if feeling for his keys. Jennings watched in silence, taking shallow breaths. This was the moment when it could all turn to shit. A van could pull up. Men with guns could appear, shouting and grabbing Jorge. He waited. Nothing happened. It was time.

He left the safety of the shadows and walked in long steps to the trash barrel. Still watching the old man, he reached in and pulled out a second garbage bag tied shut at the top. Hands now shaking, he undid the tie and plunged a hand in. It came out holding a thick wad of twenties. He strode quickly out of the park to where Jorge stood, still patting his pockets. He handed the old man two twenties.

Shorty pulled up. Jennings tossed the bags in the back and jumped into the front. He gave Shorty a thumbs-up. Shorty checked his mirror, put on his directional and drove slowly away.

Forty-Six - Crunch Time

McGuire looked at his watch and yawned.

“You tired?” Gomez asked.

“Ten-four, pal. Five a.m. Only people should be up now are farmers and night watchmen.” He steered the unmarked slowly onto the Grand Concourse.

“How about prostitutes?”

“What about ’em?”

“Well, they’re up now, too. They’ve got to go to bed sometime, too, don’t they?”

McGuire laughed. “They spend their working hours in bed. They need to go back when they’re off? It’s like asking, ‘What’s a dog do on his day off?’”

Gomez removed his glasses, blew on each lens, and wiped them with a napkin. He rubbed his eyes.

McGuire knew it was one thing when you were on patrol in uniform on a late tour. You tried to stay alert, watch each street you drove down, hoping to catch a bad guy, interrupt a mugging, save a woman being raped. You could still take your eyes off the street, close them, relax for a minute, if you weren't driving. You were not in the state of constant tension the two partners had been in since hitting the street shortly after ten p.m. The strain of looking for a killer, someone who would not hesitate for a second to pull the trigger if he got a cop in his sights, was exhausting.

Their eyes moved constantly. They had not stopped to eat. Two containers of coffee from an all-night diner had been their meal, consumed as they drove to each location Dee was known to frequent. Scanning every doorway, alley, moving cars, parked cars, people coming out of subways, riding in buses. Looking for a large black man with a shaved head, who had shot at least six people.

Gomez put his glasses back on. "So?"

McGuire glanced at him. "So what?"

"So, what does a dog do on his day off?"

"How the fuck would I know? Lays around licking his balls, same as when he's working, I guess."

Gomez began to laugh then pointed to a six-story art deco apartment building. "There it is."

"Remind me again. Why are we here?"

Gomez shone a small mag light down on a manila folder. "Dee took a drug collar in '89. One of his phone calls was to Latisha McFarland, here, in apartment 6F."

"What's a nice Irish girl doing in this neighborhood?"

Gomez handed McGuire a mugshot of a black female. No beauty queen, she wore a large Afro and a menacing scowl.

"Lovely. We got a sheet on her?"

Gomez pulled two yellow papers and began reading. "Starts in '85 when she turned sixteen. Six collars—drugs, prostitution, assault, weapons—the usual."

"Wonderful. And, would this lovely lass have any wee ones upstairs?"

Gomez again flipped through the folder. "Let's see. Yeah, she's getting welfare payments for herself and five kids. This address."

"She turned sixteen six years ago in '85. And now she has six arrests and five kids?"

Gomez checked his papers. "Right."

McGuire exhaled loudly. "Her life would have been so different if only Vassar hadn't turned her down."

Gomez placed the folder on the back seat. "How do you want to handle this?"

McGuire brought both hands to his face and began to slap himself rapidly. He glanced up at the building. "I know what I don't wanna do. I don't wanna go up there and knock on the door. With our luck, he's up there. We have a shootout with him. Five babies and their momma running around? No way."

"So?"

McGuire yawned again. Rolled down the window and took three deep breaths of the cold morning air. "Does the lovely lass still have a phone?"

Gomez grabbed the folder. "She did as of the first of the month."

"Write the number down for me." He pointed to a phone booth across the Concourse.

Gomez held up his cell phone.

"No, I'd rather drive over. Get out, wake me up a bit. If she answers, I'll say I'm Child Protective Services, give her some bullshit, try to feel her out, see if I hear a man's voice in the background."

"What if he answers?"

"We don't know what Dee sounds like, other than a deep voice, but we have to assume if a guy is up there, it could be him. If so, we lock it down, call the boss, get Emergency Service, the whole nine yards."

McGuire put the car in gear.

Gomez reached over and hit his arm. "Stop."

They were on the inside service lane of the Concourse, heading south. The road, which had been modeled after Paris's *Champs-Elysees*, had three lanes in each direction. Concrete islands with some trees on them separated the service from the main roads.

"What?"

Gomez pointed toward the stairway leading up from the 149th Street subway stop.

McGuire strained his eyes. "I don't see—"

"Wait."

A head appeared just above the sidewalk level, then disappeared back down the stairs. "Got it. Mugger waiting for a victim?"

"Could be. How you—" Gomez stopped mid-sentence as the head again appeared. This time, the body followed. A large body. The head was now shrouded in the hood of a puffy-black down jacket. "Shit. Think that's Dee, John?"

"Could be. Big enough. Has to be six-four or five."

The man walked south, away from them. Gomez reached for the radio.

"Got no time to wait for backup," McGuire said. "Hell, if it's Dee, he could disappear on us. We gotta check this guy out now." He drove forward slowly.

"This is a good block, Joe. The whole right side is Hostos College. I doubt any doors are open this early. We do our usual felony stop." When they were ten yards behind the man, McGuire stopped the car. Gomez got out, gun in hand. As he quietly closed the door, he looked back. "Be careful, John."

McGuire nodded, put the car in gear, and drove past the suspect. Fifteen yards beyond him, he pulled to the curb and stepped out. He had seen what he wanted. A large-brown metal mailbox, not the type the public puts letters in, but the solid box postal workers used.

He took a position behind it as the big man slowed but kept moving toward him. McGuire now had a tactical advantage, something which had been drilled into him at the police firing range.

"Cover, find cover. Put something, anything between you and the shooter. Combat crouch. Two hands on the gun. Don't think about using the sights. Point the barrel, center mass. Squeeze the trigger, don't yank it."

With his secondary vision, he could see Gomez trailing the suspect, staying in the street, giving him an angle to not endanger McGuire if Gomez had to shoot, and keeping himself out of harm's way should McGuire have to fire.

The suspect was now in the area where McGuire wanted him. He had walked past the last of the parked cars. Gomez was now behind it on McGuire's right, his gun stretched over its hood.

Across the sidewalk was the school's solid brick wall. McGuire and his partner had cover, the suspect was in the open with nowhere to go. The Kill Zone. McGuire looked, but the hood concealed the man's face. It might be Dee. It might not. He let the man get a little closer.

McGuire, who had been leaning on the box trying to appear nonchalant, now crouched behind it and brought his service weapon over the top. He pointed the gun at the big man's chest. "Police. Don't move. Take your hands out of your pockets."

The big man froze in his tracks. He was looking at a mailbox with a head and a very large weapon.

"I can't do that, Officer," he said softly.

"Why not?"

"Sir, I cannot take my hands out of my pockets without moving."

Shit. He's got me on that one. "Okay. Keep your hands where they are. Very slowly walk toward me."

The man complied. When he was ten feet away, McGuire said, "Stop. Now, real slow, take your left hand out of your pocket."

The man complied, holding up the hand to show it was empty.

"Now, nice and easy, reach up and pull the hood back so we can get a look at you."

When he did, McGuire felt the tension rush out of him, like someone had opened a valve in his belly. The suspect had hair, salt and pepper. He looked to be in his mid-fifties. Twenty years older than the bald Dee. Still, McGuire did not let his guard down.

"Right hand, easy, out of pocket."

The man stood with both hands raised.

"Toss him, Joe."

Gomez holstered his weapon and came out from behind the car. He ran his hands over the man's arms, legs, body.

"He's clean."

McGuire stepped from behind the mailbox, gun still in hand. Just because this wasn't Dee, it didn't mean he wasn't wanted for something else. Many a cop had died after making this bad assumption.

"You can put your hands down. We stopped you because you were acting a little suspicious back there."

"Suspicious?"

"Yeah, back at the subway," Gomez said.

"Suspicious?"

"Yes, suspicious. What are you a ground hog or something?"

The man flashed a perplexed look.

Gomez continued. "I saw your head, up the stairs, back down, up, back down. Finally, up for the third time, you walked away."

A broad grin crossed the big man's face. "Officer, if it's suspicious, you got me. I come home from work this time every morning. Get off the train, it's dark out, streets empty."

"Where you work?" McGuire asked.

"*The New York Times* on Forty-third Street. Paper handler. Load the trucks. Eight p.m. to four a.m."

"Okay, but why the groundhog act?" Gomez asked.

"Officer, I'm scouting the terrain. I been robbed twice, right on this block."

McGuire checked out the man. "What are you six-five, two-thirty? Who's gonna rob you?"

The man pointed to McGuire's gun. "Heard once 'God made every man different, Sam Colt made them all equal.' I ain't taking on a midget if he's got a piece pointed at me."

"What made you come up out of the subway after checking twice?"

"'Cause, I saw what looked like an unmarked police car sitting there."

"You made us?" McGuire asked.

"I was pretty sure when I saw the car. Either cops or a gypsy cab. But after you drove past me and got out, I was positive you were the man."

"How's that?"

"C'mon. Bet you the first white man to lean on the mailbox since John Lindsay was mayor."

McGuire holstered his weapon. "Scouting the terrain? You a military man?"

"Yes, Sir. Two tours in 'Nam."

"What branch?"

"Army. Special Forces."

"Thank you for your service." They shook hands. "What's your name?"

"Clyde."

"Clyde, I'm sorry we had to come on so strong, but we're looking for a really bad dude. Big guy like you. We thought you might be him."

"I understand. These are some mean-ass streets. You got a job to do. I don't have no problem."

"Since you live around here, maybe you could do us a favor?" McGuire pulled Dee's mugshot from his jacket pocket. "Ever see this guy?"

Clyde looked closely at the picture and began to laugh.

"What's so funny?" McGuire asked.

"Oh. I seen this guy plenty. Not recently, but I seen enough of him to know I never want to set eyes on him again."

"Why?"

Clyde took the picture from McGuire. "Officer, this here guy is a thug and a gangster. A no-account human being. Dwayne Dillon. Calls himself Dee."

"How do you know him?"

"I'm ashamed to tell you this. He's my nephew."

Forty-Seven - The Take

Pooh Bear Jennings and Shorty Brown drove back to the Webster Avenue safe house. Shorty found a parking spot. They both got out.

Pooh opened the back door. “Shorty, grab a bag.”

Shorty hesitated.

Jennings turned to him. “Yeah, I trust you. I also need one hand free. Lot of thieves around here.”

They each took a bag.

Jennings swung his onto his left shoulder, his right hand inside his coat gripping the .9mm Glock. They entered the project, got into an open and empty graffiti-covered elevator. Jennings pushed the button for the fourth floor. The door was slowly closing when a man’s voice called, “Hold the elevator, please.”

Shorty moved toward the panel.

“No,” Jennings hissed.

The door was almost shut when a hand from outside suddenly seized it. Jennings pulled Shorty into the corner behind him and brought the Glock out, holding it against his leg. The door shuddered twice and slowly opened. An old, white-haired black man picked up his full laundry basket and started to enter. He stopped short in the doorway.

"Guess you boys didn't hear me." He eyed both men suspiciously.

Jennings turned so the gun was hidden. "No, Sir. I did. I was trying to get my bag down and the door shut. I'm sorry."

The door began to close. It stopped when it hit the old man's arm.

Shorty pushed and held the open button.

The old man looked directly into Jennings's eyes. He hesitated, then stepped in.

"No problem. I'm a little grumpy tonight. Arthritis kicking up."

"Doing your laundry awful early, Sir," Jennings observed.

"I do it when I feel like doing it. Like having the machines to myself. Even if I have to walk down and back up one floor." He seemed to sense Pooh's puzzlement. "Elevator stops going to the basement at ten p.m. Keeps the riffraff out. Starts again at six in the morning."

Jennings was about to ask the man if his late-night trips to the basement laundry room ever ended in his being robbed.

"Don't have all night. Could you push three for me?"

Shorty pushed the button and the door closed.

At the third floor, the man got off. "You boys have a nice night."

"You too, Sir." Jennings stood with his back keeping the elevator door from shutting, watching the old-timer limp down the hall.

The man turned.

"Just keeping an eye on you, Sir. Make sure you get into your apartment with no problems."

The man smiled and shook his head. "Your momma raised you right, son. God bless." He continued walking.

"That she did, Sir, that she did."

When the man was safely inside, they continued to their floor. They entered the apartment and dropped the bags on the kitchen table. Jennings opened one of the bags and pulled out a wrapped stack of twenties. "Looks like Flaco's been to the bank."

He took out a second stack and examined it closely. Each bundle had one-hundred bills, two grand. He looked then in the second bag. All tens, fives and ones. Thank God, most of them were wrapped.

"Let's start counting."

Shorty picked up a stack of twenties and began to examine each bill.

"What you looking for, bro?"

"How you know they ain't trying to be slick? Put a twenty on top and bottom of a stack of singles?"

"And what if they did? What we gonna do, call the cops? The Better Business Bureau? What we got is what we got. Start counting, my man. You do those. I'll take the small bills."

An hour later, they finished. Jennings had taken the loose bills and put them in stacks of one hundred, like those in the bank wrappers.

Once more he counted. "I get ninety-six thou."

"You sure?"

"Went over it three times." He made a pile of ones, fives and tens. Counted them twice. Pushed the stacks down the table. "This is you, Shorty. Six grand."

"But—"

Jennings gestured to the pile. "I know I told you five, but I'm giving you the small bills and a little bonus. Makes it an even ninety for Dee and me to split. This our last job." He held out his hand. "Always knew I could count on you, my man."

Shorty grabbed Pooh Bear's hand and pulled him in for a hug.

"Listen to me now, Shorty. You gotta get Dee at the motel at eight o'clock. Get back to your crib first and hide the cash. If Dee asks, tell him we got ninety-five thou. I gave you five. Only five. Make sure he knows you don't have it on you."

"You think I gotta worry about Dee?"

"You gotta be careful with Dee. Last job. He don't like no loose ends."

"Loose end. Like what he did to Rontal. You remember?"

"Only every day."

"You worried?" Shorty frowned. "Want me to cover your back when you meet Dee for the split?"

"No need. I can handle Dee. I ain't worried. But I will be careful."

* * *

McGuire and Gomez were back at the squad with Dee's Uncle Clyde and the entire task force team. Six a.m., their tour was over. McGuire briefed Sergeant Ramos on their discovery of Clyde Dillon and the man's willingness to help them find his nephew, Dee.

"Can we trust him, John?"

"Yes, Sir."

"You sure?"

"Yeah, he's a legit guy. Vietnam vet. Works for *The Times*."

"Why's he want to help us find his own nephew?"

"'Cause he's a good guy. He didn't have to tell us he knew Dee. We'd have sent him on his way. Can't stand Dee. Called him a thug."

"Think he can help us find the current whereabouts of said thug?"

"That's what we wanna find out."

Ramos rubbed the heavy stubble on his chin. "The guys are all dragging ass. I really want to send everyone home to get some sleep."

"They'll perk up quick if Clyde comes up with some new Intel."

Ramos sighed, held up one finger. "You got an hour. Tell everyone to stand by. I'll clear the overtime with whatever captain is covering the night watch."

* * *

McGuire returned to the squad and passed along the sarge's order.

Gomez was talking with Clyde. The rest of the team banged away at typewriters documenting their night's activities.

McGuire turned to new detective, Ty Crawford. "Ty, do me a favor? Go down to the desk and see if we can use the Auxiliary Police Office to talk with Mr. Dillon."

Crawford pointed. "Why don't you just bring him into the War Room?"

McGuire had been about to sit. He hovered over the chair with a pained expression on his face.

Gomez jumped up. "I got it, John." Without a word, he beckoned Crawford to follow him to the door.

Once out of the office, he led Ty down the hall to the staircase where Gomez stopped. "Ty, that was a rookie mistake."

Crawford looked surprised. "What? What did I do?"

Gomez adjusted his glasses. "You know who that guy is, right?"

"Yeah, Dee's uncle."

"And, why do we want to talk with him?"

Crawford let out an exasperated sigh. "Well, obviously, we want to find out everything he knows about Dee."

"Right. We want to find everything he knows about Dee."

"Yeah. So, what did I do wrong?"

"The War Room? Put him in there? What's in the room?"

"Our Intel on Dee."

"Right. So, in the room, on the walls and easels, is everything we know. Where Dee lived. Where he took collars. Who he was collared with. Where they lived. Who he called. Who visited him in prison. Past associates, girlfriends, family members. You made all those charts up. You know what's there."

He saw a baffled look on Crawford's face. "We want to find out everything Clyde knows about Dee, not show and tell him everything we know about the psycho."

Ty began to blink rapidly. "Yeah, but John said Clyde is a good guy."

"Don't matter. He goes in there, he starts playing detective. He'd tell us what he thinks we want to hear. He'll walk out knowing everything we know. We have to question him. Pick his brain first. See if he corroborates any of our information. If he does, then we have a good idea he's legit. *Comprende*?"

Crawford hung his head. "Shit, Joe." He looked up. "I'm sorry. Last thing in the world I want to do is disappoint you and John. I'd still be in Narco if it wasn't for him. Hell, I'd probably be dead or in jail without John's looking out for me."

Gomez reached out and patted Ty's arm. "File it under lessons learned, *mi hermano*. Come on."

As they walked down the stairs, Gomez asked, "You still playing on the department football team?"

"Yeah. My fifth season coming up."

Gomez stopped. "John told me you're quite the player." He paused and looked intently at Ty. "But, maybe this season, you might want to think about wearing a helmet."

He pointed down the stairs. "Now, go down to the desk and see if we can get the key to the Auxiliary Police office, Sherlock."

Ty laughed and started down. After two steps, he stopped and turned. "Joe."

Gomez looked back.

Ty mouthed one word. "Thanks."

* * *

Sergeant Ramos entered the squad. "Listen up, guys." The clatter of the typewriters died down. "We're all on the clock until seven."

A groan rose across the room. Generally, overtime was something every cop sought. Helped pay the bills. This morning, after having worked all night, frustrated by their lack of progress in finding Dee, they wanted to go home and hit the rack.

"Keep typing, guys. I want fives on everything you did last night before you leave. Salt and Pepper, you, too. You were detectives last night."

Noticing Clyde, he stopped. "Where are you interviewing Mr. Dillon, John?"

Crawford came through the door holding a key. "Got it."

McGuire stood. "Ty, can you take Mr. Dillon down and get him a cup of coffee? I'll be right there."

When the two left, the sergeant continued. "While we wait to see what John and Joe come up with, the rest of you knock out those fives. Everything you did last night, where you went, who you talked to, put it on paper. Remember, 'If it ain't on a five, you got nothing but jive.' Everything, guys.

You leave out any steps, and we can end up duplicating our efforts. We have to bag Dee. Clear five homicides. Get our clearance rate up."

Salt and Pepper looked on wide-eyed. The two young, uniformed cops had never been exposed to the inner sanctum, the mysterious shroud the detective squad worked under. Although part of the precinct, the detective squad was very much an entity unto itself, with its own customs, rules, and jargon.

"What's a good clearance rate for homicides, Sergeant?" Pepper asked.

Ramos laughed. "Well, Pep, one hundred percent would be good, but it's never going to happen. Sixty-six percent is the clearance rate headquarters wants."

"Sixty-six percent is good?" Pepper looked mildly askance. "So a lot of murders go unsolved?"

"Solving homicides is not as easy as it looks on TV. Especially in precincts like this one. Good people are scared to come forward. Bad people don't give a crap. Sometimes it seems like we're shoveling shit against the tide and nobody cares. Who gives a fuck if some crack dealer gets whacked or some junkie ODs on some bad dope?"

Ramos walked over to the desk where Salt and Pepper were sitting. "Am I right? Have you guys ever heard any of the cops say, 'Who gives a fuck? Let them kill each other."

Salt and Pepper suddenly found something of interest on their shoe tops.

Ramos slapped the desk and startled everyone. "You know who gives a shit?" His voice rose. Taking a deep breath, he brought his broad, former boxer's shoulders up under his ears, swiveled his head from side to side and exhaled. "I do. And so do these guys." He pointed at Gomez, McGuire, and Cutrone.

Salt and Pepper hung on Ramos's every word. "Seven years I been doing this. Know what I found? Yeah, a lot of the people who get killed had it coming. Play with fire, and you're going to get burned. Nobody retires from the drug trade. They end up in jail or in a box. And, most times, when you knock on some project door to notify the next of kin, you see the dead apple didn't fall very far from the tree. Skells, for the most part, breed skells. But, every now and then, good, hard-working people have the bad luck to get killed or have a relative who fucks up and ends up dead."

Ramos leaned over the desk, getting closer to the two young cops. "It's what we're doing with this case. All our victims, with the exception of the kid working in the bodega, are skells. But, you can see we're working it hard, right?"

Salt and Pepper both mumbled, "Yes, Sir."

"And it's why it's important to treat every murder the same, whether the victim is a junkie or the parish priest." He tapped both cops' chests with a meaty index finger. "Don't forget it."

He stood, retrieved his coffee cup. "End of speech."

McGuire cleared his throat. He looked at Ramos and winked. McGuire knew the sarge thought highly of the two young cops. He wanted to make sure they didn't develop the "us against them" attitude some of the young officers had. They would remember the usually soft spoken Ramos's speech for the rest of their time on the job.

"We'll be down speaking with Mr. Dillon." As McGuire and Gomez walked out, Angelo Cutrone handed McGuire a sticky note. "Call ADA Gina Torelli."

McGuire stopped in his tracks.

Forty-Eight - The Final Split

Shorty Brown left the safe house with a garbage bag containing his six thousand dollars. He drove to his apartment over a Blockbuster video store on Fordham Road, where he divided his take into two piles. After shutting off the water and draining the toilet tank he placed the first, still in the garbage bag, in it. The second pile went into his freezer. He left two twenty dollar bills on the kitchen table, hoping that if a junkie broke in while he was gone, he'd grab the bills and take off.

He left the apartment, checking all three locks on his door to be sure they were engaged, and drove to the Yankee Inn. He stood to the side of the door to Room 20, knocked once, then twice, then once again.

A deep voice from inside asked, "Who?"

"Shorty."

The door opened a crack. Shorty saw one eye and the muzzle of a gun.

"C'mon."

The door opened. Shorty entered and saw Flaco, both hands cuffed behind his back, sitting on the edge of the bed.

"How'd it go?" Dee asked.

"Good. We got the cash, no problems."

"How much?"

Shorty hesitated and looked at Flaco.

"How much?" Dee repeated.

"Close to what we asked for."

"We asked for a hundred grand. What'd we get?"

Shorty looked at the .44 Bulldog revolver Dee held. His mouth went dry. "Nine." He swallowed hard. "I think ninety-five grand."

Dee stood and began waving the gun around the room. "And you think ninety-five grand is close to a hundred?" He sat down and let out a deep chuckle. "Be five grand short. How bout, since you say it's close, we take the five outta your cut?"

Shorty's mouth moved, but no words came out. He could not take his eyes off the gun.

"How much you getting?" Dee asked.

"S, S, five."

"Survive? What the fuck did you say?"

"Five. I said five."

"So, you wanna take nothing? Make up for the five grand this spic's people shorted us."

Flaco stood. "Please, I can get more. Just—"

Dee sprang, smashing his gun into the side of Flaco's head. The Puerto Rican fell face-up onto the bed.

"Stay the fuck down while I have a discussion with my associate, Poncho." He looked at Shorty. "So what do you say, little man? You take zero stead of five, even things up?"

Shorty looked at Flaco, blood running down the man's face, his eyes open wide, looking for help, for mercy.

Shorty looked at the floor. "I need the money."

Dee laughed. "Thought so. Five grand ain't much unless it's coming outta your pocket." He pointed to the door. "Go wait in the car, little man."

Shorty tried not to, but shot a glance at Flaco and left.

* * *

Dee picked a dirty pillow off the floor.

"No," Flaco cried out, but Dee was quickly on him, pinning his head to the mattress with the pillow. He put all of his 240 pounds into the arm on the pillow as his right hand holding the gun slowly worked its way up.

Flaco's cries were muffled. He began to kick and buck, but without the use of his cuffed hands, he was no match for his overpowering opponent.

Dee now had the gun under the pillow against Flaco's head. He began to squeeze the trigger. He stopped. Flaco's bucks and kicks seemed to be growing weaker. *Fuck it. This will work. No noise. No ballistics for the cops.*

He brought his gun hand over the pillow and pressed even harder with both arms. The kicks became less frequent, weaker and weaker. Finally, after a quick flurry of both heels on the bed, they stopped completely. Dee did not let up. He continued putting maximum pressure on the pillow until his arms grew tired. Slowly, he pulled the pillow back. Flaco's lifeless eyes stared up at nothing. Dee rolled him over, removed the handcuffs and rolled him back onto his back. He then placed the pillow under Flaco's head, threw a blanket over the body, and re-holstered his gun.

After checking the room to make sure they had left nothing, he closed and locked the door behind him.

He got into the car. "Drive."

"Flaco's not coming?"

"No. He likes this place. Said he'll check out later." Dee began his deranged chuckle. "Yeah, motherfucker got the late checkout."

Shorty cleared his throat, nibbled at his lip, and put the car in gear. "Where to, Dee?" His voice broke.

"Tiebout Avenue. The old crack house."

"You want me to take Webster Avenue or the Concourse?"

Dee shifted in his seat and glared at Shorty. "How much you say you gonna get for this job?"

Small beads of sweat now glistening on his upper lip and brow, Shorty stammered, "F, f, five thou."

"Five grand? Five grand to drive a fucking car for a few hours?" Dee snarled the words and shook his head in disgust. "Well, drive the fucking car and stop asking me stupid fucking questions, you midget moron."

Only two blocks later, a clearly rattled Shorty almost rolled through a traffic light's yellow warning.

"Stop," Dee bellowed in aggravated disbelief.

Shorty slammed on the brakes then backed out of the crosswalk he had stopped in. "Sorry." He wiped heavy sweat from his face and neck with the sleeve of his jacket. His trembling hands then clamped tightly onto the steering wheel.

Dee's head was on a three-sixty swivel, checking to see if they'd attracted any unwanted attention. He swung back around to face Shorty with his right hand inside his coat. "You sorry? You know that every fucking cop in the Bronx is looking for me? And you gonna blow a fucking light on the Grand Concourse?"

"I'm sorry, Dee. I s, swear I'm sorry."

Dee opened his coat, revealing the holstered .44. "You gonna be a lot more sorry if we get stopped by the cops 'cause a your fucked up driving."

His deep basso a serpent's rattle, Dee then snarled. "'Cause after I shoot them, I'm gonna shove this gun so far down your throat, the muzzle will be tickling your balls. You understand?"

"Y, Yes, Sir."

The light turned green.

"Drive. And remember, if we get stopped—"

"I'll be careful." Shorty continued up the Grand Concourse, staying under the speed limit, stopping well in advance at another red light.

As they waited, Dee asked, "Where you turning?"

"At 181st Street."

Dee pounded the dashboard with a huge fist. "Are you the dumbest motherfucker in the Bronx? Do you want me to shoot you right now?"

"Dee, what, where do you—"

"If you make a right on 181st Street, what's the next block you hit?"

"Ryer Avenue."

"Yeah. And you never noticed the three-story, red-brick building on the corner? The one with the blue and white cars parked all around it? The Forty-sixth fuckin' police precinct."

"Dee, I—"

"Put your blinker on, shit for brains. We turn here."

Shorty, his hands shaking, slowly made the turn.

"When we get there, you're coming in. Me and Pooh Bear gonna have us a little talk 'bout giving you five grand. Man, you about the biggest loose end I have ever had to deal with."

Shorty nodded his head. "Whatever you say, Dee."

He knew the Tiebout crack house was where Dee had killed his and Pooh's good friend, Rontal Cheery. "Yes, Sir, whatever you say."

Ain't no way I'm going into that house. I got three blocks. Three blocks.

Forty-Nine - The Meeting

McGuire was alone in the squad room. His exhausted team had headed home to get some sleep. The day tour detectives were out on a case. He was grateful to have some privacy as he dialed ADA Gina Torelli's number. He was glad she'd called, but nervous as he waited for her to answer.

After exchanging greetings, Gina said, "You must be a happy man today."

"Why?" It was all his tired mind could come up with.

"Weren't you and your partner just cleared of any wrongdoing in the drug/ homicide case you're working on?"

"You knew? You never said anything to me."

"John, I'm an officer of the court. You knew I couldn't reveal any information. You were the subject of an active investigation."

McGuire let out a long sigh and smiled. He'd thought Gina's coolness toward him the last time they spoke was due to his getting drunk and ruining their night at Elaine's. While it certainly had been a problem, he now knew why she had been so cold toward him. He had been under investigation.

"Gina, what did you hear—"

"John, I'm giving my closing in a robbery trial in ten minutes. Are you still working? Looking for your killer, Dee?"

"No. Just went off duty. We struck out again last night. Coming back in at six tonight."

"Well, if you're not too tired, I should be free in about an hour. If you want to come over, we can have some coffee and talk."

McGuire was exhausted but wanted to see Gina, wanted to smooth out the problems between them. "Sounds good. See you in an hour."

He hung up, feeling much better than he had five minutes before.

* * *

Sergeant Ramos came out of his office. He was surprised to see McGuire still in the squad room. "Thought you went home, Johnny Mac. Why are you still here, and why do you have that shit-eating grin on your Irish mug?"

"I'm just feeling good, Boss."

"About what?"

"Start with Joey and I being cleared on the corruption bullshit. Add on seeing the fat piece of shit, Hanlon, being led away in cuffs by IAD."

Ramos grinned. "Had to feel good."

"And, last but not least, I just love doing what I'm doing."

"Doing what?"

"Being a cop. Working homicides. Locking up scumbags. Getting a front-row seat to the greatest show on earth."

Ramos sat on the edge of McGuire's desk. "Now you're losing me. What'd you mean?"

"Sarge, I got friends. Work on Wall Street. Make ten times what I do. You know what they do for excitement?"

"I don't know. Bang beautiful young models?"

"No. Well, they may do that, but the ultimate rush for these guys, their biggest thrill, is on weekends they go out to the Island, go into the woods, and play fuckin' paint ball."

"So. What's so bad about playing paintball?"

"It ain't bad. But compare paying to run around like kids, maybe getting shot with some paint, to what we do. Last few nights, we've been hunting. Trying to bag a known killer. You know the Hemingway quote they have hanging up in the Homicide Squad? 'There is no hunting like the hunting of man, and those who have hunted armed men long enough and liked it, never really care for anything else.' This is what I'm talking about."

Ramos only had a high school diploma, but when his family arrived in New York from Puerto Rico, he'd spent countless hours in the library on the Grand Concourse perfecting his English. He learned not to clip words and to pronounce every syllable when speaking. He devoured books. Hemingway was a favorite author.

"Don't love it too much, John. I have another quote from Papa on the subject, something like, 'When pursuing evil, do not get too close. You may become what you pursue.'"

"Ten-four, Sarge. I get it."

"Good. Take it, go home, and get some sleep."

"Will do. Gotta make a quick stop at court first."

"Going by the court? Want to do me a favor?" Ramos ducked back into his office and came out holding a large envelope. "The Four-six called a few minutes ago. They've been beating the bushes looking for Dee. They asked for more photos. There's a hundred mug shots in there."

"No *problemo*. I'll drop them off on my way to court."

"Thanks. And, after court, straight home. Right?"

"Yes, Sir."

Ramos put a meaty hand on McGuire's shoulder, looked him square in the eye. "I know you're going through some hard times, but I need you. At your best."

McGuire nodded. "The Four-six, court, straight home. See you at six, Boss."

* * *

McGuire drove his car to the Four-six, double parking in front of the old station house.

There was one spot open at the curb, but he knew if he took it, when he came out he would be blocked in by a sector car. It never failed. He gave the photos to the squad commander, filled him in on the latest news on the search for Dee, and headed out.

He drove up Ryer Avenue, pausing at a stop sign. He looked to his left, then his right, and began to go when something caused him to look left once more. One block away, on Valentine Avenue, he saw a car stopped with the driver and passenger doors open, with two men running from it.

Hail and bail was his first thought. People frequently flagged down a gypsy cab, negotiated a fare, and then bailed out and ran away without paying when they got near their destination. He looked again. It appeared a big man, who must have been the driver, was chasing a smaller man. He really didn't want to get involved, but McGuire had empathy for cab drivers who worked so hard for very little money, often killed by robbers for chump change.

He turned left. *If I can catch the little prick, I'll cuff him and take him back to the Four-six. One of the uniform cops will be happy to take the collar.*

As he got closer, he could see the little man had won the race. He had turned right onto Tiebout Avenue. The driver had given up, but strangely, he wasn't walking back to his car still sitting in the middle of the street with the doors wide open, but stood catching his breath in the intersection. The man turned left and began walking.

McGuire caught his full profile. He was a very large black man with a shaved head.

McGuire's heart raced. He knew he was looking at Dee.

Pulling to the curb, he got out, jogged to the corner, and glanced around a building. Dee was walking down Tiebout Avenue with his back to McGuire. The big man looked back once, then bounded up the steps of a burned-out house. McGuire recognized it as the crack house, scene of a shooting which had produced two bodies weeks before.

Dee pulled up on a piece of sheet metal, which served as the front door, and entered. McGuire looked around, praying for a sector car to drive by. None appeared. There was no phone booth on this corner. For the first time in his life, he wished he had a cell phone.

His options were very limited. Dee could walk through the crack house and disappear out the back door.

McGuire had no choice.

He had to go in.

Fifty - The Showdown

McGuire jogged across Tiebout Avenue, drawing his off-duty .38 caliber Colt Cobra revolver as he did. He climbed the crack house stoop, stopped at the top step and listened. Hearing nothing, he gently pulled back the sheet metal covering the door. It gave a metallic "twang" McGuire thought could be heard in Brooklyn. Easing his way inside, he paused to let his eyes adjust to the darkness.

Voices came from the back of the building. He very slowly shuffled toward them, gingerly, one foot at a time. He had to be certain that the floor, which he could not see, could support his weight. Between the traps crack house operators often put in to foil police raids, and the damage the fire had done, he was operating without a net.

As he moved forward, the voices grew louder. When his eyes adjusted, he saw a wall about six feet in front of him with an opening in its center. The voices came from the other side. He made it to the wall and moved to his right, nearing the opening. He could now clearly distinguish two voices, one raised in great anger.

"Fuck your man, Shorty. Running off, leaving me out on the street. He gets nothing."

A softer voice answered. “Calm down, Dee. He got nervous is all. I’ll give him something from my cut.”

McGuire, crouched low, peeked into the room. Shafts of sunlight, radiating through a hole in the roof, gave the area a surreal, church-like aura. He could clearly see Dee.

Someone else stood facing the big man. McGuire could not see his face, but spotted a large bag at that man’s feet. He watched and listened intently as the heated conversation grew even hotter.

“I just told you. The motherfucker left me out on the street. And you wanna give him some o’ your cut? Fuck him.” Dee paused. “And you. Hooking me up with a midget retard, when you know half the pigs in the NYPD be looking for me. You trying to get me caught?” Dee then gazed up at the light coming from the roof, and shook his head.

McGuire could see the gears turning inside the violent man’s bald head. This wasn’t gonna end well.

“You know what?” Dee’s words were tinged with pure venom. “Fuck you, too, Mr. Pooh. I’m takin’ it all.”

Pooh started to object.

McGuire saw Dee’s right hand move inside his coat. Clearly, the man was going for a piece.

It’s showtime, ladies and gentlemen. McGuire stood. From his vantage point behind the wall, he leveled his gun into the room, and shouted, “Police. Don’t move.”

Both men whirled in reflex to where the voice had come from, but, apparently, could see nothing but darkness.

“We have the place surrounded,” McGuire announced. Then, in his most strident voice, he commanded. “If you run, you will be shot. Now, slowly, raise your hands over your heads.”

The man called “Pooh” immediately complied with the order. Dee took a bold step toward the voice. “Officer, we ain’t doing nothing—”

"Freeze!" McGuire pulled back the Colt's hammer. The metallic click of the gun being cocked stopped Dee in his tracks. "Do exactly what I say, or I will shoot you."

Dee slowly raised both hands over his head.

"Now, both of you, keep 'em up, turn around, and walk slowly to the wall behind you."

When they were three feet from the wall, McGuire yelled, "Stop! Lean in, hands on the wall above your head. Assume the position. Spread your legs. Wider. Wider."

He had the suspects in the classic police wall frisk position. With a good portion of their weight on their hands, it would be tough for either of them to make a sudden move. McGuire reluctantly left the relative safety of his cover and slowly shuffled toward them. His gun still in his right hand aimed directly between them, he fished his handcuffs from his belt with his left.

He decided to get Dee's right hand behind his back and cuff it to the other guy's right hand. If they tried to resist, or bolt, they would end up facing in opposite directions. Then, despite the terror of the moment, he had one additional thought. *I wish to God I carried a second set of cuffs. I'll never call Joey Inspector Gadget again.*

Dee and the other guy were now lost in the shadows on the wall. McGuire could not see them as well as when they had been in the bright light.

* * *

Dee had to make his play. It was now or never. The wall frisk position gave him the perfect opportunity to drop his head and peer discreetly under his left arm. Looking past the shoulder holster that held his .44 Bulldog, he watched as the cop crept toward them. His mind was made up. When the cop stepped into the shaft of sunlight, Dee's right hand came off the wall. He spun to his left, pulled his gun, and went into rapid fire.

* * *

McGuire saw the move, dropped his cuffs, and stepped to his left. In one smooth motion, he crouched, thrust his weapon straight out, and began squeezing the trigger. Instinctively, his aim centered on the muzzle flashes a mere six feet away. He had no idea how many shots he had fired, or how many rounds he had left.

Suddenly, he felt as if he had been hit in the right shoulder with a sledgehammer. The blunt force spun him completely around and left him half-sprawled on the filthy floor. His ears rang, and he shook his head, trying to clear it. He spotted his gun to his right on the floor. He tried to reach for it but realized his arm wasn't working. Then he saw the hole in his jacket. He felt no pain, but was stunned and unsure of what to do next. Next thing he knew, the other man, Pooh, appeared and grabbed McGuire's Colt.

"Shoot him, Pooh. Kill the motherfucker!" Dee screamed. He was on his knees. Both hands covered with blood pressing a wound in his stomach. His weapon lay a few feet in front of him.

"Shoot him, Pooh. Shoot him." He reached for his gun, but was stopped by a searing jolt of pain in his belly. He reached again.

The second man, the one Dee had been calling Pooh, looked from McGuire to Dee. Dee's hand was now very close to his gun.

"Kill the mother fucka!" Spittle flew from Dee's big mouth.

Pooh raised McGuire's gun and pulled the trigger.

A fine mist of blood filled the room. McGuire fell backward onto the floor. He rolled onto his side in time to see Dee, half his head gone, crash face first at his feet. McGuire looked up in disbelief.

"Why'd you—?"

"S, S, Shit happens." Seeing the shock on McGuire's face, he added, "If he got to his gun, he would have killed us both."

"Did he have any bullets left?"

"Don't know." Pooh held the Colt out to McGuire.

"Do I have any?"

Pooh pointed the gun to the roof and pulled the trigger. The hammer clicked on a spent round. "No. You out." He handed the gun to McGuire and knelt to look at his wounded shoulder. He pulled the jacket back. "I ain't no doctor, but looks like you got lucky. It ain't bleeding too bad. Got an exit in the back."

"I can't move the arm."

"A .44 caliber bullet went through you. You lucky the arm is still attached. Had to break some bones." The man looked around. "Where's your boys?"

"Aren't any."

Pooh drew back, then smiled. "You came in alone? You either very brave or very crazy?"

"Think you could go out, find a phone, dial 911, and tell them an officer needs assistance here?"

"You letting me leave? How you know I'll come back?"

"Don't come back. Make the call, and get in the wind. I owe you. You saved my life."

Pooh gestured to Dee's body, McGuire's shoulder. "How you gonna explain this?"

"What's to explain? I saw a wanted killer. Followed him in here. We exchanged gunfire. I won. I'm a hero. Just promise me you'll make the call. I'm feeling weak."

Pretty much wasted, McGuire put his head down on the floor. He didn't see Pooh pick up the garbage bag, and he didn't see him leave. But, one minute later, he heard the approaching siren.

* * *

Three Weeks Later

Joe Gomez entered McGuire's room in Jacobi Hospital carrying a clear, plastic dry-cleaning bag.

"What's that?" McGuire asked.

"Your dress uniform. Had it cleaned yesterday. They want you to wear it when we leave."

"Joe, I told you I don't want any hoopla. Told Sergeant Ramos, too. I just want to get out of here."

"Out of our hands, Partner. Orders from the Police Commissioner. He's going to be here, along with the Chief of Detectives, some politicians, sixty or seventy cops in their dress blues and the Emerald Society Pipe Band, in full regalia. They're calling it a Hero's Walkout."

McGuire sat up. "Bring the car up to the emergency room. I'm getting out of here now."

Gomez shook his head. "John, in a couple of weeks, they're going to promote you to second grade. You'll probably get the Medal of Honor. Don't screw it up. Go along with the program. They'll wheel you out, the cops will be formed in two lines, everybody will clap, the pipers will play 'Irish Soldier Boy,' the PC will say a few words, you'll thank the doctors and nurses, and we'll be done. I'll drive you home."

McGuire sank back on the mattress. "What time does this show start?"

Gomez looked at his watch. "Two hours. Noon. They want it live on the three local network news shows."

McGuire pointed to his right arm with the shoulder heavily bandaged and the arm in a cast and sling. "How we getting this into my uniform?"

"Don't worry. We'll figure something out."

"It's been a long three weeks, Partner."

"Count your blessings. You're alive. The doctors say with a lot of physical therapy, you should get full use of the arm back, and you're a hero. Could have been a lot worse. Still, I know it's been a tough three weeks."

It had been. The initial cops, responding to an anonymous 911 call of "Officer Shot," had found McGuire unconscious. Luckily, one of those cops was EMT qualified. He had examined the wound and found a considerable amount of blood trapped inside McGuire's leather jacket. The cops picked him up, carried him to their car, and rushed him to Jacobi where doctors pumped two pints of blood into him. They had a large supply. Over fifty on- and off-duty cops had rushed to the hospital to donate as word of the incident spread.

Once he was stabilized, the doctors began to work on the shoulder. One surgeon mentioned he hadn't seen anything similar since Vietnam. After the initial treatment, the NYPD brought in the top orthopedic surgeons in the country. Two operations were performed. One more was scheduled when McGuire was stronger. Because bullet wounds leave dirt and grease behind, he was hooked up to different antibiotics to prevent infection.

It had been a long three weeks.

McGuire beckoned Gomez closer. "I should stop bitching. I know it's been tough on you, too. Thanks."

Gomez had virtually lived in the hospital since the day of the shooting, going home only for quick showers and visits with Raysa and the kids. No matter how often McGuire told him to stay home for a while, he rushed right back.

Gomez patted McGuire's left hand. "You don't have to thank me. It's what partners do. You know the two toughest things I had to do here?"

"Empty my bedpan and give me a sponge bath?"

Gomez laughed. "No. Number one tough assignment was making sure Cathy and Gina didn't come up at the same time. When one of them was with you, I sat in the lobby. If the other came in, I grabbed them, told them you were out of the room having tests done, and took them to the cafeteria until the coast was clear."

McGuire smiled. Cathy had visited every day. She told him her Wall Street fling was over.

"You were right, John. He was a phony. We ended up hating each other."

"Going to be uncomfortable for you, working for Mr. Phoney, ain't it?"

"Not going to be a problem. I had an offer from our biggest competitor a while back. I called them. It was still on the table. Start with the new company next week with a little more money, and a bigger office."

She had moved back to an apartment in Brooklyn. She asked McGuire if he wanted to give their marriage another try.

Gina had visited nine times. Each occasion lifted his spirits and made him laugh with her Italian humor. On one visit, McGuire complained to her about the bland food the hospital offered.

She came into his room the next day holding a large brown paper bag. Pulling his tray table next to his bed, she placed the package on it. Paper plates and napkins followed.

"Gina, what do you have in there?" McGuire pointed at the bag.

She ripped it open to reveal a large hero sandwich. "I stopped at Sal's. I don't think anyone would consider a Frank Sinatra sandwich bland. And, before you ask, I cleared it with your nurse. She was okay with it, just this one time."

They shared the hero and many laughs, with Gina making fun of McGuire's manhandling the pronunciation of the various Italian ingredients.

"It's pronounced brichute. Not pros-i-cutto."

"You tell me, Gina, how does a meat that starts with the letter P, end up sounding like it begins with the letter B?"

"It's an Italian thing. You wouldn't understand."

They both laughed and dug into the hero.

He really liked Gina and was happy she said she cared for him and would like to see him again. He also had loved Cathy since they were kids.

He had no idea how this would all work out.

Gomez handed McGuire a razor. "You missed a few spots. Right side of your face."

"You try shaving with your left hand." McGuire got up and gingerly walked into the bathroom.

"So, what was the second hardest thing, Joey?"

"Keeping your large teammates from the football team and your Emerald Society friends from turning this room into a kegger every night. They don't bring flowers or candy. They bring Guinness and Buds. I had to keep telling them the doctor said alcohol would mess with your antibiotics and could lead to infection."

"It shouldn't stop the boys from having one to toast me. It's an Irish thing."

"Half your football buddies are black."

"Yeah. Well, it's also a football thing."

"And, they're like the Easter Bunny. Putting cans of Guinness under your pillow, under the bed, in the bathroom for you to find later. I had to search this place, top-to-bottom every night."

"Find much?"

"John, I have two cases in the trunk of my car."

"Good for you, Partner. *Sláinte*. Enjoy them." McGuire knew a case of beer would last Gomez into the next millennium.

"I'm proud of you. Three weeks without a drink. Think you might continue the streak?"

"Joe, I've been buzzed on painkillers since I got here. And the docs made the whole 'booze and antibiotics don't mix' thing very clear to me. I kinda like having two arms."

"You're better without it."

"I don't know. I just don't know. We'll see." Finished with shaving, McGuire walked slowly back to bed.

Gomez swung a chair close to him and sat. "Something puzzles me. Can we talk?"

"Sure."

"The docs said you would have bled out in another couple of minutes if the Four-six cops hadn't gotten to you when they did."

"Yeah."

"And it was just you and Dee in the crack house, right?"

"Right."

"So, whoever made the anonymous 911 call saved your life?"

"Probably."

"So, who made it?"

"I don't know. Ten shots were fired. Lot of noise. Somebody must have heard it."

"That's the funny thing, John. I listened to the tape. The caller doesn't say, 'Shots Fired.' He says, 'Officer shot. Officer needs assistance.'"

"So?"

"Well, if you and Dee were the only ones in there—"

"Maybe someone saw me go in. Knew a white guy heading in there had to be a cop."

"And hears the shots and figures the white cop must have been shot? And the guy who makes the call, from a phone booth one block away on Valentine Avenue, who definitely sounds like a male black? He didn't say, 'Cop shot.

Send help.' His exact words were, 'Officer Shot. Officer Needs Assistance.' NYPD speak. The way a cop would call it in."

McGuire reached for his partner's hand. "Joe, listen to me. Dee is dead. I'm alive. Those are the only facts which should matter to you. Don't play detective with this. Let it go."

Gomez was about to answer when a young, attractive nurse entered the room. "How are we feeling today, handsome?"

"I'm fine. How are you?" Gomez answered.

The tension broke.

"All the VIPs are waiting downstairs. Looks like you're going to get the royal send-off, love." The nurse smiled. "I know you have some visits scheduled with the ortho doctors next week. Make sure you keep them and your rehab appointments."

McGuire stood and hugged her. "Thanks for everything, Annie. You've been terrific."

She started to pull back, then leaned in and gave McGuire a quick peck on his cheek. "Don't be a stranger now you're leaving."

"I won't. I'll see you when I come back for rehab and ortho."

"Good. Now I'll go get the wheelchair while Joe gets you dressed."

"I can walk, Annie. Forget the chair."

"Hospital rules. Can't have you taking a fall and undoing all the good work we did these last three weeks."

When she left, Gomez helped McGuire into uniform. They were able to get his dress jacket, called a Summer Blouse by the NYPD for some long-forgotten reason, over his shoulder and buttoned with his arm inside. Gomez had already pinned McGuire's badge, with its tall rack of medals, onto the blouse. Pants on, shaved, hair combed, he was ready.

Annie returned with the wheelchair. She looked at McGuire and fanned herself with her hand. "Be still, my beating heart. You cut a much nicer figure in the uniform than you did in the hospital gown, Mr. McGuire."

He smiled.

She gestured to the wheelchair. "Your chariot awaits, Sir."

McGuire got in. They took the elevator to the ground floor. The commissioner and the president of the hospital sat at a long table covered with microphones. Annie pushed him over. Both men stood and shook John's left hand.

The PC gave his stock speech about the plague of gun violence. The hospital president told of the extraordinary efforts his medical team had performed in saving John's arm and his life.

The microphone was pushed in front of McGuire. He calmly took a sheet of paper from his jacket pocket, glanced at it once, looked straight into the cameras and began speaking. He thanked everyone who had helped him by name, beginning with the two cops who had rushed him there, continuing through every doctor and nurse who had treated him. He finished with a special thanks to his partner and his special care nurse, Annie Connelly.

As he finished, he saw Annie and Joe wipe tears from their eyes. Press conference over, Annie took the chair and guided it to the front door. McGuire could see a line of cops on each side of the driveway. The Emerald Society Pipe Band waited ten feet from the door. They would lead him to his waiting car.

Annie leaned over and kissed his cheek. "Your partner can take you from here, love." She turned and went outside.

Gomez grabbed the handles of the chair.

McGuire looked up. “Fuck it. I’m walking out of here.”

The door opened. He stepped out to the sound of sixty pairs of hands, draped in their white dress gloves, applauding. Sergeant Ramos and the rest of his team, all in uniform, very gingerly, gave him hugs.

Ty Crawford whispered to him, “It’s taken care of.”

McGuire took a step.

Ramos touched his arm. “One second, John.”

The sergeant and the team fell into formation. Ramos barked, “Detail. Ten Hut.”

The applause stopped. Heels clicked. The formation stood at attention. Ramos nodded.

McGuire took a step.

“Present Arms!” Sixty white-gloved right hands snapped up to their hat’s visors in salute. The band began marching with “Irish Soldier Boy” wailing from the pipes.

McGuire felt goose bumps cover his body. He wasn't alone. When he reached the end of the drive, McGuire did an about face, looked at the throng, raised his left hand and mouthed “Thank you.”

Ramos followed with, “Order Arms. Detail, dismissed.”

The ranks broke. They all came by to shake McGuire’s hand and wish him luck on his recovery. After ten minutes, things quieted down. McGuire and Gomez stood outside McGuire’s car.

Ten yards away, Ty Crawford leaned on his.

“You ready, John?” Gomez asked.

“I am, but slight change of plans. You don’t have to drive me home. I’m fine.”

“You only have one arm. How you going—”

McGuire snaked his left hand behind Gomez’s head and pulled him close. “You’re my partner, and I love you. I want you to go home and give Raysa and the kids a big kiss from me. I've taken you away from them for the last three weeks."

Gomez looked unsure.

"Joe, the car has power steering. I'll be fine." He pointed to Crawford. "Ty can drop you back at the house."

"John, I can't–"

"Yes, you can. It's what I want."

Gomez shook his head. "I know better than to argue with my thick-headed, stubborn Irish partner. Okay, John. If it's what you want. If you need anything, call my cell."

"Yeah. The cell phone. You know, I'm actually thinking of getting one of those now."

Gomez smiled. "About time. I'll buy you one. An early promotion present."

They hugged once more, and Gomez left in Crawford's car. McGuire took a deep breath. He took off his summer blouse and threw it on the back seat. It felt good to be alone, to be out of the hospital, to be alive.

He drove onto the Triborough Bridge, having some trouble for the first time in his life, paying the toll as a lefty. As he left the toll plaza, he was faced with a choice. A very big choice.

A right turn would take him into Manhattan, where sweet Gina lived. Straight ahead was Queens, then Brooklyn where Cathy now made her home.

He pulled to the side of the road, put the car in park. He sat, torn, mulling his options.

I don't know. I just don't know.

He turned and knelt on the front seat, reached into the back with his left hand, and moved his summer blouse. Ty Crawford had come through. A small Styrofoam cooler, filled with ice and four pint cans of Guinness. He plucked one out, turned back into the driver's seat. He placed the can against his forehead. It's felt so cool, so familiar. He looked up the highway.

Right or straight?

Cathy or Gina?

His fingernail played with the pop top.

"I don't know. Dammit, I just don't know."

About the Author

Bob Martin served the NYPD for 32 years in a wide variety of commands. These include the fabled Tactical Patrol Force (TPF), the Street Crime Unit, Mounted Unit, the 72nd, 69th, 6th Precincts, Queens and Bronx Detectives, and finally as the CO of the Special Investigations Division. Martin was a charter member and played for a dozen years with the NYPD's Finest Football Team. He served for twelve years on the International Association of Chiefs of Police (IACP) “Committee on Terrorism” and traveled extensively, in this country and abroad, speaking on the subject. He retired as a Deputy Inspector in 2000 and began writing. His stories have been published in numerous magazines and newspapers. Bronx Justice, based on an actual case, is his first novel.

Made in the USA
Middletown, DE
12 November 2017